THE CITY OF A THOUSAND FACES

WALKER DRYDEN is the pseudonym for writing team Mike Walker and John Scott Dryden.

JOHN SCOTT DRYDEN

John Scott Dryden is an award-winning writer and director best known for his work in audio fiction. He created the popular podcast series, *Passenger List*, a mystery thriller about a plane that disappears mid-flight between London and New York. He has written and directed many audio drama series for the BBC including the thrillers *Severed Threads*, *Pandemic* (winner of the WGGB Award for Best Original Radio Drama Series), *The Reluctant Spy* and the highly successful audio version of *Tumanbay*. John is a recipient of the prestigious Peabody Award for the radio drama, *The Day That Lehman Died*, which he executive produced and directed.

MIKE WALKER

Mike Walker has written series on Caesars, Plantagenets, Stuarts and Romanovs for the BBC. He wrote the BAFTA award-winning interactive play *Dark House* and has published *A Long Way Home*, on the Botany Bay convict Mary Bryant, *Powder Puff Derby* on women pioneers of flying, and a thriller: *Bad Company*. He teaches creative writing at Lambeth's Morley College. Over the past few years he has worked with John Scott Dryden bringing to life the world of Tumanbay.

THE CITY OF A THOUSAND FACES

A Tumanbay Novel

Walker Dryden

ORION

First published in Great Britain in 2020 by Orion Fiction,
an imprint of The Orion Publishing Group Ltd.,
Carmelite House, 50 Victoria Embankment
London EC4Y 0DZ

An Hachette UK Company

1 3 5 7 9 10 8 6 4 2

A CIP catalogue record for this book is
available from the British Library.

ISBN (Hardback) 978 1 4091 8701 1
ISBN (Trade Paperback) 978 1 4091 8702 8
ISBN (eBook) 978 1 4091 8704 2

Typeset by Input Data Services Ltd, Somerset
Printed and bound in Great Britain by Clays Ltd, Elcograf S.p.A.

MIX
Paper from
responsible sources
FSC
www.fsc.org   FSC® C104740

www.orionbooks.co.uk

MW
For Octavius

JSD
For Ayeesha who came on the journey with me,
Hugo & Leela-Grace who appeared along the way,
and Cairo who we lost

'After I had labored for two days and was covered with sand and loose earth, I picked out several sheets of different old scrolls and manuscripts, but I did not find any use or information in them – who knows what lies underneath – for I was tired of searching.'

Jacob Saphir, Talmudist scholar and traveller, 1864

'We came upon a great desert, four day's journey in width, where a wind called *simoom*, or poison wind, blows. Those unfortunates caught by this wind invariably die. And it is said that when a man is killed by this wind and his companions try to wash him for burial, his body falls apart. There have been many such deaths and we were warned only to travel by night when the wind does not blow.'

Ibn Batuta, traveller, 1304–1369

Characters

al-Ghuri, Sultan of Tumanbay, came to power following the untimely death of his brother, the previous Sultan.

Shajah, Sultan al-Ghuri's First Wife, previously married to his brother, the murdered Sultan. She grew up in poverty, arrived in Tumanbay as a slave and soon learned to exploit her dazzling beauty in exchange for power and wealth.

Madu, the Sultan's nephew and only son of Shajah and the former Sultan.

Maya, widow of a deceased governor of Amber Province and leader of the rebel movement.

Effendi Red, Maya's envoy.

Grand Vizier Cadali, the Sultan's chief advisor.

Commander Gregor, head of the elite Palace Guard and the Sultan's spymaster. He arrived in Tumanbay as a slave-child with Qulan.

General Qulan, Commander of Tumanbay's armies.

Manel, Qulan's teenage daughter.

Ibn Bai, slave trader and recent arrival to Tumanbay. His wife and daughter are travelling by ship to join him.

Sarah, a slave with a baby whom Ibn Bai purchases in Tumanbay's slave market.

Daniel, Sarah's brother, also purchased by Ibn Bai.

Basim, an officer in the Palace Guard.

The Frog, Basim's son, a young boy with prophetic powers.

Slave, an escaped slave from a ship bound for Tumanbay.

Wolf, leader of a proudly independent band of warrior-horsemen.

The Hafiz, symbol of religious authority in Tumanbay.

Bello, a priest and the personal assistant to the Hafiz.

Prologue

The journey to Tumanbay had been long and arduous. The envoy, riding a mule and accompanied by a small party of believers, moved mostly at night to avoid the heat of the desert. But such was the urgency of his mission, on the final day, they had continued in the sun. Even though they were still a day's long march away, the city appeared to rise out of the sand, shimmering like water in the heat.

If anyone had seen this small caravan moving towards Tumanbay, nothing about it would have caused suspicion or alarm. There were so many traders travelling to and from the city and many checkpoints along the way. Their papers were in order.

By sunset he could clearly see the towers and minarets, the palaces like glittering islands in an ocean of green and blue roofs, and the great walls reputed to be impossible for any army to breach.

And yet, with help from believers within the city, the envoy had entered in darkness, unnoticed by the gatekeepers, and was now, on this auspicious morning, making his way on foot to the Sultan's palace. Even though he was weary from the journey and the sack he had slung over his shoulder was beginning to feel heavy, he didn't stop for rest or refreshments at any of the cafes or stalls that lined the street. He kept his eyes fixed on the imposing gates of the palace ahead. If he had looked about, he would have seen a bustling scene – donkeys and carts, camels, traders, soldiers, slaves, thieves, shoppers, layabouts and lovers – the citizens of Tumanbay going about their daily business as they had for centuries, unaware that their world was soon to change.

They hardly noticed him. There were so many from so many different parts of the Empire and beyond, each with their own dress and style – a short, bearded pilgrim in red and black robes was nothing unusual.

There was a disturbance ahead, like dust or smoke blowing around in circles beside the entrance to a small lane. People were crossing the road to avoid it. As he approached, the envoy paused and watched. Despite the crowds, the street was deserted here, except for this swirling, humming mass, which he could now see were wasps. Perhaps their nest had been disturbed or destroyed and they were disorientated and anxious, unsure of where to go, a danger to all.

He stared, transfixed. This was a sign, surely, that he must carry out his task without fear. Like the wasps, these people would soon be scattered about the world; their wondrous city, in which they had put their trust and belief, would be shown to be as empty and meaningless as a dead nest.

He clutched the sack and crossed the road.

Part One

There's a city far away . . . My parents often spoke of it as if it had always been there and always would be . . . I had seen it in paintings, I had read of it in stories, the richest, most powerful place on earth . . . the centre of everything. It drew people from every corner of the Empire and beyond, hungry for wealth and power, or in some cases, more wealth and more power. They were dazzled by its brightness. And like moths drawn to a candle . . . many were burned alive by its fire . . . Tumanbay . . .

I

Basim

The child's eyelids were flickering, but everything else remained still. Unnaturally still. Even his breathing seemed to have stopped. Basim shook him gently.

'Wake up, my little Frog. Wake up.'

The boy's eyes snapped open, terrified and confused at first. Then he saw his father smiling down at him and he relaxed.

'It was just a dream,' Basim said, gently stroking his son's damp forehead.

It was still dark, Basim's favourite time of day, when the air was cool and the only sounds were the cicadas and the preachers calling across the city.

'Don't go today, Papa,' the boy said, sitting up. 'Something bad will happen.'

Basim smiled, continuing his preparations. 'Is that so, my little Frog?'

'And they will chop off your head and you will never see us again.'

Basim considered this for a moment.

'I will miss having my head,' he said, checking himself in the mirror and adjusting his uniform. 'I think it's rather a handsome one, don't you?'

These dark dreams had been coming regularly for several

moons now and had changed the character of the child. He had become less inclined to play with other children and, whereas he used to delight in going to school, where he excelled as a gifted child, now he was angry with and resentful of his mother, Heba, for making him go. Heba had sought help from the wife of another officer, a woman known in the compound for her healing powers, and had been told not to worry, that he was just a boy with a vivid imagination.

Basim often came home from the palace to find the Frog sitting alone in the passageway outside the apartment, lost in thought. The other day when Basim asked him what was wrong, the Frog had said, 'I was thinking about how they see down there.'

'How who sees, where?'

'The underworld. The people who live there.'

'There's no underworld,' Basim had said. 'It's just a story.'

The previous evening, their neighbour Khalida had reported her cat missing. The Frog had insisted on going over to her apartment to tell her that he had knowledge the creature was now 'buried in darkness amid the grains of sand'. This caused her to cry uncontrollably and, as several of the neighbours gathered round to comfort her, the Frog just stood there in the passageway staring, as if he was oblivious to the pain he had caused her.

But now, seeing the Frog through the mirror lying on the couch, Basim's heart went out to him. He may have been a strange child but he was *their* child, a precious gift from God, who had been a long time coming to this world after Heba had delivered three whose fates were not to be of this world. They wanted, above all else, for their surviving child to be happy.

Basim felt a hand on the back of his neck. He turned to see Heba.

'You hear that?' Basim asked.

'What's that?' she asked brightly.

'The Frog's had another one of his dreams.'

'Something bad,' the Frog added.

'Oh really? Well, you can tell me all about it after you've had your breakfast,' she said and busied herself preparing food. They had agreed to try not to look concerned in front of the child.

Basim attached his sword – an elegant curved sabre carried only by the officers of the palace guard – and kissed the Frog on the forehead.

'Be good. Obey your mother.'

Heba followed him to the door.

'See you when we see you,' she said, looking deep into his eyes. 'And try not to worry. He'll be fine, I'm sure of it.'

'What makes you so sure?'

'I took him back to see Mistress Talum. She gave me some medicines and said expect the dreams to get worse at first and then they will disappear completely. Perhaps by the time you return.'

He wrapped his arms around her and kissed her on the forehead.

'You both mean so much to me,' he said.

'Foolish man. Don't you think I know that?' she replied. 'Now go, or something bad really will happen.'

Basim made his way through the narrow, but ordered, passageways that formed the compound where the families of the Palace Guard were housed. As he passed Selim the shoemaker's shop on the corner, he heard the plaintive wailing of a cat. He stopped and went back to investigate. Next to the shop, and at the end of every alley, was a small storage unit where grain was delivered for the inhabitants of each section. Basim pulled the latch and peered inside. As he did so, a cat shot out like an angry djinn from the infernal world and disappeared along the passageway towards its home.

Basim continued out of the compound. As he crossed the vast Square of the Martyrs, the Gates of al-Suliman Midan were opening, and men were rushing out from their morning prayers. Basim quickened his pace. He was late. He had usually crossed the square by the time the faithful dispersed.

When he got to the palace, it was light. He had been away for two days. He would be on duty for another ten before he saw Heba and the Frog again.

Or so he thought.

2

The Girl

The sea was empty. Just blue water, sun in the girl's eyes, the endless creaking of the ship, the boom of the huge lateen sail bellying out under another gust of wind, the white wake reeling out behind them as every moment took her closer to Tumanbay.

It was all so unfair!

She leaned against the bulwark beside the brass cannon on its swivel mount. Maybe they'd be attacked by pirates and she could escape to a life of adventure; anything would be better than being the wife of a merchant in a city she didn't know, in a country she didn't want to be in. Yes, a pirate queen with her own crew of blood-soaked rogues, terrifying the Middle Sea; but it wouldn't happen because things like that never happened outside the stories, and certainly not to the daughters of merchants. Besides, there were no pirates any more. Tumanbay made sure everyone obeyed its laws and her father had assured her that its navy kept the oceans peaceable. And who wanted peace? Merchants and, she supposed, merchants' wives. It wasn't fair, it just wasn't fair.

Behind her, the captain bellowed and sailors began climbing the rigging to reset the sail. Canvas cracked in the wind as the sail shivered, the helmsman leaned on the big wheel and the whole ship began to come about, the bowsprit tracking across the blue horizon until it met a smudge of land.

She couldn't even run away to sea and become a sailor – girls weren't allowed, oh no, they had to stay at home and do what they were told and . . . get married to . . . who? What if he was hideous or old or both? Her father had written and said he was a 'fine young man', and she knew all too well the kind of boys he thought were 'fine'. She looked down at the sea racing by. Maybe she should jump. Here and now. That would show them all!

She stepped up onto . . . she didn't know what it was called but some kind of iron thing they tied ropes to, and leaned further over the side – the sun was making patterns in the waves, making her dizzy – she eased herself further up, further out . . .

'What are you doing without a cloak? The sun and wind will . . .'

Too late! She stepped back onto the deck.

'And don't lean over like that, you might fall into the sea and then where would you be?'

'I would be in the sea, Mother.' Fat chance.

Her mother sighed with exasperation. 'Put this on.'

'I'm hot, I don't need it.'

'You need it.'

Her mother didn't need to give a reason. It was obvious she thoroughly disapproved of the crew and captain ogling her daughter. She also knew the precise value of every commodity and didn't want her daughter's pale skin darkened and roughened by the weather before the deal was done. She draped the cloak about the girl's shoulders and, taking her arm, walked with her to the stern where they stood looking at the white wake and the seabirds swooping and taking scraps from it as someone emptied a bucket of kitchen waste from a port below. They stood together in a silence that the girl was determined not to be the first to break.

Eventually, her mother said: 'Are you going to talk to me?'

'I am talking to you, Mother.'

'You know what I mean. You've been sullen this whole trip. Don't you want to see Tumanbay? It's the greatest city in the world.'

The girl silently mouthed the words along with her mother, she'd heard them so often by now and, yes, in a way, she did want to see this city . . .

'But not this way,' she burst out.

She knew her mother thought that once she was married she would settle down, but she didn't want to settle down. There were so many things she'd read about in her father's library – castles built on mountain peaks, spice cities, the great inland sea, the riders of the plains in their thousands – and now she would never see them. She would be shut away behind . . .

'What about your father? Don't you want to see him?'

'Of course I do, just not like this.'

'Not like what?'

'You know, Mother.'

They'd had this conversation a hundred times and it never went anywhere except round and round and round.

'He's a fine young man, your father says. Don't you trust your father?'

She wanted to shout: No, of course I don't, not where boys are concerned, but she said, 'Of course, I trust him, I just don't want to—'

'There you are, then,' her mother said, as she'd said before and would no doubt say again and again until the day the contracts were signed.

The girl was about to make the same answer she usually made when she heard the creak and shriek of one of the deck hatches, the furthest away, being thrown open. There was a terrible smell for a moment before the wind snatched it away. The girl hurried forward to the rail by the ship's wheel where she could see down on to the deck.

'Wait . . .' her mother called, then came after her as someone was pulled from the darkness below decks by a couple of burly sailors: a big man, dark-skinned, wearing breeches and no more. His wrists were manacled in front of him. He blinked in the sunlight, momentarily blinded after his time below decks, and stumbled. His captors pulled him brutally upright and rushed him to the foot of the big central mast, where they secured his wrist chains to a line and pulled them up, above his head, so he was virtually hanging from the iron cuffs.

'You should go back to your cabin, ladies,' the captain growled.

'Why, what's happening?'

'Nothing that need bother you. If you'll just . . .'

'Indeed it will not,' her mother snorted. 'I have seen slaves punished before, Captain. It's the nature of the business.'

'Perhaps your daughter . . .?' the captain offered.

'Nonsense. It's time she learned a few facts of the life we lead. She will watch too.'

If anything was going to send her back to the gloomy cabin it would have been her mother telling her to stay where she was, but something about the slave caught her attention. He didn't seem to be frightened for a start, but neither was he struggling. He hung there, his powerful fists gripping the wrist chains, the muscles on his arms expanding as he pulled himself up a fraction to ease the cutting pressure.

'What do you think he did?' she whispered.

'It doesn't matter,' her mother said. 'It is necessary sometimes.'

'Is that what Father does to his slaves?'

'Of course, it's the only way.'

The slave's body jerked as a whip was brought down with fearful force. Blood and – the girl's hand went to her mouth in horror – lumps of flesh were torn from the slave's back. And yet, as the whip rose and fell, he made no sound – his face was rigid, displaying neither anger nor fear, as if he was somewhere else and this wasn't happening to him at all.

'Why isn't he crying out? It's like he doesn't care. How can he not care?'

'They come from beyond civilisation. They don't feel pain like us, they're barbarians.'

'Then what's the point, Mama?'

'What do you mean?'

'If he doesn't feel it, why whip him at all?'

The sailor with the whip paused and shouted up to the captain: 'Enough, Sir?' The girl just knew he was going to say: 'More.'

She burst out, 'Enough, enough ...' feeling tears brim her eyelids. The captain looked at her and paused.

Then he nodded.

'Enough, take him down.'

The ropes were loosened, the line slackened off. The slave lowered his arms and stood, legs apart, solid on the deck as if nothing had happened, as if the blood and flesh scattered around him and being washed away with buckets of seawater, as if the horrible white glint of bone through the gore on his back, were nothing to do with him at all. Ignoring everyone, he turned and walked back to the open hatch and went below.

How could he do that, the girl wondered – just hang there while they flogged him and then look at them as if they were the ones who had been punished?

If only she could find that kind of courage to stand up to her mother, her father ... to stand up to all of them and say *no*! But she couldn't even throw herself over the side of the ship when she had the chance. She was just a coward.

Her mother coughed – she had been coughing a lot lately.

'I'm tired,' she said irritably. 'Come and read to me while I rest.'

3
Ibn Bai

Ibn Bai had always thought of himself as a reasonable man but, faced with more delays, he was beginning to lose patience as his builder announced: 'Effendi, who could have foreseen that the wall would develop a crack and set things back to such a degree. It's in God's hands, we have to do the best we can.'

Ibn Bai felt like telling the builder that he should have foreseen the problem when he put too much weight on a wall that was obviously never meant to bear that sort of load, and that accordingly he should lower his price and work extra time to make good the damage he had done to Ibn Bai's beautiful new house. But, of course he would say nothing, nod, agree and ask when the work might be completed because even finding a half-good builder in Tumanbay was something of a miracle and, once you had him, you kept in his good graces.

'So, Arem Effendi, tell me, how long will it take to fix the wall and put in the extra bracing for the balcony supports?'

Arem, a thin fellow, though surprisingly strong even so, flexed his hands and grinned.

'Only a day or two, effendi. Of course, there will be the supports to pay for but I know where I can get some at a very good price?'

He stopped, his head cocked on one side, waiting for Ibn Bai to say: 'Yes, of course, go ahead.'

'Then we should be out of your way by the sickle moon.'

'Three weeks?'

Arem shrugged. 'That's if all goes well.'

'Why should it not?' Ibn Bai asked, feeling increasingly irritated.

'Well . . . the fountain of al-Dar ran red the other day.'

'So?'

'Auguries of blood, they say!'

'They say anything that comes into their empty heads. They say there are giraffes in the palace! I am more concerned with practicalities. My wife and daughter will be here any day now. I had hoped to have the house ready for them – painted and furnished.'

Arem sucked his teeth. 'It is in the hands of God.'

Ibn Bai recognised the moment they had both been circling for a while – the moment when the deal is finally made.

'There would, of course,' Ibn Bai said, 'as is the practice where I come from, be a finishing bonus payable upon early completion of the job. A recognition of the craftsman's skill and efforts on behalf of the customer.'

This time Ibn Bai sucked his teeth and waited. The builder mentioned a figure, Ibn Bai agreed, smiles and handshakes were exchanged, the builder went back to his crew and Ibn Bai could hear him cursing their laziness and shoddy work and driving them on to a completion in a mere seven days. He had set the bonus money aside at the beginning of the contract and had, in fact, paid a third less than he'd expected so, all in all, his mood was a little improved. He thought he might take the cart along to the port, enquire whether there was news of his ship and perhaps see if there were any goods worth picking up.

Before setting off for Tumanbay six moons ago to establish home and business, Ibn Bai had read much about the city, and by far the majority of the accounts had extolled the great walls that protected the landward side, stretching beyond sight in either direction, and the four massive gates, made of the thickest oak, banded with iron, studded with brass spikes, opened each dawn, closed each dusk. The walls and gates were, without a doubt, an impressive sight, one of the wonders of the world, but Ibn Bai somehow preferred the other side of Tumanbay, the harbour that looked out through the Gulf of Winds towards the Middle Sea.

This was how many newcomers first saw Tumanbay, how he had seen it himself from the deck of a dhow, heeling in the breeze, passing the long arms of the harbour walls, jutting three leagues or more out into the gulf, closing to an entrance no more than five ships wide, a fort on either point with mighty chains draped down, under the water, that could, if necessary, be winched into position across the entrance, effectively sealing the port.

Entering the harbour, Ibn Bai reflected that never in all the harbours he'd visited – and he had done business in a good few – had he seen as great a volume of shipping in one place at one time. The expression 'a forest of masts' had come to him from some tale he'd read and he realised that it was no exaggeration: there were thousands of them rising from the decks of ships uncountable. Dhows, triremes, tubby merchantmen, stately galleons, fishing boats of every size from the smallest to those able to chase and catch the great monsters of the Middle Sea. And darting between them, like insects skittering across a pond, tenders and skiffs transporting the host of men and women who pursued their trades here and whose skill and labour made the whole vast machine function. It was exhilarating. Ibn Bai had felt a dozen years younger; there was nothing in the world that could not be found and bought and traded in this vast arena, and he longed to be a part of it.

And so it had turned out. In the six moons he had been in the city he had found and bought an old house which he was having virtually rebuilt, he had established a network of contacts, sorted out a decent marriage deal – though his wife Illa was oddly silent in her letters on his daughter's enthusiasm for the project. Surely any young girl couldn't wait to get married? He had good business premises and was making a place for himself in the slave markets. He was already in profit, trading with his old associates across the Middle Sea. Once this marriage business had been settled and he was in partnership with a Tumanbay merchant, he would be on a firm footing and well on the way to success.

As always, the harbour master's office was crowded and Ibn Bai had to wait a sandglass or more before he saw the assistant clerk (and that had cost him a bribe, but then everything in Tumanbay was oiled by a little something for your trouble) and was able to ask if there was any news of his ship, the *Gullswing*, from the forts and observation points along the coast.

'From Cyrene, you say?'

'Exactly so, effendi. With fortunate winds, she might dock within seven days or less.'

The clerk flicked through the reports that were constantly arriving via the couriers who rode along the coast from fort to fort with news of incoming vessels.

'*Gullswing*? Nothing here. Once she passes the Mad Sultan we'll probably get word. Come back next week.'

'I have a cargo on board.'

The clerk gave him a smug look. 'Of course you do, everyone who comes here enquiring has a cargo on board. And do you know what they all want?'

Ibn Bai didn't like the fellow's manner but neither did he want to antagonise him.

'No, what do they want?'

'What you all want, without exception, is to get your papers stamped in advance so the cargo can be processed with less trouble and greater speed when it does arrive. Correct?'

'Correct. But you see, my wife and daughter are on the ship and I hope—'

'And so do I.' The clerk sighed. 'I truly do hope your wife and daughter make the happiest of landings but until they do, you will have to wait like everyone else. And when your ship comes in, I or another clerk will count the cargo, tally the list, you will make your mark, and the papers will be stamped. Is there anything else I can aid you with?'

'No thank you, effendi. Good day to you.'

Ibn Bai's good mood evaporated as he pushed his way out of the office. He was annoyed with himself, not for making a fruitless attempt to short-cut the landing process but because he didn't know how to short-cut the landing process. He knew very well, as did the smug clerk, that there were avenues but so far, as a newcomer, he hadn't found them and he hadn't found anyone, yet, who would show him the correct pathway. What he needed was a patron. That was how business was done: you found a person of power for whom you could be useful and they, in return, dispensed favours and influence. Well, it would come with time and he was, as he'd told himself only this morning, a patient man. He decided to take a walk through the harbour market and see what was available. Tumanbay had half a hundred markets but the harbour was the first he'd got to know and traded in and he still had a fondness for it.

As always, the market announced itself to his nose first: the stink of bodies, excrement, decaying food and the incense burned unsuccessfully to cover the stench. He nodded to a couple of dealers standing by cages of silent, bewildered, truculent or even enthusiastic slaves trying to draw attention to their virtues. The better quality goods were generally to be found in the city at the bigger markets but it was possible, still, to find the odd bargain at the harbour.

'What are you after?' asked one of the dealers.

Ibn Bai realised he had been standing looking into one of the cages for too long to escape attention.

'Domestic? Labour?' the dealer approached.

'Nothing,' Ibn Bai replied. 'Just browsing.'

'Of course. Please . . . take your time,' said the dealer, stepping back.

He was a typical salesman, Ibn Bai thought: chewing paan, spitting, and his hair an unnatural red. It was a current fashion among the merchant classes of Tumanbay for older men to apply henna to their hair in an attempt to appear more youthful and virile. Ibn Bai was repulsed by it.

'Anything you want to know, just ask me,' the dealer added, and positioned himself close by ready to assist at a moment's notice.

Ibn Bai peered into the cage. A girl was looking back at him, her eyes widening slightly in fear . . . or was it appraisal? He dismissed the thought; slaves didn't appraise, dealers did that. She held a baby protectively to her chest. She wore a coarse shift but she wore it as if it had been something infinitely finer. Ibn Bai could see the marks left by rings on her fingers and her ears had been pierced. Behind her, a young man looked at him levelly. No fear in the blue eyes, no hope either.

'My name is Mitra, by the way,' said the dealer. 'I have the best stock in the market. Ask anyone.'

Ibn Bai dismissed him with a tut and continued along the row of cages. Mitra followed.

'I have four slaves from the Asir Mountains,' he said, pointing into one of the cages. 'Quite rare. Easy-going, good with children. Quick to learn.' Ibn Bai's eye drifted across to the adjacent cage, where three boys stood staring out at him, their bodies hard and fit, their gazes defiant. 'They're marked for the army already, came in through Villeppi.'

They were no more than children. How had they come to this, Ibn Bai wondered.

'Volunteers,' Mitra said, as if reading Ibn Bai's mind.

'Volunteers?'

'Life is so hard in the mountains there, many abandon their children to the elements. It's a custom in those parts. The strong survive and the weak . . . Well, the weak are no good to anyone, so it's better that they . . .' He shrugged. 'Anyway, they are not for you, my friend. But these four here . . .'

'I'm really not looking to buy anything today.'

'Of course, of course,' enthused Mitra. 'But just have a look . . .' He clicked his fingers at an assistant, who came running with a ring full of keys and started unlocking a cage. 'You will be amazed,' Mitra promised.

'No, I told you already, I'm not interested,' Ibn Bai said firmly.

The assistant stopped, looking to his master for instruction. Mitra shrugged and was about turn his attention to another potential customer when Ibn Bai pointed back to the first cage.

'But these two . . . The blue eyes. Where are they from?'

Ibn Bai approached the cage again. The girl was still looking at him.

'She has a baby?'

'She can come with or without the baby. No problem.'

'Do they . . . understand? Do they speak our language?'

'That you will have to take a chance on. I haven't been able to get anything out of them.'

There was something about these slaves. Ibn Bai sensed it.

'Give me a moment,' he said, waving Mitra away.

'Of course. Take all the time you need. Just don't get too close to the cage, eh?'

And he scurried off to join his assistant, who was unlocking a cage for another potential customer.

Ibn Bai beckoned to the girl. 'You, come closer.' She didn't move but the flicker of her eyes told him she understood his words. 'It's all right, you want to keep your baby. Fine, I have a child too. I understand. Come, closer ...'

She moved a few hesitant steps.

'You're something special, aren't you?' he said. 'You used to wear a ring on your left middle finger. You're educated. It's all right – I'm not going to tell anyone. I just notice these things.'

She remained still, expressionless, just staring back with her striking blue eyes.

'What about you?' said Ibn Bai, turning his attention to the male, who waited in the darkness behind. Ibn Bai pressed his head against the cage-wire to get a better view. 'Are you related? Are you the father of the child?' The slave approached slowly.

'That's right,' Ibn Bai said encouragingly. 'Come. You can talk to me. Tell me who you—'

He wasn't able to finish because, within the blink of an eye, the slave leaped forward, roaring and clawing at the cage-wire and gnashing his teeth. Ibn Bai was so shocked he tripped backwards and fell to the ground. He lay there for a moment as Mitra and his assistant rushed over and started beating the slave back with sticks.

'Are you all right?' Mitra asked when things had calmed down. He helped Ibn Bai to his feet. 'Did he touch you?'

'No,' Ibn Bai said, brushing the sand and filth off his clothes. 'I warned you.'

In the cage, the girl had reached out and touched the male slave on the arm. He calmed and stepped back into the shadows.

'I think I'll end up selling him to the fighting pits if I can't tame him,' continued Mitra. 'Not so much money, but—'

'I think I can tame him,' Ibn Bai said.

Mitra's head jerked round. He and his assistant stared at Ibn Bai, amazed.

Yes, Ibn Bai thought, staring back into the cage, there was definitely something there.

The sight of Ibn Bai's cart with the cage on the back excited no comment as he drove through the narrow streets of the port quarter in the direction of the grand trunk road, as wide as a dozen elephants, that circled the outer city and from which branched all the smaller, interconnecting streets that made up the arteries of the vast body of Tumanbay. The new slaves crouched behind him, holding on to the bars. Neither had spoken a word since Mitra had shooed them into their new confinement. It made Ibn Bai uncomfortable – even after all these years in the business – to have them squatting behind him where he was unable to see what they were about. To calm his nerves, he talked. His wife Illa always said he talked too much, especially to the goods, but that was his way; better by kindness and encouragement if possible, and only then through punishment.

'You're lucky – to have been bought by me. I have contacts in the royal palace. You'll fetch a good price there because you're both educated. Education can get you anywhere in the world. That's why I'm here. I know things. And you do too, so you'll probably be all right.'

He paused. No response. He went on: 'I'm new here myself.

Well, not as new as you but I've already learned a thing or two, and that's important in Tumanbay. You know the Empire is ruled by slaves . . . Well, they came as slaves and now they run the place – everyone's a slave here. Well, I'm not. I'm a free man. You're lucky – anywhere else you would have been a slave forever. Here, if you have the right attitude, you can be anything, anything . . . A shopkeeper? Perhaps not for you. A general, an artist if you have the talent, even a Sultan . . .'

He was babbling. Illa was right, he should try and keep his mouth shut. Ahead he could hear the roar of the traffic along the big road. Once they reached it, there would be no more conversation, the noise and dust would see to that.

'My baby?'

'What? What's that?' He looked over his shoulder. The girl was right up against the bars.

'What will happen to my baby?'

'What is it, boy or girl?'

'Girl.'

'Well, she can be a doll.'

'What?'

The tone was sharp, unusual in a slave. They didn't make demands. He looked back. The man was leaning against the bars at the back of the cage, looking at him calmly. The girl's face was concerned. Dust was beginning to rise around them.

'You know . . . the princesses? In the Sultan's hareem. They need dolls. To play with. She might end up a friend. A good friend, a confidante. But of course, she might get broken, thrown away, who knows. Life is chance here. There's everything to gain, but nothing is certain. You should cover your face, it's going to get dusty. The baby too.'

She did as he bid her. The man stayed looking levelly at him with his cold, blue eyes. As the chaos and confusion of the trunk road rose all about them, Ibn Bai reflected that these two were certainly different – the question was, could he make a decent profit out of 'different', or would he be forced to let them go at, or just above, cost? And then a further thought struck him: that somehow, he wasn't driving the cart at all, but that those two in the cage on the back were actually holding the reins and directing everything. He shook his head – nonsense – and gave all his attention to avoiding a camel that had broken free of its train and was running crazily through the dust, its load of rocks slipping dangerously to one side.

4

Basim

It was a day like any other. Basim spent the morning in the eastern section, the administrative quarters of the Palace Guard, working on the guard rota for the coming few weeks, then inspecting a consignment of new swords which had come in the previous day and needed approval before payment to the supplier could be authorised. He had always been good at taking care of the everyday business, the detailed work – it's why he had been plucked from the regular army to join the elite ranks of the Palace Guard. He liked being organised and he took pride in doing a job well.

What Basim didn't like were loose ends. There was one such loose end that he had been putting off dealing with all morning: a messy situation with one of the palace butchers who was suspected of reselling offcuts of meat on the side. Basim liked the man and hoped that the rumours weren't true, because if they were it would mean almost certain death for the butcher who, like Basim, had a young family dependent on him.

Basim made his way down to the meat store and saw the butcher at work, happily chatting away to his assistants, unaware that he was being investigated and would soon be hauled off for questioning. He watched them for a moment. The butcher had a cleaver in his hand and was chopping through bone. He said

26

something and his assistants erupted in laughter. Would this be the last joke of his life, Basim wondered.

As Basim approached they became silent and stood with their heads bowed respectfully.

'Akin,' Basim said, 'I need to discuss a matter with you.'

Basim noticed the butcher's hand tighten over the meat cleaver.

'What matter, effendi?' he asked with a hint of belligerence.

'We need to inspect the orders for the coming weeks.'

'They're all in the register.'

Basim kept his eyes on the meat cleaver. Had it been wise coming down here, at this time, without support? He had been thinking all morning about what the Frog had said. What did he mean? Could there be some truth in his dreams?

The butcher sensed Basim's hesitation.

'I'll come with you if you like,' he said, and started pounding the meat, 'but there's much work to be done and there will be a lot of hungry officers come mealtime. It's up to you.'

He stopped, tossed the cleaver into the chopping board and stood there solidly, challenging Basim to make the next move.

'No,' Basim said after a moment. 'Report to the guard's office when you have finished your shift and ask for me, Officer Basim. Bring the register.'

'As you please, sir,' he said sullenly.

Basim turned and walked away down the stone corridor, his sword rattling in his belt. He could have used it, forced the butcher to come with him. The kitchen staff would be laughing at him now. He was a peacock in all his Palace Guard finery, a soldier for display, impotent, fake.

When he got back to the guardroom, he found his comrades standing to attention. Commander Gregor, Master of the Palace Guard, was passing through with another officer. His eyes darted around the room – interested, intelligent, cruel eyes. They fixed on Basim, who stood at the door.

'Who are you?'

'Officer Basim, Commander.'

Gregor appraised him for a moment.

'Give Officer Basim the job,' he said. 'He seems like a dependable fellow.'

Then he moved through the line of officers to the door at the far side.

As soon as he disappeared from sight, the room was buzzing with anxious excitement. One of their own had been detained, Basim learned – dragged away just now from his station. No one knew exactly why but there were rumours: he was a traitor, claimed one officer, and had been overheard criticising the Sultan; he had been neglecting his duties, claimed another, and sneaking off to see a girl in the town. Basim had missed the drama and was more than curious to know what he had just been assigned by the commander to do.

'Khalid's job, of course,' said one of the officers.

'Because he's no longer available,' said another, getting a hearty laugh from the others.

'And what was Khalid's job?' Basim asked.

Basim made his way to the eastern gates accompanied by a small retinue of guards. As they marched in formation, people got out of their way, but as they approached the city gates, the crowds thickened and their progress was hampered. Getting in and out of the city could be a lengthy process for normal citizens; papers had to be inspected, taxes paid and there were often, as there were today, long queues. Basim ordered his men to wait by the custom house and went inside to see the guard on duty, who was sitting at a small desk with a ledger open in front of him.

'A delegation from Amber Province, due in today – has it been sighted?'

'From Amber Province,' the guard said, raising his eyebrows, somewhat surprised. 'Where the trouble is happening?'

Basim nodded and the guard checked through his ledger.

'Nothing yet,' he said.

Basim proceeded past him up some stone steps. After climbing several flights, he emerged onto a wooden platform at the top of the city walls. From here he could see Maduk Highway, with all its traffic stretching away from the city far out into the desert towards the Gates of Dawn.

This was the first time he had been responsible for receiving official visitors, let alone a party from a rebellious province. It was rumoured that the wife of the recently deceased governor of Amber had made a bid for power, and that the representative sent out by the Sultan had been put in chains and paraded about the streets. Now it seemed Maya, as this widow was known, was racked with remorse at what had happened, and had sent her representatives to Tumanbay with gifts to beg the Sultan for forgiveness.

Whoever they were – and Basim suspected that if they were from this distant province on the edge of the Empire, they would likely be a self-satisfied bunch of ignorant officials – they would need to be rehearsed in the protocols for being in the presence of the Sultan. That was Basim's job, something he had studied meticulously, even though he had never actually been in the presence of the Sultan himself, or even into the Hall of a Thousand Pillars where visitors were received. In fact, Basim had only once set eyes on the Sultan – long ago when he was still in the army. It had been at a military parade and the Sultan – a surprisingly frail-looking man, with a long white beard and a bejewelled turban – was sitting on a white stallion some distance away, inspecting the troops.

Gazing out into the desert, Basim noticed what looked like a merchant caravan approaching through the haze, its heavily laden camels in a long line slowly weaving across the sand to join the highway. Could this be the delegation? It occurred to him that he had no idea what a delegation from the provinces should look like. Would they have a flag of some sort, he wondered.

'Officer Basim?' came a voice from the doorway. It was the guard from the custom house. 'Message from the palace.'

'Yes?'

'Your guest is waiting there.'

Basim frowned.

'It seems he came in earlier. Effendi Red is his name.'

'And the others? The delegation?' Basim asked, confused.

'I don't know about any others. I'm just the messenger. You are to return straight away.'

Basim pushed past the guard and ran down the stairs three steps at a time. He was about to run back to the palace alone, when he remembered the soldiers he had left. He found them waiting in the shade under the main gate.

'Come with me. Quickly,' he ordered, and led the way through the crowds back towards the palace.

5
Ibn Bai

The builders were still working when Ibn Bai arrived home with his latest consignment. At least that meant the agreement was holding up and his new house would be finished for the arrival of his wife and daughter and the celebration of their daughter's marriage. He would need to start finalising the agreement; he didn't want his partner getting cold feet and backing out.

The doorkeeper had spotted the cart and the big oak gates were swinging open as he approached. Both slaves were silent, although he could occasionally hear the gurgle of the baby, a sound that had always tugged at his heartstrings. The foreman of the pens came scurrying out into the heat and dust from his usual post in the cool shadows.

'Ibn Bai, we did not look to receive slaves today.'

'Why not? Aren't we in the slave business?'

'Of course, Master, and you are ever on the lookout for a bargain. No one has sharper eyes.'

Ibn Bai cut him off. 'Get the man into the pens, water him and be careful, he can be . . . unpredictable.'

The foreman flicked his fly whisk and a couple of his men unlatched the cage; the man erupted, roaring, fists flying, but he was swiftly and expertly tripped and trapped and bound around with restraints. Ibn Bai jumped down and looked into the glowering face. The man was mouthing in fury but, oddly, his eyes still seemed calm and appraising. Ibn Bai decided that the sooner he was sold on, the better.

'Take him away. If he doesn't settle, flog him.'

'If that doesn't work?' the foreman asked.

'Flog him again, you fool.' He heard a cry from the cage where the woman still waited with her baby. 'Bring her inside.'

He hurried into the house, pausing for a few words with the builder, who proudly pointed out the progress that had been made even in the short time Effendi Ibn Bai had been away conducting his business.

'Yes, yes, very good, my friend, carry on.'

In the big central room mint tea and honey cakes were waiting for him; gratefully he took a sip and told the maid to bring water and a cup. She looked surprised but understanding dawned when the young woman was led in. Ibn Bai felt a spasm of annoyance; the girl thought he was going to use the slave as men did but he never had – . . . well, not since he was married. Barring the odd lapse . . . but no man was perfect.

'Hurry, hurry, go.' Then to the slave, who was clutching the baby to her chest: 'You can sit. Don't worry, I'm not going to harm your child. There will be water for you in a moment.'

She made no movement, merely waited until the maid returned with a pitcher and a clay cup – a servant's cup, he noted – then she drank gratefully.

'Is he your husband?'

'My brother.'

'And the baby's father?'

She said nothing but her blue eyes brimmed with tears that made tracks down her dusty cheeks. She didn't wipe them away.

'Look, it's just business,' Ibn Bai said. 'There's no need to cry. I'm a merchant.'

'And I'm the business.'

'Well, yes, that's what I do. I am the merchant, you are the commodity, do you understand that?'

'I understand it very well.'

'Then you will understand . . .' The baby belched and blinked at him. 'Oh, look, the baby, she's smiling at me!' He cooed and clucked to the infant. The woman shrank back. 'It's all right, I told you, don't worry. She reminds me of my own daughter when she was small. The delight of my life. May I hold her?'

'Please, no.'

'I love babies. I . . .'

Panic appeared in her eyes and she stood and backed away from him.

'Of course, of course.' He clapped and the maid reappeared.

'Sabira, take her to the cages.'

'Yes, master.'

Spitefully, the maid grabbed the woman's sleeve and pulled her from the room, as if to say: Well, you didn't get your nasty claws in our master after all!

Ibn Bai picked up a honey cake and chewed it thoughtfully and thought that he was a fool; he knew well never to get involved with the merchandise, it was the first rule of the business. He sipped some tea and wondered if he would ever learn.

And yet, all the same, there was something about this pair. He had an eye, it was one of the first things he'd discovered when he was new to the business. He could spot talent, someone out of the ordinary, with potential, and these two had it in abundance. He would waste no time in going to the top, taking them to the palace itself and offering them to the Sultan's slave master.

6

Basim

Hot and gasping for breath, Basim stopped running and composed himself as he arrived at the assembly point. Here, those
who hoped to gain audience to the Sultan that day, or had ap-
pointments or had been summoned, were sorted out and issued
with the appropriate passes and guides.

Basim calmed his breathing and looked around the room for
the delegation from Amber. There didn't appear to be any group
without its guide, either a court official or one of the Palace
Guard. He pushed through the crowd, circling the room for any
unattached delegation. Nothing. Then he saw a figure sitting
on a window embrasure. He appeared to be sleeping, his head
hanging to one side, saliva dripping into his beard. One man,
dusty, travel-stained – could that be it?

'Effendi Red?' Basim enquired.

The man grunted and his head jerked up. He looked around,
uncomprehending, for a moment, then nodded and rose to his
feet. He was shorter than average and clearly a devout man,
Basim thought, as he was dressed entirely in red and black, the
colours of a holy man or pilgrim of some sort.

'I have been sent to escort you, effendi. If you will accompany
me ...'

Yawning, the envoy indicated that Basim should lead the way.

Often visiting officials were nervous, even shaking at the prospect of coming face to face with the great Sultan al-Ghuri, but Red seemed indifferent. Basim knew that an important part of his job was to impress his guest – and perhaps intimidate him too – with the scale and grandeur of the palace before he came face to face with the Sultan.

'The menagerie . . .' Basim announced, opening a door to a vast covered courtyard filled with trees and exotic birds. 'The Sultan designed it himself.' A giraffe strolled by, chewing on some eucalyptus leaves. Great and small birds flew lazily overhead. 'It's where our beloved Sultan comes when he needs to relax and think. A kingdom of nature within the walls of the greatest city on earth,' he added.

Red nodded politely.

A family of small monkeys scurried towards them, expecting food. They stopped a few paces away and Basim noticed several pairs of eyes looking out from under their mothers' bellies. The male of the group approached and held out a hand.

'Don't be alarmed,' Basim said reassuringly. 'They are tame.'

But he wasn't certain of this and as a precaution quickly guided the envoy out before the monkey got any closer.

They continued through corridor after corridor, each opening on to chambers more extravagant than the last.

'The Gold Room,' Basim announced, 'containing treasures from across the Empire and beyond.' He was confused by Red's reaction. He barely gave them a look.

'And here the hall of mirrors . . .' Basim said, throwing open another door.

Perhaps, Basim thought, the man had some religious objection to looking at himself in a mirror for he hurried through, his head down.

Now they were making their way through a huge vaulted gallery.

'This, effendi, is the Sultan's collection of sculptures from the ancient world . . .'

They seemed to impress Red even less than the hall of mirrors. Basim felt frustrated not to be able to share his knowledge with this visitor, who seemed too uninterested to enquire about anything. For most people the chance to see within the palace would have been a rare privilege.

They arrived at a reception room, already crowded with those who would have an audience with the Sultan that morning. There were ambassadors in the exotic costumes of their many nations: religious leaders, sombrely dressed for the most part; merchants from the city itself and also from further afield, some wearing the furred robes of the eastern lands which must, Basim reflected, be impossibly hot; others came from the exotic forests beyond the southern mountains and sported feathered head-dresses and robes like the wings of exotic birds. All of them were here to offer submission, alliance, trade, all to become richer or more powerful through their relationship with Tumanbay. Basim gestured towards a jewel-encrusted divan, inviting the envoy to sit. Red remained standing.

'When the time comes,' Basim said, 'the doors will open and I will announce your name. Only then step forward. The guards will assist you.' It was also his job to explain the protocol. Usually guests were eager to know how to behave in front of the Sultan. 'There is a crescent moon in the centre of the throne room floor where you should stand. The guards will guide—'

'You're new, aren't you?' interrupted Red, looking directly at Basim for the first time. 'Recently promoted.'

'How did you know?'

'You seem so . . . fresh. This is an opportunity for you, isn't it? You . . . what . . .?' He came closer. 'Came from the ranks of the army?'

Basim nodded. The Palace Guard were supposed to be efficient and polite, but unreadable. He was annoyed with himself for being so transparent. He was annoyed with himself for handling the butcher so badly. And something else was bothering him . . .

'It must be a great honour. To be so trusted.'

'Yes,' Basim conceded. 'One more thing – when we enter the throne room, it is important that you keep your head bowed at all times.'

'You know what interests me about Tumanbay?' Red continued. 'Even in the short time I have been here, I've noticed the way everyone scurries around looking over their shoulders all the time. Why is that?'

'I . . . don't know what you mean, effendi.' This was becoming dangerous talk. Basim was not going to let himself be drawn into it. 'We are fortunate to serve under such a mighty and benevolent ruler.'

'Of course you are.' Red's eyes were piercing, knowing.

Basim felt a trickle of sweat roll down the back of his neck. He felt the presence of the guards at the door.

'Tumanbay is the greatest empire on earth,' he proclaimed. It was a phrase drilled into every servant of the Empire. 'And all I desire is to serve my Sultan.'

He said this loudly enough for the guards to hear. But all he really wanted was to get away from Red. Something about this man made him uneasy. He had cold, unimpressed eyes. He was impossible to read. He didn't seem like a man who had come to beg forgiveness.

Red sat on the divan looking down at the mosaic floor, while Basim stood some distance away. They didn't speak again as the various delegations entered and left. Red was obviously not considered to be of any great importance, as most of the morning

37

had passed before a court chamberlain attracted Basim's notice and beckoned with a lazy forefinger.

'Come,' Basim beckoned.

The envoy got up and tucked the silk-covered box he had been carrying under his arm. It was then that Basim realised what had been troubling him.

'Gifts are usually handed to the slaves to be presented later,' he said, pointing at the box.

'You want me to entrust this to one of your slaves?'

'It's what visitors normally—'

'This is a diplomatic gift from my queen. I am an official of—'

But before he could finish, or Basim respond, two guards took hold of Red and pulled him forward into the adjoining room, holding his head down so that all he could see were his feet.

The audience chamber was vast, known as the Room of a Thousand Pillars. There may not have been quite that number, but pillars and intricately decorated arches led away in every direction, avenues that tricked and confused the eye until the beholder simply stopped trying to orientate themselves and gave in to the sheer size and magnificence of the space.

Red was dragged into position and forced to kneel before a gold and pearl-embroidered curtain.

'Effendi Red,' Basim announced, his voice faltering slightly, he was so overcome by the magnificence of the moment. 'Emissary of Maya, wife of the late governor of Amber Province.'

After a moment, the curtain started to ripple, then swept open to reveal the golden throne, surrounded by the Sultan's personal guard, not one of them less than half as tall again as the average man, their swords the weapons of giants, their ornate headgear lending them even greater height, their robes glimmering like the sun itself.

And at the centre of all and everything, Sultan al-Ghuri, Lion of Lions, Sultan of Eagles, Destroyer of Enemies, Father of the Peoples, Protector of the Poor, Sword of the Faith, lounged on his throne. It was the first time Basim had seen the Sultan close to: his skin was creased and leathery like an old saddle, but his clothes were bright and youthful. A gold and diamond chain hung from one ear. He had about him the aura of power, as if there was nothing he could not command. Basim felt a wave of loyalty wash over him. This small, elderly man was the earthly embodiment of the whole great Empire of Tumanbay. Centuries of dominance had their centre here, on this throne, in this hall. For a moment Basim could almost feel it, as if he were at the centre of a great whirlpool of stars, each point of light a great sultan or general, scientist or artist from the storied past, whirling away into the vast distances of time.

Red rose to his feet.

'May the Almighty guide and keep you,' he called out. 'I trust Your Majesty is in good health.'

Basim leaped forward and pleaded with the envoy to get back on to his knees. But there was no need; a guard had already grabbed Red by the shoulder and was about to force him down when someone standing close to the Sultan clapped his hands. Immediately the guard backed away.

'His Majesty would like an explanation.'

Basim knew this to be Cadali, the Grand Vizier, the voice of the Sultan on many public occasions.

'An explanation?' Red enquired, calmly unruffling his tunic.

'His Majesty would like an explanation,' Cadali repeated.

'I have not come prepared to discuss any business that is not—'

'Well, I suggest you get prepared,' Cadali said, 'because that is what the Sultan wishes to discuss.' The rolls of flesh on his neck rippled with barely suppressed fury. 'And may I suggest you choose your words very carefully. His Majesty is a patient man but this . . . this outrage has—'

'Stripped naked! My chosen representative!' The Sultan was now up on his feet, seething, his eyes popping out of their sockets. 'Paraded through the streets with a bucket of manure on his head!'

Red paused before replying.

'Regarding that incident—'

'That outrage!' corrected Cadali.

'I have no specific details or message to convey from my queen, Your Majesty.'

'Your "queen"?' Cadali lurched back as though he had been slapped in the face.

'I think you can take it that her message is implicit in the –' and he nodded at Cadali – 'the "outrage", if you wish, itself.'

Sultan al-Ghuri sat back on the throne and beckoned Cadali over. They spoke urgently, just out of Red's earshot.

After a moment, Cadali turned back and spoke quietly.

'His Majesty would like to know the purpose of your visit?'

'I've come to convey my queen's detailed instructions.'

'What are you talking about?' the Sultan asked, leaning forward. 'Instructions for what?'

'The surrender of the city. The procedure for handing over control of the palaces, the army, the law courts, all the arms of government . . .'

Basim looked around the throne room, where the court officials were in various states of bafflement and shock. How could anyone dare to speak like this, he wondered. And without fear or any outward signs of concern.

'And of course, His Majesty will wish to know how best to prostrate himself in front of Queen Maya when he presents her with his swords.'

Several guards had stepped forward and were waiting for the signal to drag him away or spear him. Basim felt a deep sense of alarm growing in the pit of his stomach. Should he act? He hadn't been trained for this.

Then al-Ghuri started to laugh. The courtiers, Cadali included, joined in, hesitantly at first. Basim, overwhelmed with relief, started to laugh too.

'And tell me,' al-Ghuri mocked, 'what will happen if I fail to obey your "queen"'s instructions?'

'She will destroy you,' Red answered without hesitation.

The throne room was now echoing with laughter. Red was an entertainer surely, brought here to amuse them all, a gift from their benevolent Sultan, and they must show their appreciation.

Al-Ghuri raised a hand for silence. Immediately the laughter stopped. Cadali approached the throne. Another whispered exchange. Then Cadali turned back to the envoy.

'Your "Queen" –' he let the word hang like a condemned man – 'seems to be confused.'

'Oh yes? How so?'

'She is the mere widow of a dead provincial governor. She has no authority to rule in Amber. The Sultan decides who governs his provinces. Over two years we have been sending messages and have had no replies. And now this . . .'

Red shrugged.

'I understand your frustration, Majesty—'

'I don't want your understanding! Tell your whore-bitch queen I'm going to send Qasaba, governor of the Eastern Province, to smash her. Cadali, send orders out to him at once.'

Cadali nodded and scurried towards the doors.

'Don't bother,' Red said, glancing down at the silk-covered box tucked under his arm. 'Why don't you consult Qasaba on this matter now? I can wait.'

Al-Ghuri frowned and looked at Cadali for an explanation.

'What is he talking about?'

Red loosened the drawstrings of his box. Instinctively Basim rushed forward.

'Please, sir. No gifts here—'

'What are you doing?' demanded the Sultan. 'What is he doing? Stop him!'

The guards were approaching from across the room.

'Leave your gift, sir,' Basim pleaded, pulling Red by the arm. 'You need to come with me now.'

Red smiled at Basim reassuringly. 'It's all right. Really. You have nothing to be alarmed about. He's here.'

He reached into the box.

'Majesty, why don't you put your heads together now?'

Grasping a clump of dark oily hair, he pulled a severed head from the box and tossed it at the Sultan.

Al-Ghuri recoiled, tripping on the plinth beneath his throne. The head of his most trusted ally landed with a crack and rolled slowly towards him, eyes wide open, staring, empty.

Dazed, Basim found himself stumbling along a corridor. He imagined what must now be unfolding in the guardroom. Questions . . . Who was responsible for ushering the visitor into the Sultan's presence? What was his connection to the rebels? He imagined the cold fury of Commander Gregor, pacing back and forth, demanding arrests, witnesses, collaborators. He imagined the interrogation he was sure to receive, enhanced by some contraption of pain. He thought about his beloved Heba and the Frog and the life they now faced through their association with him. Perhaps they would even be brought in front of him and tortured until he confessed his treachery. He caught his reflection in one of the vast mirrors – he fancied it was as pale and lifeless as the severed head. He realised he could no longer save himself, he had to save them.

Instead of continuing towards the guardroom, he found himself darting down a flight of stone steps. He nodded at the soldier stationed at the side door, then he was striding across one of the service courtyards leading to the outer gates. None of the guards there seemed to notice him. No doubt they hadn't yet heard what had happened. He needed to act fast; as soon as he was reported missing from duty, every officer, spy and informer in Tumanbay would be out looking for him.

Now he was on the street, retracing his steps of the morning. It seemed like a lifetime away. And he was back in the narrow lane and could see the Frog sitting alone.

'Papa?' the child muttered, surprised.

Basim scooped him into his arms and carried him up the stairs to their apartment. Heba was hanging up clothes on the landing.

'Basim? Why are you . . .?'

Grabbing her hand, he pulled her into the apartment and closed the door. Heba stood motionless, sensing catastrophe, as Basim put the Frog down.

'I want you to wait here,' he said as reassuringly as he could. 'I need to talk to your mama.'

He led Heba into the other room and started to bundle up some possessions.

'You have to leave.'

'What?'

'Don't go to your sister's house. They will come looking for you. Go to one of the travellers' hostels in Mashuka Street until you can find lodgings. You need to just disappear—'

'I don't understand!' she cried, tears streaming down her cheeks.

Basim lifted a floorboard and pulled out a purse.

'Take this. It's everything I've saved. I'm sorry. I'm so sorry. I've made a terrible mistake . . .'

Heba reached out to touch him.

'It's all right,' she said tenderly. 'If it's some mistake, surely—'

But Basim pushed her away. He couldn't afford to be weak now.

'No, it's not all right,' he said, keeping his composure. 'I'm going to be arrested. And then they will come after you and our little Frog. So that's how it is. I'm sorry. That's how it is. So go . . .' He propelled her back towards the front room. 'For the sake of our child. Go—'

'Basim!'

She tried to embrace him.

'Don't! It's too late—'

'When will we see you?'

He noticed the Frog standing close by, staring at him.

'Your mama is taking you out,' Basim said, trying to smile.

'Where?'

'A surprise. Go with her, little Frog. You need to hurry.'

Basim could see tears welling up in the child's eyes. He was shaking.

'But, Papa, I don't want—'

'You'll enjoy it. Go,' he said, ushering them both to the door.

'I want you to come,' the Frog protested.

'I'll join you tonight,' Basim reassured him.

'No, you won't.'

'What?'

Basim stopped. He recognised the tone, the way the Frog spoke when he described his dreams.

'You won't, Papa.'

Basim stared at the child. He tried to control his breath, to not . . . break. But he could feel his strength dissipating.

'What should I do?' he whispered.

'There's nothing you can do, Papa,' the Frog replied.

At that moment there was a loud knock on the door. Basim, Heba and the Frog froze. Could it really be the Palace Guard? Would they have already noticed he was missing?

Another knock, louder. Basim guided Heba and the Frog through to the back room. The window was open and he stuck his head out to inspect the passageway. It was empty. He helped his wife up and she clambered over the edge. It was only a small jump down. Then Basim lifted the Frog and handed him down to her.

'Come with us,' she urged.

'I'll follow.'

'But how will you find us?'

'The travellers' hostels, Mashuka. I'll find you. Don't worry. Go, go!'

He shut the window. The knocking at the front door was more urgent. Basim collected himself, then went through to the front room and opened the door. There were two officers of the Palace Guard waiting.

'Officer Basim?' one of them enquired coldly.

Basim nodded. 'Yes. I'm ready. I'll come with you now.'

He stepped out onto the landing, closing the door behind him.

7
Qulan

The blade of the spade bit into the black soil. Qulan grunted and lifted the weight, twisting the shaft, dumping the earth onto a waiting pile. He stepped back and regarded the hole he had dug. The sun beat down on his naked shoulders and he took a rag from a bucket of water, held it above his head and squeezed out the drops, then wiped his face. He measured the hole with the spade to check it was deep enough and, thrusting his hands into a bulging hessian sack, scooped up a pile of manure, scattering it carefully where it wouldn't touch the tender roots and burn them but would provide food for growth.

'Well, well, General Qulan, caught at last with shit on his hands.'

Qulan grunted and turned back to the sapling which he placed carefully in its bed, kicked soil in until the ground was level and then took the bucket and watered the earth.

'So, what brings you to my garden, brother? Have you came to arrest me and carry me off to your torture chambers?'

Gregor stood under the leaves of an olive tree. Even so, his cold dark eyes glittered in the shade, his gaze level and chilly in the sun.

'As far as I know it's not a crime to plant an orchard. It could, of course, only be a matter of time.'

Qulan gently tamped down the damp earth with the sole of his sandal and nodded, satisfied with his work. He took up his shirt and the bucket, threw the spade to his brother and set off back towards the house.

'You can carry that, do some honest work. You might even get some honest dirt on your hands for a change.'

He laughed drily. As he crossed the courtyard he stopped by the fountain and leaned under its spray, washing the sweat from his back and chest, before putting his shirt on and going inside.

Gregor leaned the shovel against the base of the fountain and followed him in. Manel, Qulan's daughter, stood waiting in the shady room, a smile on her face.

'Uncle, welcome. Mama is at the market but I know she would wish me to give you her salutations.'

It was rare in Tumanbay to find an official's wife who still did her own shopping. It was considered demeaning, a shameful thing, but General Qulan had never been a man to follow either fashion or the common rule; he went his own way and took his family with him.

'Manel, you are cool water on a hot day. I'm sad that you are too old to enjoy sweets any more, otherwise I would . . .'

Her expression was comical and he couldn't help smiling as he produced the silver-wrapped *mamoul*.

'I can see through you every time, Uncle.'

'Then why the look of discontent?'

'Because it's what you expect, of course!' She laughed. So did he. Was he that transparent to this sixteen-year-old girl?

'You are wise beyond your years, Manel. You should be the general and your father could give his time to his gardens.'

Quietly she said: 'Sometimes I think he'd be happier if he could. But go through, there will be coffee.'

Gregor reflected that the only time he ever laughed was in his brother's house, but that was the price of the life he had chosen. He and Qulan had taken different routes in their lives, the private and the public, but had always supported each other even if they rarely agreed about anything other than their personal survival. It helped, perhaps, that neither had any illusions about the other.

Qulan had once said: 'No one can lead men and women successfully unless they have a heart.'

Gregor had replied: 'And no one can torture information from them unless they haven't.'

Qulan's room was a cool darkness lit only by fugitive bars of sunlight falling from the shutters. Motes of dust danced in their brightness.

'Sit. You'll have coffee.' It wasn't a question and he didn't wait for an answer.

A servant placed the small cup in front of his brother and left the room silently. A tiny rock of sugar-crystal lay in the bowl of a silver spoon in the saucer. It was how he always served it to Gregor, a reminder of who they once were and where they had come from.

Gregor dipped the spoon into the thick, black liquid, watched the sugar-crystal darken, then crunched it and for a moment saw himself and Qulan as the boys they had been when they had first arrived in Tumanbay.

Two child-slaves sitting in the kitchens of their new master, wondering if the life-and-death struggles they had endured to reach this place would be worth it or if they would have done better to die on the icy passes of the mountains they had crossed. Their master had entered and placed in front of each of them a crystal of sugar and a needle.

He had said: 'Tumanbay is your world now. You make of it what you wish – eat the sugar or prick yourself with the needle and escape to Paradise. A willing slave is worth a hundred who are not. If you choose to die, I will have lost a few gold coins but if you stay, I will expect a return for my investment. I will want your loyalty now and later. In Tumanbay, a wise man makes allies of those he buys, a fool will walk alone. A willing slave can rise to any heights, an unwilling one may as well die for all the suffering he will endure. I give you this gift of choice. Take it.'

And Gregor had looked at Qulan – two boys who had come from the cold lands in search of hope – and together they had picked up and crunched the sugar.

'From now on you will be as brothers,' their master had said. 'You will trust and help each other with all things. If you do that, you will survive and thrive in Tumanbay.'

Now, in these days, Qulan was a man with many allies; Gregor had always walked alone and yet together, they had survived.

'So, why are you here, Gregor?'

'Does there have to be a reason?'

'With you, there's always a reason. Always has been, always will be.'

'You've heard about this uprising in Amber?'

'Of course. Maya, wife of a dead governor, challenging the Sultan's authority ... His representative insulted. Buckets of horse shite. From what I recall, the governor was a useless fellow – one of the Sultan's favourites, promoted way above his ability. Should have got rid of him when he was still alive and there wouldn't have been any trouble.'

'Well, there's trouble now, Qulan, a shite load of it.' Gregor went through the events of the morning for his brother.

'Aren't you supposed to stop this kind of thing?'

'I wasn't there. Fortunately. It was simply a normal audience session, people from all over the Empire come to offer loyalty, gifts, present petitions and apologies.'

'But not severed heads on the marble floor. Very untidy, doesn't look good, Gregor. Looks slack but then it is slack.' Qulan stood abruptly and walked to the windows. He threw open the shutter and sunlight flooded in. He stood with his back to Gregor, looking out as if he could see all the way to Amber. 'The whole damned Empire is slack. The way they've treated the army is only one indication. Frankly I'm surprised there haven't been more revolts and insurrections out there in the marches. When the centre is weak and corrupt, people start to see opportunity.'

'It sounds like you've given it some thought, brother?'

'This empire was built on its soldiers, Gregor, on the skills and the loyalty of a slave army in which any man or woman could rise to the top through their own ability—'

'As we did,' Gregor said.

'And I should have added cunning. But yes. That's what made Tumanbay what it is. Now, from what I hear, that woman Shajah has plans to install her brat as heir to the Sultan.'

'Rumours breed rumours. I am more concerned with today and tomorrow – and so should you be, Qulan.'

'Go on.' There was an edge of suspicion to Qulan's words.

'We have the officer who ushered the envoy into the presence of the Sultan. He was a fool but knows nothing.'

'I doubt that will save him,' Qulan muttered. Gregor shrugged.

'The Sultan will want something done and done quickly. He's been made to look weak and word will get out soon enough. There's going to be a war council, probably first thing tomorrow. Grand Vizier Cadali will try and use it to his advantage. He wants me out of the way, just as he has sidelined the army and its commander.'

'And forewarned is forearmed – is that what you're saying?'

'This is a way back for us, brother. If we care to take it.'

'I serve Tumanbay, Gregor, I always have. You know I'm

not interested in power for myself. I want what is best for the Empire. I've told you before, do not try and snare me in whatever deceptions you weave.'

Gregor reached out and took another crystal of sugar from the bowl. There was no more coffee so he crunched it dry.

'You say you want the best for the Empire? Who is the best? The First Wife and her son, who is the talk of every bathhouse and brothel in the city? Cadali, a man who would and has betrayed anyone and anything for power? I think one day he'll even betray himself out of sheer love of duplicity. Are they the best of Tumanbay or are we, you and I? I leave you with the thought.' He stood. 'I'll see myself out.'

Qulan stayed by the window as Gregor left. He heard him bid farewell to Manel. This was a narrow path that Gregor proposed and yet duty called him on. He loved the army and was deeply wounded by the way its needs had been ignored over recent years. Yes, Tumanbay had waxed fat, trade flourished, gold showered down upon the merchants, horizons seemed limitless and yet beyond the horizons there were always new threats and dangers to be faced. As far as Qulan was concerned, this problem wasn't unexpected at all. This Maya woman was hardly likely to be a real threat, but she was a symptom of what had gone wrong with the Empire. The provinces had stopped paying attention. They no longer feared; they smelled Tumanbay's lack of resolve, its greed. In former times, any dissent had been held in check by the power of the army. It had stood at the centre of things, the Sultan's fist, ready to reach out and strike wherever and whenever it was necessary. Not any more. Qulan had always believed that, in the end, peace was won, and died for, by a platoon of soldiers. Maybe their time was coming round once more.

8

The Girl

The shoreline was within sight and the girl could clearly make out a tower on a headland. It seemed to be windowless, with a stone staircase spiralling around the outside to a small platform near the top.

Some hours had passed since the flogging and she had persuaded her mother to leave the stuffy cabin and come back up onto the deck, where the wind was freshening.

'How long before we reach port, please?' she asked the captain as he passed by.

He stopped and smiled politely at the girl, aware that her mother was sitting close by in the shade watching them.

'See the tower there,' he said, pointing. 'Right at the point of the spit? They call it the Mad Sultan. When we reach it, we'll be in home waters. Just a few days, given a favourable wind.'

'Why do they call it the Mad Sultan?' she asked.

'They put a sultan in there once. Bricked up all the doors and windows. There was just a hole to pass food in. They say he's still in there and if you listen carefully –' he put his fingers to his lips and with his other hand, indicated the tower on the spit of land – 'you can hear the screaming. Listen . . .'

She listened. She could hear the wind whistling through the rigging, making a high-pitched hum, but . . .

'Can you hear it?'

'No,' she replied.

'Well, when you hear the screams, you'll know we are in safe waters.'

'I don't believe you. It's just the wind.' She resented being treated like a child. 'You seem to know a lot about Tumanbay, Captain. Are you from there?'

'No, not I. Not many are actually born within the city walls. Everyone goes to the city for one reason or another. Some of them are lucky – most aren't.'

'It sounds like a cruel place.'

'That it is. But show me a place that isn't.'

'It's not where we come from.'

'Then you are most fortunate, young lady. But if that is so, why did you leave?'

The girl was wondering how exactly to answer the question when she heard coughing and saw her mother on the other side of the deck, leaning limply against the side.

'There's a chill, always is this side of the line,' the captain said. 'Perhaps you should go to your cabin, madam.'

The girl took her mother's arm and helped her back to the cabin. By the time they reached it, the fit had passed but her mother was still short of breath.

'You should lie down,' she said. It wasn't like her mother to show weakness and she felt suddenly concerned. 'You don't look well, Mama, is there something I can get for you? Water, some—'

Her mother screamed and dug her hand like a claw into her daughter's arm.

'Mama, what is it?'

The captain was through the door in a moment – they were, after all, important passengers. She was pointing at the hem of a cushion – lying in its shadow was a rat. A rat as big as a cat but unmoving. The captain laughed.

'Don't worry, ladies, this fellow is dead. Ships and rats, rats and ships, they go together.' He took hold of the beast's tail and held it up. It was indeed a monster. 'When I was a lad there were times aplenty when I'd dine off a fine fat fellow like this,' he laughed.

'There's blood on its mouth, blood . . .' the older woman managed to murmur before she vomited explosively and collapsed.

The captain called for a sailor to clear up the mess but was himself summoned by the mate to another matter on deck. The girl settled her mother and read to her until she fell asleep. Her forehead was hot to the touch despite the chill of the night, and she moaned and muttered, waking occasionally with a cry or calling out for Ibn Bai, her husband. She gave her mother cool water and wiped her sweating face, then sat beside her, until she herself fell into a deep and dreamless sleep, waking with the dawn, to the sound of a cry from outside. Had they met another ship? Was there something wrong? Wrapping her cloak around her against the chill of dawn, she went out onto the deck.

The cry was coming from the ocean. The girl ran to the side and looked down. A man was struggling to keep his head afloat as he was being sucked under by the wake of the ship. She ran towards the foredeck.

'Captain, Captain! There's a man overboard!'

The captain, who had been occupied with several sailors, stopped what he was doing and looked down at her, shaking his head as if she was an interruption, as if what she was saying wasn't important enough to waste his time on.

Then she was distracted by another cry. Another sailor was in the water, his arms flailing. He crashed into the side of the ship and then disappeared from sight.

'You need to do something!' she shouted. But the captain remained still.

'Go back to your cabin,' he said firmly.

Clearly, he didn't understand the gravity of the situation. Perhaps he hadn't heard her – her voice was so tight with tension, it was noisy on deck.

She clambered up the ladder towards the foredeck. The captain moved to the top of the ladder to block her way.

'I said go back to your cabin,' he repeated.

Between his legs she could see the front slave hatch was open. The crew were pulling slaves out, many of them chained together in groups of five or six, and herding them, using swords and pikes, to the side of the ship. The bulwark had been removed and there was nothing to stop them from falling overboard into the water in a tangle of chains and bodies.

The girl froze, her eyes wide with fear. 'Your men are throwing slaves overboard.'

'Better to lose the cargo when there's sickness on board.'

'What sickness?'

'Plague.'

'How do you know?'

'I've been transporting slaves long enough to know when there's plague aboard. They get pustules. Under the armpits, in the groin. There's nothing we can do for them.'

She continued up the ladder and tried to push past the captain, but he held firm.

'And if one of your men had that?'

'There is nothing we could do. Once the pustules burst, the sickness spreads. I have to save the ship and those on board.'

She had no words – and there was nothing to say because the procession of the doomed had stopped. The mate came over, his face grey with effort and fatigue.

'That's the last of them, Captain.'

'Burn the brimstone, I want every space below decks smoked till it's brown. No chances, now, Sadique, it's our heads on your thoroughness.'

The mate hurried away, calling sailors to his side, sending them off to various tasks.

'How is your mother?' the captain asked, tilting his head slightly and holding the girl's gaze. She backed away down the ladder.

'She is . . . recovered. Just tired.'

'I was concerned,' he said, following her down the ladder to the main deck.

'No, she's fully better.'

The captain nodded. 'Good.'

She felt his eyes watching her as she made her way back towards the cabin.

The room was stuffy after the cold on deck. Her mother's pale face hung in the darkness.

'What was it? What's happening?'

'Nothing, Mama. Are you feeling better?'

'I think so, my dear. Some water.'

The girl held the bottle while her mother sipped from it and then dried her lips with a cloth.

'You need to eat. Shall I get you—'

A noise – something falling in the large cupboard in which their clothing was stored. Her mother's eyes widened.

'What was that?'

The girl realised she would have to look in the cupboard, if only to reassure her mother. As she approached there was another sound, like two bits of metal rattling together. She twisted the handle and pulled at the door. It held firm, as if stuck. She pulled harder and it juddered open.

'What is it? A rat? Please, God, not another rat.'

She retched slightly and held the sheet to her mouth.

The girl was calm. 'No, it's not a rat.'

'What is it, then?' her mother persisted.

But the girl didn't reply. She was staring at a pair of large brown eyes belonging to a bare-chested man. His face was dirty and gleamed with sweat. He lifted the palms of his hands in a gesture indicating that there was nothing to fear. There were shackles on his wrists.

'Who are you?' she asked. 'What do you want with us?'

9
Gregor

Gregor had been lying on a couch when the officer came with the message. It had been a long night of interrogations. When he eventually returned to his private apartment – a windowless, cell-like collection of rooms along one of the access corridors in the basement of the palace – he was too alert to rest.

He paced for some time, then sat on the couch and, just as tiredness pulled him towards sleep, there was a knock on the door.

'Enter.'

'You asked me to let you know, effendi, when they'd be calling for you.'

'I did.'

'And they are. In the Water Garden.'

Gregor nodded and the man left. He didn't require formality or ceremony from his Palace Guard, only efficiency. He dashed water in his face, changed out of his work clothes – the Sultan liked his officers to look the part – and left.

Blinking in the harsh sunlight, he made his way to the garden and joined a group of courtiers and palace officials. They were gathered around Sultan al-Ghuri, who was lying on a palanquin. He seemed agitated and at the same time listless, jerking up to bark an order and then collapsing back, exhausted. A slave

58

kneeled beside him, trying to soothe his brow with a damp towel.

Theros, the physician, was hopping about administering floral remedies, trying to calm the Sultan.

'Take this,' he purred, pushing a small jar towards the Sultan's nose. 'It's one of your very own creations – "Queen of the Night".'

Al-Ghuri brushed it aside.

'But, Your Majesty,' Theros pleaded, 'it will calm your nerves.'

The other courtiers nodded with expressions of deep concern.

'I don't need to calm my nerves, I need the war council. Cadali! Cadali!' he bellowed on seeing the Grand Vizier Cadali waddling towards them across the lawn as fast as he could. 'What's happening? Is everyone ready?'

'Yes, Majesty,' Cadali said, catching his breath. 'Allow me to escort you.'

He offered his arm to the Sultan, who struggled to get up. Without all his finery, Gregor mused, the Sultan was no longer the great warrior, the Sword of the Faith, just an irritable old man. How many of those present had similar thoughts, he wondered. Such thoughts, if ever expressed, were enough to condemn a man to a most brutal death. One that it would be Gregor's job to provide.

'Where's my nephew?' the Sultan asked. 'I want him to attend.'

Several servants were dispatched to find the young man.

The physician stepped forward, tentatively holding out a hand.

'Majesty, these emeralds are from Samarra – hold one, keep one in your pocket. They will emanate strength and wisdom.'

Al-Ghuri grunted, then reluctantly took them. As Theros backed away into the gathering of sycophants, he caught Gregor's eye and acknowledged him with a nervous smile. Gregor had often enlisted the services of Theros to help with interrogations, using his knowledge of certain chemicals and herb extracts to prolong life – and therefore suffering. He had also, on occasion, sought the physician's help to 'deal with' certain enemies in the court. Gregor knew things about Theros that kept him loyal.

The Sultan's nephew appeared at one of the doorways, looking distinctly queasy. He was led by two anxious servants.

'Ah, Madu. Where have you been?' Al-Ghuri beckoned the young prince over. 'I want you by my side in the war council. You will learn how decisions are made.'

Madu collapsed into a chair and looked around dreamily. A couple of peacocks caught his eyes and he watched them for a moment as they strutted by.

Al-Ghuri frowned. 'Sit up. You need to be attentive.'

Madu turned to the Sultan and smiled, surprised, as if he had only just noticed him and proceeded to tell him about a dream he'd had.

'A snake entered my room,' he said, 'through the open window.' He leaned forward as if reliving the dream. 'I tried to find something to shoo it away but everything I grasped hold of fell from my hands – just slipped out. So, the snake came closer and entered into my body and tried to come out of my left eye . . .'

The courtiers shuffled, glancing nervously from Madu to the Sultan, who had remained impassive during the speech, and now fixed his nephew with an icy stare.

'Are you . . .? Have you been . . .?'

But before he could finish, Madu's head sank between his knees and with a heave of his shoulders, he threw up.

The Sultan leaped back, disgusted.

'Get him out of here,' he ordered. 'Doctor, attend to him.'

The physician put his arm on the young prince's shoulders and asked him to breathe deeply.

'I suppose you've been up all night with your friends?' the Sultan asked.

'No. It wasn't that, uncle, I—'

'I'll deal with you later.'

Al-Ghuri turned and was about to take Cadali's hand and proceed towards the palace, when he spotted Gregor.

'So, what have you got to report?' he asked.

Gregor eased Cadali aside and walked beside the Sultan. He had been expecting this question but didn't yet have a complete answer. Maya's envoy should never have been allowed into the inner chambers of the palace carrying gifts, let alone a severed head. No one, no matter what their status, was supposed to get close to the Sultan without several searches.

So how did it happen? His brother Qulan had been right – it was his responsibility to keep the Sultan safe. But what was the point of being in charge if you couldn't push the blame on to someone else?

'We are at this very moment,' Gregor said in his most re-assuring tone, 'questioning the officer who escorted the envoy into your presence, Majesty. I am dealing with him personally,' he added.

'Good. I want to know how this happened. I want to know everything.'

A pair of doors opened, manned by two bare-chested Sibian slaves, and closed elegantly after they had passed through.

'How could my most loyal governor have been defeated with-out our knowledge?'

Cadali pushed past Gregor. 'On this I have some news, Maj-esty. It appears Qasaba wasn't defeated exactly.'

'What do you mean?'

'He was killed in his own palace by someone close to him. One of his wives, a servant . . . we don't know yet. His head was smuggled out in the middle of the night before anyone even knew he was dead.'

Al-Ghuri stopped.

'A spy?'

Cadali nodded gravely. 'One of Maya's, we believe.'

Gregor could see a glint in Cadali's eyes. The self-satisfied bastard. How had the Vizier managed to get this news before he had?

'Isn't it your job, Gregor,' he asked innocently, 'to know about these sorts of things?'

Gregor nodded to the Vizier and spoke out in a firm voice.

'Indeed it is, and I have the report on my desk at this very moment,' he lied. Cadali raised an eyebrow, disbelieving. 'But, knowing His Majesty's dislike of rumour and uncertainty,' Gregor continued, 'I was not going to present it until I had corroborated the intelligence. No point in rushing off to follow a false trail.'

The document could be fabricated easily enough and after the war council, the Sultan's mind would no doubt have wandered to other matters.

It was, however, a concern that Cadali's people had been quicker than his. Perhaps he had been too complacent in recent months, or was he bored? Whatever it was, he hadn't kept his eye on the rapidly moving arrow – and the arrow was going to strike him in the head if he didn't move out of its path. That's if Cadali didn't get him first. The Vizier was pale with fury but could reveal nothing in front of the Sultan. He smiled at Gregor with all the amity of an assassin's blade and, taking Al-Ghuri's arm, escorted him to the Council Chamber.

Gregor usually found these war council meetings entertaining. Often the Sultan would single someone out – an official whom he would berate for corruption or disloyalty – and have them dragged away in front of everyone to be tortured or executed. Gregor just hoped it wasn't his turn to be singled out. Surely his loyalty to the Sultan was never in any doubt – at least outside his own head.

The Sultan settled himself onto the throne. Gregor thought of chickens and eggs, then resolutely thrust the image away as Qulan entered the room and bowed.

'Majesty, I am late, please forgive my tardiness.'

He was in full ceremonial fig – the uniform of General of the Army, with the sash and the various medals and orders he had been awarded glittering about his person.

Al-Ghuri waved the apology aside. 'General, I take it you are informed of the situation?'

'I am, Majesty. An unforgivable insult to Tumanbay. We should stamp on these rebels, show them no mercy, make an example.'

'But General Qulan, isn't it the weak man who reacts at once?' Cadali said. 'The strong man bides his time.'

Cadali made it his business to take the military commanders to task, endlessly questioning their every proposition, as if to demonstrate to them that he was, as far as they were concerned, the voice of the Sultan. It had been his advice that had led to the reductions in the army.

The Sultan would usually just listen, staring blankly into the distance, nodding occasionally as his ministers gave their separate opinions, but today he seemed impatient with the discussion.

'This is a small provincial uprising,' Cadali continued, warming up to his theme. Al-Ghuri started to shift in his throne and beckoned one of the officers of the Palace Guard. 'A province on the very edge of the . . .'

Cadali, who was only really performing for the Sultan, was

thrown by the whispered conversation now going on between the Sultan and the officer.

'. . . No, not down there.' The Sultan was getting excited now. 'Bring him up here. I want everyone to see it . . .'

The officer nodded and strutted off to one side, where he gave instructions to several of his subordinates, who then turned and disappeared down a side passage, the one that led, as Gregor knew all too well, straight down to the dungeons beneath the throne room.

As the soldiers disappeared from view, the Sultan called out to the officer in charge, 'And get the doctor. I don't want him to die too easily . . .'

He turned back to Cadali who, like everyone else in the room, was paying close attention – silent, anxious, frightened.

'Yes?'

'Yes?' Cadali echoed uncertainly.

'You were saying?' al-Ghuri prompted.

'Ah yes,' Cadali composed himself. 'What I was saying was that we have nothing to fear from this self-appointed "queen". Let us bide our—'

'Who said anything about fear? I'm not afraid.'

'No, of course not, Majesty, I merely meant—'

'I want that bitch's head on a pole so I can see it from my bedroom window.'

'Yes, absolutely.' Cadali nodded.

'"Yes, absolutely" what?'

Gregor was enjoying watching Cadali squirm. The rolls of flesh on his neck were turning a pinkish colour. His voice began to falter.

'I agree with everything you—'

'Enough!' The Sultan waved Cadali away. 'Gregor, you have nothing to say?'

Al-Ghuri's irritation now swivelled slowly and precisely like a cannon towards his spymaster.

Gregor stepped confidently into the middle of the room where the Sultan could see him clearly. He lowered his head for a moment as if trying to find the words to express a carefully considered, deeply felt response.

'General Qulan and the Grand Vizier both make sound points.'

The trick, Gregor had learned, was to avoid committing to one side of the argument or the other, while not appearing indecisive. In the end the Sultan would make his decision on a whim. Once, his instincts had been sound and his decisions generally good, but those days were past.

'And which point do you find the most convincing?' al-Ghuri probed.

You never knew which way the Sultan would go. To express an opinion might put you in opposition. However, Gregor was a master at choosing the right words at the right moment.

'We need . . .' he said, as if he had thought this through for some time. He sensed the Sultan leaning forward. He sensed the whole room leaning forward. 'We need to punish her.'

'Yes!' Al-Ghuri leaped up, excited now. 'At last someone is talking sense. We need to send a new governor, someone to sort it out and do what I want them to do.'

Gregor stepped back. He could see Cadali staring at him thoughtfully. The Vizier was not done yet. He leaned close to the Sultan, speaking almost into his ear, as was his right as chief advisor.

'Gregor has brought whole kingdoms under our control.'

This was true. Gregor had established his reputation as a capable and harsh administrator over many years in far-flung corners of the Empire. He had suffered many miserable journeys across the desert and the sea – for he didn't travel well – and degrading living conditions in barbarous lands, all for the glory of Tumanbay.

'Ah, it seems such a long time ago, Majesty. And I cannot take the credit . . .'

'Why not appoint him governor of Amber Province?'

The Vizier might as well have said: Why not leave him to rot out there in the provinces, while Cadali worked his way ever closer to the throne here in the city?

Gregor looked at Qulan, who had stepped forward.

'Majesty, as always the Grand Vizier speaks great wisdom but I wonder on this occasion . . .' He paused.

'Go on, General.'

'In my garden, when I find pests on the fruit I grow, I pinch them out, destroy them. They are tiny insects but over time they can destroy a tree, they can bring down an orchard.'

Al-Ghuri stared at Qulan, frowning.

'I think,' said Cadali, 'the general has been spending too much time tending his plants. Perhaps if he—'

'Our provincial armies haven't fought for a long time,' Qulan continued. 'How long is it since we've called on the provincial governors to muster their men? This is an opportunity to bring them in line – in case they have any thoughts of their own about rebelling. We should call on them to provide men to help fight Maya.'

'But,' Cadali said, pushing himself between the general and the Sultan, 'to do so would send a signal to the provincial governors that we are panicking. That the central authority is weak.'

'No. It would show them that they owe their power to our Sultan. I need—'

'What do you need?' the Sultan asked.

'Total authority – over all provincial governors and district commissioners.'

'But, Majesty,' Cadali pleaded, then paused to collect himself. He smiled, calmly, statesmanlike, looking about the room for allies. 'If you were to grant these powers you would be going back on the treaties that you yourself—'

'The provincial governors have had it too good for too long. They are fat, lazy, self-obsessed peacocks,' Qulan said, staring at Cadali. 'They spend too much time admiring themselves in the mirror. They are the reason we have left ourselves open to attack.'

The room went quiet. All eyes were on the Sultan, who sat motionless, his head resting on his hand. After a moment he looked up.

'Go and do it,' he said quietly to Qulan. 'You have my authority.'

Cadali slid to the Sultan's side 'Majesty, if, as your Vizier and chief advisor, I may just—'

'You may not, Cadali,' the Sultan snapped. 'Prepare the letters for the general and bring them to me to sign as soon as they are ready.'

Cadali smiled and stepped away. Qulan glanced at Gregor and turned to leave.

'Where are you going?' the Sultan asked.

Qulan stopped. He was confused by the question.

'To my army, Majesty, to prepare—'

'You don't want to see the entertainment first?'

The Sultan gestured towards an officer who was waiting by one of the side doors with the physician.

'Get the envoy up here,' he ordered. 'Let's start.'

The condemned man was escorted in and chained to a metal ring in the centre of the throne room. Gregor watched, interested.

So this was Effendi Red, Maya's envoy, the fanatic on a suicide mission. It was one thing not to fear death, but the death he was about to face was, everyone knew, going to be painful and protracted. Red looked calmly about the room as if he had arrived at an official function and was the guest of honour. He was shorter than Gregor had imagined.

The physician hovered some distance behind, waiting for it to begin. He had some experience of the Sultan's prolonged executions. He had a medical bag with him, full of potions and vapours. If the victim fainted he was quick to revive them, so that they would not miss any of the agony that their bodies were suffering.

'Your Majesty . . .' The envoy's voice was confident and strong. 'Why am I being detained? I am a mere messenger . . .'

'Of course,' al-Ghuri acknowledged with a reassuring smile. 'I know that.'

Gregor heard a chair move. He turned as his brother brushed past him and stepped into the centre. He bowed towards the Sultan.

'Your Majesty, I must return to my men—'

'Sit, General Qulan!' the Sultan barked. 'You will stay and watch.'

Gregor could see Qulan's nostrils flare. They always did this when he was trying to control his anger. He knew how much his brother hated the Sultan's proclivity for torture as a form of entertainment, and took some satisfaction in Qulan's discomfort.

'Yes, sit, brother,' he said. 'You might enjoy it.'

Qulan glared at him. Of course, Gregor thought, Qulan would have no hesitation in sending a thousand men to their deaths in battle, but that, he would argue, was different.

Qulan sat and kept his eyes focused on the floor.

Al-Ghuri now stood up and approached the envoy.

'You say you are a messenger,' he said gently. 'Well, I would like to send a message to your ... "queen".'

'Of course. Yes,' replied the envoy.

'So you agree?' Al-Ghuri was still smiling.

'Agree? Yes. Give me any message you like.'

'He agrees!' proclaimed the Sultan to the whole room.

Gregor knew how much the Sultan enjoyed playing with his victims before killing them.

'He agrees!' he repeated, cueing a ripple of laughter. 'So let me convey,' he mocked with an exaggerated sweep of his arms, 'to your "queen" my response to her demands.'

It had become customary at these events for a scribe to be seated nearby. His job was to document the final moments of the victim's existence in this world, to record his final words or cries of pain. The account would be returned with the dismembered body, giving clarity to the message the Sultan wished to convey.

The Sultan was now standing in front of the envoy, looking into his eyes.

'Let's begin, then,' he said.

On a signal from Cadali, two bare-chested men with black hoods stepped forward and began laying an array of metal implements in front of the prisoner. Al-Ghuri looked disappointed that the envoy still showed no sign of fear.

In fact, the envoy looked strangely relaxed.

'You won't kill me,' he said almost wearily.

Was he delusional, Gregor wondered. Had he managed to take some drug to numb his anxiety?

'And why is that?'

'The ovens,' the envoy continued. He had the Sultan's attention. 'In the palace kitchens. Were they causing some trouble yesterday? Was a dead rat found in them?'

Al-Ghuri turned to Cadali. 'What is he talking about?'

'And last week. Did the water in the fountain in front of the Al-Dar gate run red?'

This was true. It had. But it was common knowledge.

'So, you have a good network,' the Sultan sneered.

'Oh yes. Even in the privacy of your own bedchamber.' Al-Ghuri, who was moving back to his throne, suddenly froze. 'I know for instance, Your Majesty, that your First Wife, Shajah . . . She had a disturbed night last night.'

Gregor could see the Sultan faltering – he didn't know how to react. His rule was based on fear. He had never had to deal with a prisoner who seemed so fearless.

'What was it? A dream that she was being attacked by mosquitoes?' Each new revelation seemed to affect the Sultan deeply. 'They were everywhere, all over the kingdom.'

Al-Ghuri turned and faced the envoy.

'Who are you?' he asked.

'You need not fear Maya and her armies,' said Red calmly. 'Tumanbay is a kingdom that will be destroyed from within.'

The room fell silent. After a moment one of the hooded torturers turned to Cadali and asked if they should begin their work. Cadali hesitated, waiting for a sign from the Sultan.

Eventually al-Ghuri nodded.

'One moment.' The envoy waved his torturers aside as they were about to attach a cage-like contraption around his head. 'Did I forget to tell you, Your Majesty, about your nephew . . .? Madu, isn't it? Was he feeling unwell this afternoon? What did he have for breakfast? Was it his usual dates brought daily from the orchards of the Zaghloul Plains?'

Al-Ghuri felt a growing sense of panic, a feeling he hadn't experienced since his youth when he had lost his way in the desert and encountered a pack of hyenas hungry for meat. With his bare hands he had wrestled the creatures. He had sustained grave injuries, but he had survived. He understood the situation he was in – a fight for survival. It was him or them, and he embraced it and had triumphed through cunning and brute strength. But something was going on here that he didn't understand.

'He hasn't got long, I'm afraid,' the envoy continued. 'There is a poison working in his blood now. He will die within two days.'

Al-Ghuri looked from the envoy to Cadali, who had nothing to offer.

'Unless . . .' continued Red. His voice was no more than a whisper now.

'Unless what?' al-Ghuri asked, also in a whisper.

'He is administered the antidote.'

'What antidote?'

'The one that will be found in the palace – don't worry, it will be found – once I have passed through the Gates of Dawn unharmed, and am on my way back to Amber Province with my comrades.'

Gregor became aware of movement behind him. One of his officers had entered the room and was quickly approaching.

'What is it?' he asked, and leaned close as the officer, white-faced, delivered his message. When he had finished, Gregor looked up and caught the Sultan's eye.

'Majesty . . .' he said. 'The First Wife requests your attention.'

'I can't be disturbed now,' he replied irritably. 'Cadali, you go and see what—'

'Majesty, I think you will wish to go in person,' Gregor said firmly. 'It's your nephew.'

The Sultan froze. Had events moved so fast? Had this small rebellion been able to inflict such a heavy blow to his very family?

Red stepped forward. 'Don't think you can use your torturer, Commander Gregor, to make me divulge where the antidote is – I don't possess that knowledge. It is not in my gift. Only when I am safe will the antidote be revealed to you. How will it be revealed? That is a question for my queen. We have very little time, Majesty.'

Al-Ghuri looked about wildly to the generals and courtiers watching impotently. He was the most powerful ruler in the world and no one could help him.

'Majesty, time is of the essence. Your nephew will live if you do as I say.'

His head was a fog of confusion. There was no room for anger or fear. He had no children of his own and he doted on his nephew, despite his shortcomings.

'Majesty!' It was Qulan, who had been silent up to now. 'Think about this,' he said gravely into his ear. 'If Tumanbay were to surrender to such threats from this rabble, the consequences could be significant and long-lasting.'

The Sultan brushed his general aside. He knew exactly what he must do. Clarity at last. There was only one course of action available to him.

'Release him!' he shouted to the guards. 'Escort him to the city gates. Go! Go! Go!'

The room erupted as officials and courtiers rushed about like a cloud of wasps whose nest has been threatened. Al-Ghuri kept his eyes firmly on the envoy, who was having his chains removed. Who was this magician? How had he performed this trick with such apparent ease? Red bowed towards him and his general, thanked them for their indulgence and took his leave.

'Spies!' screamed the Sultan, turning to Gregor. 'It's your job, Gregor, to find them. All of them. I want the spies rooted out. I want them lined up in front of me and . . . and . . .'

He stumbled and fell. Cadali rushed to him and tried to assist him to his feet. But the Sultan pushed him away.

'Gregor, you understand me?'

Gregor stepped forward and met the Sultan's gaze. He nodded firmly.

'It will be as you say, Majesty.'

10

The Captain

A fresh northeasterly breeze caught the great lateen sail and helped disperse the stink of sulphur rising from the forward hold. The mate, a cloth tied across his nose and mouth, clumped across to the foot of the quarterdeck ladder.

'Fore-hold empty and scrubbed now, Captain.'

'Don't have to ask if you burned the brimstone,' the captain said. 'They'll smell that in Tumanbay. Nothing in the aft hold?'

'All clear there. We still have half the cargo.'

'Well, keep an eye and any sign at all, overboard with . . .'

The captain never finished the sentence. The door of the passenger cabin clattered open and the girl came out. She was pale, her face a white blob against the darkness behind. He muttered a silent prayer that her damned mother hadn't got the plague or he'd have to throw both of them over the side.

She shouted against the wind: 'Captain!' Her voice was strained.

'Is everything all right, little miss? How is your mother?'

'Captain, launch the boat.'

Ahh, so she was scared of the plague. Just like a woman! He bellowed a relieved laugh.

'No need for that. Everything has been taken care of, there's no more plague. We are out of danger and . . .'

74

Behind her the darkness moved and an arm snaked around her throat, jerking her head back and exposing her white neck. The voice was strong and certain.

'Launch the boat now or I'll cut her throat.'

There was a shard of broken glass in his left hand. The captain recognised him as the slave who had been flogged earlier and he had no doubt he was deadly serious. The girl hung limp in his grip.

The captain growled to the mate: 'Go forward, get help.'

'Stay where you are! No one moves or she dies.'

'Then you die too!' the captain shouted.

'Your choice, Captain. Do you want to arrive with a dead passenger?'

'If you let her go, I'll launch a boat, you can have your freedom.'

'The same freedom you offered my brothers when you threw them in the sea?'

'They were dead meat, the plague had them already. You can live and be free. I give you my word.'

The arm tightened around the girl's neck; her feet left the deck.

'Your word is worth nothing. This girl is worth everything. Launch the boat, put food and water aboard.'

The captain could hear the ocean hissing alongside.

'We'll have to trim the sail, we're moving too fast.'

'Then do it.'

He growled to the mate: 'See it done.'

'I could have a man with a bow in the shrouds, Captain? We could take him down.'

The captain recalled something his father, also a sailor, had once said: 'There are old captains and there are bold captains but there are no old, bold captains.'

He wasn't going to take any chances.

'No bowman, just bring us to, Mate.'

'As you say, Captain.'

The crew swarmed into the rigging and within moments the ship settled. Now he could hear the waves slapping against the hull and the panicked breathing of the girl.

'Launch the boat.'

The boat was heaved over the side and fell to the water with a crack. One of the crew held the painter to keep it close; everyone else backed away.

'There, it's launched. Let her go.'

Still holding his captive clear of the deck, the slave moved carefully out of the cubby, to the ladder.

'Everyone, go forward except the one holding the boat. You stay.'

The captain had seen slaves uncounted during his long career and considered himself a judge of men and this man, he reckoned, was used to command. Gods knew how he'd ended up here – just so long as he went with as little trouble as possible. Maybe he could take the mother too? The captain suppressed the thought immediately.

'I don't want to go . . . Please, help me, I don't—'

The girl's voice was choked off as the slave dumped her over the side. She thudded into the boat and moments later her captor was beside her, once more holding his arm round her neck, the shard of glass glinting evilly in his hand. The captain looked down at them.

'All right, you're in the boat, there are provisions. Let her go now.'

'Do you think I'm a fool? The girl will be released once I get to shore.'

The mate was at his shoulder. 'Cannon's loaded, should we fire?'

'No.' He shouted: 'Let go of the painter, set the main lateen!'

They still had half a cargo and though the main loss would come out of the merchant's profits, the captain and crew would lose a percentage of their fee too. Above all, he didn't – couldn't – take time out to pursue the girl, in case the plague broke again. He needed to get the rest of his load to land as fast as humanly possible. What happened to them after that – plague or being sold on in the markets – was no business of his and that, he told himself, was what it was all about: simply business.

Feet sounded on the deck behind him and within moments the ship began to make way, leaving the small boat astern. The slave stood looking at him, still holding the girl, who was no longer struggling.

'Where's the mother? Someone should go and check on her cabin.'

'Aren't we going to chase them?' the mate asked.

'There's nothing we can do. Keep to your course, we still have a cargo to land.'

A scream sounded from the cabin: anger, fear, rage and despair. The captain hitched up his trousers.

'I'll talk to the mother.'

She was lying on the bed, her eyes glittering in the hot darkness. As soon as he entered she spat at him: 'Where is my daughter? Where is that man? What happened? Where are they?'

'There was nothing we could do, madam.'

'What do you mean?'

'He took your daughter, in the boat. He would have killed her. We did what we could but . . . I'm sorry.'

'Sorry? Oh no, Captain, you don't know what sorry means but you will, I swear it, if my daughter is harmed in any way, if you don't turn around now—'

'Go about, madam. The shipboard term is "go about".'

77

'I don't care what it is!' she screamed. 'Now, turn the ship, stop them, get my . . .'

She groaned, doubled up on the bed in pain and then vomited over the floor. The crewman pushed the door open and the sunlight fell on the vomit.

A croak of horror came from the woman: 'Blood, there's blood . . .'

II

Red

Light was fading as the small party made its way along Maduk Highway, the thoroughfare that cut straight through the myriad lanes and passageways that made up Tumanbay's famed market district and led to the city's eastern gates and beyond. Red, riding a short-legged horse provided by the palace stables, kept his eyes fixed on the road ahead. He was escorted by several officers of the Palace Guard and when they reached the city gate they were waved straight through with none of the usual searches or requests for papers.

Once outside the city walls, Red took a deep breath, savouring the air. Within a few hours they would, God willing, pass through the Gates of Dawn. He would take leave of his escort and join his companions and a small group of Maya's best horsemen, who had been camped there, waiting for Red to return. They had never had any doubt that he would return.

Everything was as it had been written.

Part Two

12

Gregor

'You are all going to the cells, don't think that you're not.'

Only a few moments earlier, the kitchen staff, who had been happily chatting and preparing to retire for the night, had been told to leave their stations and gather in the refectory, where they were now lined up in front of Gregor. Some shuffled, their heads bowed. A few were unable to contain their fear and wept openly; others just fixed him with terrified stares.

'You will tell me everything because if you do not, my men will apply torture and, believe me, it will not be pleasant. So save yourselves pain, save your lives and be totally honest.' He paused to make sure he had everyone's attention.

Those who had been looking down now looked up, forty, maybe fifty pairs of eyes fixed on his own.

'Some of you may be completely innocent of all this,' he continued. 'But you've got to go, you're already tainted. So make no mistake, your jobs, your lives within the palace are over. Once you leave prison, if you leave prison, there will be a new life for you far from here. Does anyone have any questions?'

Silence. Once hope had gone, Gregor had always found, there were never any questions. He nodded towards an officer of his elite guard, who had been standing by the door to the kitchen. Now that he had prepared the ground, they would begin their questioning. They would discover everything about everyone: whose hands had been on the dates; who had brought them into the palace; who had stoned them; who had added the rose-water; who had ground the herbs; who had carried them to the young prince's rooms. By morning he would know all of this and more.

'So, shall we start?'

The guards divided the kitchen staff into groups. They would be taken one by one for questioning and then thrown into cells to await their fate, which Gregor would eventually decide upon. There had always been a big turnover of kitchen staff at the palace. But then there was always a plentiful supply of replacements, brought in from across Tumanbay's vast Empire.

The interrogation had been going on for some time, Gregor personally supervising much of it, when he noticed the Sultan's First Wife standing at the back of the room. He got up and bowed.

'Gregor, why are you wasting time on this rubbish?' Shajah said. 'You should be looking for the antidote.'

Gregor had been aware that even if they found a culprit – and he thought that many hands might have been involved – there was little chance of saving the young prince's life unless, of course, the envoy had been telling the truth.

'My Lady, we must wait.'

'Who can wait. My son is sick. He is dying. And you are just asking questions?'

'My men are everywhere, and as soon as the antidote appears—'

'And you believe this so-called ambassador?' she scoffed, looking at Gregor with contempt.

He resented her haughty manner. Like him, she had come to Tumanbay as a child slave and worked her way up through the palace. They had been close once, had flirted, shared intimacies, and Shajah would never have been in the position she was in today without his help. She had always been ambitious but it had been Gregor who taught her how to act on that. He had mentored her through a succession of court lovers, had got her into the previous Sultan's hareem, helped her rise within to a position of influence. But marriage to the previous Sultan, the birth of a son, the Sultan's death, her marriage to his brother, the current Sultan . . . She had become more remote to Gregor with each step upwards.

'His Majesty believes this envoy,' he said calmly. 'Who am I to question what the Sultan believes?'

He felt Shajah looking through him. She knew his inner thoughts like no one else.

'You are a snake, Gregor. If my son dies, I will have your head—'

She was interrupted by a sound. It was a long, deep tone that filled the air even though it came from far away. After a moment it subsided, then rose again – this time accompanied by the ring of a closer bell within the palace compound. It was the signal; the envoy had passed through the Gates of Dawn, the outer perimeter of the city's domain.

'So,' Shajah said, staring at Gregor with what he thought was a hint of disgust, 'where is the antidote?'

The door crashed open and a servant came running in.

'Highness! You need to come quickly!'

Shajah turned and ran, her elegant gown sweeping behind her. Gregor followed. When they got to the prince's rooms they found Madu sitting up on a couch surrounded by his physician, several servants and Sultan al-Ghuri himself.

'It's extraordinary,' the physician declared. 'He's lost a lot of liquid and I don't understand how he can be so—'

'I'm hungry,' Madu mumbled.

There was a collective sigh of relief from those gathered and

Shajah wrapped her arms around him, saying, 'My dear, dear son. What a scare you gave us.'

'What did you give him?' al-Ghuri asked the physician.

The physician, sensing where this question might be leading, turned pale and awkward.

'Nothing,' he said.

'You must have,' said Shajah, turning on him. 'You were attending to him all this time. So what did you administer?'

'I swear,' said the physician. A trickle of sweat ran down the side of his neck. He was an elderly bearded man, nervous by nature. Doctors tended to be the first suspects in any poisoning. 'Perhaps the vomiting emptied his stomach of the poison, but I can't be sure. I have never seen such ...'

Gregor stopped listening to his protestations – he was too obvious a suspect and he surveyed the room for others. There was a young woman standing on the other side of the couch – a slave, Gregor thought, of the hareem. He watched as Shajah ordered her to bring water. She turned and disappeared into one of the side rooms, then returned a few moments later carrying a jug.

Al-Ghuri was now sitting on the couch beside Madu, who seemed confused about where he was and how he had got there. The Sultan was reassuring him and telling him to drink. The room was bustling with activity, with Shajah asking her attendants to get this and that.

'Who else has been with him?' Gregor said, taking Shajah to one side. 'Apart from the physician here?'

'No one. Just me,' Shajah replied.

'Who's she?' he asked.

Shajah followed his gaze to the young woman with the jug of water.

'That's my maid ... Ayeesha.' She stared at her and seemed

momentarily lost in thought. 'No, no, she's been with me since she was a child.'

'Does she have access to—?'

'No. No ... Not without my supervision. She assisted the physician when asked to ... Oh, you think ...?'

But Gregor was already moving through the gathering towards the young woman. She had turned away and was heading back to the side room, but stopped when Gregor caught her shoulder. She turned to him and smiled.

'Do you know who I am?' he asked.

'Of course. You are Master of the Palace Guard,' she answered, her head tilting slightly, her eyes wide, questioning. She had never been addressed before by such a senior palace official, apart from her mistress, of course.

'Come with me,' he said, beckoning with his finger.

'Now?' she asked with a look of panic. 'But, my lady needs me to—'

'Go with him, Ayeesha.' Shajah said. 'I give you permission. Go.'

The slave put down the jug of water and followed Gregor out of Madu's chambers and along a corridor.

'Thank God our beloved prince is better,' she said brightly.

But Gregor didn't respond. He stopped beside a stairwell and gestured for her to proceed down. He followed. It was a long way down. Centuries of building and rebuilding the palace at Tumanbay had created a substantial network of subterranean passageways with many hundreds of rooms leading off them.

Gregor stopped outside one such room. A guard appeared from the shadows and on seeing Gregor saluted him. Gregor pulled a key from his tunic, unlocked the door and gestured for the maid to go in.

It was a small suite lit by torches. A den, of sorts: a couple of rugs, a couch against the wall and several chairs.

'Sit down, please. I apologise for the mess,' he said, glancing towards a small side table where there was some half-eaten bread and fruit. 'This is where I spend much of my days . . .' He lowered himself onto one of the chairs. 'And nights,' he added.

Despite it being a bare, airless place, this is where he felt most at ease.

'Do you know what I like most about being down here?' he asked.

The maid shook her head.

'The knowledge that when I'm here, no one ever disturbs me.'

He spoke slowly and deliberately, watching her face for any sign of unease. But she held her polite smile. Interesting, Gregor thought. He had had hardened criminals down here trembling with fear by now.

'Are you comfortable?' he asked.

'Yes, thank you.'

'Good. Now tell me who you work for?'

She frowned. 'My lord, what are you—?'

'No questions – leave that to me. Just answers. Who do you work for?'

'Lady Shajah, of course.'

'You seem nervous. Are you nervous?'

'Wouldn't you be in such a situation?'

'What situation?'

'Down here. With you. I feel I am . . . being accused of terrible things.'

'If you are innocent, you have nothing to fear.'

She shifted her position and then stood up.

'What are you doing? Stay seated!' he said. But she was approaching him, a hand reaching out . . .

'But, my lord. I want to show you something—'

'Step back!'

She clasped her arms around him in a tight embrace and brought her lips towards his face. He pushed her back with such force she stumbled and fell against the couch.

And then he heard it – the clink of something landing on the flagstones. He looked down to see a small vial that had fallen from her hand. Poison!

'Were you trying to poison me?' he asked, pulling out his sword.

Crouching down, he examined the small bottle, careful not to touch it. A green liquid was seeping out of it onto the floor.

'What is it?' he asked. 'Flying death? Moon seed? Hemlock?'

'They are among us,' she whispered.

'Who?'

'First a few, and now many. One of them is inside you too. She will wake inside your head.'

'Who?'

'The queen,' she said, as if the answer were obvious. She was back on her feet now and seemed calmer. She was smiling. 'You might have seen her in your dreams. You think her armies are nothing, but this is an empire that will be destroyed from within . . . All you can do is save yourself.'

'Save myself, how?'

'Find that thing which Maya desires. Take it to her.'

Gregor had heard rumours of strange occurrences about the city in recent months. His network of spies had also informed him of hints of a secret sect with a growing number of converts. Was this maidservant one of them? There were many sects in the city, many beliefs, old and new, most of them completely mad, some dangerous, the majority harmless, but this was the first time Gregor had heard anyone in the city claim to be a follower of Maya. She was not considered to be any sort of threat to Tumanbay until her envoy had delivered the severed head a few short hours ago.

'What is it that Maya desires?' he asked.

'The heart of the Empire.'

'You need to be more specific. Tell me.'

But she was silent. Gregor held his sword to her throat and she looked up at him.

'If I tell you will you let me go free?'

'Of course,' he said. 'You tell me everything you know about Maya, her followers, how she operates within the city and I will personally ensure your safety.'

'But how do I know I can trust you?' she asked.

'If you co-operate and give me the information I require, why would I want any harm to come to you?'

Now, Gregor felt, he was on familiar ground. He had handled so many interrogations like this. It was like taming a horse; once it was established who was in control, things followed a predictable pattern.

'Maya doesn't want the palace, or the Empire,' she said quietly. 'She wants what she can hold in her hands.'

'Which is what?'

'I don't need to tell you. You're inquisitive. You're powerful. You can find it if you want to.'

'How can I find it if I don't know what it is?'

Gregor noticed she had slumped a little to one side.

'If you tell me,' he continued, 'I can help you.'

She started to laugh. Gregor grabbed her by the shoulders.

'Look, you can make this difficult for yourself or you can make it easy. I can make you talk.'

'No . . . You can't,' she said, shaking her head.

He let go of her and she fell to her knees. It was then he

noticed a pink rash spreading from her lips, up towards her cheeks. He recoiled backwards.

'Moon seed,' she said.

'What?'

'The answer to your question. Moon seed. I would have liked to take you with me but it was not to be . . .'

He knew the poison well. He had used it himself in interrogations. In small doses, it was effective in calming the most violent prisoners and forcing them to focus on his questions. It had the unique effect of keeping the mind sharp to the very end, while the muscles slowly died.

'The time has come . . .' she said.

'No! Wait!' He shook her violently. 'You will tell me . . .'

But she was drifting away, away to another place, another time. She was no longer of this world. If he had been better prepared, he might even have had the physician on hand to administer something to prolong her stay in the world.

As he was mulling this over, there was a knock on the door. It was one of his guards.

'Excellency,' he said, 'Officer Basim of the Palace Guard is ready for you.'

This meant the fellow had been 'prepared' for the questioning – suffering enough torture to make his duty to confess clear. In these cases Gregor found the preliminaries boring and preferred to start on the main course, as he put it.

'Good. I will come shortly and . . .'

The interrogation of the maid had left him thoughtful and a little lethargic. He yearned for a bath. Could he really be bothered to talk to this hapless officer who hadn't done his job properly? The fellow was merely incompetent, Gregor was sure of it.

'No. Just execute him,' he said.

The officer stared at Gregor, open-mouthed.

'Yes? What is it?' Gregor asked.

'But I thought you wanted to interrogate him, Excellency?'

'I've changed my mind,' Gregor said, making his way down the corridor. 'He has nothing of any use to me.'

He was about to go up the stairs when he remembered something. He turned to the officer once more and said, 'Oh, the girl in there. She's dead. Dispose of her . . .'

13
Ibn Bai

There was the city and then there was the palace. Ibn Bai was never quite sure if it was the heart of Tumanbay or if that lay somewhere else, hidden from history, but one thing was for certain: he'd never seen anything like it, and he had spent time in the fabled Spice Cities of the East, each a state in its own right. Legend had it that the palace had not been built by mortal hand, that a djinn had conjured it out of the void at the very beginning of time and since that moment it had been growing, changing like something living, and that while its many towers challenged the clouds, there were as many passages hidden like roots beneath the ground and that unmentionable things, half human, half something infinitely worse, scurried around down there in the perpetual dark.

He shivered despite the sun and drew the cart to a halt before the Gate of the Tradesmen. As always, the Palace Guard controlled entry and exit and, as always, he felt a spasm of fear as he handed his papers over.

And as always, the papers were returned, minus the bribe, the sergeant nodded him through and the gate swung open silently on oiled hinges. He jerked the reins and the cart started forward into the outer wards of the palace.

He unfolded his map – it came with his membership of the

Guild of Slave Traders and he would have been lost in the inner palace without it. As it was, the sun had moved a good distance before he came at last to the Head Eunuch's office where his business would be carried through. He looked briefly back at the cage as he climbed down; the woman was sitting with her baby resting on crossed legs, the man lounging as if he didn't have a care in the world.

There was a common belief that eunuchs inevitably went to fat, replacing the sexual appetite with gluttony; this was not the case with Ramos, the Comptroller of the Office of Slaves. He was built like a wrestler and moved with easy confidence. It was rumoured that he had more than one mistress in the palace, though how that worked was beyond Ibn Bai.

He unlocked the cage and ushered the slaves out. The male wore ankle and wrist irons, the woman only light wrist restraints.

'Blue eyes. Unusual. Where did you procure them?'

'I've been a slave merchant all my life, Excellency. I have travelled far and have contacts in every port.'

'And you haven't answered my question.'

'I chanced upon them at the slave market near the harbour. I like to be early, you know, snap up . . .' He was talking too much. 'And of course I thought of you at once.'

'Very considerate,' Ramos said, disinterested, then, turning to one of his clerks, he asked if his next appointment had arrived. The clerk went scurrying off to find out.

'It's obvious they are quality goods. Look, impressions of rings on her fingers. They are educated, read and write –' he hoped – 'speak our language, many languages. An ornament to any home, an intelligent slave.'

Ramos peered closely at the male.

'He says you are educated – is that so?'

The male leaned forward, as if he were going to whisper something into Ramos's ear. Then his knee jerked up and crashed into the eunuch's groin.

Alarmed, Ibn Bai rushed forward to control the slave, but he was too late. Quick as a snake, one of the eunuch's fists flashed out and the male was lying in the dust, blood dripping from his nose.

'I'm so sorry, Excellency. Are you all right?' Ibn Bai gushed apologetically.

Ramos didn't move.

'Was that supposed to hurt me?' he asked, starting to laugh. 'Those went a long time ago. I assume you still have yours. For now . . .'

'But look at his spirit, Excellency,' Ibn Bai added.

Ramos turned to the woman.

'Brother and sister,' Ibn Bai explained.

Ramos appraised her. 'I'll take them both. See my assistant, he'll take care of the paperwork. Usual rate . . .'

'I was thinking . . . perhaps a little higher, they are, after all, unusual . . . The blue eyes . . . uhm . . .' Ibn Bai fell silent.

'Unusual in that the male launches unprovoked attacks? Now I have other traders to see.'

He walked away along the corridor as a clerk brought over a ledger for Ibn Bai to place his mark upon.

'And the baby?' Ibn Bai asked.

He heard the woman suck in a frightened breath, almost felt her grip tighten on her child.

'The baby?'

Ramos stopped and turned. It was as if he had only just noticed the child in her arms.

'I thought it could be a doll, for one of the princesses—'

'Oh no, we have no use for the baby.'

'But . . . But the princesses . . .' Ibn Bai said plaintively. He was almost pleading now.

'We have enough,' Ramos said, walking away. 'Throw it to the dogs.'

The woman howled as her brother moved to her side. Ibn Bai could see this going very wrong; he could lose the sale just like that. He stepped between the woman and the guard who was now leading them away, and held up his hands, palms out and empty, unthreatening.

'It's all right, I'll take her – find a use for her.'

The women's knuckles were white with strain, her eyes wide with fear.

'No, I don't trust you.'

'You must, you have to, there's no choice.'

'No. No.'

She was frozen. Carefully Ibn Bai reached out and just touched the infant's shawl. He spoke slowly and clearly, looking into her eyes, those disturbing blue eyes.

'If she goes down to the cells with you, they will take her away and who knows what will happen? This is her chance to live, to have a life . . .'

The guard moved forward; the assistant was waving his paperwork.

'Give her to me. I promise I will see she is looked after.'

Convulsively, she handed her baby to the man who had just sold her into slavery. Ibn Bai did his best to comfort her.

'Naima,' the woman muttered.

'What?'

'Her name . . . Naima.'

In a moment she was pushed and jostled away, along with her brother, and Ibn Bai was left alone with a wailing baby in his arms.

*

The builder was wreathed with smiles when Ibn Bai entered his compound. He gestured towards the courtyard like a magician and said: 'Behold, Ibn Bai. Now watch this!'

Ibn Bai waited, wondering what he was supposed to be watching. The sleeping baby in his arms was decidedly smelly and he was asking himself for the thousandth time: *What have I done? What will my wife and daughter say?*

The silence stretched out. The builder bellowed: 'Arnett, you dolt, open it up, *now!*' then smiled apologetically. 'My nephew. What can you do, eh? The boy's a fool but . . .'

There was a grating coming from the courtyard, then a long watery hiss.

'At last. Behold, Ibn Bai!' the builder beamed.

The spray of the fountain rose up behind him, catching rainbows from the morning sun, gradually filling the bowl of the ornamental pool. For a moment Ibn Bai forgot the morning, the baby, everything, in the delight of the builder's skill.

'It's beautiful, my friend. You have done all you promised.'

Ibn Bai had always been a quick thinker, able to put a deal together on the move, and he remembered something the builder had mentioned at the very beginning of their acquaintance.

'Arem, my dear friend, I need you to do me a small favour, something that may well be to your advantage. At least, to your wife's advantage and a happy wife means a happy home, you agree?'

Suspicion crossed the builder's face but he didn't disagree. Favours meant favours in return; that was how business was done in Tumanbay.

'You said your wife regretted never having had a daughter?'

'Daughters are a burden upon a man, Ibn Bai. They eat his food and deplete his purse and attract young men like flies around goats' meat on a hot afternoon.'

Maybe this wasn't going to be as easy as he thought.

'Daughters are a delight to a man, Arem Effendi. They are like cool water to the fevered brow of a busy father and . . . a buffer between a man and his wife when such things are needed. And as for making marriages and, of course, business alliances . . . and in old age they are a great comfort . . .'

'I take it we are referring to the child in your arms that is presently stinking up the compound worse than a plague of camels?'

'Hmmmm . . .'

'There will be a cost, of course. Nothing in this world is for free, except the mercy of God, and even then, it helps to have the odd gold coin to pay over.'

'I will need to be sure she is well kept, Arem.'

'Well paid is well kept,' the builder said.

He looked down at the child nestling in her blanket and thought of his own child, how precious she was to him – and this baby was to be given away? Even in this short time he had become attached to her but what would he say to Illa when she arrived? No, little Naima had to go to her new home.

She was given to the maid to be cleaned up and the builder took her away, his purse somewhat heavier than before.

Ibn Bai looked at his new fountain with pride and pleasure. Yes, he had been momentarily weak but that was all sorted out. He had still made a profit and in a few days, he would be showing their new house to his wife and daughter and all would be well with the world.

14
Gregor

Gregor made his way through the crowded forecourt of the palace's own slave market. The turnover of slaves at the palace was high and a system of acquiring new ones to clean, cook and serve had led to the palace having a market within its walls. Here, merchants brought only the most desirable goods, the ones who could fetch the highest prices. There was always a demand in the palace for intelligence, strength and beauty.

Sweeping past a line of waiting merchants, Gregor made his way to the door of the Head Eunuch's office, only to find his way was blocked by a guard.

'He's busy. You'll have to wait your turn like everyone else.'

Several traders seated around the room lifted tired eyes to see what was going on. The Head Eunuch ran this place like his own kingdom. Ramos the gatekeeper – that's how he liked to be known.

Gregor turned to the guard, smiling. 'You have no idea who I am, do you?' He said this with such casual authority, the guard became suddenly very, very apprehensive.

'Ah . . . What . . .? Who . . .?'

Gregor was about to rebuke him, but decided he couldn't be bothered. He had enough on his mind. The suicide of Shajah's maid had unsettled him. She had been in control of the

99

interrogation all along, he thought, looking back on it. She had laughed at him as she died.

So what could he learn? That she possessed a belief that fortified her against the fear of death. No, against death itself. He had known many who laughed at death from a safe distance but when it came to the moment, the brutal fact of it, they changed and begged for mercy. This maid, Ayeesha, had not. It was something he had only seen a few times in his career and never in a woman so young – who, like the many thousands of slaves in the palace, was virtually invisible as she went about her work. How many like her were there, he wondered.

'Effendi . . .'

The stuttering guard was indicating that he should go ahead. He swept into the office. It appeared to be empty. But as his eyes adjusted to the darkness – for the shutters were closed – Gregor saw movement at the far side of the room.

'Wake up,' he said.

Startled, the Head Eunuch sat up.

'What . . .? Jamal, I told you not to—' But then seeing who his visitor was, he got off the couch and adjusted his clothes. 'Your Excellency. What an honour—'

'The Sultan's First Wife, Lady Shajah, needs a new maid. As I handle the security arrangements for the Sultan's household it's my duty to find a suitable candidate.'

'I see, Excellency. But I thought—'

'What did you think?' Gregor snapped.

He didn't like Ramos much. He knew what he was – a self-important bully. And he was a fool too – he didn't realise Gregor had spies in every corner of the palace, reporting back to him on everything and everybody. Gregor knew of all Ramos's excesses and they were only possible because Gregor tolerated them. Ramos was useful to Gregor . . . for now.

'I thought she had a maid.'

'Not any more.'

'Oh . . .'

Ramos knew better than to ask what fate had befallen the First Wife's maid. Slaves came, slaves went, that was a fact of life in Tumanbay. The good ones rose to the top, the others . . . well, they were never spoken of again.

'I need someone clean and new, someone untainted by all the politics of the palace. Do you have any candidates?'

A smile grew across Ramos's face.

'It just so happens . . .' he said, then stopped. 'No, let me take you to her . . .'

A few moments later, Ramos was leading Gregor down some stone steps, clutching a chain of keys.

'She's been wailing for her baby ever since she arrived,' he said. 'I was thinking of putting her in the kitchens.'

He unlocked a heavy wooden door and they continued along a long corridor, one of a maze of underground passageways that linked different parts of the palace.

'Baby?' asked Gregor.

'Oh, don't worry, Excellency,' Ramos said soothingly. 'I had no use for it, so the merchant took it away. Ah . . .'

He stopped beside another door, opened a small hatch cut into it, and beckoned. Gregor stepped forward and peered through the grate into a dark cell. When his eyes had adjusted he could see it was occupied by several females, crowded together, most slumped asleep against the walls. One of them had stood up on hearing the hatch open and fixed Gregor with piercing blue eyes.

'That's her,' said Ramos. 'She's from the north somewhere. Educated. Clearly, she was someone once.'

'When did she arrive?'

'A few days ago. Blue eyes, good manners. And she's pleasing to the eye too – but that, unfortunately,' he chuckled, 'is no longer something I can act on.'

Gregor knew that was a lie. Reports from his spies confirmed that, whatever the Head Eunuch's limitations, he had an insatiable appetite for female slaves.

'But perhaps Your Excellency might . . . enjoy . . .'

He waited for some affirmation from Gregor, for some wink or secret male acknowledgement that they understood each other. But Gregor gave no such sign. He was thinking just how much he disliked Ramos, and how he must remove him from his elevated post one of these days.

Gregor stared at the female and she held his gaze. Unusual, he thought. Self-possessed. Intelligent. Angry. What was she, he wondered.

'Hey, girl! Girl!' Ramos called, causing her to look away from Gregor. 'Come forward.' He gestured with his finger. But she remained still. 'Girl! I said—'

'It's all right. There's no need,' Gregor said, moving away. 'Send her to my quarters for interview. This evening.'

'Of course, Excellency,' Ramos said, delighted. 'What did I tell you?'

Gregor made his way back along the corridor.

'And if you should need any more female slaves "for interview",' Ramos called out, 'I can provide you with a regular supply, Excellency.'

But Gregor had disappeared from sight.

15

The Hafiz

Dust. Everywhere dust. Even behind the tightly closed curtains of the carriage, little trickles of the everlasting Tumanbay dust found a way through. At least the sun was excluded and it was pleasantly dark inside. Madu took a sip of water from the crystal bottle and swilled it round his mouth. He was still feeling distinctly shaky, though this time he had no cause to hide the reason; he had been poisoned by the enemies of the Empire. He was a casualty of war, which surely meant he should at least be spared this dreary business.

'Why,' he asked his mother, 'are we doing this? He's a stupid, dirty, smelly old man who never cuts his fingernails.'

Swathed in silken robes from head to feet, seemingly oblivious of the heat and dust, his mother muttered: 'He's the Hafiz and you will show respect.'

She had an annoying habit of never quite answering his questions.

'He wasn't shown much respect in his own country, they kicked him out. Uncle just uses him for state occasions. If he didn't have you he probably wouldn't even eat decently.'

'He's the direct descendant of the Teacher. A pure line. Respect that if you don't respect him. He's called by God.'

103

'Called by the spirit more like, since he's drunk most of the time!'

Shajah laughed – a deep throaty chuckle, almost a gurgle, that he loved to hear. One jewelled hand slipped from the silk and lightly tapped his cheek.

'You are a naughty boy, Madu. What am I going to do with you?' She didn't require an answer and, as the carriage juddered to a halt, she went on: 'Besides, he is our security.'

He screwed up his eyes as a groom opened the carriage door and heat and light flooded in.

'Come on, Madu.'

Reluctantly he followed her out. It had been a good few years since he'd been here and it hadn't got any better in the meantime. Maybe it had once been a great temple but now it looked closer to a ruin, with hundreds of tiles missing from the walls, giving the front a toothless, ancient look. One of the minarets was surrounded by – possibly supported by – wooden scaffolding, and Madu reckoned it was a long time since anyone had summoned anyone, never mind the faithful, from those rickety heights.

'Do people ever come here?'

'Not any more. The Sultan has forbidden it.'

A guard stood at the door.

'The First Wife, to see the Hafiz.'

The guard nodded and ushered them towards a second door on the far side of the atrium, also guarded. Madu reflected on the oddity of setting guards over a ruined temple. Surely only in Tumanbay. The door opened as they approached, allowing them into a hallway, musty and dark but in reasonable condition.

'Highness, Highness, we are honoured beyond all our expectations and deservings.' A short fat man in brightly coloured robes, his stubby fingers heavy with rings, fluttered across the room, puffing and bowing as he came. 'Your brightness is a light in our darkness.'

'Good day, Bello. Is he here?'

'As always. I see you have brought the young prince, how fine he is, how he has grown.'

'As always, Bello, you see too much. If you wish to keep your eyes, curb your tongue.'

'As always, at your service, Highness. This way . . . He is, as you ordered, sober.'

Casting a sly and knowing glance at Madu, the fat man showed them through into a small room which smelled powerfully of the Hafiz, just as Madu remembered. Like the building, the old man hadn't worn well with time. He regarded them out of gummy eyes, his face as seamed and cracked as a dried river bed. He rose unsteadily and the smell rose with him.

'You've come. I'm so glad you've come.'

The voice was still strong and if you hadn't seen the man, you might have thought that here was a person of consequence.

'First, Holiness, a blessing for my son. He has been unwell but God has delivered him.' She took Madu by the shoulder. 'Kneel, my dear.'

The pressure of her grip made it clear it wasn't a suggestion. He kneeled.

The old man held out a hand with nails long and twisted. Madu was sure he'd had nightmares of being touched by those nails as a child. He screwed his eyes shut as they became briefly entangled in his hair and the Hafiz muttered some ritual and sprinkled water from a bowl being held by Bello.

'Done? Good,' Shajah snapped.

Bello handed Madu a cloth to dry himself.

'I hope to serve you as I have served your beautiful mother. You have only to call upon me. I am known for my discretion.'

Bowing, he retreated and pulled a curtain across the entrance; they were alone with the Hafiz.

'How are they treating you, Holiness?' Shajah asked, concern in her voice.

'All right. For a prisoner.'

So the old man was still shrewd enough to feel resentment, Madu thought.

'The food?'

'It could be better.'

'I'll see what can be done. Perhaps increase your allowance. Now why did you call me?'

'I think they should be with me. With respect.'

Madu noticed the glance his mother shot in his direction. He turned and studied a mural of the Battle of Somewhere as if he were distracted. If his mother was concerned about him overhearing, it was something he should be hearing, or so he reasoned. She continued her conversation, evidently reassured.

'With respect, Holiness, I think not.'

'I should be with them, I am their guardian, I am nothing without them.'

It sounded like he was weeping but Madu didn't want to chance a look. He kept his eyes on the mural, which he now decided was the Ascension of Somebody to Paradise.

'But as we agreed,' she said firmly, 'when I agreed to look after your interests, we agreed that I would be best positioned to keep them safe, so no man could find them, not even the Sultan.'

'Yes, I know but I am nothing without—'

'Oh, please, stop this humiliation.' Madu recognised her tone from far too many occasions. 'They will stay with me, in my care. That is best.' She turned her back on him. 'Madu, we are leaving.'

The door opened before they reached it; Madu glimpsed Bello grinning in the shadows, actually winking at him as they passed.

Behind them the rich voice of the Hafiz boomed improbably out: 'It is written, that the Word is sharper than any sword and will cut even to the soul and spirit, joints and marrow. It judges the heart of a woman and—'

The door slammed and cut off the last words.

Madu said: 'It's odd that the Sultan should post guards here. The place is a ruin and so is the Hafiz.'

She didn't answer and hurried down the steps and back into the carriage. Only then did she say: 'The guards are mine.'

'What's it all about, Mother?'

She unwrapped herself from her robes and sat back and took a deep breath.

'To the palace,' she called, and the carriage moved off.

In the closeness Madu could not fail to notice a delicious perfume suffusing the air.

She took his hand and, as if reading depths of his mind beyond even his ability to plumb, said: 'It's about time we found you a wife.'

'I'm not ready, Mother – besides, I have you.'

'No one is ever ready, my dear. You are my son. It's no secret you are your uncle's chosen heir but a Sultan without an heir is vulnerable. Al-Ghuri has no son, but he has you. You have nothing.'

'In the old days it would have been General Qulan or the Vizier Cadali who succeeded, because they are both ruthless and have the experience necessary. I have and am neither.'

'You have me, my dear sweet boy, and I am both and more. You are of royal descent twice over – after all, your father, commend his soul to God, was also Sultan.'

Commend his soul indeed, Madu thought, since you were the one who sent him to Paradise.

What he actually said was: 'I'm just a slave, Mother, from slave stock, as are we all here.'

16

Gregor

'Why don't you sit down?' Gregor said.

The slave remained standing. She had been delivered to his rooms a few moments earlier by one of the Head Eunuch's assistants, who was standing at the door.

'You may wait outside,' Gregor said to the assistant, who nodded and left, shutting the door behind him.

It was important from the beginning that the slave understood there was no choice in her life. If she was told to sit, she sat.

'I told you to sit down. Do so.'

His voice was level and quiet – threat implies at least the chance of resistance, confidence says there is no choice.

She sat.

'What is your name?'

He knew this from the documents provided by the eunuch, Ramos, but knowledge wasn't the point here, control was. She said nothing. He waited. In the silence he could hear her breathing, agitated, uneven; he could smell her sweat. She was frightened and confused. Good. Was she also intelligent enough to realise that she would answer any question, in time, either voluntarily or with the encouragement of pain. If the latter, she was no use to him. Any spy must have a relationship with their handler; they must come to trust them and trust can only be won through reason, not fear. Even so, she had to make the first step. So he waited. In his business, patience was an investment.

It paid off when she burst out: 'Sarah, my name is Sarah.'

'Thank you, Sarah. You are wise to co-operate with me. It will go better for you that way.' A simple exchange: give me something, I give you something.

'This is where I live in the palace,' he said. 'It's a small apartment, but then I don't need much. I don't have a family or anything like that. I live alone. It's necessary . . . for what I do. Now I would like you to tell me where you come from, about your family, how you came to be here?'

I tell you something, you tell me something.

After a pause, she did. Telling a tale of pirates and fire and rapine, brother and sister captured and sold and sold again, a child born in loneliness and pain, arrival in Tumanbay to be sold once more. It was a story worthy of the great collections of ancient tales that could be bought at any market in the city – and probably about as truthful, he concluded. There was a baby, there was a brother, she was obviously of the merchant class, maybe higher, she had been enslaved; she was also intelligent enough to provide him with what she thought he wanted. She was, therefore, not a fool and could be of use if they could enter into an agreement. When she had spoken of the child her eyes had flickered away from his for a moment and when she looked back, they were damp.

'Would you like some wine?' he asked, pouring from a jug on a side table. 'It's all right. You can drink wine here if you want. No one will arrest you. Certainly not me. It's spiced with honey.' He held out the goblet. She took it but didn't drink. 'I am not your enemy,' Gregor said quietly. 'You must understand that. Drink if you wish or if you do not . . .'

He turned away as if to allow her some privacy to make her

decision, but watched her reflection in a shard of mirror hanging on the wall. She was looking at a ledger that lay open on a table nearby – her striking blue eyes narrowed in concentration, moving from right to left.

'So you can read,' he said, spinning round to face her.

She stared back at him, neither denying or admitting.

'Did you see anything interesting? About my work? Do you know what my work is?'

She shook her head.

'Please, Sarah, don't take me for a fool. You have a chance to make your way in this city. Slavery is no bar to ambition here. Stupidity is. Do you know what I do?'

'You find things out. You frighten people. The eunuch was scared of you even though he tried not to show it. The guards at his slave pens, they were frightened too. They said there are stories about you. You find things out and you use them.'

'What do I use them for?'

'I don't know. To protect the Sultan?'

'To protect the Sultan. Very good.' She had no more than moistened her lips with the wine. 'Drink more if you wish. I also have water.'

'Water, please.'

He poured it from a plain bottle into a pewter cup. That 'please' was a concession from her, a step towards normality. She drank the cup down and he poured again. This time she sipped.

'Thank you.'

Hasten slowly, Gregor, he thought. He sat on the couch that stood against the wall. He was now on her level, looking at her as if she were an equal – though they both knew that was not true.

'Do you know what I've learned in all the years I've been here in the palace doing this?' he asked. 'No, of course you don't. Everyone wants something. Knowing what you want and striving to get it – it keeps us alive. *What* people want can change from day to day. *What* people want doesn't matter. That they want *something* does. For instance, this evening, right now . . . do you know what I want?'

'No.'

'I want a trustworthy pair of eyes on the Sultan's First Wife, Shajah. And do you know how I can get that? If her new maid were to report everything that happened to me. Why would she do that? Because she wants something too. What does she want . . .?'

He got up and poured himself another goblet of water. Once again they were sharing. He drank, put the cup down on the floor beside his foot, giving her time to ponder. He never got bored of playing this game of persuasion.

'You see,' he said finally, 'this is how the world works. People need prizes. What is your prize? That your baby might live . . .'

Her face betrayed her desperation. For the first time since she had entered the room, real, raw emotion. Pure gold in his business.

'If you help me, work with me, Sarah, you will do well and thrive in Tumanbay.'

Help me, work with me – he was giving her what appeared to be a choice. She would work for him because she believed she wanted to, not because she must.

'My baby . . .'

'Will be looked after, that I promise. And you will be able to see the child. Do well and she will be returned to you in time.'

He needed to be sure the infant was still alive, of course, and could be recovered. It would be inconvenient if that were not so. This slave was talented, he could tell, and he did not want to lose her services.

'This First Wife, she will be powerful. She will have suspicions of a new maid. If I am caught, what will she do to me?'

'You will not be caught, Sarah. And you are right, she will have suspicions because everybody spies on everybody in this palace. Actually, my brother Qulan is the only person I know in the court who doesn't.'

Once again he was giving her something of himself, making a relationship between them, vital in the creation of a good spy.

'But you are new to the palace, you have no history, as far as she is aware, no alliances. She will cultivate you, Sarah, she will try to make you hers. Good – that is all to your advantage.'

She was thinking. He had seen this moment often before: the choice. What happens if I refuse to do this man's bidding? She took a sip of water and cleared her throat.

'If I say no?'

'Then this conversation never happened. You can go back to Ramos's cells, you'll be assigned a place in the palace, who knows where. It will be out of my hands.'

'You will not harm me if I say no?'

'I will not harm you.'

'But . . . my baby?'

'You give me something, Sarah – I give you something.'

She was going to be his spy in the First Wife's hareem. And Gregor knew she wouldn't let him down.

He unbolted the door and instructed the head eunuch's assistant to take Sarah back and have her prepared for her new duties. With a new sense of purpose he strode down the corridor. He would seek out the slave merchant and retrieve the child.

17

Ibn Bai

Ibn Bai considered himself a judge of men; he had to be in this business. But the man who came calling, late on the sixth day after he'd sold the two slaves and foolishly taken the baby home before getting rid of it to his builder, was quite beyond his experience and frankly the most frightening person he'd met in a long time.

The gatekeeper had appeared, leading a tall, dourly dressed man who waited by the door while he was announced.

'Commander Gregor of the Palace Guard would like a word with the merchant Ibn Bai, if that is possible?'

One didn't mess with the palace.

Ibn Bai stood and said: 'Please, come in, Excellency, sit if you will. May I send for tea or anything else you may require?'

'Water only, if you would be so kind.'

Ibn Bai sent the gatekeeper off to wake the servants. The commander took in the room – Ibn Bai had no doubt he would be able to describe it in detail tomorrow or the next day, or the next year, for that matter.

'How may I serve you, Commander?'

Had his bribes not been large enough? Had the blue-eyed man caused more trouble? He could feel his heart racing – he hated being at a loss.

'You came to the palace to sell two slaves, Ibn Bai, I believe, some few days ago.' The tone was polite and yet as disturbing as a sword blade in a nursery ... and it was to the nursery that the conversation was heading. 'After the sale, when you left, you took the woman's child?'

'Yes, Commander. She was disturbed, I was soft-hearted. I was a fool. It was no business of mine.'

'Do you still have the child?'

'I gave her into care. My builder's wife had always wanted—'

The commander held up a hand and Ibn Bai fell silent.

'I require you to get the child back and look after it. You will be paid for your trouble. You will report on its retrieval and health to me alone. I shall visit you here to receive your reports. You will tell no one else of this arrangement. Do you have a family?'

'A wife and daughter. They ... uh ... They will be joining me in a few ... a few ...'

The commander placed a leather purse on the table; the flap was open and Ibn Bai could see the milled edges of gold coins.

'Please me and you will find you have a friend for all weathers. Disappoint me in any way and I will destroy you, your family, and I will burn your house to the ground and salt the earth. Are we in agreement?'

Ibn Bai nodded. His throat was too dry to allow him any words. The maid came scurrying in with a tumbler of water. The Commander took it from the tray and placed it in front of Ibn Bai.

'Your throat is dry – fear can have that effect. Drink some water and you will soon feel better. Goodnight.'

He stood and left the room.

Ibn Bai drank the water. He didn't feel better.

What if the builder had got rid of the baby? What if ... the baby simply was not to be found? What then?

*

As the first call to prayer sounded, Ibn Bai burst into his builder's house, barely noticing the new tiles which were exactly the same as his new tiles, or the new wrought iron which was . . .

'Where is it? Where is it?' he bellowed at the sleepy, disgruntled and obviously irreligious builder, who staggered into the hallway rubbing his eyes.

'Ibn Bai?'

'The baby – where is the baby I gave you?'

'Hardly gave, Ibn Bai. As I recall—'

'The seven gods piss on your recall. Do you have the baby? Here. Now. I need that baby—'

'No.'

'No – what?'

'No, I don't have the baby. It isn't here.'

Ibn Bai slumped onto a convenient low table. Cups and plates cracked beneath him.

'Where is it, Arem?'

'You're sounding croaky, Ibn Bai. Would you like a glass of water?'

'I need the baby. Where is it, Arem?'

'Well, none of my wives wanted it so . . . uhhm . . . I sold it on. Are you sure you don't want a drink. Some green tea, perhaps? You're not looking well at all.'

'The baby, just the baby.'

'I gave it to Recif the butcher.'

'The butcher?'

'The butcher.'

'And where might I find Recif the butcher?'

'The Street of the Butchers. Third shop along. At the sign of the cleaver. You didn't say it was valuable, the baby. You seemed to want to get rid of it, Ibn Bai, so that's what I did.'

'Recif, the butcher?'

'Street of the Butchers, at the sign of the . . .'

Ibn Bai was, as Arem was later to tell his wife, gone like the hot desert wind that comes out of the east in the height of summer and takes whole trees and occasional camels in its passing.

The Street of the Butchers was in full swing when Ibn Bai finally got there, sweating far too much for a man of his size and age. He made for the third shop along, at the sign of the cleaver, and burst in through the curtain just as a huge silver blade cleaved through a joint of meat and buried itself in a bloody wooden block.

'The baby you got from my builder Arem?' he bellowed.

'Don't shout, it's not good for the meat.'

'The meat can't hear.'

'The goats in the pens at the back – they don't like disturbance. It affects the quality of the meat and we only sell the best here. How can I help you?'

'The baby . . .'

'What of it?'

'I need it back.'

'It's too late,' the butcher said, cleaning his blade on a dirty cloth.

18
Shajah

Shajah looked in the mirror. Something was missing.

'Bring the belt with the gold thread,' she instructed her new maid. Sarah went over to the couch, where a small sample of the First Wife's wardrobe and accessories had been laid out earlier by one of her women. 'Also the diamond-studded one,' her mistress called out.

She picked up the two belts and held them up for her mistress to see. Shajah took the diamond-studded one and wrapped it around herself. It sparkled against the crimson silk gown she wore.

'No, I will wear the gold tonight.'

'Yes, madam.'

'Let me show you,' Shajah said. 'You loop it around like …' but seeing Sarah skilfully weaving the gold thread through the delicate straps of the gown, she held her tongue. Clearly this maid knew things.

'Shall I bring the azure kameez now, madam?' Sarah asked.

'Don't ask, just do. I will tell you if I am dissatisfied.'

Shajah had been impressed with Sarah so far. She had been an attentive but not overbearing presence. She'd had maids who always seemed to be there when she didn't need them and then not there when she did. She'd had maids who were always one step behind, never quite anticipating what was required when it was required. They never lasted long. Sarah seemed altogether different. Clearly, she had served a high-ranking lady before – or was she herself a high-ranking lady from some distant land?

'I was a slave too, you know,' said Shajah as Sarah carefully unfolded the kameez. 'Everyone's a slave, I suppose. Even the free men are slaves – slaves to power, slaves to money, slaves to . . . This is how it is in Tumanbay.'

Sarah offered the kameez.

'May I, madam?'

Shajah nodded, allowing Sarah to drape it over her shoulders.

'How did we come to this place and this time?' she sighed, admiring herself in the mirror. How indeed had she, a mere slave who could neither read nor write, who at twelve years of age had been sold by her mother to camel traders, become wife of, not one, but two sultans? 'How did we begin the journey?' she continued, watching Sarah in the mirror. 'You and I, in this place, at this time. We have such different lives but we have a similar journey, I feel.'

Sarah didn't respond but continued her work, threading a needle and now carefully stitching her mistress's dress up at the back.

'So you were taken by pirates, I understand?'

'Yes, my lady.'

'And before that?'

Sarah was silent.

'Where is your family from?' Shajah persisted.

'My father was a merchant from a small kingdom in the north.'

'What kingdom? What's it called?' She knew the answer before it came.

'Kassek,' Sarah said quietly.

'Kassek. Ah . . .'

'It's very small. You won't have heard of it.'

Shajah smiled. She was going to find out everything about this maid. Her mistake with the last one was trusting those in the palace responsible for ensuring slaves were loyal, were doing their jobs properly. Clearly, they weren't, and now she needed to look after things herself.

'Actually I have heard of Kassek,' she said. 'How is his excellency Ivane Kaas?'

Sarah's head jerked up and Shajah held her gaze in the mirror.

'Ivane Kaas . . .?' She seemed flustered.

'Your king,' Shajah said firmly.

Had it been so easy to unpick the girl's story? She felt disappointed. She liked Sarah and now it seemed she was not who she claimed to be and would have to go.

'But . . . But . . .' Sarah stuttered. 'Surely you must know, my lady, that Ivane Kaas is dead. Killed by his son, Ilkin.'

Shajah had not known this.

'Ah, yes. Yes,' she said casually. 'It escaped my memory.'

Shajah had not heard of Kassek or its insignificant rulers until earlier in the day, when she had been delivered a report by the librarian at the palace scriptorium. She had asked him to research a few details relating to the maid's story so that she could put her to the test. She made a mental note to have the librarian firmly reminded to keep his records up to date in future.

'Life is so fragile,' she said. 'We think we are safe and then suddenly . . .' She snapped her fingers.

'Ilkin was not so kind to my people as his father was,' Sarah continued. 'We had to leave in a hurry to find a new home.'

'And were captured by pirates?

'Yes.'

'And here you are.' Shajah held her arms out to the maid. Sarah flinched momentarily. 'Don't be frightened,' Shajah said, smiling. She held Sarah's head in her hands. 'You have suffered great hardships. But now you are safe. You are my maid and I will look after you.'

She released Sarah and moved towards the door. She was late for the reception. The Sultan would be waiting for her. He hated her not being by his side. Just as she was about to leave, she stopped and turned to Sarah.

'Do you know why you are my maid?'

'No, my lady.'

'Why do you think you have this job? You're from nowhere. You know nothing. Why did I allow that man to place you in my household? Don't you want to know?'

Sarah nodded.

'Because I had no choice in the matter. You see, I'm a slave just like you. In essence, I have no real power. Not really. I live my life for the Sultan. And you ...? Well, the only thing I ask of you is total and complete loyalty.' She was no longer smiling. 'Because if you're not loyal, you will suffer. You think you have suffered already, but believe me, you know nothing of suffering. Here in Tumanbay, we have had centuries to perfect the art.'

She paused, waiting for a nod or some acknowledgement from the girl, to show she understood what this meant – that she had a choice, that she was being offered the chance for something.

'Madam, what is it for?'

'What?'

'The celebration.'

'A wonderful new perfume created by my husband, the Sultan.' She swept up her kameez and went out of the apartment to join her ladies, who were waiting to escort her to the banqueting hall.

When Shajah entered, the room was full. Sultan al-Ghuri was already seated on a throne, receiving guests who had come from all over the Empire to celebrate the creation of his latest perfume.

'You don't like it?' she heard him ask one of them.

'I love it!' the guest exclaimed. 'I absolutely love it, Majesty!'

'My nephew Madu helped me develop it,' the Sultan said, delighted. 'I call it "Life". Quite simply, "Life".' All about the room were smiling, nodding faces. 'To celebrate his recovery from the clutches of death.'

'Very good, Your Majesty.' It was the Vizier Cadali's turn to congratulate the Sultan. 'It's similar to the . . . er . . . the one you created for . . . er . . .'

'For the king of Assaria?'

'Yes. That one.'

'Or the scent I made to celebrate the Feast of the Sickle Moon?'

'Yes. That one too—'

'But they are entirely different,' the Sultan said, eyeing the Vizier suspiciously.

Cadali chuckled nervously. Shajah enjoyed seeing him squirm. And now all the sycophants in the room were staring at him, no doubt hoping to see him being led away by guards for some degrading and humiliating punishment. But if Cadali knew anything, it was how to handle the Sultan's volatile temper and fragile ego.

'My ability to distinguish such subtle differences in smell . . . uh . . . scent . . . is far less developed that yours, Your Majesty. It is really quite a unique and . . . and wonderful gift you have.'

Shajah surveyed the room. She saw Madu smiling, talking animatedly to one of the male servants. Didn't he understand that servants were there to serve, not to talk? When he saw her frowning, his smile melted away and he said something to the young man, who carried on with his duties. Madu nodded to his mother, then disappeared from view into the crowd.

'May I be the first to congratulate you?'

She turned to see Gregor, smiling broadly, a mischievous twinkle in his eye.

'What for?'

'Your husband's wonderful new creation,' he said.

'Oh, that? They all smell like horse dung to me. But then I wasn't born here.'

The Hafiz, in all his finery, was being led into the room by his acolyte, Bello. He had been summoned to bless the Sultan's new scent. Cadali was shepherding them to their assigned places ready for the ceremony to begin.

'I heard you visited the old man the other day,' Gregor said. It irritated Shajah that he knew this, but she didn't react. She knew he had his men watching her. 'I didn't know you were close, you two.'

'We're not. I felt sorry for him.'

'That's very unlike you, madam. A soft heart?'

'I thought you knew me better, Gregor,' she said. 'You did once.'

She caught his eye and they shared a momentary memory of something long past but not forgotten.

The room had gone silent. Sultan al-Ghuri rose to his feet and addressed the guests.

'I have commissioned the great Masoud Shah to compose a special piece celebrating the creation of life itself,' he announced.

There was a muttering of satisfaction as a single soaring note from a *ka-vard* filled the room. After some moments the note exploded into a tune as a curtain was drawn, revealing the musicians. The guests applauded enthusiastically.

Shajah could see her husband looking around. She excused herself from Gregor and went to join him.

19

Gregor

Gregor observed Shajah as she took her place beside her husband. She looked ahead, emotionless. The Hafiz was now speaking about the Sultan's extraordinary qualities, and how his new scent might spread harmony and strength across the Empire. Many of the guests were wearing the Sultan's new perfume and Gregor was finding it overpowering. He slipped out of a side door, unnoticed, and made his way to a passageway which opened onto the grand courtyard, where fires had been lit in a row of braziers to take the chill off the unseasonably cool night. He leaned against the banister and took a few deep breaths. The lingering smell of the Sultan's new scent made him feel slightly sick.

This is an empire that will be destroyed from within . . . Both the envoy and the maid had said those same words. What did they know? Everyone at the palace, from the Sultan down, was behaving as if nothing was wrong. But Gregor sensed a great deal was wrong. Perhaps even the First Wife was part of it.

His thoughts were interrupted by the spectacle of Cadali waddling along the corridor.

'Good evening, General,' Cadali said.

He was addressing Qulan, who was standing nearby talking to some guests. Gregor moved closer, unseen by either of them.

'And how is the most powerful man in the Empire?' Cadali enquired. 'Enjoying the celebrations?'

'I have an army to build, an empire to defend. Do you think I should be wasting my time here?'

'Oh dear, yes. Power is not just about big armies and strong men, General. It's about confidence.'

'What do you mean?'

Cadali's eyes twinkled. 'Confidence is strength. All this will no doubt be reported back to our enemies, wherever they may be. Spies, General. They need to see that Tumanbay is confident, that our glorious Sultan is ... well, in control.'

'My brother, Gregor, is dealing with the spies.'

'Oh no. He's not,' said Cadali. 'He can't. Spies are like cockroaches. You can kill them all day long and just when you think they have all gone ... you find one in your bed sleeping beside you ...' And with that he continued towards the banqueting hall.

'Aren't you coming in, General? I think the Sultan is about to cut the cake.'

Qulan didn't move.

'Why the pained look? This could be your last chance to enjoy civilised company before your long march to the provinces. Anyway, all you have to do is make sure the Sultan sees you, compliment him on his new creation, and then you can be on your way.' Chuckling, he disappeared.

Qulan stood for a few moments looking out at the night, then made his way towards the banqueting hall to do his duty.

Gregor was about to join him when he noticed ash from one of the burning braziers drifting past. For a moment he was back in the mountains, snow falling, one of a small group of children struggling over a treacherous pass. Gregor was helping another child whose leg had been injured by a bear trap. He was crying, asking to rest, and Gregor was encouraging him with soothing words, but knowing in his heart that darkness was drawing in and the worst was still to come. From way ahead Qulan was calling back to them, 'Come on, come on. We have to hurry or we will die.'

Gregor felt a hand on his shoulder.

'Brother?' It was Qulan. 'I'm soon to march out with the army. You need to watch my back. You need to watch Cadali.'

Gregor nodded.

'I just told him you are dealing with the spies. Are you?'

'It's what I do, brother.'

'It's what you are meant to do, but from what I hear, not very much is actually happening.'

'It's a dark world. Spies, informers, who works for who – it's quite probable there are people out there who believe they are spying for the Sultan when all the time they are working for Maya or any one of half a dozen other interested parties.'

'So if even the spies don't know what they know, how does the spymaster discover the truth?'

'A good question. It's why we go to the iron.'

'What exactly does that mean, Gregor?'

'You know what it means.'

'Torture, in other words?'

'In other words. A tool of my profession. A few screams from down the passage can be amazingly encouraging to a reluctant memory.'

Qulan shook his head in dismay.

Gregor took his brother by both shoulders and looked into his eyes.

'Dear Qulan, you are probably the only man in the city who is not betraying someone to someone – everyone is a spy, even if they don't know it. Apart from you. That's what I saw in the mountains when I crept up on you trying to cook that half-starved rabbit over your pathetic fire. I saw a boy who was absolutely what he was and nothing else. If I hadn't seen that, I would have killed you there in the snow and taken everything.'

Qulan reached up, took Gregor's forearms in his hands and forced the arms down. Neither man's gaze faltered.

'I heard the creak of your foot pressing the snow. I had a dagger in my hand and that pathetic fire saved your life. You would not have survived that night on the mountain without it.'

Gregor knew this to be true. Why Qulan had allowed him to join his small party all those moons ago, when they had so little food and provisions, he had never been able to bring himself to ask. For certain it had saved his life; without Qulan he would have starved, or frozen, or fallen to his death as the others had.

'Be careful, brother,' Qulan said.

'I'm always careful,' Gregor replied.

'Are you? What about her?' His voice dropped as a courtier walked past.

'Don't worry, I already have a spy in her chambers. I know everything that goes on in the hareem.'

'Then be careful, above all, of yourself,' Qulan said. 'It is when we are most certain that we are most vulnerable.'

'You should have been a preacher, brother, it suits you. I have one request.'

'Yes?'

'Let go of my arms, Qulan, so we can go in and compliment the Sultan on his wonderful new fragrance. Oh, and one thing further.'

'Yes?'

'I don't think this is a minor incident in a far-off province any longer. I think it's something infinitely more serious. Maya's followers hide in plain sight. If they are here in Tumanbay already, we don't know how many provinces have been infected.'

'As a soldier, I always expect attack from the least expected direction,' Qulan said.

'Attack from an enemy you don't know is there? Who is unafraid of death?'

Qulan lowered his arms and looked towards the banqueting hall, from where the sound of applause and cheering was coming.

'Let us go in and do our duty to sycophancy.' He paused and grinned. 'So we can then leave and get on with our duty to Tumanbay.'

20

Ibn Bai

The sea sparkled under the morning sun as if a great swarm of silvery fish were passing beside the quay. There was still a little of the cool of dawn present but Ibn Bai knew it would soon vanish, just as the momentary peace while many of the dockers and sailors – a notoriously superstitious lot – were at morning prayers, would soon be replaced by the crash and thunder of a busy port. The vast chain that stretched across the harbour entrance overnight was being lowered. Beyond it three merchantmen were already jockeying to enter, their sails shivering as they were raised in expectation; but no sign yet of his ship, bearing wife, daughter and a valuable cargo which would establish him in the slave markets of Tumanbay as a man to respect.

He walked over to the harbour master who presided, splendid in the blue and gold colours of the city, on the raised terrace of the custom house. He was surrounded by half a dozen clerks who were dispatched as the waiting ships entered the harbour, to check cargoes and contraband. Each was accompanied by two or three port police, who would, if necessary, enforce the regulations.

'The *Gullswing*, Excellency – when is she due?'

'She'll be due when she's due, Ibn Bai. As I told you yesterday.'

'Yesterday you told me she'd been seen off the Gold Dome.

Doesn't that mean she should have been waiting to enter with those other ships this morning?'

'You're not a sailor, are you?' the harbour master said. Ibn Bai shook his head. 'If you were, you would know that the sea has its ways. A sudden squall, a rogue tide, a lost spar, who knows – things happen out there. She will come in her own good time. Though I grant you, I would have expected her this morning. Why don't you go . . . have a glass of tea, a honey cake and come back in an hour?'

'If you don't mind, I'll wait here.'

'It's your time, my friend.'

He turned his attention to a clerk who had arrived with a manifest, running his eye down it and pocketing the bribe it concealed with professional ease.

Ibn Bai wandered over to the quayside and stood looking down at the sea, as it moved sluggishly against the wooden pilings with its carpet of flotsam – shards of wood, an amphora, a dead fish or two, torn nets and cork floats, a broken lobster basket, a gull's wing, – all the rubbish of a port, heaving down there in the last surge of some ocean current that was even now delivering his ship and cargo to a happy return.

The sun was nearing its highest point – the heat was intense – when Ibn Bai's musings were cut short by the harbour master's bellow to one of his clerks.

'Zlatan, ship coming in! *Gullswing*. Ready your people and go aboard . . .'

And there she was, the beautiful *Gullswing*, slipping through the harbour gates, sail set, white water shearing back from the prow as she dashed for shore.

'Will she dock alongside the quay here?' Ibn Bai called.

'She'll anchor at the buoy there until the paperwork is complete.'

'Can I go out with the clerk and his men on the skiff?'

'Not allowed.'

'It's been a long time since I saw them – I have so much to say . . .'

For a moment, an uneasy thought of the baby laying in an improvised cot back home entered his mind. The butcher had exacted a high price once he'd realised how badly Ibn Bai needed the child, telling him how much his wife doted on the little sweetheart, but recalling the dour man who had visited his house and threatened his family, the merchant paid up and felt he had got off lightly. How Illa would feel about it once she arrived was another matter entirely and he put the thought aside. He'd deal with that when everyone was at home and settled.

'I told you, no one is allowed aboard any vessel—'

The harbour master stopped in mid-sentence and stared out at the approaching ship. It was coming in fast, there was no doubt about it. Even Ibn Bai could see that. The harbour master shaded his eyes with his hand and sucked his teeth.

'What are they doing, the idiots?' he muttered.

'What do you mean? What's wrong?' Ibn Bai asked, hearing alarm in his voice.

Ignoring him, the harbour master leaped up onto the quay and bellowed through his speaking trumpet: 'Master of the *Gullswing*, give way! Give way!'

He watched for a moment. The ship continued its frantic dash towards them, narrowly missing a fishing boat heading out to sea. Its crew lined the rail, bellowing insults.

Turning back to his assistant, the harbour master shouted, 'Zlatan, raise the signal!'

'What is it?' Ibn Bai asked. 'What's going on?'

'The sail, man! They haven't lowered the sail, they're coming in too fast!'

A signal cannon boomed behind them; smoke drifted across the platform. But the ship ploughed on, closer and closer, running down a skiff, crashing into the prow of a merchantman, breaking the fore rope, bringing the foremast crashing down on to the deck. It slowed the headlong progress a little, but not enough. It was now making directly for them. Ibn Bai and the harbour master ran back towards the custom house and leaped clear just as the *Gullswing* hit with a splintering of wood and a deafening shriek of iron, and then came to rest with its bow perched high on what remained of the quay. The aft mast shivered and swayed but stayed upright, at a crazy angle.

Lying in the muck where he had landed, Ibn Bai looked around, aghast. For what seemed like an age everything was still, everything was silent. Then he heard someone shouting, 'Oh my God! My wife, my daughter . . .' It took a moment for him to realise it was his own voice. Then he heard others: 'Shore it up, take the ropes . . .'

He scrambled to his feet. The harbour master and his assistant were running towards the wreck. He followed.

'No one to board!' the harbour master shouted. 'Hold the quay, no one else to approach.'

But Ibn Bai was already close behind, scrambling over splintered planks that may have been part of the quay or the ship. When he got to the top he could see what remained of the foredeck and jumped across, missing his footing and slipping onto his back. He crashed down, hitting a fallen spar, which knocked the breath from his body. The deck in front of his face was stained with something dark. He shook his head, took a deep breath and struggled to his feet.

'Illa! Illa!' he kept shouting as he pushed his way through the tangle of ropes and sailcloth. He could see no signs of the crew or his beloved wife and daughter.

133

'Zlatan,' the harbour master called, 'keep watch on the slave holds. I want them contained until we know what happened here. I'm going below.'

Ibn Bai followed him down to the lower deck. The wooden steps were splintered and broken; at the bottom the heat was unbearable and the shadows pressed close around them.

'Hello? Hello?' the harbour master called out.

'Illa? Illa?' Ibn Bai echoed.

It was eerily quiet.

'Where are they all?' Ibn Bai asked.

The harbour master pushed at a door but it wouldn't shift.

'Help me.'

Ibn Bai put his shoulder against the weathered wood and they shoved together. The door crashed open and they both recoiled, choking. The stench of rotting flesh was like something solid coating lips and throat. The harbour master covered his lower face with his sash of office and moved forward. Ibn Bai clapped a hand over his nose and cautiously followed him.

He stepped onto something soft, turning his ankle, and lurched back as a rat, screeching, scurried away. As his eyes adjusted to the dark he could see movement as if the floor were rippling; the cabin was overrun with rats, hundreds, thousands, scurrying everywhere. Ibn Bai knew rats were always found on ships, usually hidden away in the bilges and behind the walls, but these were bold; the ship was their kingdom and Ibn Bai and the master were the intruders. On the far side of the cabin they had formed themselves into a great writhing mound, tails and bodies entwined – then he saw it: a human hand poking out from under the mass, the arm no more than a shred of raw, bloodied meat. He ran back out the door, his gorge rising, and vomited in a corner. The stink, the dreadful stink of rat and corruption, was everywhere. He spat and wiped his mouth. The harbour master had also emerged and was crouched beside a hatch, peering through. There was a pulsing, buzzing, humming . . . Ibn Bai went to look.

'Don't,' the harbour master said.

Ibn Bai looked and wished he had not. He saw bodies, so many bodies, some in hammocks, others on the floor. Most were in advanced states of putrefaction and all were crawling with flies and speckled with millions of eggs, many already hatching out into writhing white maggots.

'Master!' came a shout from above. The harbour master moved back towards the deck.

'The slave holds are empty,' the assistant informed him. 'Scrubbed clean. Washed out with brimstone.'

Ibn Bai followed the harbour master back into the sunlight.

'What's happened?' he asked plaintively.

Ignoring him, the harbour master addressed his assistant.

'They must have unloaded the slaves at sea and then tried to . . .'

He stopped and gestured towards the quarterdeck. A man was standing there at the wheel, looking down at them. A silence had fallen, or maybe it was just Ibn Bai who was hearing nothing except the thudding of his heart in his ears . . .

'Why doesn't he say something?'

'He's dead, Ibn Bai. Tied himself to the wheel and died there.'

'But where is everybody?'

'You saw them. Down there,' the harbour master said.

'No, you don't understand. My wife, my daughter . . . They must be somewhere, we have to find them.'

The assistant looked at him and said something but no sound came out of his mouth. His face was white and he was backing away.

'My wife, my daughter . . .' Ibn Bai started forward. The

harbour master grabbed him; he tried to shake himself free. 'You don't understand, my wife and daughter, I have to get to them.'

'Look at the wheelman,' the harbour master hissed. 'You can see it from here … Look at his neck, look at his throat. Plague. This is a plague ship. It's a ship of the dead.'

'I have to find them, don't you see, my wife, my—'

They dragged him, still shouting, begging, pleading, back onto the devastated quay. Port workers were frantically poling the ship clear, pushing it out into the harbour where other vessels were backing up, using oars, cables, anything they could to get away. They knew what was going to happen; they knew if they didn't they would burn too.

'Light it, light it up!' the harbour master shouted.

Half a dozen bowmen were igniting oil-soaked arrows at a fire which Ibn Bai had noticed earlier but dismissed as of no interest. Now it was the engine of the loss of everything he held dear.

He struggled, but he was not a strong man and as the fiery tracks arced across the water and descended onto the ship, he slumped as if all the bones had been torn from his body. Fire began to dance across the deck, little rivulets of pale yellow flame that leaped up and took the fallen sail in a great sheet of brightness – and everything became blurred behind his tears and he wished, begged for darkness and death himself but it didn't come and after the ship burned to the waterline, the harbour master spared the clerk to see him safe home.

He stood looking at the fountain, the water playing over the beautiful tiles he had ordered from the artificers of Pireas. He walked through the front door, sandalwood and brass-studded, into the cool hall, the afternoon light falling so softly, so kindly through the coloured glass of the high windows. He went into his library and wondered where, in all these words, these scrolls and books, he might find one tiny shred of comfort – and there was nothing. He passed into the main room with its copper tables, beautifully patterned, its carpets with colours so deep and designs so intricate that you couldn't believe men had made them – and it all meant . . . nothing; nothing, nothing, nothing. He sat . . . somewhere on something and stared at nothing as the shafts of sunlight moved across the floor and the day fled into night and there was no comfort. And some time, in the darkest watches, there was a sound, urgent, demanding of no delay: the patter of slippers on the oak floor, a glow of light passing. He stood and followed the light and saw the hired nurse, Mala, lifting the child.

'I am sorry, master, I did not mean to disturb you,' she said in her native tongue – it was one of the old languages of Tumanbay and which Ibn Bai had taken pride in having learned – 'but the baby, she was hungry and needed changing.'

'Yes, yes, of course, Mala,' he said.

Something he had forgotten came back to him. As the woman Sarah was being led away, she had spoken . . . At first, he had thought it was only a cry but no, there had been words, surely there had. She had said the name of her child . . .

'Ibn Bai, is there something I can do for you?' The maid's face was pale against the darkness.

'The baby,' he said. 'She is called Naima.'

21

Shajah

The arrival of her new maid, and the story of her plight, had led Shajah to become reflective of late and to think about the circumstances in which she herself had come to Tumanbay. She came from nowhere, had nothing except her good looks and a determination to rise to the top whatever the cost. The girl Sarah, on the other hand, had come from some court, she'd had status and wealth, probably – and then lost all this and now seemed defeated and compliant. And what of Madu? She had spoiled him, she knew, from the day he was born. She didn't want him to go through what she had suffered. He had been given every advantage in life but now . . . now she wondered if that had been an error.

'More ambergris, my lady?'

Shajah looked up at Sarah, taken out of her thoughts for a moment.

'Yes.'

The maid poured and Shajah allowed the heavy amber liquid to run over her hands and down her arms and into the warm water of her bath.

'Do you think it's different for boys?' she asked.

Sarah paused. 'Madam?'

'Don't stop. Love. Women. Sex. For boys?'

'I can't say, madam.'

'Is it just hygiene, tapping off some male excess, something they have to do before they can do something more important?'

She stood and indicated the gleaming jugs of fresh spring water. Sarah began to pour, sluicing away the soap.

'I remember being twelve years old, riding into Tumanbay with a caravan of traders. Someone, I can't remember who, had traded me to them for copper or goats or ... I remember the city walls and beyond them the towers rising out of the shimmering heat, I remember riding astride a camel, blood on my thighs from my first time as a woman – seeing even then, men's eyes following me and thinking – here, here I will become myself.'

Sarah was now wrapping towels around her mistress.

'And so you have, madam, you have become the First Wife of the Sultan.'

'Not bad for a twelve-year-old whore on a camel, eh? And yet ...'

Her thoughts turned back to Madu. He was sixteen already. Why were no little whores scuttling around his apartments? Was he too soft, too weak, too easily led? She would need to do something about him before it was too late.

'Fetch me the lilac dress and the rose veil.'

Sarah walked through to the wardrobe chamber, stopping for a moment to open a wooden blind a crack and hang a length of cloth, blue with a border artfully embroidered in gold, from the window. She positioned it carefully and was about to walk on when she felt a breath on her neck. She turned to face her mistress.

'What are you doing?'

'The girdle, madam, it ... It was ... wet. I thought to dry it, that is all.'

Shajah held her hand out. She said nothing. Sarah unhooked the cloth and handed it to her. In the silence both women could hear drops of water hitting the marble floor.

'Very well. Now bring me the dress.'

22

Gregor

You can't police a feeling any more than you can take a breeze and tie a knot in it as if it were a cord, but all the same you know the wind is blowing and you know the feeling is subtly altering everything you are observing. And Gregor was looking very carefully at the palace and the city of Tumanbay. He had thousands of informants scattered through every enterprise and household in the city, most of them unaware that the gossip they passed on in the market, at the laundry or the public baths or the public jakes, at the games, at their workshops, in their regiments, temples, schools and hospitals was collected by his agents and passed back to his ministry, where it was analysed by a small legion of clerks adept in picking out the loose thread, the odd note, the misplaced word. These reports were collated by his senior officials and the chaff winnowed out; the remainder, the heart of the matter, was passed on to him for his consideration.

It was here that he felt those almost intangible movements as the atmosphere began to change and the tone of conversation and gossip was … altered. He couldn't yet put a finger on it. Those citizens who had been interviewed at greater depth had no information to give, no names to name; they were simply feeling differently about their city and the way things went on in this world of Tumanbay. They could say no more than that.

It was a change in the wind, only by a minute amount but it was there all the same. The interesting question was: would it all blow over or were these the first breaths of a coming storm?

That was the public side of his life of spying. Nothing yet to report to the Sultan beyond his instincts. The other side, the more urgent side – finding the spies within the palace and keeping a watch on the First Wife – was, so far, equally unproductive but was, at least, functioning well.

He had set up a system by which the slave girl, Sarah, could make contact by leaving the end of a cloth hanging from a window in the hareem. According to the particular cloth and the amount visible, the time and place could be set and he would then meet her and take her to a safe room to deliver her report.

He said, 'Here, eat, drink if you wish.'

There was always fruit, wine, water for her but she never ate or drank.

'You know what I want. I want to see my baby.'

'You ask that every time.'

'And every time you tell me I can't, not yet.'

'You will see her. I promise. She is well looked after.'

He hoped that she was – and made a mental note to check as soon as possible.

'How do I know I can trust you?' There were tears in her eyes, her hands clasped together, the tendons standing out. 'You're a liar!' she burst out. 'A liar who employs liars to lie. Everything is a lie in this place.' Now she openly wept.

He didn't touch her; he waited. He knew the tension of her position in the First Wife's hareem was intense, as was her need for her baby. He felt for her as he had felt in the past for many of his agents; those in the position of greatest risk who offered potentially the greatest reward.

When the tears stopped he silently offered her a cloth. She wiped her face.

'I can't prove anything here and now. When you do see your child, you will know I have been telling the truth. Then you will trust me. I can only ask you to believe. You know I am a practical man. Yes?'

'Yes.'

'I want results. I deal in information and secrets. My spies obtain them for me. You could say my spies are the tools of my trade, and any workman would be a fool who did not treat his tools well and with respect.'

He took the knife he wore concealed in his sleeve. It was small, thin and very sharp. He held her arm. She flinched but he did not let her go. Gently he shaved the golden hairs from the pale skin, then released his grip.

'The knife is my tool. I keep it sharp as a barber's razor. The blade is poisoned – if it had so much as broken the skin you would be dead by now. That is its purpose. If I let it go blunt, let the poison dry, it would no longer be of any use to me. So it is with you – your purpose would not be served if you didn't work willingly for me. That depends on your baby's health and life. I would be a fool not to ensure that.'

'Do you remember what you said the first time? "I give you something, you give me something."'

'Ah, but you haven't given me anything yet.' He paused, waiting for her to respond. 'So . . .?'

She reached into a pocket and pulled out a piece of parchment. 'I have no choice, do I?'

'Who does?' he said. 'Even the Sultan is driven by necessity. Now read me your report.'

She did so. A litany of the everyday. Shajah kept careful accounts for the hareem. Her eunuchs were trained to note everything down: buttons and thread, lengths of lace, personal items, court items, food, drink, medicines . . .

The report droned on: oil of cloves for toothache; sumac, verjuice and lemon; African rue; white henbane; ambergris; foot scrapers and tweezers – fifty from the metalworkers at cost price for the palace; Sogdian musk from the merchants of Khorosan to excite the jaded appetite of a lover; one copy of al-Nurwayri's *History of the Eluites*; one book of riddles . . .

'Do you want me to ask you a riddle?' she said.

'If you wish.'

'How is it possible that two women could meet two men and say, "Greetings to our two sons and our two husbands and the sons of our husbands."?'

'I am no good at riddles. Go on with the list.'

'I don't understand. What is it you want?'

'I don't know yet,' he said, 'but when I hear it, I will. Continue.'

'Al-Ghurabi figs, a rhinoceros ear soaked in urine, a tent for hunting . . .' She went on for some time and when she finally came to the end she said, 'I've done what you want, now what will you give me?'

He stared into her blue eyes. No one made demands of the Commander of the Palace Guard; she was either a fool or something rather special.

23
Madu

A sea gently lapping at the beach, waves lazily unwinding along the sand as he walked into the water, looking down at his shoes which for some reason he was still wearing but it didn't seem to matter; the sea was so clear and warm and welcoming that he decided there was nowhere else he wanted to be, and besides he could wade out to the great ship that lay at anchor in the bay, its vast red sails shivering in a breeze that had not yet reached the shore.

The first slight tremors disturbed the surface of the water, like wrinkles crossing blue silk ...

On the boat they were calling to him: 'Madu, come to us, hurry, be quick, there isn't much time.'

He realised he needed to get aboard and started wading out to them, only the water was impeding his progress. How could that happen? He had to climb aboard before ... before ... He looked down and saw seaweed, great black tendrils reaching out, wrapping themselves around his ankles, climbing up his legs, more and more of it, dead hair in the water, holding him back.

'Wait!' he shouted. 'Wait!'

But they were going and he was being pulled under by ...

He came awake with a cry. Seaweed ... No, hair, that was hair ...

'What in God's name?'

He scrabbled up the bed and saw a face, framed by abundant black hair: a girl's face, a pretty face, smiling at him, jewels glittering in her raven locks as she hovered over his groin. Leaping out of bed, he gathered the silk sheet, blue as in his dream, about himself.

'What are you doing here, girl? Are you one of my mother's maids? No, not dressed like that.'

'My Lord?'

She smiled and was beautiful. And professional. Not thrown at all by his panicked reaction.

'Who are you?'

'My name is Shamsi, My Lord.'

She stood at the foot of the bed. Not tall, slim but well made, wearing . . . of course.

'You're a whore?'

'Of course I am, what else would I be?'

'Is this a joke? Did one of my friends put you up to this? It's not my birthday.'

'Do my clothes bother you, Lord? That's no problem.'

With a little shiver she let them fall and stood naked as a pin.

'Is that better?'

'A moment, girl, wait.'

Grabbing a robe that hung within reach, he stepped out of the sheet and moved across the room, away from her.

'Is there something else you'd prefer? Something special?'

'Ahh, Shamsi . . . It is Shamsi, you said?'

'Yes, Lord.'

'It's my mother, isn't it? She sent you.'

'Yes, Lord. Look, it's easy enough. Just lie back, I'll make it happen. You won't even notice.' She smiled again, waiting for his response. 'If you'd prefer I could get a boy and we could—'

'Enough, girl. Shamsi, whoever you are. This isn't going to be.'

In a moment her face crumpled and she wept.

'Stop it, stop it now!' he shouted.

'It's my job to prove your manhood. I must obey or she will have my head. I don't want to die, please, Lord.'

She was at his feet, sobbing and clutching the robe, leaving a trail of snot on the velvet. Well, he'd been there himself a few times, weeping and desperate in half a hundred taverns and worse places in the city – it was such an ordinary thing that he couldn't help but laugh, even though the anger against his mother was still boiling up.

'I won't let her hurt you. Just stop wailing, will you?'

'She's the First Wife, Lord, she can do anything.'

'I know, she controls my allowance.'

'Then you should want to please her.'

'That's the difference between us, Shamsi. You have to please – I don't. Wait here. No, wait in the annexe through there, I have to get dressed and see a woman!'

The door was unlocked – it wouldn't have made much difference if it had been barred and bolted; Madu went through hardly breaking pace. A slave was folding clothes by the window and gave him a startled look with her striking blue eyes.

'Where's my mother?' he barked.

'My Lord?'

'Are you deaf or stupid? My mother, girl.'

Shajah entered from her private chambers.

'You may go, Sarah,' she said.

The maid turned the clothes over her arm and hurriedly left the room. He waited until she was gone. He owed his mother that much.

'What do you think you are doing, Mother?'

147

She shrugged, her face a mask of innocence but he knew that face too well.

'The whore you sent to my rooms. You can't do that. My life is my own business.'

'You know that's not true, in Tumanbay and in this palace in particular. Now do sit down, you are so very loomy for a short man. I recall your father was loomy too, when he got angry.'

She sat on a seat by the window and looked out over the city to the east.

'I can assure you and anyone else who might be interested, that if and when I want to have some girl, I will make my own choice in my own way. Please look at me, Mother.'

She did, her almond eyes wide in feigned surprise.

'It's just that, as I said the other day, you need ... a bastard or two ... People like that sort of thing in their young princes. People need to know that if ...' She let the words lapse.

He sat on a couch facing her. 'If what?'

'If we are going to change things, go against custom, if you are to be your stepfather's successor ...'

Leaning forward, he looked into her eyes. 'You say this is all about being a man, yes?'

'Yes.'

'Well, it's simply not manly to have these things arranged. When I need to produce an heir or any number of bastards, I can assure you I will – and I will do so because I wish it, because that is what a man does.'

She considered for a moment.

'You're right, my dear. I am sorry, I shouldn't try to manipulate you. I can see you are indeed a man and that you need to make your own decisions.'

'Thank you, Mother. I'm glad you understand.'

Did he feel vindicated? No – somehow, he felt trapped. His mother never gave in this easily.

'Which is why,' she said, a smile haunting her eyes, 'General Qulan, at the request of the Sultan, has arranged for you to join the army. And I have given my blessing.'

'I won't go.'

'It's a man's job. It's what you wanted. You'll work under Qulan. It will be invaluable experience for you.'

'I simply will not . . .' A fist closed somewhere in his bowels, cutting off his words.

'And it will be useful for us. Qulan has influence and if things go the way they seem, he'll soon have more.'

Madu took a series of deep breaths and gradually the pain in his guts settled. He felt he could stand up and face her down.

'You can't make me. I have things to do. Things I need to do.'

'Because I am your mother, my dear, and have in the past overlooked various indiscretions, scandals, scrapes or whatever you care to call them, do not for a moment think that I will change my mind on this. We are all of us in a terribly serious game.'

'The army is hardly a game.'

'I have a certain position, a certain influence, but you have only me. Also, you could be used against me. You must make allies of your own, make your own way and then we will stand together as a power in Tumanbay. Qulan has offered to take you and train you. You will accept that gift with the grace I expect of my son.'

'And if I refuse?'

'In Tumanbay everything has a use. If it does not, it is thrown away.'

24

Gregor

The child was crying. Ibn Bai picked her up and gently rocked her as he had done so often with his own daughter. A pain like a dagger in his heart drew a silent cry from his lips, and he felt he was about to weep again when the maid entered the room.

He said: 'I told you that I should not be disturbed when—'

'So, the slave trader becomes a nursemaid.'

The man from the palace was standing behind the girl, a dark and menacing presence. How had he got in? Ibn Bai had not heard the gate bell ring. This Gregor was obviously one who disdained doors and gates.

'As you commanded, I have the baby.'

'Look after it, your well-being depends upon it.'

Ibn Bai laughed bitterly. 'My well-being?' The words were a challenge. It was quite clear that at this moment Ibn Bai gave not a fig for all this man's threats. 'Yes, I am so fortunate I have all this. My house, my business, my library. It is celebrated, did you know that? Scholars used to come to my home in Cyrene to consult my books, my manuscripts. It has taken years to assemble and now ... my wife, my daughter are ... Do you see? Nothing, it all means nothing to me!' He was shouting and the tears had come as they had threatened. He stood shaking with emotion. 'I was so fortunate. I had everything and now, nothing.

Plague has taken them from me. My life is over.'

Gregor nodded and when he spoke, his words were uncharacteristically gentle.

'Truly, my friend, the plague cares nothing for any one of us. It takes poor men and princes alike, it takes the loved and the hated. It is death's best servant. In war and intrigue men make decisions that are good or bad and we prosper or suffer as a result, but plague simply plucks us and throws us away.'

'I could not even bury them. I stood and watched as they burned.'

The baby belched loudly in Ibn Bai's arms.

'May I?' Gregor took the child.

'Naima.'

Gregor was staring intently at the tiny face as another belch came.

'What?'

'Her name. Here, she has wind, she bolts her milk. Let me.'

He took her back, laid her against his shoulder and rubbed and patted. After a few moments more milky belches followed.

'She has blue eyes like her mother,' Gregor said.

'And her uncle. They both had blue eyes. Highly valued in the business.'

'The business?'

'The trade. Slaves. It is said that blue eyes first came from the cold lands to the far north where there were giants. Here, I'll show you.'

He called for the maid and gave the baby into her care, then led Gregor along a corridor – 'Be careful, effendi, the plaster is still a little damp.' – into a well-lit room lined with books and scrolls and liberally provided with reading desks.

'Here . . .' Ibn Bai pulled a large volume from a shelf, laid it on a lectern and opened it where a feather marked the place, to reveal a beautifully rendered world map. 'It is very old but see how vibrant the colours still are.'

Gregor leaned close, obviously fascinated. Ibn Bai pointed to one corner, where mountains of ice and strange horned fish were depicted.

'I think they are Bulgars from the land beyond . . .' He stopped and slammed the volume shut. 'What am I saying? Rightly is it said the mind of man is a monkey and leads us where it will. I have lost everything and yet I chatter on about pictures!'

'Tell me about the other one.'

'Other what?' The slave trader was still lost in his own self-contempt and misery.

'Tell me about the brother.'

'I sold them both to the palace. I think he was sold on to the army. A waste really, he was educated but hard to control. I would have—' The sound of the baby crying stopped Ibn Bai in mid-sentence. 'Excuse me, I must—'

Gregor detained him with a hand on the shoulder; the grip was not hard but insistent.

'Ibn Bai, listen to me. I came here today simply to be sure you had done what I asked. I found a man in deepest despair, a man who told me he had lost everything. That is not true. After the fire burns the forest, new life arises from the land and must be tended. The child matters to you, I can see it clearly. So tend her well. She is useful to me, as are you. And so long as that lasts . . .' He let go his grip. The menace was none the less for being implied. 'I will see myself out. You should go to the child. I will come again soon when I have need of you.'

25
Madu

It was vast. He'd had no idea the place was so huge. Why would he? He'd never had any reason to be here until today, until his mother's ultimatum: join the army or ... There was something frightening about the unstated threat of that 'or', and so here he was in his mother's coach crossing the streets and squares of a section of Tumanbay closed off to most of its citizens; an area known as the Army Quarter.

On the far side he could make out barrack buildings, row upon row of them, some of the windows and doors boarded up but many obviously still in use. He'd heard the army was not what it used to be but from the many groups of recruits being marched back and forward or practising spear work and other manoeuvres he didn't recognise, there was still no shortage of slaves to fill the ranks. He saw a vast tortoise composed of shields held above the heads of crouching men. He saw boys in the rough skins of the mountain dwellers being taught the rudiments of swordplay. He saw men falling off camels and horses and siege engines, and simply falling off their own tangled feet as they tackled a variety of obstacles, all of them driven on by the batons of the sergeants whose bellows could be heard clear across the parade ground. In its own rough way it was all rather exciting and Madu began to feel that maybe this wouldn't be such a bad thing after all.

He was, if he was honest with himself, of two minds about his mother's plans for the succession. He was the son of one Sultan, the nephew of another; his mother had been the wife of both and the death of one. He was here to fulfil her ambitions but there was no reason why he shouldn't use this opportunity for himself.

Maybe if Madu were on General Qulan's staff, a rising, capable young officer, he could charm the old lion – making friends was, after all, one of his greatest skills. Yes, he could see his way now. A brilliant career in the army, a following of young firebrands in uniform, the benign approval of the general – even his mother would find that difficult to deal with. It would give him a bargaining position, something that was vital for survival in the jungle that was the court of Tumanbay.

The carriage came to a halt before a massive tent with banners flying from the tops of the many poles that supported it. Was everything here built on the grand scale, he wondered as he stepped down onto a stool placed by the coachman's assistant.

'Shall we wait, effendi?'

'No, this is my home now. Go back to the palace.'

The unrelenting sunlight was diffused inside the big command tent. Qulan and his staff were leaning over a map table scattered with papers, pens and ink pots, rulers and brass dividers for measuring distance. The general stamped his seal on an order and handed it to a clerk.

'Have it copied at once and delivered to all governors. And tell the messengers to get a receipt.'

'At your command, General.'

The messenger took the scroll and left, passing a young man who was entering. Qulan turned back to the table.

'All these orders go out under the seal of the Sultan himself,' he said. 'There will be no backsliding. We'll need . . .' The young man had wandered up to the table. 'What do you want?'

'I've come to join you, General.'

'To join me?'

'Madu.' He raised an eyebrow as if to say that surely Qulan should know who he was. 'I am the son of Shajah. The First—'

'I know who she is. I was not aware that she held any military command.'

Madu held up a hand. 'I agree, General. I just happen to have been sent by my mother to assist you in any way you might need assisting.'

The staff officers around the table shifted uneasily and backed away a little.

Qulan said: 'So, Madu "sent by my mother", what exactly are you going to do for me?'

'Well, I have to say, General, I was really impressed by what I saw this morning crossing the Army Quarter.'

Neither Qulan nor any members of his staff said a word. Madu reckoned he had their attention.

'I know I have no experience and no training, but I do have a great admiration for our army, for the soldierly virtues that made Tumanbay what it is.'

Still no one else uttered a word. Madu plunged on.

'I think I can help you, General. Simply put, I know everyone and everyone knows me. I can talk to people, I can write a half-decent poem, I can be your mouthpiece. I can speak for the army, win you friends, explain to the enemies we defeat why they should welcome Tumanbay, explain to the enemies in the court why they should support the army, write of our victories so the common people can learn of . . .' He held up his hands, palms to the room, as if to say: there's nothing I can't do for the army. 'Simply, General, I'm here to help.'

In the long silence that followed they could hear the wind ruf-
fling the canvas of the tent, the sound of marching from outside,
a sergeant bellowing: 'On the balls of your feet when you thrust
with the blade!'

Qulan looked at his staff. They looked at him. Everyone
looked at Madu.

'Simply,' Qulan said, 'you want to join the army.'

'Yes, General.'

'But things in this world, young man, are rarely simple and
never so where your mother is concerned.'

'It was her idea, General, I grant you, but I am my own man
and I intend to make my own way. To rise by my own virtues. I
don't want to call on privilege and start at the top. I am prepared
to work my way up.'

'From the bottom?'

'Yes.'

'Good. We agree. I welcome your help, Madu.'

'Splendid.'

'You can "help" in the latrines, there's always room for a willing shovel there. Sergeant . . .' The door guard came to attention.
'Impress this volunteer in the 10th Foot Regiment and escort
him to the shit-shovellers detail.'

Madu stood frozen. This wasn't supposed to happen. When
the sergeant's hand gripped his shoulder he let out a squeak but
no words came.

'I shall send word to Shajah,' Qulan said, 'that you and I have
come to a satisfactory arrangement for your military career.'

It was a long walk from the tent, across the parade ground,
skirting the various training areas, waiting while a phalanx of
straining half-naked men struggled to set the catapult arm of a
trebuchet, passing through the barracks and the kitchens and the
armouries until they reached a field where stinking fires burned

over many pits. By then Madu's voice had returned.

'Look, I need to send a message. I can pay. You don't know who I am.'

'You're right, I don't. But I do know who this is. Sergeant Ban'th.' He came to attention, as did his fellow sergeant. 'Good day, Ban'th. Old Stone Face says one more for your merry band.'

'Thank you. You may leave him with me.'

Madu protested, 'This is stupid – my mother—'

'Shagged a camel, strained it through a cheese cloth and got you.' An evil grin split Ban'th's seamed face.

'You can't—'

Madu got no further. The sergeant's staff flicked out and Madu found himself face down in the sand with an intense pain in both his calves.

'You, Blue Eyes, what are you doing?' Ban'th called to a soldier wielding a shovel – from the sour expression on his face, a fellow he'd never liked.

Without looking up, Blue Eyes shouted back: 'Shovelling shit, Sergeant!'

'Well, I've found a use for you. Here's another lump of shite for you to look after.'

Ban'th pulled Madu to his feet and shoved him stumbling towards the trench.

'What should I do with him, Sergeant?' Blue Eyes asked.

'Do I look like I care? Throw him in the shit pit if you want. We'll be marching for the provinces tomorrow. Get this lot burned and covered and remember, you are responsible for this turd too.'

26

Shajah

From her position on the couch, with her head flung back, the approaching army outside appeared upside down. Shajah was in the Sultan's apartment, the Sultan on top of her and the armies of Tumanbay below, parading past, beginning their march to the provinces. Somewhere out there, Shajah was thinking as her husband grunted above her, was her son Madu, now a foot soldier. How would he be coping with his new status in life, she wondered.

'Turn around,' the Sultan growled, giving her a sharp slap on her naked thigh.

His sexual appetite had increased, she'd noticed, since she had presented him with a rare and difficult to source musk from Sogdia.

She got on her knees as he positioned himself behind her. Her afternoon visits to the Sultan's apartments were an essential part of her daily routine – and a vital one, when she could find out about the business of the Empire. It gave her all that she needed to keep her position and make her decisions – who was in favour, who was out, what was on the Sultan's mind – information to which even Gregor didn't have access. She enjoyed it too, because she and al-Ghuri had a long and intimate history together. They'd had true passion, deep secrets; they had plotted and killed together, had seized the throne together, and now . . .

'Move your head a bit,' he said, thrusting into her with his gaze firmly fixed on the movement outside.

The armies were directly below the balcony now and the sound – the horses, the boom of the marching drums, the blaring trumpets, the bellowed commands – filled the room. The Sultan seemed particularly full of vigour today, she thought, after days of brooding over all that had happened recently – the severed head of his most loyal governor thrown at his feet, and Maya, that wayward provincial governor's wife who seemed to think she could intimidate him with her outrageous demands.

'There's nothing like a war to bring the blood to the boil,' he said, thrusting harder and faster. 'Look at them as they march by, look at the flags, the lances . . . My army . . . *My armeeee!*'

This was it. It had happened much faster today, and in a little while he would roll over onto his back and sleep until she woke him with rose-water and sherbet.

'Majesty, truly you are a man among men,' she said.

'Yes. Put some clothes on.'

She got off the couch and started to dress.

Musks and herbal stimulants could only do so much. The Sultan was an elderly man after all, approaching seventy, and she was under no illusions that if he were to die now, her position in the palace would be anything but secure.

'Boy!' the Sultan called out.

From an alcove at the far side of the room, a slave approached.

'My army needs to see me. Fetch my armour.'

The slave disappeared into another room and returned a few moments later with two others who helped the Sultan dress.

'Where did it come from, this ingratitude?' he asked, turning to Shajah.

Panic filled her head. Had her husband learned of her visit to the Hafiz's palace?

'Husband?'

One of the slaves was now helping him with a chain vest and he impatiently slapped him away.

'Maya ... I put her there – at least I put her damn useless husband there. I gave him the governorship of Amber Province! For his loyalty. And what happens ...?'

He waved his hand at the slaves, who retreated.

'Come ...'

Taking her hand, he led Shajah towards the balcony. Dust was rising from the army in a great cloud and the smell of horses and sweat was drifting into the room. It stuck in the back of Shajah's throat and she badly wanted to cough, but resisted.

'Well, we'll do this again,' he said, 'with the whole army marching by and the bitch's head on a tray ... right there.' He gestured towards an ornate side table at the foot of the couch. 'So she can see me in all my manhood ...'

'I look forward to it.'

They stepped onto the balcony to a deafening cheer and the low bellow of horns that echoed about the grand courtyard as the procession threaded its way towards the city gates and onwards into the desert – bowmen, the camel division, the cavalry, even men on elephants and of course the foot soldiers, thousands of them, the invincible might of Tumanbay. And among them, somewhere lost in that mass of men, her son ...

'I sent Madu with General Qulan.'

Al-Ghuri looked at her quizzically. She had been waiting for an opportunity to mention this to him and now it had presented itself.

'It will be good for him. He'll learn about life, about how to obey and how to command. General Qulan will be a fine teacher and when Madu returns, perhaps, My Lord, you could take him on to your council so he could—'

'You want him to be my successor.'

'I'm just saying—'

'No, don't answer, it isn't a question.'

There was another shout and then, as one, the soldiers came to a halt and turned to look up at the Sultan and his First Wife.

Another shout and then the reply from all: 'WE SERVE AND DIE FOR TUMANBAY!'

Al-Ghuri raised his arm and waved, beaming. The army responded with a deafening cheer as the procession moved forward once more.

'Like ants on the march, they seem to go on forever,' Shajah said in awe.

'Not yet forever.' His mood had darkened. 'But once the provinces muster their forces, yes, we'll roll over her, crush her like a grape and the blood will run between our toes.'

'My Lord, are you . . .? You sound . . . sad,' she said, increasingly concerned with what might be on the Sultan's mind. 'I hope I do not make you sad.'

She brushed her hand against his and was relieved when he took it.

'Moments,' he said. 'There are moments when I forget . . . when I am a man as other men but then . . . Don't you understand? No one is safe now. Not even within these walls. If my nephew can be poisoned . . .'

She stared into his eyes. There was still kindness there, he needed her, she had been worrying unduly.

'Shajah, this kingdom is full of people who think they can rule in my place. Even Qulan . . .' He gestured towards the head of the procession, now well in the distance. 'There, there he is . . . leading his men—'

'Leading *your* armies,' she interjected.

'No, even he, that paragon of honour, when power presents itself, he'll reach out for it. Gregor, he has ambitions. Cadali. All of them. Nobody is proof against the desire for power. Power is everything, power gives everything and power is worth risking everything for.'

'Then isn't it safest to keep it within the family . . . to have a successor you have trained, who is of your own brother's blood, My Lord.'

'You talk about my brother's blood when I shed it for you?'

'I'm talking about your brother's son, Madu. He's like you in so many ways. Name him your successor and all the jealousy, the in-fighting and plotting will cease. The future will be certain.'

'The only thing certain about the future is that we will all die. And the only questions are when and how. And the only tactics are survival. Now, here, this moment, I could have you sent away for your own safety to a monastery in the desert to spend your days in a cell praying.'

She felt suddenly alarmed. It could happen here, now, out of nowhere. Her husband's behaviour had been strange all day. Had he become aware of something she had said or done, some casual remark perhaps . . .? This was Gregor's doing, surely.

'Guard!' al-Ghuri shouted. She was aware of an officer approaching.

'No,' she said firmly. 'I am loyal, I'm loyal. You must know that, husband. I loved you when I was your brother's wife—'

'When you betrayed my brother.' His face was like stone.

'For love of you, My Lord. I never knew love until—'

She was stopped by his hands rising and settling on either side of her face.

Fixing her with a cold stare, he said, 'Just remember, everything you have and everything you hope for Madu, depends on me.

However clever you are, you will not last as long as a butterfly's life if you lose my favour.'

She nodded in acknowledgment. Satisfied that she understood, he waved the guard away and walked back into his apartment. Shajah waited a moment, shaking not with fear but with intense, unbearable, rage.

After a few moments she turned to go back inside but walked straight into the maid, Sarah. How long had she been standing there, she wondered.

'Is there anything I may get for you, madam?'

'Yes, have them prepare my carriage.' Shajah brushed past her, then paused. 'Actually, no,' she said, turning back to the maid.

'Madam?'

'Don't. I will be fine. Leave me.'

The last thing she wanted was more rumours going about the palace. She would make her own arrangements.

27

The Artists

In a small workshop in a district of Tumanbay called the Street of the Illuminators, where the ancient buildings leaned crazily towards each other creating a perpetual shade, an argument was taking place, or perhaps an argument was continuing as it had done for most of the lifetime of the brothers – identical twins, tall, thin, bearded, robed with their sleeves pulled back to leave their arms and hands free – who flitted back and forth through the beams of light that entered the workshop from a high window, placed to catch the sun.

Parig appraised the curved wooden panel on which he was working. Behind him, peering over his shoulder, Panik said, 'That's not right.'

'What's not right? Pass me the thin silk brush, will you, the number thirty-five.'

'The haunch isn't right. Are you sure you want the thirty-five, wouldn't the forty be better?'

'The haunch is fine,' Parig said, 'when you consider the point of view of the viewer. The box will be on the floor and thus observed from above. The thirty-five.'

'I don't know,' Panik muttered through his beard. 'Even so—'

A knock at the door stopped Panik in mid-sentence. The brothers looked at each other.

Panik said: 'Is there someone due to collect today?'

'No one.'

'You're sure?'

Parig turned the pages of the big ledger. 'Of course I'm sure, you oaf!'

Again the knock, loud, peremptory.

'Well, how can I be the oaf because there is definitely someone there?'

'Well, look, Panik, look through the peephole. That's why it's in the door.'

Panik marched across the shop and lifted the peephole cover, peered through and reared back.

'Gods, it's her! Shall I let her in?'

'She's the Sultan's First Wife, what are you going to do – tell her to come back tomorrow? Yes – no, wait . . . We can't tell her it's almost done.'

'But the work is good. I mean she wouldn't, would she?'

Parig held up his hands in a gesture of resignation.

'Once it's finished, we're finished. You know what these people are like. We need to get paid and get away before it's handed over. You know that!'

'Why did we ever come to this accursed city?' Panik wailed – but quietly as another knock sounded.

'For this, brother – a job so well paid that we'll be made men for life. Just as long as we can hang on to life for time enough to enjoy it. Let her in. We have to keep her happy but not so happy that she thinks the job will be finished tomorrow. Now, do it.'

Panik turned the ornate key, tumblers fell and clicked in the antique lock, the door swung open and Shajah swept into the workshop.

'Honoured madam, please enter our humble—'

'I am not accustomed to waiting in the street.'

'Of course, madam.' Parig bowed. 'Brother, what are you thinking of? Get madam a glass of water at once. Only the finest water, madam, cooled by the snows of—'

'I do not need water. The work?'

'Ahh, yes, the work.' Parig smiled obsequiously – he hoped.

'Is it done?'

'Almost,' Panik said.

She turned and faced him. He blenched.

She said: 'Almost?'

'Finished,' Parig said. 'That is to say almost finished, madam. But not finished.' He gestured to his brother.

Panik said: 'We are awaiting the . . . actualiser.'

'Exactly, the actualiser. You will understand, madam—'

'I neither care about nor am interested in this actualiser. Show me what you've done.'

'Panik, the drawer.'

Panik pulled open a long narrow drawer to reveal two scrolls, each partly open, the illumination glowing even in the dark workshop, casting a light as if an inner fire burned within the vellum. As Shajah reached forward, Parig stayed her hand with a gesture – taking care not to touch her.

'No, madam, please don't disturb them, we are at a most delicate stage.'

All three stood in a sort of wonder.

Shajah said: 'They are very fine, aren't they?'

'The finest we've ever had in our workshop,' Panik muttered. 'They are very old.'

'As old as time,' Parig said.

A beam from the highlight fell across the scrolls and for a moment it was as if they had burst into flame. Parig slid the drawer closed.

'The box, too, madam, is almost done. We await the lapis from

Samarkand. They are always slow in Samarkand.'

'You have a week. I want it finished by then. Do you understand?'

'It will have our full attention,' Parig said. 'I am certain that Samarkand will have . . .'

Shajah walked to the door. Panik skipped past her and pulled it open so she did not have to pause in her progress.

'Gracious lady, I assure you of our . . .'

And she was gone.

He closed the door and leaned against it, exhaling as if he had just climbed a mountain.

Parig said: 'Brother, we need a plan.'

'We had a plan, brother. Your plan. We go to Tumanbay and get rich.'

'Well, it's working out so far, isn't it?'

'You know, I wish I'd never seen the place.'

And he turned the key in the lock as if that might actually keep them both safe.

28

The Girl

The girl awoke to the excruciating brightness of sun on sea. Her mouth was dry; her back ached but not as badly as her neck, which felt as if it had been wrenched halfway round, like a chicken she had once seen the cook kill. She pushed herself up and felt the heat falling on her back as she shifted out of the shadow of the tiny sail hanging limply from the mast. And in that one shattering moment she remembered where she was and ... and what had happened. She felt sick and scrabbled further into the prow of the boat, turning fearfully to look back at him. The slave – the one who had taken her from her mother, from her future, from everything to nothing. She would have cried if she had any tears, but all she managed was a croak.

'Where ... where are we?'

'Here,' he said, his face like stone under the filthy hair.

Her stomach gurgled in sheer horror; he was everything she had been taught to fear. She could smell the sweat and ... blood rising off him. She wanted to cry, she wanted to scream, more than ever she wanted her mother but she was never going to see her again, never going to see any of them ...

'Drink.'

He threw a water skin at her. It was filthy but without

hesitation she picked it up and pressed it to her lips; the water was the sweetest she'd ever tasted.

'With care,' he said. 'We don't know how long it'll have to last.'

After another swallow she threw it back to him.

'If you move along the boat into the shade of the sail you'll feel cooler.'

She didn't move.

'What's your name?'

She turned away from him and looked out towards the horizon. It was hard to see where water ended and sky began in the glare of the sun.

'What's your name?'

She didn't move, didn't answer.

'Look, girl, I don't need you. I needed you to get off the ship but I don't need you any more. It wouldn't take much to break your neck and throw you to the fish and there'd be more water and food for me, so you can talk or you can swim, it's up to you.'

Was he moving towards her? She could hear him shifting his weight and the boat rocked. She spun round.

'Stay where you are. Heaven, it's Heaven.'

He settled back against the stern and laughed, like he didn't have a care in the world.

'What's funny, why are you laughing?'

'I'm in a boat with Heaven.' He shook his head. 'Strange indeed are the ways of fate.'

She pulled her robes tightly around herself and covered her head against the sun.

'Stop it. I have to go home, I mean I have to go . . . I have to go back, please take me back?'

'To the ship?'

'My father's a merchant. He can pay you. There'll be a reward.

You have to take me to a port, take me to somewhere and there will be someone there, an agent, someone who will give you money.'

He leaned forward, took up the oars that rested along the boat, fitted them into the locks, shifted his position so his scarred back was to her, and began to row.

'Why aren't you listening to me? You'll be paid. Gold, don't you understand?'

He went on rowing; she looked at the muscles of his arms swelling with the effort as he moved easily back and forward. He could kill her just like that, without thinking about it. At last he looked back over his shoulder.

'What is gold to me. Can we drink it? Can we eat it? Can we make a bigger sail than this rag to catch the wind?'

'What do you mean?'

'Look around you. What do you see?'

'Nothing.'

'That's right. Nothing. And my name is Slave.'

'That's not a name. It's a thing, I mean it's . . . It's . . .'

'Then we have something in common, Heaven's not a name either, it's a place.'

He turned away and resumed rowing in long measured strokes that barely seemed to disturb the turbid water around them.

Time passed – was it two days or three, or longer? She knew it got dark and then the pitiless sun rose again; she knew she was hungrier and thirstier than she'd ever been and Slave doled out the water and stale bread in tiny measures so her feelings passed from fear and annoyance to hate. He said little and rowed doggedly on, always away from the rising and towards the setting sun. At night they drifted, though Slave lowered the rag of a sail to catch any dew that came with the inevitable dawn.

She thought: we're going to die here in this stupid boat on this stupid sea under this stupid sun.

And then one day the sun was hidden behind cloud and there was a breeze rippling the surface of the water and the sail began to fill and after what seemed another long age, she looked up and saw a grey beach before them.

With a couple of pulls, Slave drove the boat into the sand and jumped out. His face was grey with exhaustion and he walked stiffly up the beach. He didn't look back or call or anything. She jumped out of the boat and waded ashore after him. He sat on a dune that had scrubby grasses growing from it. There was nothing else, neither trees or buildings, nor bushes with fruit on, nor a stream – nothing!

'Well, what now?' she said.

He didn't answer.

She went on: 'There's nothing here, this isn't any better than the sea.'

'Then go back to the boat.' He lay back on the grass and shut his eyes.

'This is stupid. You should have found a proper port where there's people and food and something to drink. This is just stupid.'

He opened one eye. 'You've already said that. Twice.'

'Well, what are we going to do?'

'I got you to shore. You can do whatever you want. Me, I'm going to sleep.'

He closed his eyes, his breathing became deep and regular and then he began to snore. She would have shaken him or kicked him but she didn't want to touch him. She walked to the top of the dune. Nothing! She sat down and realised that she was tired, deeply tired; she blinked and slept.

When she woke the sun was gone and there was a darkness

rising on the horizon. She kicked Slave and he woke with a grunt.

'Still here?'

'Is it a sandstorm?' she asked. 'Should we find shelter?'

Slave kneeled and pressed the palms of his hands to the ground.

'Not a storm,' he said. 'Feel.'

She did and through her palms she felt a rhythmic thudding, like . . . like rain on a thin roof.

'An army,' he said. 'It's an army.'

Part Three

29
Madu

Madu had never thought there could be too much walking, even going at marching pace, but by midday his thighs and calves were in agony. He was in the rear rank, beside the tall blue-eyed soldier who had more or less ignored him since they had set off. He seemed to have no trouble marching at all, stepping out in time to the drummers who rode on camels beside the endless columns. Maybe it would have been better at the front of the army where the dust would be less, but Madu doubted it. Despite his every effort he began to lag behind and once he stumbled and would have fallen if Blue Eyes hadn't grabbed him and pulled him up.

'You need to keep marching or you'll be flogged,' he said.

'They won't, they can't,' Madu gasped.

The Sergeant bellowed: 'Keep it up, step it out and keep it up!'

'They'll flog you and they'll flog any man who doesn't keep up.'

'I shouldn't be here.'

'Save your energy.'

'It's not right.'

On they marched, as the sun crawled across the sky. Every so often water skins were passed around and some of the men had food they ate on the move. The land around them was featureless – a few bushes, dunes and more dunes, groves of trees that offered the hope of shade that was always denied by their relentless progress and the agony in his legs becoming worse and worse until he found himself weeping from the pain and the unfairness of it all.

Blue Eyes rested a hand on his shoulder.

'Keep marching, don't look at the ground, look at the horizon and you'll get through this.'

The tone was brusque but the kindness behind the words almost brought the tears to his eyes again.

'I can't,' he said, 'I can't,' and fell to his knees.

The sand seemed very hot. Then Blue Eyes pulled him up and shouted: 'Get up, get up! March!'

'I can't.'

'You can. Rest on my shoulder.'

Water splashed his face; it too seemed very hot. He looked up and saw the burning sun, then shut his eyes but it made no difference, the sun was there too. Whole armies of suns dancing in the darkness. He felt himself falling and heard a shout: 'Man down!'

The voice of the sergeant.

'Man can't march, man can't fight. This army needs fighters. Keep moving.'

'Sergeant, he's only a kid.'

'Then he'll only be a dead kid and no loss.'

Madu tried to see what was happening but half a dozen suns still danced in front of his eyes. Were they leaving him behind?

Excruciating pain in the back of his neck, Blue Eyes' long fingers crushing and blue eyes staring into his.

'Look at me.'

Somehow the suns went away and he was looking into that long stern face . . . Yes, stern but not without compassion.

'I'm going to leave you now. You're going to die here. Can you hear the vultures? They've learned to follow armies. It's like they know there'll be pickings for them. They go for the eyes first. Shall I kill you now, to make it easier? I can cut your throat.'

Could he feel the edge of a blade against his flesh?

'Close your eyes. It'll be quicker.'

'No, I won't, I can't ...' From somewhere beyond himself, as if something were sitting on his shoulders digging in claws of fire and making him croak: 'I won't ... I won't die. May God curse you, Mother, I will not die.'

Lurching to his feet, Blue Eyes still holding, pulling, one foot in front of the other, on and on and on ...

The two tiny figures, one pulling the other along, were dwarfed by the immensity of sand across which the army was passing; and yet that army was no small thing itself. Under great clouds of dust kicked up by their boots, ten thousand men marched doggedly on to orders bellowed by brass-lunged sergeants, their pace controlled by drummers swaying atop camels, hammering their kettledrums in a remorseless chest-quaking beat.

Rank after rank of infantry, armed with short stabbing swords and heavy shields, burdened with backpacks that contained everything any man might need on the march, in battle or after. Behind them, pikemen, their lances a moving forest, the vicious steel heads glittering above the dust. Each also carried a needle-thin, needle-sharp dagger to thrust through gaps in the armour of the mounted warriors their lances would bring down.

Flanking the main body of the troops were skirmishers mounted on swift horses bred to cope with noise and confusion. These riders were expert archers, able to aim and shoot from the saddle while galloping at full tilt; their task was to scout out the terrain ahead of the army and, in battle, annoy the enemy with a thousand pinpricks and drive him into rash moves in response. They regarded themselves as the aristocrats of the forces of Tumanbay, their heads held proudly above the dust that enveloped the sword fodder.

In fact they were all the same: Tumanbay's army had, for centuries, been formed – like every other aspect of life in the Empire – from slaves. Every slave had it dinned into them during their first weeks of training that General Qulan himself had arrived in the city as a boy slave and worked his way up through hard work and talent at killing enemies, to the very summit of power, and that if they too strove with all their might and main, the same hill was open for them to climb.

On that hot day as the soldiers marched and sweated and strained until they thought their backs would break and their legs fold under them, there was another army on the move – this one far less warlike and proud but equally vital to the success of the Empire. Marching a few arrow-flights back, out of the immediate dust, it was a caravan of workshops and kitchens that provided the stuff upon which armies march and fight. Their blades were the knives and cleavers of the butchers, receiving a constant stream of carcasses from the mobile slaughterhouses. Their lances were the poles and rods of the surveyors, who plotted routes and planned where to set camp. Their short swords were the razors of the barbers who cut and shaped the hair of the army – and there were many fashions that swept through the thousands of men: plaits one day, shaven with a crest the next, mustachios for the plains, knotted beards with ribbons entwined for the snowy passes. Their kettledrums were mighty brass kettles tended by a legion of cooks, sending a forest of steam into the sky twice a day at dawn and dusk, stirring their pots with ladles as large as battle hammers.

And further back beyond this shadow army, was another: a

shanty of carts and smaller tents, some gaily hung about with feminine garments that are not usually hung about, others more subtly hinting at ale and wine, forbidden on active service but always available; yet others occupied by families who chose to follow their men and lived in a hundred ways off the leavings of the army. There were whole clans of children who swooped like predatory birds and scooped up everything that fell to the ground or was not tied and strapped safely in a backpack. Many of them would become soldiers of Tumanbay in their turn, and not all by any means would be boys, for in an army where any can rise, then any can serve. General Qulan himself had decreed: 'Don't tell me who he or she is, tell me how they can fight.'

And even this was not the end, for beyond the beyond were the shit-shovellers, and as any shit-shoveller can tell you, that many men and women leave an awful lot of shit to shovel! And in one of his few lucid moments Madu, potential heir to the throne of Tumanbay, thought: truly, I am starting at the bottom. From shit were we raised and to shit will we fall.

'Keep going, just keep going,' the tall soldier said.

Madu laughed, though it came out as a croak.

'What is it?'

He shook his head and staggered on. There was, after all, nothing else to do.

30
Gregor

Sarah was attending to her duties in the First Wife's extensive wardrobe chamber when Gregor materialised out of nowhere. She was about to scream when he slapped his hand over her mouth and strangled the sound. He turned her to face him.

'There's nothing to worry about,' he said quietly, calmly, 'nothing is wrong. I'm going to take my hand away now. Are you all right?'

He allowed her room to nod and took his hand away. She sucked in a deep breath and collapsed on a chest.

'Where . . .? How . . .?'

'I could say it was magic but there is no magic in this world, only what we make for ourselves. One of the Sultans many years ago had the palace rebuilt and installed passages behind all the walls to enable the servants to pass without disturbing him and his court. His successor, who used the passages to bring about a revolt – the Sultan was boiled alive in his bath – had them closed off and they were soon forgotten. Very few people know about them now. I am one of them, you are another. See how I trust you, Sarah. And yet you do not trust me.'

'I don't understand.' The colour was returning to her face but her breathing was still disturbed.

'You are late with your report. You left no sign for a meeting.

You have done nothing for me – what, then, should I do for you?'

'You promised,' she cried out, 'My baby.'

He said nothing.

She went on: 'I was taking notes in the Stewards' Office when the Vizier came in. I . . . I was scared. I didn't want to be away in case he said something and my mistress became suspicious . . . Do you see . . .? If she knew I reported to you—'

'You probably underestimate Shajah. Everyone in this palace is like the walls – they have hidden areas, they make secret journeys to unknown destinations. What happened?'

'I had sent the Steward to buy sweetmeats for the mistress. I was copying the daybook as you desired when he let himself in. He had a key. He took some sugar plums.'

'He shouldn't have been anywhere near the hareem without permission.'

'Maybe he did have it?'

If that was the case, Gregor thought, the permission must have come from the Sultan himself. That was an interesting and dangerous thought. On the other hand, Cadali could have been acting on his own behalf; it would take little effort to sow suspicion of the First Wife in al-Ghuri's mind. Al-Ghuri and Shajah had been illicit lovers, had murdered his brother the reigning Sultan and taken the throne. It might be convenient for al-Ghuri to mount a plot to get rid of Shajah . . . in which case the only others left with knowledge of the events were the Vizier and Gregor himself. Time to tread carefully.

'Did he see the list?'

'Yes, he read it.'

'What did he say, when he wasn't stuffing his face?'

'Only that he was surprised I could read and write.'

'Only that? Hm. Very well. He'll probably try and recruit you to spy for him. If he does, accept.'

He took the list from her and began to scan it – it was long, covering three sheets.

'I still don't understand. It's just a list. Like all the other times.'

A marble table stood near them. He ran the flat of his hand over the top, his fingers spread.

'I'm looking for a flaw in the marble, almost invisible to the naked eye until the delicate –' his hand stopped moving – 'sense of touch tells you there's a crack. Then you look more closely and . . .'

He tapped the paper and passed it to her.

'What's this?'

Sarah looked down at the item on the list.

He said: 'Angellotti Brothers.'

'I don't know.'

'Unusual name. Artists, I believe, calligraphers. The Sultan has had work done by them, I think. Does your lady have a lot of calligraphy done?'

'She delights in fine work and don't you all believe you have the best craftsmen in the world in Tumanbay?'

'We have indeed. Now what does your mistress have to do with these two, eh?'

'I don't know, Excellency.'

'Of course you don't. Is she commissioning work? Something for the Sultan's delight, perhaps? Well, let's see. And don't be late with the list again, it will not go well with you.' He stepped between rows of hanging dresses, the delicate materials wafting in his wake. 'Your mistress will be wondering where you are, you should go.'

'Wait.'

Gregor stepped back into the room. It wasn't good practice to allow a spy to dictate anything but perhaps she had more to say.

'Well . . .?' he asked.

'My baby. It will be a moon at my next report, when we meet. I want to see my baby. You promised.'

'Yes, I did.'

She took a deep breath. 'I won't do anything else until I can see her. I don't care what you do, how much you threaten me, I don't want any more lies. I want my baby.'

31
Heaven

The great dust cloud crept along the horizon like a living creature, writhing and twisting as it went. Slave and Heaven lay behind the prow of a scrubby dune watching its progress, trying to make out what exactly it was, since there were no soldiers and the sound that came drifting across the open sand towards them was not of drums and marching but more of a roar and rattle – like, like . . .

'It's like a town,' she said.

'In the desert?'

'I don't know. But it's not an army and if it's a caravan, it's the biggest I've ever seen.'

'And you, of course,' he said, 'have seen everything worth seeing in your long and experienced life.'

'Well, all right, that I've ever read about and I bet I've read more than—'

She stopped abruptly and they both listened and there it was again. A bell – a goat bell, a cowbell. Both of them scrambled back down the dune to a small dry river bed that twisted past a grove of stunted bushes.

'Stay here, keep quiet,' he hissed.

'I don't think there's anyone there, it's just a lost goat.'

'It's never "just" anything, believe me.'

'Why should I?'

'Because I'm saving your useless life. And we are going to die out here unless we get food, water and some mules or camels, can you understand that?'

'Of course I can! I'm not stupid.'

Slave considered her words for a moment, then said: 'I'm going to get into the caravan and steal what we need and I'll come back. It'll probably take a while. It'll be dark and you'll have to wait. Alone. Can you do that?'

Fear rushed over her; if she'd had any food in her stomach she might have been sick.

'No, you'll leave me. How do I know you'll come back?'

'Because I say so. You'll have to trust me.'

'Why should I trust you?' The words came out almost as a cry.

'Shhhh . . . You said just now that you weren't stupid, yes?'

She nodded.

'Then you should trust me because you're still alive and not at the bottom of the sea or buried in some sand hole on the beach.'

'Give me something so I know you'll come back.'

'I was a slave – they took everything. I have nothing.'

'Then promise,' she said.

'You really are just a child.'

'And didn't you say nothing is ever "just" anything?'

'Very well, I promise I will come back.'

He threw her the water skin and in a moment he was gone.

She drank the last trickle and looked around for somewhere to hide, but the bushes were too scrubby and the river bed too shallow. She sat on a stone and hugged her knees to her chest and tried not to think about anything at all, but she couldn't stop the pictures coming and coming: of Mother on the ship, her angry face, her occasional smiles, even her pain when she was sick. She saw her father, as she'd seen him last, six moons ago, leaving for Tumanbay on his ship, standing there and waving as he left the harbour and Mother warning her not to wave so frantically like a common girl, but even she had tears in her eyes.

'I mustn't cry,' she said to herself.

Someone else said: 'Have you come to take me?'

She screamed, jumped to her feet and stumbled back.

'Stay away . . .'

'Are you the angel, come to take me?'

A boy was standing on the slope of the dune looking down at her. He was maybe ten. A few goats were following him, their bells clattering dully.

'Are you the angel come to take me to Paradise?'

'I'm lost,' she said.

'Do angels get lost?'

'I'm not an angel. Sorry.'

His face fell. 'How did you get here, then?'

He was speaking the language of the central plain that Heaven had often used when she was younger (her mother said it was common), though he had a strange accent she'd never heard before. He was walking down the dune, a staff in one hand, getting closer. She backed away.

'I told you, stay back.'

He stopped. 'I won't hurt you.'

'I was on a ship – and then I wasn't and we came here to the coast and then we walked. Can you help me? I'm thirsty and hungry.'

'Who are you,' he asked.

'I'm me.' That didn't seem to answer his question. She said: 'Can I speak to your father?' Nothing. 'Your mother?'

'I don't have a father or mother. I look after the goats, that's what I do.'

More goats were appearing over the dune, their bells clacking as they skittered down the sand.

'Who for?'

He shrugged.

'I have gold.'

Her hand moved instinctively to her waist where she could feel the belt her mother insisted she wear, with five gold coins sewn into it, under her dress.

'All right, come.'

He turned and began to walk along the river bed, the goats following him and Heaven following the goats. After a while, Heaven began to run until she had caught him up and they were walking together.

'What did you mean, have I come to take you away? Do you want to go away?'

He shrugged again. 'I thought you were an angel, that's all. Because of your hair. Angels have hair like yours.'

She tried to run her fingers through it but it was tangled and salt-caked.

'I think angels' hair is better than mine, they probably have someone to do it for them or maybe they don't need help. I suppose they don't really.'

He held up a hand and they stopped abruptly. 'Are you alone?'

'Why do you want to know?'

With a roar, Slave erupted, huge and terrifying. He grabbed the boy, slammed him down into the sand, bellowing: 'Who are you?' He too was using the central language. 'What do you want? Where are the others?'

He lifted a huge fist, ready to bring it down on the boy's face.

Heaven shouted: 'Stop it, stop it, he can't breathe, he can't speak, your hand is over his mouth! He's a boy. Stop it!'

The fist came down and buried itself in the sand beside the boy's head.

'He can help us,' Heaven said.

'And why would he do that?'

'Because you're not going to kill him. Take your hand off his mouth and nose before he suffocates. Please.'

Slave set him upright in the sand.

The boy gulped air and said: 'I don't like him.'

'Neither do I,' Heaven said.

Slave snorted. 'I might have saved your life. The boy could have cut your throat.'

'You used me as a lure, didn't you? You were never going to the caravan, you just wanted to see who was following us.'

Slave shrugged. 'It's never "just" anything.' He turned back to the boy. 'Do you come from the caravan? Who are they? What are they?'

When the boy didn't answer, Slave lifted his fist.

Heaven said: 'He's scared.' It was true – the boy was crying. 'He's only a child, stop frightening him.'

Through his tears, the boy said: 'I can help you, I swear.'

'I know you can,' Heaven said. 'Don't worry about him, he won't hurt you.'

'So now you're in charge?' Slave said, letting go of the boy, who backed rapidly away until he was well out of reach.

He said: 'It's not a caravan. It's a town.'

Slave laughed. 'In the desert, on the move, a town?'

'I'll show you, you'll see. Come with me.'

32

Gregor

The morning conference was, more often than not, a waste of time, merely a matter of reassuring the Sultan that all was well; however, all was not well and Gregor was conscious of it.

He adjusted his sash of office and entered the Council Chamber.

It was empty. He stood for a moment, confounded. The room was never empty at this time. The court ran like clockwork, Cadali saw to that ... Ahh, of course, Cadali.

The big door closed behind him. He didn't need to turn around, he recognised the scent.

'I have an appointment.'

The Vizier stood behind Gregor's left shoulder, just out of sight.

'And now you don't. The Sultan is not happy with your progress. He is a busy monarch. Matters of state. He doesn't have time to waste on your failures.'

'The Sultan will wish to be kept informed of my progress in searching out spies.'

'You do not speak for His Majesty. You may report to me. As far as you are concerned, I stand in his place.'

Cadali was almost purring with self-satisfaction. Gregor considered walking out but that would seem merely petulant; best swallow the gristle and be professional. He turned to face the Vizier, stepping close, too close, which he knew would discomfort the fat man; but not this morning it seemed. Cadali stood his ground.

'Go on.'

'Very well. I have found a number of low level operatives in the kitchens, the stables, the comptroller's office and so on. They reveal very little when put to the question.'

'Because they know very little, presumably?'

'The only high level operative we've found so far is the maid.'

'*Was*, Gregor, she *was* the maid. She killed herself, yes? And revealed nothing, yes?'

'On the contrary, she revealed that Maya has a cadre of spies who are not afraid to die – indeed they welcome it. I think we have learned something important there.'

He would never admit it to Cadali or to anyone at all, but his encounter with the spy had left him off balance. He followed the religion of the state but had never been much of a believer. He'd seen death, been death's gatekeeper, too often to think there was any mercy or any reward to come. Death was the end – and yet the young woman had gone to it with shining eyes – with hope, as if . . .

Cadali was talking: '. . . and that she was prepared to die rather than face your tender mercies is no surprise to me. I hear that our honoured physician has prepared you potions to keep your subjects alive and in agony far beyond any natural span.'

'Palace gossip, no more.'

'When I say "hear", I mean I have listened to their screams echoing from that cellar you keep down there.'

The oily bastard was enjoying it. Well, let him have his day.

'How you amuse yourself, Cadali, is no business of mine. I am waiting and looking for the one little thing that is out of place, that will lead me to the head of this group. The work of intelligence is a series of tiny steps and patience, always patience.'

'And so far?'

'The work proceeds.'

Cadali walked to one of the great windows that looked out over the roofs of the palace. He pushed the wooden shutters open and sunlight flooded in.

'I understand the Lady Shajah has a new maid.'

Gregor joined him, looking avidly at the Vizier's broad back. One hand planted in the middle, one shove, a cry, a wet thud far below. Who would ever know?

'Does she?'

'You organised it, Gregor.'

'Ye-es. Intelligent young woman, no palace loyalties. So unusual.'

'And has she come up with what you expected – or perhaps a surprise or two?'

'Come up with?'

'She's working for you.'

'I couldn't—'

'It wasn't a question, man. I know it, you know it, Shajah knows it. I imagine the boy who empties the piss-pots in the morning knows it. That's the great game, isn't it? Everybody knows everything and yet still we let slip our secrets for the ear that can hear and the mind that can solve the riddle. Yes? Oh, and surely I don't have to remind you, Commander, that no one in Tumanbay can count himself beyond punishment. No one at all. Thank you for your report. Try to make the next a little better than inadequate.'

Gregor didn't bother to answer; there was nothing to say and there was somewhere else he needed to be.

33

Ibn Bai

Ibn Bai knew Commander Gregor would come back but some weeks had passed and he had begun to believe that perhaps he would be left in peace, doing no more than delivering a weekly report to an anonymous official at the palace while he tried to come to terms with his terrible loss. He was, of course, fooling no one, either about the intensity of his grief, which became sharper with each passing day, or about this Commander Gregor who, once again, announced himself with a thunderous knocking at the compound gate.

Ibn Bai waited for him by the fountain as the gatekeeper unlocked and admitted not the man alone but a smaller figure, a woman, swathed from head to toe. Once the gate was closed, she threw back her head covering and there were those startling blue eyes again. Her first words were: 'My baby?'

The tall man placed a restraining hand on her shoulder.

'You will see your baby. She is well cared for, isn't that so, Ibn Bai?'

The words carried the lightest possible dusting of threat but Ibn Bai had no doubt that if he had failed in any aspect of his care, there would be a price to pay.

'Everything is as you would wish, Excellency. And you too,' he said, looking at Sarah. He had made her a promise when he sold her to the palace and had kept it. 'Please, come with me.'

He led them into the cool of the house, along a tiled passage and into a luxuriously appointed room.

'I prepared this for my wife and daughter, I thought it would remind them of home. It has . . .'

His words tailed off; there was nothing to say and then the baby gave a cry. The woman, Sarah, shook off the Commander's hand and rushed to the crib, picking up the child tenderly.

'She's taking milk from the wet nurse, some solids too, growing every day,' Ibn Bai said. 'She can see properly. She smiles at me.'

The Commander said: 'I have kept my promise. You work for me and I will protect you and your child.'

Sarah ignored him but Ibn Bai wondered what her 'work' might consist of; nothing good, nothing safe – he was as sure of that as he was that this Gregor was nothing but bad news, and the gods knew, there had been enough of that in these recent days.

He said: 'The wet nurse will feed her now, if you like?'

'My milk dried up,' she said. 'I can give her nothing.'

Ibn Bai snapped his fingers and the nurse, who had been waiting at the door, hurried in. He could see with what reluctance Sarah gave up the child, how hungrily her glance rested upon it as it took the breast.

'Ibn Bai, a word, if you would be so kind?'

Ibn Bai took Gregor into the library. He looked around, a half smile on his face.

'I can see there is a whole world of knowledge in this room. If a man knew half of it, Ibn Bai, or even one quarter, he would be wiser than any other man living, I should think. But then there is not the time in a whole life to learn it.'

'That is the thing of it, Commander. A man does not need to

know the answer, he only needs to know where to go to find it.'

'Then, my friend, I have come to you for an answer to my question. You buy many books and scrolls?'

'Too many, my wife always— Yes, I do.'

'Angellotti Brothers, illuminators, restorers of ancient texts – where might I find them?'

An odd request, Ibn Bai thought. Why this sudden interest in the fine arts and religion?

'In the Street of the Illuminators,' he said. 'It is beyond the market, under the temple walls, the sign of the crossed brushes.'

'Very good, Ibn Bai, thank you. I have some business to attend to. Remember, your head on my slave still being here when I return.'

34

Heaven

She hated the way they nibbled at her robe. Goats had never been her favourite animal – were they anyone's? They followed the boy without a command, though he did sometimes talk quietly to them as they crossed the desert, drawing closer to the dust cloud and whatever was making it. When she'd asked him his name he'd said: 'Boy, my name is Boy.' She told him that Slave's name was Slave, just like his, but he said Slave was nothing like Boy. She'd given up after that and simply followed him.

The town, as Boy called it, began to solidify out of the evening haze. At first she'd thought it must be a mirage: there were flags on long poles, waving above the swirling sands, each with a highly coloured sigil painted on it. Below, looming out of the dust storm, what appeared to be whole buildings appeared. Most were tents, vast and many poled, highly coloured, swaying and bucking as they crept forward on hundreds of wheels. Among them were other structures, made of wood in fantastic shapes. She thought she saw a spiral staircase for a moment before it vanished into the swirling sand, and a peaked roof and a spire with an onion dome beside it; and beyond these, she could see yet taller tents, higher banners and great squat shapes that must have been carried on dozens of carts, each hauled by straining teams of oxen. Among all this were people, swathed from head to toe in robes against the sand – crowds of them, as if the town were a busy market, passing up and down and in between the teams of sweating animals. And rising out of the whole ungainly mass, smoke. Blue smoke from hundreds of wood fires, and also something thicker: dark, oily smoke writhing like serpents into the blue sky, staining it in a horrible way.

'It's a town, see?' Boy said. 'With tents and temples and inns and other places and streets and they even have baths and everything, it's everything.'

'But it's moving,' Heaven said. 'How do they do that? Does it go on? I mean, do they . . . do you stop?'

'At nights and sometimes we settle somewhere and then off we go again, everything on carts and camels and oxen and backs, to somewhere else. Where we can find what we need.'

Slave said: 'What's that, then?'

'What we use.'

Heaven asked: 'What do you use?'

'I told you, everything! We find a use for it – but most of all, armies. We follow armies and after battles we make use of what's left. It's what we look for. They call them the high times – a big battle and all those things to use.'

'Everything?' Heaven asked. 'What about . . . the bodies?'

Boy pointed at the town. 'You see the smoke? Not the woodsmoke, the other.'

'Thick and greasy,' Slave muttered. 'I've seen smoke like that before.'

'It's from the vats. They cook all the time, even on the move. We use it all, you see. Come on, we have to hurry, they don't like it if I'm late.'

'I'm liking this less and less,' Slave said.

Heaven said: 'It's better than the desert. We can eat, have a bath. It'll be fine, you'll see.'

She could smell the place now and it was exactly like the town where she'd grown up, or at least the market area – cooking meat, animals, spices, dung, smoke, people. She'd always had a good sense of smell, her father said; she could pick out the best tea, the finest ginger, the subtlest herbs.

'It is a town, it's . . . just like a town.'

'Nothing is "just" anything,' Slave repeated. He halted Boy with a hand on his shoulder. 'If you're leading us into a trap, Boy, I swear . . .'

'Leave him be,' Heaven said, and asked: 'How big is the town?'

'How big is big? You would need a long day to walk all around but we go this way.'

He led them past a half dozen carts piled high with multi-coloured sacks, pulled by straining donkeys; on the top of the first, three children sat eating watermelon, spitting the pips down at them as they went by. Boy's goats formed themselves into an orderly line and followed. It was a strange sensation walking through narrow streets that passed her as she passed them.

A distant horn sounded a long low note, like dragons mourn-ing in a story of long ago, Heaven thought, and around them everything shuddered to a halt. More people appeared, unyoking animal teams, hammering iron stakes deep into the sand, sling-ing ropes and hauling up masts and poles. Boy hurried them down a narrow gap between a series of low wooden arches that were settling into the sand under a platform from which steam billowed. Voices shouted angrily and delicious smells arose – she couldn't see what it was but she guessed a kitchen from the shouts; it was likely cooks were the same the world over.

'Is that it, have they stopped for the night?' she called.

'Yes. It changes, sometimes earlier, sometimes later. It all depends.'

'On what?' Slave demanded.

197

'How would I know that?'

He trilled something and the goats streamed past him into a small paddock area and settled down. There was a tent going up as they approached, the roof pole rising as a stocky man, as wide as he was tall, heaved on a rope. A woman in wine red robes decorated in silver was carrying things from a wagon into the tent even as it rose around her. A second cart had a cage on its flatbed and two enormous dogs peered levelly through the bars, following Boy as he crossed the paddock and rubbed their muzzles. Heaven wouldn't have gone within ten leagues of any of them; they looked like killers to her.

'I have brought guests, Master Rajik. They were travellers astray.'

The stout man wrapped a rope around a stake and turned to face them, hands on hips, the muscles of his arms swelling. He wore a sleeveless leather jerkin lined down the front with bronze studs. He looked, Heaven thought, rather like a pirate captain from one of her favourite stories. He regarded them with a cool gaze.

'Who are you?'

Slave said: 'Who are you?'

A silence fell between them; all around the noise of establishment went on but the two men stared at each other and neither moved until . . .

'Rajik, these are travellers, guests, and guests are sacred to our kind.'

It was the woman who had been carrying goods into the tent. Close up, she looked motherly, generous, hung about with enough bracelets, baubles and charms to furnish a jewellery stall in the market. Heaven decided she liked her.

'Are we not all travellers through this world? Why, she's hardly more than a child, this beauty. Come, my sweet, you must be exhausted. I will heat water for you, you must wash away the sand and the aches and pain. Rajik, where are your manners, husband!'

Rajik gave them a narrow smile, displaying two gold teeth, strode across the paddock and stuck out a huge hand. After a moment's hesitation, Slave took hold of it.

'Forgive me, brother. Of course you are welcome.'

It didn't sound to Heaven like he meant it.

The woman swooped on her and wrapped her round in a scented and robed embrace.

'I am Pamira, you are safe now, my sweet.'

Unable to help herself, Heaven burst into tears. She allowed herself to be led into the tent as behind her, Rajik was saying: 'We're all running from something here, big man. You want to come in, fine. You want to stay outside or go on your way, that's fine too.'

He loosed his fist from Slave's grip and went inside.

Boy said: 'It's all right, I swear.'

Slave said: 'Nothing's all right, I swear.'

35
The Artists

Parig and Panik were for once in harmony as they ate lunch together. Neither were big eaters but during their childhood mealtimes had always been oases of quiet when their father, an irascible man in life, would tell tales of his adventurous youth in the mountains of the far north, where there were giants and white bears and all sorts of other wonders. Neither brother was ever quite sure how true these tales were, but they enjoyed their father's enjoyment and their mother was happy that there was peace in the house.

Peace in the shop was shattered by a knock at the door heavy enough to rattle the hinges and send the dust flying. They looked at each other.

'The First Wife?'

'Too heavy, Panik.'

As if to underline the words, the knock came again and again the door rattled.

'Better go and see,' Parig said.

'Why don't you go?' Panik said. 'I always go.'

'Well, exactly, you always go.'

'It doesn't mean it's immutable.'

'I am the elder and that, brother dear, is immutable. Answer the door.'

Chewing the last of his chickpeas wrapped in flatbread, Panik shifted off his stool and went to the door, where he lifted the cover over the peephole.

'It's a man.'

'See, I told you. Ask him what he wants.'

'I imagine he wants to buy something, we are a shop after all.'

A shout came from outside: 'Angellotti Brothers?'

'Yes, what do you want?'

'I have been sent by the Lady Shajah, may I come in?'

'Shajah, you say?'

'Yes.' It was a bark rather than an answer.

Panik unlocked the door and ushered the visitor in. A tall man in dour clothing with a steady, hooded gaze that gave nothing away.

'She sent you?' Parig asked, easing himself off his stool.

'The Lady?' Panik supplied. 'You come from the Lady?'

'Only,' Parig put in, 'we don't know you, do we?'

'Never seen you before.'

'Not from Samarkand, are you?'

Panik said: 'Course he's not. Look at that colouring. You've nice colouring, my lord.'

'Besides,' Parig said, 'she knows it's not ready. Only last week, when she came to inspect the work . . .'

The visitor produced something from under his robe. About the size of a gold coin, it bore the crest of the city. All officials of higher rank carried such things.

He said: 'Unlike your questions, my patience and my time are both limited. She wants a progress report.'

'You have to understand, Excellency,' Parig said in tones suitably obsequious, 'we are artists and art cannot be hurried.' He crossed to the large wooden store cupboard and began to ease out a drawer. 'Your mistress might find a hundred mere artisans who would do the work and promise Paradise in weeks but she is wise ...'

Panik took up the refrain. '... for she knows that for work of this quality only the best will do.'

He gestured at the drawer his brother had now opened and at the scrolls, partially unrolled, resting there.

'The very best,' Parig said. 'Every brushstroke, every inlay, must match the original so there is no difference to be seen.'

The visitor leaned over the scrolls, obviously drawn by their strange beauty.

'Such is our artistry,' Panik said. 'But it takes time.'

'Time,' echoed his brother.

The visitor muttered: 'These are very ancient?'

'Precious,' from Panik.

'Rare,' from Parig. 'We've never seen the like and we have seen everything. These are a wonder.'

'So I shall tell the lady that the work proceeds and will be complete in ...?'

'By the sickle moon,' Parig said, 'or a day or two after.'

'Thank you. Please, close the drawer – as you say, they are precious indeed.'

And he was gone like a shadow from the shop of the Angellotti Brothers at the sign of the crossed brushes.

36

Ibn Bai

The slave, Sarah, was playing with her child when Ibn Bai brought her some mint tea and honey cakes. He put the tray down near to where she kneeled on the floor with the babe.

'Please, eat if you wish.'

The baby reached out a pudgy hand and she said: 'Not for you, my sweet. Not yet.'

Ibn Bai found an onyx and silver seal on a chain and held it up so it glittered in a sunbeam.

'She likes this,' he said, and handed it to the woman.

The baby immediately began to reach for it, chortling.

'You said earlier, your wife and daughter . . .'

It was as if a sharp blade had cut across Ibn Bai's face. He shook his head and turned away.

'I'm sorry if I caused you pain.'

'No, not you. I had forgotten for a moment, watching you with your child . . . I do that, I forget and lose myself in a book or my accounts or some such everyday thing and then I remember again – they are dead, the plague, somewhere at sea they died. My daughter was going to be married here. She would have had a family. Babies. They were on a ship, or did I tell you that? A ship of the dead. I watched it burn in the harbour here. Their pyre.' He sat down and, without thinking of it as he talked, took and ate a honey cake. 'I have discovered something. That for each one of us in this world there is one thing that is . . . everything. For some it is their honour, or power or gold. For me it was my family.'

'And for others, their freedom, perhaps,' she said.

'Yes, their freedom.'

Reaching for the bright pendant, the baby began to struggle.

'She'll be strong,' Ibn Bai said, 'and she's already beautiful. She has your eyes. Her father's eyes too, perhaps?'

'His eyes were full of lust.' Her voice was flat and cold.

She was a slave – what did he care what this man's eyes were like? What did she or her freedom matter to him? Ibn Bai should have stood up and left the room and kept guard until Commander Gregor returned, but he did none of these things.

He said: 'What happened?'

'I can see his face hanging over me . . . I can remember the pain and the fear and the hope I would die there and then.'

'But you didn't. No matter how much you wanted to . . . Maybe you even tried to end it yourself?'

'The heart is a traitor,' she said. 'When I hold Naima in my arms I can feel the love flowing out of me. Shouldn't I hate her? Only I can't. Maybe you are right about family.'

'Life has a way. I say – you are finished, Ibn Bai. Your life is over. I've said it a thousand times since . . .'

A scent arose, the rich, teasing aroma of a milk-fed baby releasing her bowels into her diaper cloth. They both smiled and Sarah said: 'And yet she needs to be changed.'

The wet nurse brought water and a clean cloth and together they changed the child and put her back into her crib.

Outside the bell rang.

'Commander Gregor,' Ibn Bai said. 'I'll go to him, give you a few more moments.'

'Wait. Do you trust him?'

'Say nothing.'

Ibn Bai left her there and hurried to meet the commander in the hall.

'All is well, Excellency?'

'She is still here?'

'Yes.'

'Then all is well. Are there pens, ink, paper in the library?'

'Of course.'

'Then come with me.' As he walked the commander held his hands apart as if cupping something. 'This wide, old, definitely old, torn a little, vellum with an ivory sheen . . .'

They were in the library; Gregor took paper and pens.

'Top and bottom a script, letters something like so . . .' The pen scratched against the paper. 'Not a form I have ever seen. And centrally, representations – green, blue, violet, red, gold picked out, travellers perhaps . . . and a ship on a starry sea – again, a style I am unfamiliar with. Borders and divisions . . . Moons rising and setting . . . So and so.'

He sketched hastily.

'Margins?' Ibn Bai inquired.

'Like so.' Again the pen dashed across the paper. 'Symbols of some sort. Snakes and lizards entwined. I only saw one length of each. There was a lot more I didn't see.'

Ibn Bai felt his heart beating faster – the excitement of a collector of fine things – but he looked again. Could it be?

'No, impossible.'

'What?'

He hadn't realised he'd spoken aloud.

'From what you've shown me here . . . There are a number of copies of this, you'll find one in every great temple in the capital city of every nation that follows the faith. I imagine this copy was damaged, perhaps from much use, and is being mended. Even the copies are considered holy and thus valuable, of course.'

'Of course, what?' Gregor said.

'Of course, considering what they are.'

'And . . .?'

'They are copies of the Great Book, the message the first Hafiz received from . . . from God, I suppose.'

'Could they be original?'

Ibn Bai laughed. 'You may know many things, effendi, but you don't know your own religion. They were lost in the great fire. When the barbarian hordes destroyed the Temple of the Mount – a thousand years ago? They were burned and the second Hafiz rewrote them from memory, and his acolyte Abdul al-Hazred made a limited number of further copies. These copies are still of incalculable value and they are always blessed by the Hafiz of the day – wherever he is, so is the heart of belief. So they say. I mean . . . there are many beliefs in this world.'

'But if these scrolls were real?'

'If they were real, the original from which all other copies descended . . . the mother of them all? No, such a thing is impossible.'

'Thank you.'

The commander folded the paper and slipped it under his robe.

He called, 'Sarah, we are going now.'

She was waiting in the courtyard by the fountain. The commander strode past her and indicated that the gate be opened. Ibn Bai looked at the woman and she looked back and in that moment they made an agreement. God alone knew what might come of it, but as the gate closed behind them, Ibn Bai felt, for the first time in many days, that perhaps there was a path before him now.

*

In the street, as he guided the shrouded Sarah through the crowds, Gregor began to feel something stirring inside him, that sense of excitement he had always experienced, even as a child, when he had begun to fit separate parts together into a whole that only he could see and use. Secret knowledge, Gregor's knowledge, his power to impose control on the confusion of the world around him. These scrolls, they meant something. They were more than copies, even his blundering eye could see that, could feel the power radiating from them like the heat of an intense fire. Or maybe they were only scraps of old parchment and worth nothing much at all except to priests and collectors. He almost chuckled, not that he was given to mirth, at the prospect of the chase and the possible reward. He, Gregor, would have these things or be damned for it!

He felt a touch on his arm and spun, reaching for his sword. It was the slave.

'Thank you,' she said.

Her glance was direct, her blue eyes somehow disturbing his thoughts about the chase. He nodded, grunted and walked on, his head down.

37
Madu

Time passed in a haze of pain. Madu couldn't even have said how many days had gone by; there was marching and there was sleeping and then marching again and sleep and marching and as soon as camp was struck, he fell asleep on the sand and knew nothing until morning when horns woke him and he looked around, at the camp, at the men going about their morning tasks, at . . .

Blue Eyes, who was sitting cross-legged watching him. He said nothing, only pushed across a water skin and some gruel in a bowl. Madu pushed it away but drank deeply. Blue Eyes leaned close and took his hand, slipping two leaves into it. They were very dark green, probably dried.

'Chew them, they'll help dull the pain. Also you must eat or you won't make it through the march. You've had virtually nothing for three days.'

Madu was about to say it would make him sick when he realised he was actually hungry. He hadn't eaten since he'd arrived in this hell on earth. He grabbed the bowl and swallowed the warm, gluey mass gratefully.

'Thank you. Was it so long? Three days? I don't remember.'

'Ah, so you can talk as well as whine. I've taken care of your stuff, dug your shift – double work for three days but that's it. After this you sort for yourself.'

'If I get through today.'

'Oh, you will. You've broken its back now. I thought for a time you were a dead man. We watch out for each other. That's the army. Daniel.'

'Madu.'

The sergeant was bellowing, the camp was vanishing around them; bedrolls were secured, field kitchens loaded aboard carts, fires extinguished . . . and in a moment, it seemed to Madu, they were marching again, into the sun.

Whether it was the leaves he was chewing or the wet cloth Daniel gave him to wrap round his head and shield his eyes, the day was bearable. By the end of it his legs were marching for themselves and he was beginning to notice what was going on around him and was even able to make a show, if not much more, of digging latrines with the rest of the detail.

Next morning the marching was a little easier still. Perhaps he was getting used to it. That was scary but he began to think he might have a future. After they'd been going some time, he asked Daniel: 'How did you come to be here?'

They were climbing a long dune and Daniel didn't answer until they eventually crested the brow and started down the other side.

'Things happened.'

'I didn't mean to pry.'

'Then don't.'

'But you weren't always a slave?'

Madu wondered if Daniel was going to ignore him, so long was the answer in coming but eventually it arrived.

'I was born a free man.'

'And . . .?'

'And what?'

'What are you doing here. How did you become a slave?'

'I was travelling home from Salmania.'

'In Amber?'

'So?'

'So nothing. Just curious, that's all.'

'You talk too much.'

'So they tell me,' Madu said.

The conversation lapsed but Madu felt he'd established a bridgehead, as the general might have said. He knew he was going to need Daniel's knowledge and support to survive and was determined to make a friend of the man. It was one of his skills – one of his few skills – but, when he worked at it, there weren't many who could resist him. He hoped.

When they made camp with the fall of night he pulled a full shit-shovelling shift and was ready for his rations. He and Daniel sat at a small fire of scrub wood that burned weakly and gave little heat against the cold desert night.

There was something intractable in his gruel and he spat it into the flames.

'What do they put into these rations?'

'Best not to ask,' Daniel said, 'Someone makes money out of it, that's all.'

'The general?'

'I don't think so. He's a hard bastard but I trust him.'

Madu laughed bitterly. 'I'd sooner put my hand in a bag of snakes.' He swilled his mouth with a gulp from the water skin but he could still taste the vile gristly something he'd spat out. 'So you were in Amber?'

Daniel grunted.

'And did you ever see Maya? Isn't that where she comes from?'

'Uhuh.'

'So what's she like, this governor's wife? They say her followers are prepared to die for her.'

Daniel said nothing for a long time, then: 'She's like ...' He shook his head. 'I didn't really see her at all. Not that much.'

Madu took a chance. 'I don't believe you. I think—'

A violent pain in his back. A soldier's boot kicking him aside. 'Move it, boy, this fire's taken.'

Madu had seen the fellow shovelling; he and his mates kept to themselves and took what they wanted but hadn't bothered Madu until now.

Without looking up, Daniel said: 'Taken by us, Ursu. Go and find your own fire.'

'I wasn't talking to you, Blue Eyes. Don't want no trouble with you.'

Ursu's mates had arrived from the food line and stood behind him. All big, hard bastards.

Ursu went on: 'What are you doing here, boy? You're no soldier.'

One of his mates stepped forward.

'He's from the court. He's a spy, ain't you, kid?'

He pulled Madu to his feet and shoved him towards the others ... This was beginning to look like it had all been arranged, Madu thought, as he bounced from soldier to soldier.

Daniel looked up, his eyes icy blue in the firelight.

'Leave him alone.'

The words were quiet but clear. Madu's whirling progress suddenly stopped. Ursu held his arm in one vast meaty hand.

'You reporting on us, shorty? Run off back to the general, do you?'

Ursu leered into Madu's face and a wash of foul breath almost made him vomit. Instinctively he struck out, grazing the big man's face. With a roar, Ursu switched his grip to Madu's throat and lifted his feet clear of the ground.

'Know where you're going, palace boy? In the shit.'

His mates were laughing and then they weren't and Ursu's roar was of pain, not anger, as he tried to scramble out the fire, blood pouring from his nose. His mates started patting down his smouldering uniform.

Daniel was standing, looking down at the struggling man. There was a slight smile on his face and when the sergeant arrived, bellowing, striking out at random with his staff, he nodded as if he'd been expecting him all along.

'Stand back, stand back. What happened, you?'

Ursu mumbled through bloody lips: 'Blue Eyes, he started it, Sergeant, him and the boy.'

'That's a lie!' Madu burst out.

The sergeant grinned. 'Seems you can't keep out of trouble. Is it true?'

Half a dozen voices supported Ursu's words, adding little details of their own, that they had, presumably, rehearsed earlier: 'He's trouble, that Blue Eyes – Insulting the General, they were – stealing rations – the kid's a dirty spy.'

'And you, what do you say, Blue Eyes?'

'I say never get on the wrong side of the sergeant.'

'I'd say you was right there.'

Sergeant Ban'th pulled out a whistle and blew an ear-piercing blast. Half a dozen members of the Watch appeared out of the darkness and took hold of Daniel and Madu, who shouted: 'You'd better not touch me. There'll be trouble, I promise you that.'

Daniel shook his head. 'Be quiet, Madu, let them do what they have to.'

'What do you mean?'

'You should listen to your friend,' the sergeant said. 'Fighting in camp – mandatory punishment, flogging before the regiment, fifty strokes. Take them to the Watch compound, and I don't very much care what condition they arrive in.'

The Watch were experts in inflicting the maximum amount of pain while leaving a man still able to stand and march if he had to; as Sergeant Ban'th had said, a soldier is no good to anybody if he can't fight.

Gregor waited until the Vizier had smirked his way from the room.

'May I sit?'

'I prefer you standing. I ask again, what do you want?'

'Spies, that's what I want.'

'Then you can't be wanting anything here.'

'Your last maid was a spy.'

'In this palace that's hardly exceptional. The interesting thing is that she was a spy for Maya and you had no idea. She had to practically throw herself into your arms before you arrested her.'

'When I was questioning her—'

'Before she killed herself?'

'Something she said . . .'

'Go on.'

'Look at me, Shajah. Why won't you look at me?'

'You know why.'

Oh, it was so dreary, she thought, and so predictable, the way men never quite managed to grow up and accept that their toys were no longer theirs and, perhaps, were never theirs in the first place. It was demeaning.

'I could serve you if you'd let me.'

'Spy for you?'

'You know I don't mean that. We all need—'

'Sarah!' she called, cutting him off, she hoped, before he made an appeal to past times and stale couplings. 'Gregor, we no longer know each other.'

'But we did, and alliances can be built on that.'

The maid entered.

Shajah hissed: 'I am the First Wife. There is nothing to say and do not, for one moment, Gregor, think to apply pressure upon me in any way.' Then she raised her voice. 'I will have more coffee, Sarah, tell them to heat it.'

'Will his Excellency . . .?'

'His Excellency will not be staying.'

'It was about the Hafiz.'

'What?'

'The maid. Maya's spy. She talked of the Hafiz.'

Really, would she? Could she? Or was he simply fishing for what scraps he could get?

'I am hardly responsible for whatever rubbish fear draws from your victims.'

Besides, her informants had told her the maid said virtually nothing about anything. Gregor was dissembling as usual, but why?

'When the Hafiz came here, where did he come from?'

'You know that very well.'

'Did he pass through Ghabrell?'

'I believe so. Is there any point to this?'

'He was desperate, relying on the generosity of strangers by the time he got here and threw himself under your protection.'

'Sarah, you're an intelligent girl. What do you think Gregor wants?'

'I would not presume to know, madam.'

'Exactly, and neither would I.'

'Just questions, Shajah. I have to update my records.'

'I never really saw you as a bookkeeper. Sarah, you may show His Excellency out.'

Gregor bowed and walked to the door.

'I know my way. Oh, and I imagine you would have no objection to me seeing the Hafiz. For my records. Given that he's under your protection.'

And I, she thought, am under the Sultan's hand and Gregor cannot go against it. So that's what he wants, to talk to the old fool – but why does he want it?

Gregor slipped back into the room, producing a sheet of parchment from some concealed pocket.

'In which case you might put your seal on this warrant for me?'

He laid it down. If she did not, she was telling him, as sure as there were two moons, that she had something to hide. But if she did?

Gregor smiled.

She took the little silver tool and clipped her sigil into the thick paper. He whisked it and himself away with a nod.

'Shall I tell them to make more coffee now, madam?'

'No, don't bother, pour me some wine. I can't believe I once thought that man desirable.'

Sarah brought glass and bottle and poured. Shajah lifted it to her nose – it had the heavy scent of raisins of the sun.

'Do you?'

'Madam?'

'Think him desirable? Those swarthy looks, the dashing manner, the eyes. They say women like cruel eyes.'

Sarah burst out: 'I do not like cruelty. Sorry, madam, it is not my place.'

'Interesting.' Shajah sipped. 'I wonder if that's the first honest thing I've heard you say. And if you do not like cruelty, stay away from that man. Even the things he professes to love and cherish will feel the lash of his spite sooner or later. Better to clasp a scorpion to your breast than Gregor. Now leave me.'

Alone, she sipped the heady wine – there was much to consider.

39
Heaven

The town had settled down around them. The frantic sounds of thousands of men and women clawing a handhold into the desert for the night had ceased; there was a call to prayer, groups of men and women laughing easily as they walked wherever one walked to in this place. There was the occasional pad of a horse or camel passing the big tent.

Heaven lay back against the cushions and ate another date. She was clean at last – Pamira had helped her to wash and told her how lovely she was and how good it would be to have a young woman in the tent again, like having a daughter. Heaven had felt the tears rising as she remembered her mother, and Pamira had listened and understood. Now they were in the living area of the tent, oil lamps flickering, casting highlights on copper dishes and bowls and dancing shadows in the corners of the room. Boy sat in one of these corners, quiet and attentive, eating. Rajik was drinking from a wineskin, which he passed to Slave, who held it to his mouth but Heaven didn't see his throat move like he was actually swallowing anything.

'You live well here, Mistress Pamira,' Heaven said.

'Many prosper in the town, my dear. There are always opportunities.'

'The cages outside,' Heaven asked, 'the dogs. What are they for?'

Rajik drank some more. His voice was getting thick with the wine.

'Armies need dogs bred for war. I train them.'

Boy said: 'Master Rajik traps them and breeds them.'

Rajik shot him a look, as if to say: watch your tongue.

'Fighters, strong. Muscle and teeth, they won't stop, not once you let them go. Very elegant, my dogs, bred for one thing only.' He leaned back against the cushions and spread his arms expansively. 'They have a reputation, Rajik's dogs. People come a long way to buy them for fighting and breeding.' He yawned. 'More wine. This is from the mountains.'

Pamira poured a cupful and handed it to Heaven.

'Just a little. It will bring a touch of colour to your cheeks and help you to sleep.'

She sipped it and it was very good.

'I sold a dozen last quarter, I need to get more. The price is going up, the closer we get to the battle.'

'Battle?' Heaven asked.

'For Tumanbay. Let a pack of Rajik's dogs loose in that place, you'll soon see the blood flow.'

'Will there really be a battle?'

Pamira stroked her cheek. 'Who knows. It's men's business is what I say, and not for such pretty ears as yours. Where do you come from, my sweet?'

'Mers-el-Kabire. My father is a merchant there and he went to Tumanbay to expand his business. I was going to be married to . . . someone.'

'I'm sure he'll be safe.'

Rajik belched. 'Tumanbay is finished. Everyone knows it and its people will be marched out and sold.'

'Well, you're a cheery soul,' Pamira said.

'They've grown fat and lazy.'

'Don't listen to him, dear, he's had too much to drink.'

Rajik squeezed another gulp from the wineskin and held it out to Slave, who declined.

Rajik said: 'What about you, big man, how did you get here?'

Slave looked at him but said nothing.

'You should train your slave to answer when he's spoken to.'

'He's not my slave.'

Pamira slid into the silence with her easy, friendly voice.

'And your father is a merchant in Tumanbay?'

'All we want,' Slave said, 'are some supplies, maybe a camel. We can work for them, we won't bother you for more.'

'It's no bother, is it, husband? We will be happy to help and you can pay in any way you wish. That's our code. But now you are tired, we'll let you sleep. Stay here, it is comfortable. We have our own chamber, this is yours for tonight.'

'We can find beds for ourselves,' Slave said.

'Nonsense, we are not throwing this poor child out into the night.'

Rajik snorted and clambered to his feet.

'Well, have it your own way. I'll see someone about a camel, eh? And think of what you can do to earn it. Boy, come with me.'

He stalked out, Boy in his shadow.

'I will leave you too,' Pamira said. 'Please, it is quite safe. Certainly safer here than out there. Rajik has the dogs on a free line and no one would risk their jaws.'

As if to underline her words, there was a sudden frenzy of barking from outside, followed by Rajik bellowing and the crack of a whip.

Pamira smiled. 'Quite safe.' She left.

After waiting a few moments, Slave said: 'You talk too much.'

Heaven yawned. 'I'm going to sleep. I'm tired.'

'We have to leave.'

'With the dogs out there?'

'You noticed that, then. They keep us in as well as they keep others out.'

'There are kind people in the world, you know.' She could hardly keep her eyes open.

'I've heard of them, but I've never met them.'

'You've been a slave too long,' she said.

'You've been a pampered brat too long. We have to go.'

'You go, I'm going to sleep.'

She wrapped a sheepskin around herself and let sleep take her where it would.

She woke once some time later and saw Slave sitting in the same place, his eyes catching the last light of an oil lamp as it guttered into darkness and then there was nothing until . . .

'You have to come, now.'

It was Boy, shaking her. Slave was on his feet, crouched, ready to spring at anyone who might come through the door.

'What is it?' she asked.

Boy pulled the sheepskin off her and dragged at her robes. Slave moved across the tent.

'They'll be back soon with the others, I was wrong, it isn't safe for you, they mean you harm. They want to sell you to the body men. Come, this way, I know a way . . .'

He was pulling her across the floor.

Slave was beside them. 'The dogs!'

'Chained, I chained them. We have to go.'

He pulled Heaven to the back of the tent, threw aside a carpet and lifted the hanging and opened a flap in the outer canvas. Outside it was black as pitch.

'Hurry, there isn't much time.'

He almost pushed them through. Slave stumbled, taking Heaven down with him, into straw. Behind them a door clanged shut and the tumblers of a lock thudded home. They were in the cage that had held the dogs. Slave roared and grabbed at the bars, shaking them in his rage so the whole cage moved. Rajik appeared with a lantern. With him were half a dozen men, shrouded, hooded. They gathered round the cage and lifted it as Rajik pushed the cart underneath. They lowered it into place. Slave shook the bars again and again. No one spoke except Boy, who had tears on his face.

He said: 'They won't break. Once they have you, they never let you go. I'm sorry, I'm sorry.'

40
Madu

When Madu awoke he felt as if his body was one great bruise. There didn't seem to be anything that didn't hurt and once he moved, it all hurt more. He thought the torments he'd suffered on that first day's march were the worst but this morning he had no words for the way he was feeling, so he pulled himself up. Daniel was already awake, chewing on some dried bread and drier meat. Both of them were manacled at the ankles and wrists. Daniel handed Madu a jug.

'Drink.'

Madu drank and spat out dried blood. He still seemed to have all his teeth.

'Are they going to make us march?' he said. 'I don't think I could.'

Drums were sounding. Their regiment was being drawn up in parade ground order facing two wooden frames.

'What now?' Madu asked.

'That,' Daniel said. 'Flogging.'

'No, you don't understand. I can't . . . They can't . . . Not to me. It will . . .'

'Stop that. They can and they will.' Daniel grabbed the front of his shirt and shook him. 'Face it like a man, it's all you can do.'

'General Qulan, he won't let it happen. We have to call him, get him here somehow. He'll see it's all a mistake. He knows my mother—'

'He'll be here, he always attends punishment,' Daniel said.

'Then I'll talk to him. Yes, you'll see. It'll be all right.'

Daniel grunted, pulled up his knees and crossed his arms on top of them.

'Yes, I'll see.'

The sergeants were bellowing no more, the ranks had been drawn up. A stir went through the gathered troops: General Qulan was arriving. The officers came to attention. Madu began to feel a glimmer of hope. While there was life, yes, there was hope and he could still talk. He could talk himself out of anything.

The general approached, his face stern and severe.

'Well, Madu, have you learned anything useful yet?'

'We were beaten by the Watch, General. They were set to it by the sergeant there. He hates me, he has it in for me. For both of us.'

Qulan flicked a glance at Daniel, then returned the full force of his attention to Madu.

'Is that so. Sergeant?'

The sergeant came to attention, everything about him bristling.

'Fighting in the camp, General. Punishment as per regulations: fifty lashes.'

'Well, there you have it, young Madu. This army speaks with one voice, from me, the general, all the way down through the officers, the sergeants and the corporals. One voice, one will, one victory.'

'But it's a lie!'

'That's enough. Punishment will take place. Sergeant, do your duty.'

He strode across to the dais where a few members of his staff were waiting.

Madu and Daniel were dragged forward by the Watch. Madu knew this was the last chance, he wouldn't survive fifty lashes.

'My mother will hear about this, you know she will, and when she does, she'll have you whipped through the streets of Tumanbay.'

Qulan stopped and turned. The troops called him Old Stone Face for a reason. His expression betrayed no emotion, offered no hope.

'It is for the sake of your mother that I will answer that outburst. She knows exactly where you are, exactly what has happened to you and when she hears about the flogging, she will be content that her plans are being carried out as she would wish.'

The sheer rock-face of his fate slammed into Madu in that moment; he was lost and he knew it. His own mother had consigned him to this. Well, why not? She had murdered her first husband with exquisite cruelty – getting rid of an inconvenient son would cause her no qualms at all. His arms were lifted and his wrists tied. The shirt cut from his back. He turned to look at Daniel, secured in the same way, and could find nothing to say; he only hoped that he wouldn't shit himself when it all began.

The Sergeant handed the whip to the Chief of the Watch, who would administer the punishment. He bellowed: 'Fighting in the camp! Fifty lashes!'

Madu realised Daniel was talking to him, hissing the words: 'Tell him I know Maya – tell him that.'

'What? Who?'

'The general, you fool.'

'Administer punishment!'

Madu took a deep breath and bellowed louder than the

sergeant: 'General Qulan, you asked me if I'd learned anything from my experience?'

Qulan held up a hand. The Chief of the Watch waited, his arm flexed, the whip, like an oiled and venomous snake, poised about to strike.

'Yes?'

'This man, my friend, he grew up in Amber, he knows Maya's court, he knows her world, he's met her, he knows how she thinks.'

He didn't for a moment care if it was the truth or not – anything to stop that whip.

Qulan crossed to the frames. He looked at Daniel, who looked calmly back.

'Is this true?'

After an agonising pause, Daniel said: 'It is, General.'

'You know something of how her people fight?'

'Do you know Alamut, General?'

'Her fortress? I know of it.'

'Shortly after her husband died and she took power, a prince from the plains decided to lay siege to Alamut. After all, what was Maya but a weak woman, worth no more than half a man? She invited him in, under flag of truce. He assumed it was to discuss the terms of her surrender. She took him up onto the high walls. Have you heard of them? Taller than Tumanbay's, built on the jagged crags of Jebal Raman.'

'Go on.'

'There was a company of Maya's guards escorting the party. Fifty men. She ordered them to walk off the walls. They did so, every one without a murmur, and fell to their deaths on the rock below. The prince raised the siege and went home to the plains. She had won a war at the cost of fifty men.'

General Qulan considered. 'With loyalty like that you could

rule the world. Is it her they follow, or some belief?'

'It's . . . complicated, Excellency.'

'Cut him down, bring him to my tent,' Qulan said, walking away.

'And my friend?'

'What use is he to me?'

'I won't help you unless he comes too,' Daniel said.

Qulan stopped. 'You will if I want you to. Maybe I should have you whipped after all.'

'I believe in loyalty, General.'

'Loyalty?' Qulan considered. 'Sergeant, good work in bringing this intelligence to my attention. Clean these two up and bring them to my tent.'

He strode away, followed by his staff. The regiment was stood down and Daniel, as he was cut free, grinned at the Sergeant.

Madu felt that never in his life had he met a man so cool under pressure as Blue-eyed Daniel; with a companion like that, he felt he could achieve anything!

41

The Physician

A tranquil garden. The light sound of a pair of scissors – snip, snip.

'Just one petal?' the Sultan asked his physician. He was lying in the shade of a tree in his favourite part of the garden.

'Yes, Your Majesty. That's all that is required,' the physician answered with the air of a magician. 'You will see.'

He placed the flower petal in a small marble bowl and started grinding it. Then he uncorked a small jar and poured in some liquid. Theros enjoyed these private moments with his Sultan, when they could share their mutual interest and al-Guhri was civil to him – even if they were usually short-lived.

Cadali approached across the gardens from the palace. He was sweating and seemed flustered.

'Ah . . . Your Majesty, I have some news,' he said, not noticing Theros.

'Yes, yes . . . Cadali. Smell this . . .'

The Sultan held up the potion. Cadali sniffed and reeled back, coughing.

'It's . . . It's . . . erm . . . It's wonderful. Delightful.'

Al-Guhri started laughing. He enjoyed watching Cadali squirm. Theros joined in.

'It's supposed to be terrible. One sip of it and you'd be dead. Isn't that right, doctor?'

'Without a doubt, Your Majesty. Without a doubt.'

'Well, yes ... I have something I need to—'

'Now this,' the Sultan interrupted, signalling to the physician. Theros uncorked another bottle and handed it to him. 'Sniff this.'

Cadali put his nose to the bottle and cautiously sniffed.

'It's ... It's ...' But he was too nervous to say.

'Bitter. It's bitter.'

'Yes,' Cadali agreed.

'But put the two together and ...'

Theros was now pouring the liquid from the second bottle into the bowl. He handed it to the Sultan, who held it up to Cadali. Smiling, to give the impression he was enjoying this game, Cadali placed his nose close to the bowl and sniffed. This time his nostrils filled with an odour so extraordinary and pleasant, it tickled some nerve at the back of his throat and made him laugh. He was amazed.

'You see,' al-Ghuri said, delighted. 'It's the balance of opposing forces. It's like you and Gregor. As long as we can keep the balance, eh ...?'

Cadali laughed again. The scent had certainly brightened his mood.

'Well, Majesty, I have found a way to do that. It's good news. This so-called "queen" Maya ... she wants to negotiate.'

Al-Ghuri frowned.

'What are you talking about?'

'Well,' Cadali continued, 'I have my contacts. Of course I do. It's my job. She wants to send a delegation to Tumanbay to negotiate.'

'Beg, more like. For mercy.'

'No doubt she has heard about our armies marching out to the provinces. She is awed by our Sultan's power.'

'Let her beg me *in person*! Tell that to her fucking "delegation". And have them executed! Bitch!'

Cadali nodded and turned to leave. Theros could tell the Sultan was working himself into a state of fury. The very mention of Maya, these days, seemed to have that effect.

'Who does she think she is?' al-Ghuri screamed, knocking the bowl of scent flying.

Cadali looked at the physician expectantly. Of course, Theros thought, it was now his job to calm the Sultan.

'Shall I get the smelling salts, Majesty?' he asked.

But al-Ghuri wasn't listening any more.

'I gave her dead husband a province to govern! I put him there. And now she wants to challenge me!'

'Lie back. Just—'

'Get off me! You tire me.'

Sensing danger – danger to himself – Theros backed away.

'My most humble and profound apologies, Your Majesty—'

'What is the point of you?' the Sultan demanded, fixing him with a deadly stare.

Theros's cheeks started to redden. He was a sensitive man, easily offended, with a temper that he knew he needed to keep in check if he wanted to survive. He was a relative newcomer to Tumanbay, one of the few who had come, not as a slave, but as a highly qualified professional. He had studied alchemy, medicine and herbal extraction; he also knew how to treat an abscess, had healed sword wounds aplenty, bored holes into patients' heads, carried out amputations and cut babies from their mothers' wombs. But it was his knowledge of mixtures, and combining herbs and flowers, that had brought him to the attention of the Sultan some time ago. He had been the one person in the palace who seemed genuinely interested in the Sultan's passion and so, for a while, had been a companion of sorts.

But it was a dangerous state of being. He had heard about his predecessors, and how their employment under the Sultan had been alarmingly short-lived. He was acutely aware of how quickly al-Ghuri tired of those close to him and how viciously he could turn on them.

He knew it was just a matter of time before the Sultan turned on him too, but he felt helpless, unable to do anything about it. He was the Sultan's physician and there was no escape. He couldn't exactly resign from the position. The best he could hope for was to be honourably retired. The worst was . . . Well, he tried not to think about it.

'I have no point,' he said sincerely. 'I merely exist to—'

'Yes, you merely exist,' the Sultan snapped. 'That's the problem.'

'I'm sorry if I have offended you in any way, Majesty. I am your physician. Your health and well-being are my—'

'Yes, yes, then shut your mouth!'

The physician did as he was told and stood there with his head bowed.

'Go!'

Theros turned and went.

After a moment the Sultan turned back to Cadali, who was looking down and nervously shifting his considerable weight from one leg to the other.

'Play a game with these envoys,' the Sultan said. 'Make them think we are grateful. We'll organise a reception.'

'Er . . . Of course, Your Majesty. And then?'

'We'll kill them.' The thought seemed to improve the Sultan's mood instantly. 'Send a message to my First Wife Shajah to attend. She'll enjoy that.'

*

The physician made his way through the palace, nodding politely at the various courtiers he passed – were they smirking at him he wondered – and proceeded to the east tower, and then up the narrow stone stairway to his rooms, where there was a small laboratory and his bed.

As soon as he got there, he closed the door behind him, put his hands to his face and sobbed, uncontrollably. This was becoming his routine these days. He had never felt so much unhappiness as in the last weeks when the Sultan had, on several occasions, shown him such a lack of respect that he may as well have been a slave, rather than a highly qualified professional with a lifetime of learning behind him.

He needed to get away, he knew that. Tumanbay was toxic. It had always been a place where young men and women with the optimism of youth were exploited and ground down until they became bitter or tired – or dead – but it had got far worse in recent years. People were scared to think their own thoughts. Punishments were disproportionately harsh for any small or perceived misdemeanour. The Sultan's dog, that cold, calculating official Gregor, Master of the Palace Guards, with his smug contempt for everyone, seemed to be lurking at every corner, smiling, always asking questions, his evil eyes taunting you to make a mistake, or to utter something he could use against you.

Theros had had enough. He wanted nothing more than to go back to the pleasant island he had spent the best years of his life on, studying under that old wise sage, a time when everything held wonder and potential. He cursed his youthful pride and the day he had told his mentor that he was going to Tumanbay to become someone.

He remembered the last time he saw the old man, and how

his mentor had said to him, 'I know you. I knew this day would come. You need to put aside your ambition, Theros, or it will eat you from within and you will be left less than worthless.'

He didn't understand then, but now he wished more than anything that he had taken his advice.

Calming himself, he went over to the desk on which were several glass jars and tubes and a burner. It was where all his work was done, where his medicines and remedies were forged, where he experimented with new formulas – though that had happened less in recent years. Nowadays he relied on what he knew and his curiosity had become … well, subsumed by depression.

He picked up a flint lighter and lit the burner. Then he opened a drawer and took out a small vial of powder. He poured it into a metal cup which he filled with a measure of brown liquid. Taking a pair of tongs, he held the cup over the heat, expertly shaking it back and forth, watching, hungrily, as the mixture thickened. Then he tapped it on the table several times and left it to cool. A few moments more and his mind would be in a better place. This was his only refuge, his only escape from Tumanbay.

He looked around the room – where had he left the strap? It was on a side table next to the bed. With increasing vigour he grabbed it, tied it around his upper arm as a tourniquet and took a syringe from a shelf above the desk. Carefully he placed the needle – a hollowed-out rib from the delicate paridan fish – in the liquid and pulled the copper plunger back. He slapped his wrist several times, then pushed his fingers around the green-blue bulge of his vein and carefully inserted the needle. He was well practised in this procedure. It had become a routine. He held his thumb over the plunger and began to push slowly … Yes, he could feel the warmth working its way up his arm and—

There was a knock on the door.

He paused, his thumb wavering over the plunger.

'Doctor . . .?' It was his slave.

'Didn't I tell you not to disturb me when I'm working?' he shouted.

'Yes, doctor, it's just—'

'I'm conducting difficult work. What is it?'

'The Lady Shajah . . .'

'Yes?'

'She's here.'

Theros pulled the syringe out. This was bad news. The Sultan's First Wife only ever came to his rooms when she needed his help with some despicable act. What was it this time? He would have to wait for his reward.

He put the syringe back in the tray on the shelf and opened the door.

'Madam, what a pleasure, what a pleasure.'

She sniffed. The bitter smell of his potion hung heavy in the room.

'I was preparing some sleeping remedies,' he said. 'For the Sultan. He had asked . . .'

You are saying too much, Theros, he told himself.

'I want your help.'

'Please. Sit.' He pulled out a chair and she accepted. He took a position on the other side of the desk and adopted a concerned professional look. 'Are you unwell?'

'No. I have business I need to deal with . . . discreetly.'

He shook his head as if not understanding. He knew where this was going.

'Business?' he asked.

She looked away, bored.

'There are two ways we can do this, doctor. Either we can talk in a roundabout way with me saying such things as, "I have a friend who . . ." or "Supposing I wanted to such and such . . ." Or we could get straight to it. What would you prefer?'

'My lady, I—'

She waved her hand impatiently and he stopped.

'We both know what I'm talking about. A woman in my position has many enemies. I need to protect myself. I want to talk to you about poison.'

'My lady, I am a physician. I don't—'

'Save your pious words for my husband. I know what you are.'

She pointed to the tourniquet still around his arm. He had forgotten to take it off before opening the door. His face hardened. He pulled it off and put it in the drawer. Then, noticing a trickle of blood seeping from his wrist, he brushed it against his hip, got up and walked over to the window. What a life was this, he thought; he just wanted it to end.

'What do you think the Sultan would do,' she continued, 'if he realised he was treated by a slave of the poppy?'

Theros could see the kite flyers in the far distance. The boys who risked their lives for a moment of life. But here he was, living a kind of death.

'Does it matter,' he asked, still looking out, 'if it is discovered afterwards that the victim was poisoned?'

'Hmmm ... no. Not so much. I don't care what happens afterwards.'

'That's easier then,' he said. 'There's something I've been working on.'

He turned back to the room and opened the door to his cabinet. Inside were rows of jars. He took one out. It looked like one of the Sultan's scent bottles and had a little pump on the side. He held it up and pressed it. A thin spray emerged from the bottle and hung like a mist in the centre of the room.

'What are you doing?' Shajah asked.

'Perfume. You can spray it like a perfume. You spray it in the face. It's simple, surprising . . . effective . . .'

42

Gregor

It was evening and Gregor wound his way through the bustling Street of Swords, dodging merchants and their customers,
camels, dogs underfoot, urchins above, sitting on walls fishing for
wallets with hooks and lines. He often went into the city alone
– not exactly in disguise, but plainly dressed and anonymous in
the crowd. It was his job, after all, to know what was going on
in Tumanbay, to listen to unguarded tongues, and he knew there
was no better way than to be part of it, and not above it – like
his brother Qulan, who always travelled with a military escort.

He cut through a quiet alley towards the wider, greener
and quieter streets of the Bulpass Quarter, where many of the
successful traders and merchants had built their homes, and
emerged onto a wide avenue from where he could see the towers
and domes of the Hafiz's official residence.

When he had brought up the subject of the Hafiz, Shajah had
seemed unconcerned but he knew her well enough to sense an
underlying anxiety. The old man was no more than a political
pawn of course; his lineage, reaching back to the founder of the
faith, gave him the respect and adoration of all believers. Over
the centuries, the old man's predecessors had been shunted from
place to place, wherever political power resided and required or
desired religious authority.

But that was in the past. The significance of the Hafiz had waned in recent years. The later sultans of Tumanbay had not bothered to relocate him, or his predecessors, to the city. They had lived undisturbed and unremarkable lives in the ancient walled port of Bahgred, some fifty days away across the eastern desert. Before the rise of Tumanbay, Bahgred, a thriving trading centre on the banks of the great Iffrenti river, was a centre of power with many magnificent buildings, but it had fallen into decline, exposed and unable to defend itself from the continual incursions of the tribal peoples of the forests and mountains of Parastan. The safety of the Hafiz became a concern and it was the previous Sultan, Shajah's first husband and brother of al-Ghuri, who had offered the ageing holy man, now a refugee travelling aimlessly from one city to another, sanctuary and his own palace to live in.

Gregor approached the gatekeeper and handed him the order with the First Wife's seal. The fellow looked surprised and stared at the document, then at Gregor, frowning. The Hafiz did not have many visitors clearly, certainly not unannounced and straight off the street. Eventually he unlocked the gate and waved Gregor in.

He made his way across the paved courtyard. Weeds were growing between the paving slabs and there were chips and missing stone in the steps leading up to the main entrance. As he entered, a pigeon, disturbed by the opening of the doors, took off and flew about in aimless circles high above him, the flapping of its wings echoing through the vast empty space.

'Your Excellency?' came a voice from the darkness.

'Where is His Holiness?'

The pale, puckered face of Bello, the Hafiz's acolyte, appeared like a ghost behind an approaching lantern.

'This way, my lord.'

Gregor followed him through a door and into a passageway. As they moved along it the stale smell of incense and liquor stung his nostrils. It got stronger as they entered a small book-lined room, where the old man sat at a table turning the vellum pages of an ancient text.

'What are you doing here? No one is supposed to be here.' He didn't bother to look up.

'How are you, Eminence?' Gregor asked. 'Are they looking after you well?' He placed a bottle on the table. 'Arak. The best. I hear you like the best.'

The Hafiz's bloodshot eyes moved from the text to the bottle and then to Gregor.

'I know you. You're al-Ghuri's dog. When there's dirty work to be done, you do it.'

Gregor uncorked the bottle. There was a cup beside the Hafiz with something in it. He tipped it away, poured the arak and pushed the cup into the Hafiz's hands. The old man looked scared.

'Oh, it's not poisoned. See.' Gregor took a swig and slapped his lips appreciatively. 'You are the spiritual guide to all believers, the jewel in the Sultan's turban. Why would he want to kill you?'

The Hafiz sighed, then raised the cup to his lips. He took a moment to savour the liquor.

'What do you want?'

'Just to talk. You've no objection?'

'Would it change anything if I had?' Gregor's face was hard and impassive. 'No, I thought not.'

'When you were making your way here . . . to Tumanbay—'

'Ahh, a long journey and hard too.'

'And were you alone?'

'Alone. Just me and Bello.'

Bello stood watching from the entrance and echoed, 'Just us.'

'And how did you travel. On foot?'

'Yes ... and if we found a sympathetic traveller, sometimes there was a donkey for an old man.'

'And as for resting?'

'The hard ground.'

'It must have been cold, especially the nights?'

'So cold.'

'So cold,' echoed fat Bello.

Gregor refilled the Hafiz's cup.

'And your burden?'

The Hafiz tilted his head towards him.

'Burden?'

'The things you carried with you?'

'No, no, nothing ... I had to leave quickly. There was no time, no time at all.'

He tipped the contents of the cup into his mouth and took one agitated gulp. Gregor poured again.

'Bello, tell him there was nothing, we took nothing.'

'Nothing, Excellency,' Bello confirmed.

'Not any little keepsake to ensure you of a warm welcome wherever you might end up?'

'Nothing, nothing. We were wanderers on the face of the cold earth. Is that not so, Bello?'

'It is as you say, Eminence. Wisdom was our only freight, as the poet has it.'

'But now you have come to rest. How fortunate.' Gregor rose to his feet. 'Well, I shall take no more of your time. A blessing perhaps, before I go?'

The Hafiz lifted one hand and made the sign of Oneness.

'Yes, yes, go in peace, may God give you good fortune.'

'But just in case God withholds His gifts, it is wise, is it not, to take what may not be given?'

He waited for the Hafiz to speak again, to reveal something. But the old man's attention had returned to his book.

'Bello will see you out,' he said, pouring himself another cup from the bottle.

'And you are generally accounted a wise man, are you not – for a drunk?'

But the Hafiz didn't respond.

Gregor followed Bello through the dark passageway back into the domed entrance hall.

'In our holy books,' Bello said, leading him towards the doors at the front, 'there is a verse about the wise Sultan who does not venture into the dark without a lantern so that when he needs to, he may see what is hidden.'

'And what *is* hidden, master monk?'

'Many things, but that wise Sultan—'

'With the lamp?'

'May find them out.'

Gregor observed Bello for a moment. He was well used to this doublespeak. It was the way of Tumanbay, where to say or do anything that even hinted at treason could cost you your life. But, if Gregor wasn't mistaken, Bello was offering his services as an informant.

'And this Sultan must need a lamplighter?'

'That he does, that he does.'

'Who will be well rewarded for his foresight?'

'He might hope so.' Bello confirmed, shifting nervously.

'He might indeed,' Gregor said.

Clearly the Hafiz was under Shajah's control and was not going to reveal anything, no matter what Gregor might offer as an inducement. But Bello – that was another matter entirely. He was venal. Gregor could see it in his eyes, in his gestures and expressions.

In a sudden flurry he drew his sword and lunged towards the acolyte. Bello cried out and jumped to the side.

'Hush, master monk.' Gregor said, lifting his sword into the air.

Pinned on the end was a squeaking rat, its blood dripping down the blade.

Bello chuckled nervously. 'They are everywhere here.'

'Well, here's the thing – service and betrayal, rewards and punishments. Serve me well, Bello, and you will prosper. Serve me ill and . . .'

He smashed the end of the sword against the floor. The rat came free and lay there convulsing.

'If, Excellency, if,' Bello muttered, 'if there were a burden His Holiness carried, something sacred and very ancient, something that would ensure a welcome wherever the weary traveller came to rest . . .'

Gregor waited. 'If there were, monk?'

'Then it might be better to keep it far away from the rats that gnaw and shred – in a safer place.'

'A palace, perhaps?'

Bello screwed up his eyes and shrugged. Gregor slipped him a gold coin, turned and pushed open the door.

'Good night, lamplighter,' he said, and he was gone.

43
Ibn Bai

'See, effendi, it spins so . . .' The stallholder wound a small handle that produced an odd clicking from within the base of the little globe, which then began to twirl, splashing colours onto the shaded rear of the stall. 'It is a cunning mechanism, you see, called clockwork, that has come from beyond the Middle Sea. Very fine.'

'Too fine for a baby, I fear,' Ibn Bai said with a certain regret, since he had a great fondness for ingenious machines. 'Something simpler, perhaps?'

The stallholder produced a camel in a soft material in a most un-camel-like colour.

'Now this, Excellency, is a true miracle – a lovable camel!'

They both laughed and Ibn Bai bought the ridiculous thing. And as he left the stall, feeling for once at last a gleam of content, the tall man in the dour clothes materialised out of the crowd.

'Ibn Bai, I went to your house. They said you might be here. What is this?'

'A lovable camel, Commander Gregor. The stallholder says it is a sort of miracle.'

The commander regarded the toy quizzically and then dismissed it. Ibn Bai somehow doubted that laughter was of any great importance in his life.

'It is for the baby, Excellency.'

'Of course it is. Good. I am glad you take your responsibilities seriously.'

'While she is in my care, she will want for nothing.'

'Yes, of course, but do not get too close.' The warning was like a cold hand closing around the merchant's heart. 'Now, I need your help.'

He took Ibn Bai by the shoulder, his hand digging in like a claw, as he led him through the market.

'A little mystery. You remember the scrolls I mentioned to you?'

'Yes.'

'They looked old, very old.'

'So you said, but they all look old. That's the trick of the trade – making them look like heirlooms. Almost nobody in Tumanbay has any past. We're all newcomers, so the rich love the idea of faking a past for themselves, as if they didn't begin like everyone else in the mud.'

'I have a feeling these might be different.' They had left the market and plunged deep into the maze of streets that made up the craftsmen's district. Ibn Bai had no idea where he was. 'I want you to look at them, see them with your own eyes, make a judgement. You have the experience, I do not. This could be an opportunity for you.'

Another opportunity offered by Commander Gregor was the last thing he needed – but then only days ago he'd wanted to die and now here he was, hurrying down a narrow street at the behest of this dangerous man.

He took a breath and asked: 'Why are you so interested in them, Excellency?'

'Do you know what I do for the Sultan?'

'Well, you don't look after his collection of art and calligraphy.

Oh, I know where we are now – the Street of the Illuminators. Of course, I should have known that. The sign of the crossed brushes.'

The commander hammered on the door.

'Exactly, Angellotti Brothers.'

There was no answer. He knocked again.

'No one home,' Ibn Bai said.

'One of them will always be here.'

He knocked again, the wood bouncing under the force of his fist; still nothing. He rattled the door. It didn't rattle when it was locked.

He turned the iron handle and the door swung open. Ibn Bai backed away – nothing fortunate could come of this. The commander entered. Ibn Bai could have run but doubted it would do him any good; he followed, stepping into the cluttered shop.

'Workshops like this,' he said, 'they're all along the street, churning out—'

He stopped, embarrassed. The brothers were sitting in the gloom at the rear of the room.

The commander said: 'Gentlemen, here I am again. I have brought an associate, he is knowledgeable in the . . .'

And he too fell silent. The brothers didn't move. Nothing moved in the shop except a fly, which seemed to be making an awful lot of noise. Ibn Bai was about to move closer when he was halted by the commander's raised hand.

'Stay where you are.'

Gregor approached the still forms, reached out a hand, touched the nearest, who wobbled for a moment and then fell stiffly to the floor. Leaning forward until his nose was inches from the other brother's mouth, the commander sniffed.

Ibn Bai cried out: 'What are you doing? Cover your face.'

'These aren't plague deaths. They died here, sitting at this table about to eat their lunch. There was no struggle. Something fast, very fast. There's discolouration of the lips, slight burn around the nostrils. Probably a spray in their faces, first paralysing and then ...Unable to breathe, to move, they died where they sat.'

He went to a cabinet and started pulling out drawers, most of which bore pictures or scrolls. The top one, however, was empty.

'The scrolls?' Ibn Bai asked.

'Oh, that moment has passed. Come, it would be better not to be discovered here.'

44

Qulan

The Palace of the Governor of Saraman Province, the eastern-most and largest in the Empire, perfectly fulfilled Tumanbay's ideal of grandeur. No one seeing it could possibly mistake the fact that it was here and in charge and had cost an absurd amount of gold and labour. It was a mallet, Qulan reflected, driving the population into perfect understanding of their place and the Empire's power. It was not to his taste, any more than was the governor's wife, Fatima bint Baran, which as far as he could understand meant: Fatima, daughter of no one very much. Word had it that she had come from nothing and made her way, using her charms and talents, to become the chief wife of the governor; not unlike Shajah, Qulan reflected as he dismounted before the columns of the portico. Guards regarded him from under elaborately plumed helmets. They looked impressive but he wondered how much good they would be in a fight. Well, that's what he was here to find out.

'I bid welcome to General Qulan, commander of all the armies of the Empire.'

She emerged in a flurry of robes and veils: a tall woman, impressive, her hair dressed to give her extra height still; her white hands beringed and hennaed; her eyes, above the veil she wore, glittering with . . . what? He had to admit, he could not read her at all but since she was, at best, no more than a distraction, that hardly mattered.

'Where is the governor?'

'Ah, not a man to waste words. Lord Usman will be with us shortly, as will our dear friends the governors of our neighbouring provinces.'

So, it was an ambush. They thought that through strength of numbers they would be able to mitigate his demands.

'Come, come, General. You must be tired after your long march.' She ushered him in, along a corridor. 'Do you like the chandeliers?'

It took him a moment to realise she was pointing up at a series of gold and crystal waterfalls which hung from the ceiling.

'The very finest crystal. We had them made in Vinta and brought here. It was quite an enterprise – by sea and then a caravan of wagons. Amazingly we had no breakages.'

'May I ask . . .?'

'Anything, General. Here in the provinces, we are much less formal than in the great city.'

'Why did you not bring your goods through Tumanbay?'

She chuckled, leaning close, washing him with her scent, and said with conspiratorial glee: 'Lord Usman says the import duty is so high in Tumanbay that any sensible man would think of a better way. Well, I shouldn't say such things to you, General, but it's no secret, is it really? We already pay so many taxes to the Sultan, and why should he take it all?'

She waved him through into a vast hallway hung with rich tapestries depicting foreign folk at the hunt or some such nonsense.

'Madam, all this – your husband's position, the palace, the very province he governs – it is all at the discretion of the Sultan and the Sultan alone.'

'Now, General . . .'

She spun round to face him so abruptly that he was hard put to avoid walking into her. Were her nipples rouged – is that what he could see through the silky bodice? She smiled under her veil, so flimsy it was hardly modest at all, and went on.

'We all know that's not true, don't we? The Sultan is nothing without the provinces and their governors. All things flow from us to you – except, of course, the endless demands for taxes and new laws. Ah, here we are.'

Another room, more intimate, silky and rosy with two young slaves, a boy and a girl, draped suggestively across the furniture.

'I thought you might like a little company after your long march with all those horses and men. Perhaps a bath and—'

'No . . . No. I wouldn't like. Get them out. I don't require—'

Fatima clapped her hands. 'Get out, both of you. You're not needed.'

The slaves left.

'Let me show you the bathing pool,' Fatima continued brightly, gesturing. 'It's carved out of a solid piece of marble—'

'What are you doing?' Qulan demanded, losing his patience.

'What?' Fatima asked, confused by his question.

'What – are – you – doing?'

'I'm . . . showing you—'

'No! The Empire is at war. I've come here to gather the provincial armies. Your husband should be here reporting to me. Get him!'

Fatima stared at him, as if shocked and hurt by his manner.

After a moment she said, 'Yes, of course, but until he arrives, I shall do my best to entertain you.'

'No, madam, you will not entertain me and I will not wait. I will see the governor and his fellows at my camp this afternoon at the fifth hour. Tell your husband not to be late, or I will have him fetched and believe me, neither of you want that to happen. Do I make myself clear?'

She bowed gracefully but did not bother to hide her fury. He had made an enemy of this woman, but then it was hardly likely he would ever see her again.

To get the taste of the disagreeable meeting out of his mouth – he could still smell the heavy perfume of the over-furnished palace – Qulan rode through the hills, pushing himself and his mount to the limit before heading to the advance guard of the army, where the mounted skirmishers surveyed the various routes the troops might follow, checking for possible ambush sites or natural hazards.

Their commander, a young soldier whose progress Qulan had been following keenly, reported all clear, no sign of enemy patrols as yet.

He added: 'A contingent of mounted troops joined shortly after you left, sir. Mountain people, I would say, rough as seven hells but they ride better than we do – don't tell the men – and they're bred to war. They had the Sultan's command for all to join the army, though I doubt if any of them could actually read it.'

'How many?'

'Only five hundred – I wouldn't have let any more through. The others will join over the next days, they say, up to three thousand riders.'

'You showed sound judgement. Keep any more with you here until I've spoken with their leaders. Carry on.'

'Very good, General.'

He headed back to camp, well satisfied with the disposition of the army so far – as to what happened next and how things might ultimately fall out, he would discover soon enough.

The governors were waiting for him in his tent: a gaggle

of well-fed, arrogant men, confident of their own power and standing. There was a murmur of discontent as he entered; his staff had provided a table with minimal refreshments, not enough for his guests, evidently. A group of junior officers stood in one corner, awaiting his attention. His senior staff had been attempting some sort of conversation with the governors, to no one's satisfaction if the sour looks all round were anything to go by. An imposing man, fat but solid, stepped forward; his robes of red velvet trimmed overelaborately with gold and the many rings on his fingers suggested this was Lord Usman, Governor of Saraman Province, first among equals. And so it proved to be. He bowed – slightly. The others followed his lead – just enough to stay within the bounds of politeness.

'General Qulan, Your Excellency. May I greet our great and victorious commander, a hero justly celebrated and, may I add, so sorely needed in these days of travail.'

If that was how they wanted to play it, Qulan could give as good as he got.

'Lord Usman, your Excellencies, I welcome you to the army of Tumanbay – *your* army, for I assure you, His Majesty is more than sensible of the debt the city owes to the country.'

He bowed; they bowed.

The silence in the tent was total. They could clearly hear a shout from somewhere in the camp: 'Where's my duck? I demand to know what thieving footcloth of a Circassian has run off with my bloody lunch!'

Someone laughed, then cut themselves off. A fly buzzed. Qulan watched it wobble across the tent in the humid air and land for a moment on a governor's sweating bald head.

He said: 'I welcome also the governors of the Western, Southern and Central Provinces. Excellencies, I am glad to see you here at this time of national danger.'

They turned closed faces upon him and smiled.

'I know you are all busy men so I won't waste your time. I have news – the garrison town of Kareeba has fallen to Maya's forces. We do not have any details as yet but it is clear she is on the move. The war has begun.'

A concerned buzz from the governors. Lord Usman stepped forward. He was to be their spokesman.

'And what steps have you taken, General?'

Qulan ignored him. 'I have been examining your musters, the latest you sent to the city. They are a disgrace. You have not kept up your records. Governor Usman, you have not even a glimmering of the number of men of fighting age in your province. Lord Pivane, your returns are hopelessly vague on livestock, never mind working animals. The army needs arrows. Not one of you has kept up the manufacture and storage of these, or of lances, as is expressly stated you should in your commissions.'

A general movement of governors towards him. They were angry. Usman spoke.

'With respect, General, the Sultan appears more than content with the taxes we raise for him.'

'And besides . . .' It was the Governor of the Southern Province, a small man with a limp and a black turban, which denoted membership of some religious order. 'These things are not simple. The army is straightforward. You tell a man – go there, do that, shoot them and so on. He does it. In life it is simply not that easy. Tumanbay has a glorious tradition of . . . many faiths, many peoples, many opinions. You can't say to them – attention, snap to it.'

The governors laughed, enjoying Qulan's imagined discomfort.

He said: 'And you can't say to Maya, please wait while we get ourselves into some kind of order.'

The southerner replied: 'But haven't these threats been

somewhat exaggerated, General? Of course, readiness should be our watchword . . .'

Usman joined in: 'Please do assure His Majesty the Sultan of our support but we, in our turn, would like to be assured that—'

A cup flew across the room and crashed into the table where the food had been standing, splashing some of the governors with red wine. A young man emerged from the group of junior officers in the corner. He stood a head taller than any of them and his clothes were rough but ready; he wore a thick leather belt with a long sword in a decorated scabbard, a shield strapped to his back, plaits that fell almost to his waist and he smelled of horse.

'What do you expect, General? These are not men, they are fat, pink grubs you put on your hook to catch fish!' His accent was barbaric but his words were clear.

'Who do you think you are?' Lord Usman demanded.

'I am Wolf. I come from the High Country with my riders. For centuries, we have fought as free men for Tumanbay.'

'I heard you'd come in today,' Qulan said. 'I know the Sultan had sent his call but I couldn't be sure if you would answer.'

'We don't come at any man's call – we come when we want to, for the fight. Maya the Grim is an enemy worthy of our time, unlike these worms.'

Usman spoke quietly but with authority. 'Order him flogged, General, or I will have it done myself.'

A murmur of agreement rose from his fellow politicians.

Black Turban muttered: 'And he smells of horse.'

Wolf didn't move. His figure, though slim, was tall and dominated a tent full of men used to dominating their surroundings.

'So what do you want me to do with them, General? Hang them? Waste of good rope.'

He pulled his sword: it was as if someone had uttered a deep profanity at the most sacred of ceremonies. The governors as a body shuffled away from the cold point, their heads down, desperate not to catch anyone's eye. Usman, used to command, couldn't do it; he looked up, straight at Qulan.

'That one, Commander Wolf. You say he's a grub? Spit him on your hook.'

Usman died before he knew it. He was still protesting as the sword returned to its scabbard.

'Wh-what did you do?' he muttered.

'I killed you,' Wolf said.

The life fled from Usman's body as he stood – and like old clothes it fell to the stamped mud floor, blood pooling from under the disorderly pile.

'At your service, General.' Wolf stepped back.

'Take that away. The rest of you listen to me. Your musters will be complete and correct by the crescent moon. The Governor of the Central Province will also act for Usman. He will have a further moon to complete and deliver his reports. If you fail, you will find yourself on the same hook as the late governor there. Make this known to all – I act in the name of Sultan al-Ghuri, for the glory of Tumanbay. Carry on. Wolf, I will inspect your cavalry now. I would like to see some men who want to fight!'

45
Heaven

The town was on the move. From where they sat in the dog cage on the back of a cart driven by Rajik, Heaven and Slave could see little and make less sense of the great heaving, clattering, creaking, squeaking, crashing, howling and growling mass of which they were a tiny component. Pamira was driving a wagon piled high with their living quarters; the dogs were chained to Rajik's cart and growled and slavered and eyed the two captives hungrily. Boy followed with the goats, who were meandering in a ragged line.

Heaven was crouched in a corner, her face wet with tears, her eyes slit against the dust that coated everything and left her hair in rat's tails. It was so unfair. Pamira had been so kind, so gentle, as if she understood all the horrible things Heaven had been through. She had believed it was all over, finished, that soon she'd see her father and mother again ... She'd be in Tumanbay and how silly she was, not wanting to get there when now she would give anything to be there, to be ... not here.

Slave said nothing. Since his outburst the night before when he'd tried to rip the cage apart with his bare hands, he'd sat stolid, occasionally looking around but mostly staring down at the straw in which they sat.

'What's going to happen to us?'

Slave didn't look up or answer. She repeated the question.

'How should I know?'

'I should have listened to you,' she said.

'I shouldn't have listened to you.' He looked up, looked around. 'I don't see anyone who looks like a friend. They'll sell us – if we're lucky.'

Heaven's stomach gurgled and she couldn't have told if it was from hunger or fear.

'If we're not?'

He jerked a thumb at the oily smoke. She began to cry – hating herself for it but unable to stop. He raised his voice.

'Don't worry, we're worth more alive. We'll both fetch a good price.'

'But they can't sell me, I'm—'

'No one.'

There didn't seem to be much to say after that, and they sat while the sun climbed above the dust and glared down upon them. Rajik threw them a water skin but would say nothing – not that there was much he could say in response to Slave's furious and impotent threats and Heaven's stricken silence.

After the water Heaven felt a little better.

'Do you think it's true, what he said about Tumanbay being finished?' she asked.

'How should I know? How should he know?'

'I was supposed to get married there.'

'In my country a young woman would choose the warrior she would go with.'

'Well, we're not in your country,' she snapped. 'Sorry. Where is it anyway?'

'A long way from here. Who is this man you are marrying?'

'I don't know. Someone my father chose. Another merchant.

If you want to do business there you have to have a partner who is a native.'

'No one's native in Tumanbay,' he said. 'So you're just part of a contract for your father's business?'

'They love me,' she said, and then wondered why she had said it.

He chuckled. 'You might just get sold on to your father as a slave.'

'I'm not a slave!'

'Look around you, free woman.'

He stretched out a leg and kicked one of the bars. The dogs started barking and leaping up at them. Heaven shrank away. Rajik bellowed back but they ignored him.

He shouted above the clamour: 'Boyyyyy!'

The boy walked among the dogs without a shred of fear and muttered something. They settled down and resumed loping alongside the cart.

Heaven hissed at him: 'I hate you, Boy. I trusted you.'

He wouldn't look at her and fell back to the line of goats.

Heaven wiped her nose.

'Were you free, in that country of yours?'

'I believed a man's word. He promised an alliance with his masters. I trusted him. We laid down our weapons. He lied.'

'Who?'

'Does it matter? He came with the Sultan's seal from Tumanbay. If ever I see him again, he will die by my sword and if I have no sword, I will rip his throat from his body with my bare hands.'

Looking at his face, even there in the straw among the squalor of the moving town, she had no doubt that if ever he had the chance, he would do exactly what he said.

46
Shajah

Shajah sat at her dressing table examining the restoration work the artists had carried out on the scrolls. These were precious indeed, she thought, brushing her fingers over the parchment. She couldn't read the text; it was in a language unfamiliar to her, one of the ancient languages – Amoeic, she suspected. But the illustrations – lizards breathing fire and snakes shedding their skin – kept her transfixed.

When she had taken the scrolls into her care, they were faded beneath years, perhaps centuries, of dust and neglect. She had restored them to their original magnificence. The artists she had commissioned to do the work were indeed remarkable, exceptional, perhaps the very best of their generation. She had commissioned many works of art; she had once taken on the task of curating her late husband, the previous Sultan's, collection of calligraphy, and she had never seen work as fine as this. It was unfortunate, she reflected, that Gregor poking his nose into her affairs had necessitated the untimely death of the artists. They still had so much to offer the world. But Shajah was a practical woman and, well . . .

A knock at the door.

'Who is it?' she called out impatiently.

'My lady . . .'

Cadali! What did he want? And where was her slave? She had asked the girl to fetch her favourite sherbet drink and she was taking ages.

'I need to talk to you, Your Highness.'

'My maid isn't here. Come back later when I can receive you properly.'

She continued examining the artists' work.

'I'm afraid that is not possible,' persisted Cadali. 'The Sultan has sent me.'

'Yes?' Why did Cadali always turn up unannounced like this?

'May I come in? It would be easier if . . .'

Irritated, Shajah rolled up the scroll.

'Wait one moment,' she said, placing it with the other in its ornate, wooden box – a fitting place of rest, intricately carved and inlaid with pearl, ivory and silver to resemble a palace or mausoleum. She carried the box to her cupboard of private things and locked it.

'It is inappropriate,' she said, opening the door to the Vizier, 'for you to enter the hareem without an appointment.'

'Hmmm, yes. My apologies,' Cadali said unapologetically, and bustled in looking around.

'Well?' she demanded, still at the open door.

'Yes?' He seemed unaware that she had not in fact invited him in.

'You said the Sultan . . .?'

'Yes,' he said. 'This peace delegation from Maya. The Sultan asked me to inform you that your presence will be required at the reception tonight.'

'I see. Is that all?'

'Yes.'

'I will be there.'

'Good.'

She opened the door wider and waited.

'Then I will see you this evening.'

Cadali bowed and made his way back through the door, then paused.

'There was just one other thing, my lady.'

'Yes?'

'Gregor,' he said, narrowing his beady eyes and fixing them on her.

'What of him?'

'I was hoping you might know of his whereabouts.'

'Really? And why would that be?'

'No reason . . . except, well . . . Weren't you close once?'

He didn't take his eyes off her, his pale, bald head seeming to move slowly, mesmerisingly, towards her like one of the creatures in the scrolls. He was trying to intimidate her, she knew, and she was having none of it.

'Now, now, Cadali,' she said, trying to lighten the mood, 'I didn't think you were the sort of man to listen to idle gossip.'

But he remained deadly serious. 'No, not idle gossip.'

She cocked her head. What was he getting at? Was he plotting to unseat her?

'I am the Sultan's First Wife. My husband is all my delight, always has been and always will be. Everything I do is for him.'

'Of course, of course. But you and Gregor—'

'I serve one master, Cadali – the Sultan.'

She held his gaze. She was furious. Surely he knew that he was no match for her, that she could destroy him if she so wished. Or was there something she had overlooked?

After a moment, the crinkled folds on either side of Cadali's mouth twitched and turned his expression from a scowl to one of indignation.

'I was merely enquiring after Gregor. After all, he has been rooting out the spies here in the palace, keeping us all safe . . .'

'Well, he's not here.'

'My point precisely. He never seems to be "here". Are we to believe he has rooted out all the traitors?'

'I wouldn't know about anything like that.'

'Well, no, no . . . You wouldn't, of course. We can but trust that Gregor does and that he is doing his job.'

'The Sultan trusts him. That's good enough for me.'

Cadali pondered on this and then said, 'Well, I must be off. Goodbye, my lady,' and proceeded through the door.

'Of course,' Shajah said, 'if Gregor himself were disloyal in any way . . .'

Cadali stopped. 'In what way precisely?'

'I don't know,' she said. 'He talks to a lot of people. Perhaps that's his job – watching everyone, looking for spies, as you say. But who watches the spycatcher?'

He nodded sagely. 'Just . . . Be vigilant.'

'Vigilant?'

'Especially now, with all that is happening. Better to be suspicious than to— Ah . . .'

He noticed Sarah standing in the corridor watching them. She was carrying a tray.

'Your sherbet, my lady.'

'Put it down there,' Shajah said, indicating vaguely with her hand.

Sarah carefully placed the tray on a side table. Neither Shajah nor Cadali moved; they merely paused and waited for the slave to leave.

'Is there anything else, madam?'

'No. Just go.'

Sarah bowed to Cadali and made her way back into the corridor.

'Wait. Yes.'

'Madam?'

'Tell the wardrobe master that I am to attend a reception tonight.'

'Yes, my lady.' She disappeared along the corridor.

'What do they want?' Shajah asked. Cadali shook his head, not understanding. 'This delegation from Maya?'

'Ah . . . Well, they say they want peace.'

'And what do you think they want, Cadali?'

Cadali smiled to himself. It was as if this question brought back some distant memory of his past.

'Well, perhaps we are like the child on his birthday morning waiting for his present. And there it is all wrapped up. What is it? He can barely wait. He unwraps it. He reaches in. Is it a beautiful model cannon that he will be able to fire at his model soldiers . . .? Or is it –' he snapped his fingers, making Shajah jump – 'a poisonous snake?'

47
Gregor

Gregor had one of his men watching Sarah's coming and going from the hareem. In cases of urgent need it was the most effective way to pass messages, even though there were risks involved. Today Gregor wanted to speak to her himself, and had his man tell her to report to his rooms.

'Let her know,' he instructed, 'that I have news about her baby.'

And so, just as the evening call to prayer echoed across the city, there was a quiet knock on Gregor's door.

Opening it, he saw Sarah, her head covered and her blue eyes staring up at him.

'What news of my child?' she asked.

'We will come that.' He beckoned her in and shut and locked the door behind her. 'You are serving your lady well?' he enquired, returning to the couch.

'Has something happened?'

'Just . . . sit,' Gregor said, pointing towards the one chair in the middle of the room. 'You give me something, I give you something. We will talk about what I want to talk about first. Sit.'

She sat on the edge of the chair.

'Tumanbay is under attack,' he said. 'There is grave danger.'

She looked alarmed.

'Not from armies. General Qulan will see to that. I'm

talking about an enemy within. An enemy I am responsible for countering.'

He let the words hang in the silence for a moment.

'My lord, if you think—'

'What do I think?'

'That I . . . am . . .'

'Are you?'

'No. I am a slave, my lord. You put me in my lady's service. I am loyal to you.'

Gregor rose to his feet and paced around her.

'I have reason to believe your lady is hiding something. Something that may harm us. I need you to find it.'

'What is it?'

'Two scrolls, about so long.' He held his hands half a sword's length apart. 'They have been repaired – ornately decorated. Lizards and snakes.'

She said nothing for a long time and then, finally: 'I've seen it.'

'You have?' Gregor hadn't expected this to be so easy.

'She brought the box back from the city a few days ago and she . . .' Sarah stopped as if she had said too much.

'That's all right,' Gregor said. 'I don't need to know where it is. I just need you to bring it to me.'

A look of concern spread across her face.

'But . . . how?'

'Take it when she is not there.'

'And when she discovers it is missing?'

Gregor shrugged. 'I only want to see it. For a short while. You can return it.'

'I can't, she keeps it locked away.'

'Then get the key.'

'She carries it with her. On her gold chain about her neck.'

Gregor nodded. This was typical of Shajah. She trusted no

one – but if the desire was strong enough, the fear great enough, he had always believed, any obstacle could be overcome.

'She must take it off for court functions or when she sleeps or bathes. I have wax. Use it to take an impression. I'll get a key made.'

'It will be dangerous,' she said. 'My lady is not a fool. She trusts no one, certainly not me.'

'She still believes you are loyal?' he said.

'Yes, through fear and self-interest. I don't know how long I can go on. I'm scared.'

'Things are coming to a head, Sarah. All will be well if you do as I wish. And you need to. I saw your child today.'

'How is she?' Sarah asked eagerly.

Gregor shook his head. 'I worry about that man,' he said. 'The one looking after her.'

'Ibn Bai?'

'Yes, the slave merchant.'

'Worry, why?' She was looking desperate. 'He is a good man.'

'He is a dealer of slaves, for him profit always comes first. I don't know if he is taking proper care of your little girl. She cries a lot. She's looking thin. I wonder if he is feeding her properly. Could it be that he has lost interest in her? She needs her mother.'

She stared at him silently.

'Perhaps you would like me to intervene?' He waited for a response but she just sat motionless. After a moment he said, 'Of course. Anything to help. If the child were to die, I could never forgive myself . . .'

'Give me the wax. I'll bring you the box,' she said quietly.

Gregor was the last to arrive as he joined Cadali and a small group of officials waiting in the Grand Courtyard. As he approached he could see the Vizier frowning at him.

'Not late, am I?'

'You are,' Cadali said. 'But as it happens, so are they. Busy catching spies?'

'The work goes on,' he said vaguely.

Brushing Cadali aside, he went over to one of his men from the Palace Guard to enquire about the progress of Maya's delegation. After a moment he returned and fell into line beside Cadali and the other officials.

'So . . .?' Cadali enquired.

'They have arrived,' Gregor said, 'and are at this very moment being escorted through the Imperial Gates by the Palace Guard.'

Cadali relaxed; as a rule he hated being outside, even with the current cooler temperatures. Outside was dusty, dirty, full of nasty smells. Inside was clean, predictable and could be controlled. Cadali liked to be in control.

'You appear,' he said, turning to Gregor, 'to be spending more time beyond the palace walls than behind them. What do you have out there? A secret family? A love nest?'

'The security of the palace requires a long reach.'

Gregor had had to deal with Cadali for long enough to know when he was fishing. He also knew how to shut down any line of enquiry from the Vizier.

'Day and night?'

'Yes. If I have to work day and night in the service of my Sultan, that is my honour.'

Smiling cordially, Cadali backed away.

'Of course, of course,' he said. 'Well, it is a great honour for us all to serve under such a wise and benevolent ruler.'

'It is. It is,' Gregor agreed, nodding sagely.

Cadali started to shake. Gregor watched him curiously and then realised that he was laughing. Despite himself, Gregor felt his own face tingle and twitch, before he also broke into uncontrollable laughter. It didn't happen often in Tumanbay, such was the repressive system they lived under – every word and expression had to be guarded, doubly guarded – but some silent communication had just occurred between the two men: a moment of openness, of truth, where the absurdity of the situation they found themselves in, of their lives, their existence in this strange place and time, was something they shared for an instant. It was the pure, irrational delight seen in children but which Gregor had not experienced for years.

'Why are we laughing?' Cadali asked, coming back to his senses.

'You laughed first,' Gregor said.

He noticed the other palace officials glancing at them, unsure what to make of this display of merriment.

'We are very alike, you and I, Gregor. We don't have wives, we don't have children, we live only for the glory of Tumanbay. And we are ambitious. It's just unfortunate things have not worked out for you – or your brother.'

'How so?'

'Well, clearly Maya is defeated or why has she sent her envoy to beg for mercy. That is my triumph. A triumph of diplomacy. While you have been sneaking around the palace doing – well, I have no idea what you've been doing – and your brother, the great general, has been wasting his time in the provinces building an army that isn't required, I have been— Ah, here they are . . .'

Gregor turned to see dust rising above the wall at the far side of the courtyard. There was a shout from a guard at the gates, and they swung open to admit a small delegation, a dozen or so on horses with the unmistakable form of Effendi Red at the front.

'Welcome, welcome!' Cadali cried, holding his arms out as if greeting a long lost friend. Red brought his horse to a standstill and looked around wearily.

'This is . . . a rather meagre welcome,' he said. 'One fat man, a spycatcher and a bunch of slaves.'

Cadali laughed. 'Well, after last time, perhaps we are . . . a little less open-hearted.'

The envoy dismounted and handed the reins of his horse to one of his soldiers.

'Let's get on with things. Where is the Sultan?'

'All in good time. All in good time,' said Cadali. 'Come, effendi . . .' and he led the way into the palace.

Gregor found himself walking alongside Red.

'So, have you found your master spy yet?' the envoy enquired.

'What?'

'Isn't that who you have been looking for?'

'I think you have been misinformed, effendi,' Gregor replied.

He was unnerved by Red's knowledge. Despite all his efforts, all his informers inside the palace and in the city, he had been unable to find any tangible information about Maya and her apparent army of spies. The maid was the closest he had come and she had killed herself. And yet this man, Red, seemed to know far too much about everything – or perhaps the whole thing was an elaborate fabrication, an intricate web of suggestions and lies, woven by him. Perhaps there was no Maya, just Red. He claimed to be the messenger, but what if he was more than that? After all, he was the only one they had seen.

'You are Gregor, Master of the Palace Guard?' the envoy said.

'I am.'

Gregor smiled cordially and gestured for Red to go ahead into the palace, where Cadali was waiting and giving instructions to the various attendants waiting there.

The envoy paused and said quietly, 'Then come and talk to me if you want to know things.'

'What things?' Gregor asked.

'Come and talk to me,' Red repeated. 'I can save you time and effort. It doesn't matter to us any more ...' He smiled enigmatically.

Cadali, who was looking at them with a combination of suspicion and annoyance, said, 'Would you like to follow me ...?'

Gregor moved towards the back of the group and left Cadali to accompany the envoy through the palace.

'I see you have brought no gifts with you this time?' Cadali observed drily, but the envoy didn't respond.

After a moment, Gregor slipped away. He knew Cadali was under instruction to keep the envoy waiting some time before seeing the Sultan. He would have food laid on, entertainment – dancing girls and such – for all of which Red would have only contempt. Gregor was to return after a certain number of hours and, finally, usher the envoy into the presence of the Sultan. What would happen after that depended on Sultan al-Ghuri's mood, and whatever surprises Effendi Red might try to spring this time.

48
Shajah

'The city is so empty now with all the soldiers gone,' Shajah said as she soaked in her bath. Sarah was filling a jug with her favourite unguents, a mixture of dried carrow flowers and rose petals. 'It's quieter too – it must be the men who make all the noise.'

As the girl started to pour the mixture into the bath, Shajah watched her carefully.

'What's the market place like? Is it quieter there too?' she asked.

'I haven't been to the market, my lady.'

'No? You don't go out? You don't have any . . . friends that you meet?'

Sarah put down the empty jug, crossed the room and started filling another.

'Yes, in the end, it all comes down to who your friends are. And to loyalty.' She waited for Sarah to return with the second jug. 'You remember what I said about loyalty?'

'Yes, my lady.'

'It's important that you look after your own people and that you know you can count on them. Do you remember when you first came to me, what I said?'

Sarah nodded.

'What did I say?' Shajah asked.

'You said, if I was loyal . . . you'd be kind to me.'

'And if you are not loyal? Do you remember what I said?'

She could sense the girl's discomfort, even though she remained composed. Shajah was impressed. Most of her slaves would fall apart at the mere suggestion of betrayal but then, of course, the girl was betraying her, certainly to Gregor, probably to Cadali. That was no problem, it was how things happened in Tumanbay; the thing was to ensure that, in this great game of move and countermove, her main loyalty lay with Shajah.

'I think you said you would be . . . unkind to me.'

She was a clever one, this girl, trying to defuse and soften. She would need to be disciplined at some point soon, broken in – shown, through the lesson of pain, where her interest truly lay. She was still too brash.

'No,' Shajah corrected, sitting up. 'I think I said . . . you would suffer like you've never suffered before . . .'

She lay back in the water. The truth was she had been unsettled by Cadali's visit earlier in the day. Something was going on in the palace and she didn't know what. There were always attempts by senior palace officials to outdo each other, to claw a bit of knowledge that might give them an advantage or help them survive a little longer, but this felt different. If anything were to happen to the Sultan, her position as First Wife – her life perhaps . . . no, certainly – would be in danger. Cadali was up to something, she was sure, and with General Qulan and the army far away she felt vulnerable to attack.

'I see you looking at me,' she said to the girl. 'You keep a close watch.'

'Of course, my lady.'

'To serve me better?'

'Yes.'

272

'But you are being watched too, you know?'

'My Lady? I don't—'

Shajah placed a finger to her lips and shook her head.

'Now go and prepare my dress,' she said. 'Should it be the blue silk or the gold banares? I have to meet a peace delegation. We all have to make decisions in this world, don't we?'

Sarah nodded and retreated to the adjoining rooms. When she returned carrying the two dresses, Shajah was sitting at her dressing table wrapped in a towel, applying cream to her face. The girl had taken her time, she thought. Why was it that whenever she was given a task she took just that bit longer than would normally be required? What was the girl doing? Poking around – looking through her personal possessions?

She indicated the dress she wanted to wear but did not hurry – the girl would wait as long as was necessary. All night, all day, for a week. She was, after all, a slave, that was what slaves did. Putting on her earrings, she looked sadly at the girl in the mirror.

'Where do you come from, Sarah, with your lovely blue eyes? Who are you?'

'I told you, my lady.'

'But where do you come from *really?*'

She sensed the girl's cheeks beginning to flush.

'My lady, far from here. A small country. I told you.'

She busied herself preparing the dress, avoiding Shajah's gaze.

'Yes, yes,' Shajah said, now applying cream to her arms and neck. 'But I don't believe you.'

Sarah stopped what she was doing and looked at her mistress, alarmed.

'Well, my lady, what can I say? I'm telling you the truth.'

'Are you?'

Shajah was disappointed because she liked the girl, disappointed because she was beginning to suspect her slave was part of whatever plot was unfolding in the palace. A hapless pawn perhaps, but if her suspicions were correct, the girl would have to pay. What a waste, Shajah thought, of her own time and kindness, as well as a young life.

'I came from a country in the north, Kassek. I was sent with my brother . . . as a gift.'

'Where were you sent?'

'Far away . . . We were captured by pirates.'

'Where were you sent? Where did you learn all your graces and languages, your skills? You're no ordinary slave. Where were you educated?'

Sarah remained silent.

'Don't worry, I worked this out some time ago. Why do you think I've kept you so close to me? You can be useful – if you choose – and I try never to throw away anything that can be useful.'

She picked up a gold chain from her dressing table.

'See this? It's useful, it looks beautiful and if I need to sell it I can.'

'Can I hold it, my lady?'

'Yes. If you wish.'

She handed it to Sarah, who examined it closely.

'I dare say you once wore such fine chains.'

'Yes.'

'I knew it. You see, you can talk to me. I can help you. If I choose.'

'Shall I put it on for you?'

'In a moment.'

'And may I ask you something?'

'Go on.'

'The box in the wardrobe—'

'What of it?'

'You brought it back from the market. You keep it hidden away. What is it?'

'That, my dear girl ... is my insurance. And that of my son, Madu. Think of it as our future, if you like.'

'I'm sorry, my lady, but you have no future.'

Shajah was confused. What on earth did the girl mean? She didn't have a chance to speculate. She was startled by a flash of movement. At first, she was annoyed; the clumsy girl had placed the gold chain about her neck without even asking if she was ready to receive it. She was about to reprimand her when the maid tugged hard. And then everything seemed to happen very slowly. Her first response was panic. Her hands rose involuntarily to her neck, fingers clawing at the chain as it tightened, nails scratching into her flesh. And in the mirror, she could see the maid looking back at her, lips slightly parted, blue eyes inviting her to die. She could comprehend what was happening: she was being murdered by her slave. But she could not fathom why.

Then she became aware of overwhelming pain. She couldn't breathe and felt herself biting her tongue. This was not how she'd seen her death. She was unprepared. She could taste blood. There was something hard and fleshy stuck in the back of her throat and it took a moment for her to realise it was her tongue, which she had bitten clean off. Was this how her body would be discovered?

But the pain and panic faded, to be replaced by a feeling of wonder and euphoria. She felt like laughing, but could not. She could still see Sarah in the mirror, her face strained now by effort, and it struck Shajah how delicate the girl seemed, yet how much strength she had. Here, in this deadly, fractured moment was beauty indeed. She wanted to worship her. She wanted to be received into her arms. She felt a kind of love deep in her soul for the girl, a love she had never experienced before. She was staring at her younger self, she thought, and the girl was smiling at her, inviting her to release herself from all the concerns of the palace, of Tumanbay, of this world. Tiredness swept over her. She closed her eyes and dreamed the most vivid of dreams: of camels in the desert, the warmth of the sun, a girl with ambitions to conquer the world and a city more beautiful than anything she had ever seen.

49

Gregor

'Open it,' Gregor said to the guards standing at the doors of the Azure Room. They had been waiting there for several hours, preventing the envoy from leaving. As the doors swung silently apart, Gregor could see Effendi Red sitting cross-legged on the windowsill looking out at the city, apparently oblivious of the dancers, acrobats and musicians performing at the far end of the room. He seemed to be humming to himself – or chanting – and unaware of Gregor's presence.

'Effendi,' he said, approaching. Red opened his eyes and smiled as if woken from a long, invigorating meditation. 'The Sultan will see you now.'

The envoy slid off the windowsill and followed Gregor out of the room and past various guarded doors.

'I imagine His Majesty has been busy with affairs of state,' Red said.

Gregor smiled but chose not to reply. He wondered how Red could be so relaxed. Surely he must know that Tumanbay would not tolerate his subversions and that Maya, whoever she was, would eventually be crushed, whatever new tricks the man might attempt.

'His Majesty will see you in here,' Gregor said as they arrived outside the Hall of a Thousand Pillars.

He nodded to the guards and the doors swung open. As before, two courtiers, dressed extravagantly in the crimson gowns of their position as royal attendants, took hold of Red's arms and pulled him into the room, pushing his head down, forcing him to kneel.

'Your Majesty, Effendi Red,' Gregor announced.

Sultan al-Ghuri was seated on his throne.

'So good to see you again, effendi. And how is your "queen"?'

Cadali, standing at his side, smirked.

'She is well, Your Majesty.'

'Good. I'm so pleased. I hope you have been enjoying the modest entertainment we've arranged for you? A banquet is, as I speak, being prepared in our kitchens. We had to replace the kitchen staff last time you were here, so I can't guarantee the quality.'

He laughed at this, and Cadali and the retinue of courtiers and officials standing on either side of the room dutifully joined in.

Al-Ghuri rose to his feet and moved towards the envoy.

'It's all right. No need to avert your eyes. You can look at me.' He beckoned him to rise and the royal attendants withdrew. 'Now I understand,' the Sultan said, 'that you wish to discuss terms for peace.'

'That's right.' Red straightened his black robes and looked around the room, taking in everyone there.

'Well . . .?' asked the Sultan, smiling.

'Queen Maya has instructed me to inform you that she will withdraw her armies and cease all hostilities—'

'Good, good,' al-Ghuri said.

Could the envoy, Gregor wondered, see the wink directed to Cadali, who looked on breathlessly like a child being taken to his first military parade.

'On these conditions . . .' the envoy continued.

'Conditions? What conditions would they be?' enquired the Sultan.

'That you hand over the scrolls and that the Hafiz, currently under your protection, comes to us. He will live in Maya's court under her protection and be her spiritual guide.'

Al-Ghuri frowned and looked again to Cadali, who now stepped forward.

'These . . . these scrolls?' he said. 'We have no knowledge of them.'

'It is our information that they were carried out from Bakur by the Hafiz. Bakur is now under Maya's protection. They were therefore stolen from us. We want them back.'

The conversation was not going as the Sultan had anticipated. Gregor could see his disappointment. He had wanted to play with the envoy for a while longer but he was finding it hard to contain his anger and indignation.

'Are you mad?' the Sultan asked with rising anger.

'I'm sorry . . . What, Your Maj—?'

Before he could complete his sentence the Sultan exploded.

'How dare you dictate terms to me?' he screamed. 'Our army is in the field. We will destroy you and hang your "queen" from the Imperial Gates. Are you insane, offering terms to me? We are ready to destroy your queen and raze your whole miserable province.'

Cadali rushed towards the Sultan, his arms stretched out as if to catch him should he fall.

'Majesty, Majesty—'

'Shut up, Cadali. I'm not playing this game any more. I want this son of a whore—'

'No, Your Majesty, think about this,' the envoy said, so firmly that al-Ghuri paused and stared at him, like a snake under the spell of a snake charmer. 'Yes, you have your army in the field, you are on a war footing, all for what? Because I threw the severed head of some worthless governor in front of you? Because your nephew got poisoned – or was he? Perhaps it was something that just gave him a bellyache, and he was never in any danger at all ...'

Gregor looked around the room. Everyone present was transfixed, except for the officer who had just entered through one of the side doors and was approaching him fast.

'Excellency, you need to come,' he whispered into Gregor's ear.

'Not now,' Gregor hissed.

'No. You need to come,' the officer insisted.

Gregor sensed the urgency in his voice and followed him. As he approached the side door, he glanced back to the envoy.

'Perhaps this has all been an illusion,' Red said. 'It's the paring of the nail of the smallest finger of Maya's left hand. If she really wanted Tumanbay, she would take it. But all she wants is ... the scrolls. Give her what is hers and you may keep ... what you think is yours ... For now.'

Gregor hurried along a corridor behind the officer.

'Who found her?' he asked.

'One of the eunuchs, Excellency. I came to get you at once.'

'And her maid. Where is she?'

'I don't know.'

When they reached the entrance to the hareem, the Chief Steward, Master Nergis, was waiting. He had a look of sick despair on his moon face. When a First Wife died, it was tradition for her senior staff to die with her.

'Ah, quickly,' he said, opening the door to Lady Shajah's apartment.

The rooms seemed peaceful and ordered. Gregor moved

through the apartment cautiously. The shutters were still open in the main reception room and the warm air and sounds of the city flowed through, mixed with the high-pitched buzz of the cicadas, the backdrop to every evening in Tumanbay. Scattered around were a number of the First Wife's personal belongings, on the walls the various artworks she had collected over the years. Gregor felt as though he was trespassing.

'In here . . .' the Chief Steward said, gesturing towards another room.

As Gregor stepped forward the first things he saw scattered about the floor were pieces of glass, perfume jars and ointments and an upturned stool, and then the First Wife lying on her side, naked, curled up with her head against her knees.

He crouched down and touched her shoulder. It was still warm. He turned her slightly and noticed the scratches and bruising about her neck. He placed his fingers just below her jaw to check for a pulse.

'Is she . . .?' enquired the officer who had accompanied Gregor to the rooms, and who was now standing by the entrance.

'Get out. All of you!'

He rose and pushed the officer, the Chief Steward and the various slaves who had gathered to watch, out of the room and closed the door.

He kneeled beside her and examined the bruising. Her mouth was open in a frozen scream. Blood and foam had congealed on her lips. He looked at her hands; the nails were chipped and broken. This had been a vicious struggle. He checked the dressing table – the glass on the floor had come from the mirror which had, presumably, been knocked over during the fight.

What a way to depart this world.

At least he could do one thing for her; he picked up a towel that lay nearby and covered her over.

So, Shajah had been ahead of him all the time and had paid the price.

Clever woman. You knew what Maya wanted and you had it. But . . .

He looked around. Nearby was an open wardrobe. Gregor looked inside. It was empty.

. . . someone was even cleverer than you.

There was a knock on the door. He opened it to see the pale clammy face of Theros, the physician.

'Excellency? I came as soon as I could.'

'You're too late, doctor.'

'The lady's maid. Sarah . . .' Gregor directed this to the Chief Steward, who was behind the physician, anxiously pacing.

'We can't find her, Excellency. Shall I send for the Palace Guard?'

'Yes, do that. Has anyone else been here?'

'No one. I was at my station all evening. I would have seen if—'

'When you find the girl bring her to me.'

If I'm still in this world. If al-Ghuri hasn't put my head on a spear for failing in my duty to keep the palace safe from spies and assassins.

'Now I must inform the Sultan,' he said, walking back through the apartment, 'that his favourite wife is dead.'

He disappeared into the corridor beyond.

Part Four

50
Madu

Life for Madu had become tolerable after his near flogging. He held no official rank and acted as unofficial servant to Daniel, who was spending much of his time with the general or his staff, answering questions and providing information about Maya.

Madu had asked him: 'Do you really know this stuff? Did you ever really see Maya or talk to her? Were you in that castle when her men walked over the edge?'

Daniel never quite answered, but the fact that Qulan hadn't sent them back to the shit-shovelling detail meant that he believed the blue-eyed soldier, and he was a shrewd commander and knew how to read men. That, at least, is how Madu put it to himself, and as long as the situation kept him out of the shit, he was happy.

Madu was clearing up the tent now provided for Daniel. There wasn't much mess, Daniel was naturally well organised and Madu had learned to be tidy for his sake. He was conscious for the first time in his life of another person he truly wanted to please – someone he found increasingly attractive – and yet, out here in the desert, far away from his own natural world of the stews and bathhouses of the city, he felt unsure, oddly uncertain of how to proceed. Perhaps, in this world of men, he should be content to be who and where he was and ask for nothing more.

Daniel pulled the flap back and peered into the dark interior.
'The general wants to see you, Madu.'

'What? Why?' He put down the scroll he was tidying.

'I don't know. I think we're going back to the city. And you shouldn't read in the gloom, it's bad for your eyes. Come on.'

In the command tent the general was, for once, not examining manifests or maps; he was waiting for them and stood as Madu entered.

'My boy, I'm sorry to have to tell you your mother is dead.'

A silence – or was it? He could see Qulan's lips moving, feel Daniel's hand on his shoulder, guiding him into the chair the general had just vacated. It was as if he'd jumped into a stream of slow, thick water and gone under, unable to swim or even struggle, and then he was up and out and in the world again to hear Qulan.

'. . . know any more than the brief facts. It wasn't a natural death. I have been summoned. I have to go back to Tumanbay. You are to come with me. You will come too, Daniel.'

'You don't know any more than that, sir?'

'All I know is that my brother Gregor will be having a very difficult time. We travel light, take only what you need for the journey. Commander Wolf will accompany us. He has never seen the city and the city has never seen him. We may need his particular skills.'

'What skills would those be, General?' Daniel asked.

'Killing. He's a very efficient killer.'

'Then this may not be a happy return?'

51

Gregor

The Grand Vizier met Gregor at the entrance to the Council Chamber. He had, for once, a sympathetic expression on his face.

'Not in here, Gregor, the Sultan wishes to see you in the Hall of Justice.'

Where sentence was passed on those officials who had failed their master and their city. It took all of Gregor's resolution to stand and betray nothing of the turmoil within.

'Very well,' he said, without so much as a tremor in his voice. 'I am ready.'

Cadali stayed him with a hand on the arm.

'We neither of us have any love for the other but we both serve the same cause and, over the years ... Well, I believe a certain respect has grown up between us.'

'Go on.' Gregor said. He thought: *my arse it has!*

'My advice ... if I were to offer it, Gregor, would be to ... follow the poet's words and "*give wings to your heels and shake the unruly dust from the hem of your robe, for in seeking new lands, we may preserve the old.*" I merely offer a thought. Otherwise I shall see you shortly. No ...' He took his hand from Gregor's arm and held it palm up. 'Say nothing. I owe you no less.'

And he was gone in a flurry of ceremonial robes.

Gregor considered. Was the warning well meant? It was

287

impossible to know with Cadali. Was it even a warning? Maybe it was a goad, a taunt, to make him face the Sultan. And the risk of doing that was in no doubt. Al-Ghuri would be furious, he would want revenge. The only question: would he want to achieve it through Gregor, who would find the killers, or inflict it upon him as a man failing in his duty. There was only one way to find out unless he really were to run. He recalled others who had tried it – officials who had failed and slipped away – and been caught and brought back. He had attended their 'questioning', seen their appalling suffering, for desertion was considered a far greater crime than failure. Tumanbay was eternal; human life of no more worth than the insects of spring, born to live and die in a day. There was no escape.

The room was in shadow. The figures seated along the dais were robed, their pale ancient faces peering down at him with an insulting lack of interest in who he was – all they cared about was what he had done or not done. Tumanbay's Jurists, the legislators who sat on either side of their Sultan and the Grand Vizier. They exerted their power on the Sultan's behalf unnoticed by most, though Gregor, in his work, had experienced aspects of it. He had seen their sigil, a reptile that was neither lizard nor snake but something of both, able to scale any wall or slide under any door. Sometimes he'd wondered if they were simply a myth put about by the Sultan, but not this morning, not here in this room, standing before them, waiting to answer some very uncomfortable questions.

Cadali was gently tapping a forefinger against a lectern on which rested sheets of vellum. Tap . . . tap . . . tap. He too looked down at Gregor, nodded as if to say: Well, I tried, then he picked up a sheet, read a few lines and murmured to al-Ghuri.

The Sultan simply said: 'Begin.'

'At the beginning . . .'

Gregor couldn't even be sure which of the hooded figures had spoken.

'The beginning?'

'Go back to the beginning.'

'What is the point of—?'

'You are not here to ask questions but to answer them. Who is Sarah?'

'A slave. She was . . .' He stumbled over the words. '. . . newly bought and—'

'Why did you choose her to attend the First Wife?' That was definitely from a figure at the end of the row, though the voice sounded as dry and ancient as the first speaker.

'She was untainted, you see. She—'

'Many slaves are bought every day. Why her? What made her suitable for the Sultan's wife?'

'She was special. Educated.'

'She was your spy?'

Cadali broke in, his anger almost palpable: 'Of course she was his spy!'

Al-Ghuri grunted, as if he had just woken from a deep sleep, and regarded Gregor with hooded eyes. His words were quietly spoken but freighted with anger.

'You placed your spy at the centre of my household?'

'It is my duty to—'

'Serve your Sultan, not spy on him.' The anger was loosed; al-Ghuri stood and leaned forward, his hands like claws on his lectern. 'Have a care, Commander, my patience is not infinite.'

Gregor reflected that the Sultan's patience was virtually non-existent.

'Majesty, I live to serve.'

Cadali whispered calming words and the Sultan sat and waved a hand towards the jurists.

'Continue.'

A head turned towards Gregor like an ancient insect seeking prey.

'She was your spy?'

'It is my duty to keep—'

'To keep the First Wife from harm, yes?'

There was no answer to that – he nodded.

'A duty in which you have failed.' It wasn't a question.

Cadali ran his glance down another sheet of vellum and said simply: 'Why?'

'Why did I fail?'

'Why did you place your spy in her chambers? What reason—?'

Al-Ghuri cut across his Vizier: 'Did you suspect her of treachery? Was there evidence, eh?'

'There were papers, Majesty.'

One of the jurists whispered: 'Papers?'

'I believe there were ancient scrolls in her possession which have gone missing. They were undeclared, un . . . un . . .' Was he saying too much?

'How do you know this?'

'My informants, my investigations . . . I suspected that Her Highness was – may have been – involved in a plot against the Sultan.'

Cadali couldn't contain himself.

'He's trying to save his head. Why would the First Wife plot against our beloved Sultan. She had everything, she was . . .'

He fell silent as if the emotion of the moment were too much for him.

Gregor used the pause. 'I believe there are others involved. I think these papers or scrolls have a certain importance to various parties. I think they may be at the centre of . . . the mysteries, questions that—'

'I believe – I think – a certain importance – the mysteries – the questions . . . the questions . . .' The Sultan snapped his fingers. 'These are words lost in the air, Commander. They mean nothing.'

'Give me time, Majesty. Let me find the slave, Sarah. She has disappeared. She may be the murderer or she may have witnessed the killing and run to save her life. She may even be dead. But I will solve this, I will find out who did it and why . . . Just give me time.'

'Oh, time . . .' Cadali muttered. 'We all want time but time has no time for you. There are no more excuses. Majesty.' He turned to al-Ghuri, bowed in his seat, and raised his voice. 'The penalty for such gross failure is laid down in the analects of the great jurists of Tumanbay. We all know the sentence that must be inflicted, as does the miserable Gregor, who has, in many cases, carried it out on your behalf. Now he may discover the efficacy of your mercy and we will be rid of his incompetence.'

Once again silence, then a whispering between the jurists and the Sultan. A slight smile played about Cadali's lips.

Gregor stood motionless. He was facing the ultimate choice – life or death. Oddly, he found something exhilarating in the moment. Gambler's choice. He could see why a wise government would forbid games of chance with their lethal glamour. Which way would it go? They needed him, surely – he was a tool with a good edge, he had proved himself in the past – but he still had an uncomfortable feeling that these ancients might listen to Cadali and deliver him up to al-Ghuri's wrath.

There seemed to be a disagreement between the ancients and their Sultan – dry whispers sounded like the feet of insects on vellum. Al-Ghuri half rose then sat again. More whispers and finally they turned to him. One among them spoke.

'Find the murderers, bring them to justice. Your Sultan requires results or he requires your head. You may go.'

Gregor bowed deeply, abasing himself, his nose a palm's breadth from the floor. The Sultan did not respond.

'Thank you, Majesty. You will not regret your decision.'

Gregor backed away and was almost at the door when one of the voices came again.

'Commander, this woman, the slave Sarah?'

'Yes.'

One hand was on the iron handle, the door still unopened. Was it all a torture by hope? Were they about to rescind their mercy?

'Are you quite sure about the nature of your relationship with her?'

'She was my spy.'

'About your feelings for her, Commander?'

'I used her, that's all. I used her.'

They looked at him but said nothing, and yet he had an uneasy feeling they had implied everything. What were his true feelings for the woman? Had he allowed himself to become too involved with his own spy and thus unable to see the situation clearly? It was a classic error, and shrewder men than he had been brought down by it.

He stood with his hand on the iron ring and then, after what seemed like ages, turned it and walked out. A breeze blew in the corridor; he shivered and realised he was drenched in sweat.

52

Ibn Bai

He came out of the silence of morning, announcing himself
with a hammering at the gate. Ibn Bai barely had time to throw
on a robe, dash water in his face and arrive in the courtyard
before Gregor burst in through the main gate, throwing the
porter aside like an empty sack, striding past Ibn Bai, bellowing:
'Where is she?'

'Where is who, Excellency?'

He rushed after him into the house, into the room where
the baby lay in her crib. The commander turned on Ibn Bai and
grabbed his robes at the throat, shouting into his face: 'Where
is she?' There was a tang of aniseed to his breath. 'Answer me or
I swear I'll—'

Disturbed by the noise, the baby began to cry. The commander
threw Ibn Bai back onto a settle and lifted the child from her
crib.

'Where is my slave? I swear I will dash this thing's brains out
on the tiles if you do not tell me.'

'I swear I do not know. On my life!'

'On this child's life?'

No one would have considered Ibn Bai a man of action, able
to think fast and calmly in a crisis, but in his youth, in the far-
flung and lawless lands of the east, he had often encountered

situations that demanded a cool head and clear thinking.

Now he answered in a calm, quiet voice: 'Excellency, I swear I do not know where she is. You may search the house, the grounds, you may kill me and the child and everyone here but still I will not know where she is. Now, please, give me the child. I am your man, my head on it.'

'Take her.'

Ibn Bai received the child and began to calm her, stroking her forehead, which had always worked with Heaven. By and by she fell asleep and he placed her back in her crib.

'Come into the library, Excellency. I will ask them to bring mint tea. Do you require food?'

'I require my slave.'

Ibn Bai led the way into the library, calling to the servants to bring tea – quickly.

'What has happened, my lord? There have been rumours – the Palace Guard in the streets but no word from the palace itself. The gates closed, so it's said. Something has happened.'

'Something has happened. Perhaps everything has changed. What else have you heard?'

'The First Wife . . . was executed or killed or has run away . . . You are looking for Sarah. I am not a fool. Something has been stolen, perhaps, something you wanted, needed?'

In truth, Commander Gregor's visit was not a total surprise to Ibn Bai. The word was indeed out on the street of a death in the palace, that was true; the rest was conjecture.

'Shajah, murdered by her own slave woman.'

'Who worked for you.'

Something dangerous flashed in the commander's eyes but then subsided.

Ibn Bai went on: 'But surely she wouldn't risk losing her child . . .?'

'Exactly. So, she will come here sooner or later. Take this coin and when she does appear, send it with your swiftest messenger to the Gate of the Supplicants, where he will be admitted and brought before me. Keep the slave here until I come. Do you understand?'

'Perfectly, Excellency,' Ibn Bai said.

He suspected the commander was involved in some secret game, which was why he had not brought the Palace Guard. He wondered what it could be and what to make of it. And then he realised that, in the cause of the baby, he had allied himself with Sarah.

The maid appeared at the door, afraid to enter. Ibn Bai beckoned her in.

'Ah, tea and cakes. Please, Commander, it has been a trying morning, I'm sure. Please, drink . . .'

53

Heaven

The sun's last gleaming splashed pink on the clouds over the flat horizon and already the first stars were visible high in the east. Slave rattled the bars of the cage – the ever-present dogs growled.

He shouted: 'Water! We need water, food, we won't be any good to you dead.'

Rajik emerged from the tent and threw a water skin to the boy.

'Food later,' he said. 'Give them water.'

Boy passed the skin through the bars to Heaven. He was staying well clear of Slave.

She caught his eye and said: 'I believed in you. You betrayed us.'

'I didn't want to, I had to.'

'I trusted you.'

'He didn't.' Boy pointed at Slave.

'And who was right, you little bastard? If I ever get my hands on your neck . . .'

Boy stepped away from the cage and shouted: 'But you won't! They'll sell you and then you'll be gone and it won't matter.'

Heaven couldn't see if he was angry or sorry, or maybe both. She wanted to ask him but Rajik released the two dogs' leads from the line. He held them as they bucked and slavered.

'I'm going to open the cage and get the girl. Try anything and the dogs will have you. Back away.'

Heaven grabbed the bars behind her.

'No, I won't. You can't . . . Don't let him . . .' she pleaded.

Slave made fists of his hands and moved towards the door.

Pamira emerged from the tent. With a kindly smile, she said: 'Don't let him frighten you, sweeting. It'll all be fine as long as you do what you are told. And you, Master Slave, think on it – we wish to sell her at the best price and untouched pays better than anything. She will be all right for now. If you go against the dogs, you will not.' All delivered with the same benign smile.

'Best go with them,' Slave said.

Heaven took a deep breath and stood up and walked to the cage door. She looked at the boy again as he unlocked and pulled it open and held out a hand to help her down. She batted it away.

'I don't need your help.'

She stood straight and walked into the tent, looking neither to right or left.

'See, I told you,' Pamira said, 'she's got character, that one. She'll fetch a fine price.'

The cage clanged shut. Rajik handed the dogs' leads to the boy; they were leaping up at the bars, snapping their teeth and he could barely hold them. Rajik followed his wife into the tent. Once he was out of sight the boy whispered something and the dogs settled back on their haunches.

'How do you do that, Boy?'

'Do what?'

'With the dogs,' Slave said 'Calm them like that.'

'I don't know. I just do.'

'Nothing is ever "just" anything. Can you do it with other things? Camels, horses – what about the goats?'

'They never run off, I never lose them,' Boy said. 'Why?'

'Maybe I won't break your neck when we get out of here. You might be useful.'

'It doesn't matter. You won't get out. Nobody gets out.'

A cry from the tent – Heaven's voice.

'No, no, no!'

Then silence.

Boy said: 'They're doing what they do – inspecting the merchandise.'

'I swear I'll rip that bastard's head from his body and feed it to his dogs in front of his bitch wife.'

'Is she your daughter?'

'The girl?' He laughed. 'Look at her, look at me.'

'Because you care about her.'

'Care? She's a whining, selfish . . .' He fell silent.

'It's only business with them. That's all.'

'Is that all you ever say, Boy? That's all? That's all?'

He squatted by the cage door, one hand grasping a bar.

Evening had passed into night and the star fields were beginning to cast their own cold light over the encamped town before Pamira led Heaven from the tent. Boy whispered to the dogs and they came to immediate readiness. There were tears on Heaven's cheeks, but she still walked straight and Slave noticed it.

'I hate you,' she spat at Pamira.

'Don't be a fool, sweeting, nobody harmed you. You'll still make a nice little present for a rich man or woman.'

Rajik unlocked the cage and Pamira pushed Heaven in. The door clanged shut, the dogs were retied to the line and the two captives were left alone.

Heaven curled herself up into a tight ball in the corner of the cage. After a moment, she felt a hand on her shoulder and she recoiled.

'Then for her, live for he
'You took me away fron
'Then I probably save
your strength.'
'Haven't you underst
'Haven't you? We'll
'Haven't you. Is that what
about it. Is that what
After a long mome
eyes out of her head
loaf and began to ea
'We need to wo
when he empties
help us.'
'If I can't?'
'Then we're sl

'It's
s

'
'Be
'Wh
'Wha
Looked i
was me. It
'You'll get
'Is that all y
'You can get
'Even if you fe
'You need a reas
'And have you?'
'I have to kill a mar
'The one whose word
'Only then, when I lo
back and speak it.'
'If you're going to do that
'Tell me something I don't
'All right. When they were p
was looking at them. Rajik has g
'Where? What kind of rash?'
'His throat. Red, sort of red. And
fell silent; her eyes glittered as tears a
seen them before. On the ship. My mo
She buried her face in her hands as sh
'The plague,' Slave said. 'It's here too. V
we'll die.'
'My mother . . .' she said.

r. That's your reason.'

1 her.'

1 your life. You should eat, you'll need

od anything? My mother is dead!'

be dead too if we don't do something

ou want?'

nt she answered. 'I want to rip that bitch's

As she said it, she ripped a lump from the

t.

k this out. It has to be the boy. Talk to him

he slurry. Make him believe you, make him

rry too.'

54
Qulan

The mist rose about them in swirling waves, obscuring everything, clogging their nostrils, stinging their eyes. Qulan could barely see his hand in front of his face. The tall shape of Wolf loomed out of the obscurity – and was that Daniel beside him? And Madu? The four of them, wrapped in the clouds of sweet-scented fog to the eerie sound of a peacock's cry.

Booming through the undercast like the mighty brass horns they blew at the harbour entrance on days when the sea fret came in, the voice of al-Ghuri, Sultan of Tumanbay: 'In memory of the first of all my wives, have I created a perfume of rare and delicate nature.'

'Delicate?' Qulan muttered. 'I could use this stuff in war!'

Wolf growled and swiped a hand in front of his eyes. Others further into the miasma were coughing discreetly. The Sultan went on, as he was liable to do on such occasions.

'Its name – "The Dark of Midnight Heralds the Light of Dawn". Let us remember the fragility of life, the futility of hope in the face of the inevitable end of all human striving ...'

'Through Death by choking,' Daniel muttered.

'Aye, and let us celebrate the delicate but strong power of Love ...'

'Strong stuff, this delicate fragrance,' Wolf said.

'My mother thought they all smelled of horse shite,' Madu said.

'Huh, I know horse shite and this doesn't smell anywhere half as sweet as dung on a fresh spring morning.'

Madu chuckled and Qulan reflected that the boy had got over his mother's death with remarkable ease – or perhaps not, knowing Shajah. An admirable woman in many ways, but the way of the mother was not really one of them.

A casement was opened and blessed fresh air blew into the room, shifting the scented mist and making it easier to see where they were. Al-Ghuri stood behind a great brazier from whence the perfumed smoke arose. At his feet slumped a peacock which had given up the uneven struggle. The Court, the Vizier, the doctor and others stood in reverent silence, breathing in the breeze. Qulan's brother didn't appear to be present.

Al-Ghuri added another handful of crystals to the heat and the courtiers shuffled backwards.

'Madu, my dear boy, when we sent you away to become a man, little did we guess that you would return to bury a beloved mother. Come, sit by me, we shall share with sadness the memory of a great woman.'

'General, is it all right?'

'Of course.'

'Daniel, excuse me, the call of duty.'

'Of course. We'll meet up later. You can show me the city. Don't breathe too deeply.'

'I come, Majesty. We shall join the streams of our grief in a river of sorrow that shall flow into the sea of infinity . . .'

'The boy's a natural courtier,' Qulan said. 'Do you think it's acceptable to leave at this point?'

'Matter of survival,' Wolf gasped. 'I suggest we leave the old gent to suffocate in his mourning and find some decent entertainment.'

*

The corridor outside was lined with open arches, where they stood gratefully breathing and looking out over the palace and the roofs and towers beyond.

'Have you visited the city before, Wolf?' Daniel asked.

'Not my natural hunting ground. I prefer the High Country – a man can breathe there.'

Qulan said: 'It's a matter of getting used to things and putting up with them.'

'Not our strongest suit, General. We usually cut them down and grind them into the mud.' He laughed. 'There is one thing I would like to do before I leave. Can your man Daniel arrange something?'

'A guide, you mean?' Daniel asked.

'I think something rather more . . .' Qulan snapped his fingers and a servant appeared seemingly out of the wall hangings. 'You know the palace?'

'Of course, my Lord.'

'The commander here requires some entertainment. Do you . . .?'

'If the commander will come with me, I will ensure all his needs are met.'

Qulan now turned to Daniel. 'You may amuse yourself too if you wish.'

'Thank you, General. Where shall I attend you later?'

'At my house. Sunset. Have you . . .?'

'I am provided for money, sir.' He bowed and was gone.

Briefly Qulan wondered what or who had provided him with money and then turned to face his brother who, like the servant, had simply arrived.

'I expected to see you inside, Gregor.'

'I have never liked funerals.'

'Strange, given how many you've caused in your time.'

'How were the provinces? Did you find an army?'

Gregor sat on one of the ledges and leaned back against the arch, as if to underline his ownership of this place. Qulan felt it was time to take his younger brother down a peg or two.

'What in the name of the seven hells have you been up to, Gregor?'

'My job.'

'Really?'

'Really, Qulan.'

'Which consists of what? Placing a spy right under the First Wife's nose, who can't tell you who killed the woman because – what? She was killed too? She was in league with the murderer? She's run away? Help me here.'

'There are several possibilities.'

'Shajah deserved more of you, brother. I deserved more of you. When you make a camel's arse out of a perfectly simple operation, some of the shit rubs off on your family. Were you blind or just stupid?'

A flash of annoyance crossed Gregor's face: the words had struck home.

He snapped back: 'Perhaps you should ask her blue-eyed brother, who seems to have become one of your followers.'

'I'm asking my brother. As for the blue-eyed fellow, I can assure you, I shall be keeping a close watch on him.'

'Even so, I should like to interrogate—'

'Out of the question. He's a military asset. He grew up in Maya's court with his sister . . .'

Qulan stopped in mid-sentence. His face slowly creased and he laughed, a long, loud peal.

'You didn't know! Never mind camel's arse, this is an elephant's arse. You are losing your touch, brother. I wonder if it's healthy to be seen in your company any more.'

But Gregor didn't rise to this provocation. His face drained of colour, he tried to keep calm.

'You're saying she grew up in Amber Province? In the court there?'

'Maybe you should ask Maya's envoy. I hear he's still here in the palace, being treated as if he's an honoured guest. How many spies is he recruiting, I wonder?'

Qulan shrugged, chuckled again and walked off. Just before passing through the door at the end of the corridor, he paused, looked back and said: 'And don't even think about trying to lift any of my people off the street.'

The door slammed. Gregor spat through the arch.

55
Wolf

The couch shuddered, juddered and bucked as they went at it like rabbits. Shamsi cried out, first for the money but then for the sheer pleasure of it all. The Barbarian was, he'd told her, a cavalryman from the high country and he wasn't wrong there; hung like a horse, he seemed to have the ability to go all night and then again first thing in the morning. He arrived with a neigh and whinny of joy and then collapsed on her back. She wriggled out from beneath him and went to the basin where she washed herself. Lying there on the bed, he was a truly magnificent specimen and, unlike many of her clients, had proved kind and considerate – perhaps it was all that caring for horses that did it. He'd also accepted her suggestion of a bath without rancour – indeed, with a great deal of pleasure as a result of her ministrations. If she said it herself it was no less true: she was very good at her job.

'Truly, my lord, you are a man of mighty parts.'

He turned over and propped himself on one elbow.

'I'll wager you say that to all your customers.'

She slipped on a robe and threw him a facecloth.

'I do but I rarely mean it. Most of them can barely manage the one, never mind the many. I hope it was all ... satisfactory?'

306

'More than.' He sat up and wiped himself down. 'You have a remarkable rump, my lady. I've seen less on a mare.'

'Then I worry for the mares in your service, my lord.'

He laughed and took up the wineskin, held back his head and squirted a good bottleful down his throat. Then, picking up the remains of a loaf, he began to tear it into large pieces, wrap them round lumps of meat from last night's supper, and consume them. He walked to the window.

She thought: You've a fine pair of buttocks yourself, my Barbarian, and joined him looking out at the cool dawn.

Much of the lower palace was hidden by the morning mists, only the top of the walls and the high towers visible, gilded in the early rays of sun from the east. Somewhere there was the joyous shouting of children but no one was visible.

Shamsi said: 'For as far as you can see, it's all the palace and beyond that, the city. There are the temple towers and the banners of the great houses.'

'Too much stone. I told the general, I need the air around me. Here, you couldn't smell an enemy until he was close enough to cut your throat.'

'Maybe that's why there are so many throats cut in Tumanbay.'

She rested a hand on his buttock, feeling the muscle, the sinew, the strength of the man. Yes, she decided, she liked this one very much indeed.

'They say that once you come here, you never want to leave. People live their whole lives without ever passing the walls.'

'Well, I'll be coming back here a good few times — What in the name of the devil is that!'

What looked to be a huge bat or ray swam up out of the mist and flashed past their window. A boy hung, whooping and howling, to a frame beneath the great wing. A moment later another appeared, many coloured, wide winged, with a howling girl hauling at the wooden frame, her long black hair trailing behind her like a crow's tail in a madman's dream.

Her Barbarian stepped back a pace, truly shocked . . .

'Devils,' he muttered, 'swooping for the souls of the lost.'

Two more leaped up from the sparkling sea, like flying fish, rising high and then turning on themselves, their riders swinging loose as they went heels over head and flashed down again beyond the walls that were beginning to emerge as the sun burned off the mist.

'Skyrats,' she said. 'You see them all over Tumanbay, mostly in the mornings before the patrols are about. It's called a kite, the thing they fly. They've been doing it forever. There are carvings of them in some of the temples from the earliest times. There must be ten, maybe twenty deaths every year. It's dangerous but still they do it, the boys and girls.'

Two kites passed close enough for them to feel the wind in their wake. Their gaily coloured tails fluttered after them, as did the joyous cries of their riders. And then they were gone and the call to prayer began to sound out and the mist vanished, and the daily life of the city began as it had on ten thousand similar days.

Shamsi leaned on the stone sill.

'The children of Tumanbay will dare anything. Besides, no one really minds. Even the children of the highest play such games. All life here is a chance. One day someone is up . . .'

He slipped behind her and gathered her up and carried her to the bed.

'And the next,' he said, 'they are playing the game of the two-backed beast!'

'Again?'

'Again.'

As he laid her down she said: 'You haven't told me your name.'
'Nor have you told me yours.'
'My name is Shamsi.'
'And mine is Wolf. Now may we get to it?'

56

Qulan

After attending to certain matters in the city, General Qulan made his way home in the twilight, a time he had always enjoyed, when the outlines of the buildings and towers were softened and the lights cast a magical glow, reminiscent of the puppet shows travelling entertainers gave for children, telling the stories of great heroes and wonderful travels. As a boy he had been captivated by these tales and, in the few moments his servitude allowed him, he would sneak out of his master's house and find a rickety cart set up as a stage, where the shadows moved behind a stretched cloth to the sound of flute and drum and sometimes tambourine. Nowadays, when he saw such a travelling show, he recognised the cheapness – the shoddy decorations, the crass stories, the inexpert puppetry – but then it had been a doorway into a world of infinite possibilities. And who was to say that wasn't so? Here he was, General Qulan, arriving at his high white walls, manned by his guards, that enclosed his home and his extensive gardens. Not vast and never vulgar, but big enough and tasteful and, he believed, suitable to a man of his standing and gravity.

Daniel was waiting by the gate and when Qulan dismounted he took the reins of his horse. Voices from within announced his arrival even as the gates creaked open and he entered his domain.

'Come into my house, Daniel, you are welcome here.'

Daniel bowed. 'I am honoured, General, to be received.'

Two women emerged from the house.

'Pushkarmi, Manel.' Qulan's face lit up with a rare smile. The women bowed. 'It is good to see you. This is Daniel, he will be our guest.'

Daniel bowed.

'Welcome, Daniel, I am Pushkarmi, this is my daughter Manel.'

'Sir, you are welcome.'

Neither woman was veiled and it was clear where the daughter's beauty came from.

Daniel said: 'I am at your service, madam, please call upon me at your will.' He bowed again.

'Let us go in,' Qulan said, and led the way inside.

The house was large and well-appointed but in no way showy; it reflected Qulan's soldierly nature – plain and practical with a certain elegance. It was there to do a job, house those who dwelled within it, and it did it well. Though neither woman wore the veil, the way of life was traditional. While Qulan and Daniel sat on cushions at a low table, Pushkarmi and Manel stood attending them. Qulan was asking about the work that had been done on the estate since his departure.

'The orange grove has been completed, as you desired. Will you look at it tomorrow morning, husband?'

'I will. And the watercourse . . .?'

'Has been redirected.'

Qulan laughed. 'You know my mind better than I do myself, my dear. Manel?'

'Refreshments are coming, Father.'

'And my son, is he coming?'

An uneasy silence edged into the conversation. Neither

woman replied for some moments and then Manel took a breath and said: 'He is with his friends, Father.'

'It is where he is not that concerns me. He is not welcoming his father home. When he returns, send him to me.'

'He is young, husband, you know what boys are. He probably—'

Qulan held up a hand and total silence fell. It was clear mother and daughter feared his anger.

'Of course, it shall be as you wish, husband.'

'You are hungry, I shall hurry them in the kitchen.'

It was also clear that Manel knew how to manage her grumpy father as she smiled at him, a dazzling smile that lit up her face, that lit up the room. Instantly his mood softened.

'Yes, do not keep our guest waiting.'

It took little time for the table to be filled and the men to be drinking. Pushkarmi had retired but Manel had taken upon herself the duty of cup-bearer, the better to examine their guest, for she was a young woman gifted with a questing intelligence and ambitious dreams.

As they ate, Qulan questioned the younger man; it was the first time anything other than purely military matters had passed between them and Manel could see that both were tense and very aware.

'You heard me talking to my brother at the palace? Eat, drink . . .'

Daniel took falafel and some bread. 'I couldn't help overhearing a few things before I left. He is not a soldier?'

'He has led armies but never fought battles. At least not against equal forces. He's more of a diplomat, good at controlling civilians. Nowadays the Sultan chooses to keep him close. He's Commander of the Palace Guard and responsible for searching out spies and traitors.'

'You have both achieved great things in Tumanbay, General.'

'We were brought here as children, as slaves. We were lucky, our master saw a certain potential and used it, encouraged us to succeed. That's how you get on here. Hard work, the right friends, duty, loyalty. Manel, our guest's cup is empty.'

Manel poured mint tea into Daniel's cup and then into her father's. He nodded; Daniel offered a smile and a thank you.

'You came here with your sister?'

'Yes, General.'

'She was brought into the palace as a servant to Lady Shajah?'

'So I believe. I was not there at that time.'

'It appears that she has disappeared. After the murder of the First Wife. What do you say to that?'

'There is nothing I can say. We were separated soon after we got here. From all I know of her, I think it unlikely my sister would murder anyone. She has a child ... I don't know what happened to it. Maybe she ran away to find it? But as for murder, there's no reason I can think of why she would do that.'

'Perhaps you should think harder, Daniel.' The tone was light but there was a clear threat within it.

'I have, ever since we came back to the city. The truth is, we were never close. I don't really know her at all. We were brought up in separate households, our worlds were different. We travelled together but we were strangers. We were captured together. That's all, really.'

'Maybe, maybe not. Eat – you must be hungry.'

Manel thought: Father wants to see if his mouth is too dry to eat because he's lying.

Casually, she filled Daniel's cup without quite knowing why. Daniel took bread and olives, falafel, kofta and ate with enthusiasm. He could have been in his own home, wherever that was. Only when he had swallowed everything did he drink from the tea bowl and once again acknowledge Manel.

Qulan, apparently satisfied, asked: 'From what you know of Maya, why would she send her envoy back here?'

Daniel considered. 'There is, General, in the remote hills in the north of Amber, on the higher slopes, a forest where a certain caterpillar lives. It is slow-moving and over the days and weeks spores of lichen settle on its body. But the lichen is not content to live on the caterpillar. It begins to seek out weak spots where it can enter – where it keeps feeding until all is consumed and there is only the outer shell left.'

'In the case of Tumanbay, loyalty will counter the parasites, I believe.'

'More tea, Father?'

'No more. You may leave us.' Once Manel had left the room, Qulan said: 'You like her?'

'General?'

'My daughter Manel?'

'She is very beautiful.'

'Yes, she is. But she is not for you. Touch her and I swear you will never touch another woman again.'

57
Red

The nature of the palace changed as they descended; the more ordered, understandable levels built in the recent past – seven hundred years ago or so – gave way to an earlier style of architecture which had about it something of the forest, as if the labyrinth of passages, staircases, sudden dead ends, floors that sloped one way and then another, had grown of their own twisted volition rather than been built by the hand of man. Even for Gregor, who had walked them for many years, there were whole areas that he would not have ventured into without unreeling a thread in his wake. It was hot down here too – unnaturally so – and the shadows that danced at the edge of the flaming torch he held were full of ancient threat.

Effendi Red said, 'It is very old. We must be deep indeed.'

'And the deep is where the monsters dwell, so they tell us.'

For a man effectively under detention, in the power of his enemy, the envoy showed no signs of disquiet at all. Perhaps it was time to shake him up a bit!

Gregor ducked and passed through an arch barely tall enough for a child.

'Here, I think you'll find this of interest.'

Once through he touched the torch to a brazier by the doorway. A bigger flame sprang up and, like a trick, the darkness

315

vanished. The space around them rushed outwards, giving the impression they were moving at great speed into a void – until the flames illuminated the towering walls and the cupola of a vast space in which they stood.

Red put out a hand and steadied himself against the wall as he peered upwards.

'I am impressed. You could build a town in here. What was its purpose?'

Gregor shrugged. 'No one knows. A cistern, perhaps, a temple, a circus for races? The meaning is lost in time. Very few people know of its existence. And yet even this is not the end of Tumanbay, effendi.'

'Ah, I thought there was a reason behind it all. I'm not a mere tourist, I am to receive a lesson. What, I wonder? That the power of Tumanbay has no end, or that it is a city of infinite surprises? I grant you all of those, Commander Gregor.'

'Here, look here.'

Gregor kneeled on the floor and unlatched a lock on the rim of an iron grating, which he swung upwards with a shrieking of rusty hinges. A shaft plunged away into darkness. From it came noises – groans, howls, mad laughter and a low growl.

'Always makes the hairs stand up on the back of my neck no matter how often I hear it,' Gregor said.

'What is it?' Red peered into the darkness.

'Malefactors are lowered and left to wander the caverns below. There's no way out but somehow they survive down there in the utter darkness. No one has emerged. Perhaps they eat each other.' He used his foot to slam the grating back down and flipped the catch shut. 'But enough of the darkness.'

He pulled a chain that dangled from the brazier and a lid slammed down, cutting off the flame. Gregor slipped back through the low arch.

'If I were to douse my torch and walk away, effendi, I doubt you would ever find your way back.'

'I might surprise you. I have a very good memory.' The envoy's voice was steady – still no tremor of fear. 'On the other hand, I might also be carrying a tinderbox and tow to light my own way. Maya teaches us to be prepared.'

Gregor laughed. 'Very well, then, let me show you a more pleasant prospect.'

'Are you going to tell me the magnolia tree is nourished by the blood of Tumanbay's defeated enemies?'

They were in the palace gardens. Birds and butterflies flitted among the giant ferns and branches of a small forest. Rivers and waterfalls provided a soothing background. They might have been in a park outside, but in fact walked under a great glass roof that filtered the sun's rays and dappled the marbled floor with shadows.

'No, the tree is watered and fed in the usual manner.'

'It seems a pity that it cannot grow where it naturally should but, of course, in Tumanbay there is very little that is natural.'

Gregor was becoming weary of this polite sparring, this game of riddles. He only wanted to know one thing.

'The girl,' he said.

'The girl?'

'The blue-eyed slave, Sarah. She has disappeared.'

'And what is that to me?' Red asked. When Gregor didn't reply, he said: 'I had nothing to do with the girl. Do you really think she is involved in the death of the First Wife? Surely it's more likely her body is rotting in one of those drains of which your city is so proud.'

'Is that what you believe, effendi?'

'It's one possibility among an infinity.'

'And another,' Gregor said, 'might be that there are traces of your hand in this business. Confusion, suspicion, uncertainty – are these not your tools?'

Red looked at him blankly. 'You flatter me, Commander. I am merely a messenger.'

'I doubt that. Please answer the question. I don't think you will tell me the truth but in our business lies are often a better indication of a man's mind.' Gregor's tone was cold.

'I remind you that I am still a guest in the palace. And as for your question, you know the answer as well as I do, since you have your agents watching me every moment of the day – just as you have had my chambers searched time after time. And found that I have gone nowhere and am hiding nothing.'

'Then indulge me a little further, Effendi Red. What is it about the scrolls? Why are they so important?'

'You are very direct, Commander Gregor.' The envoy had stopped by a small ormolu box on an ornate stand. He flipped the lid open. 'Sand?'

Back to a game of riddles.

'From the boots of a djinn,' Gregor said. 'So it is said. He visited one of our sultans and engaged him in guessing games.'

'What happened?'

'The sultan won, the djinn paid a forfeit.'

'His boots?' Red allowed himself a smile.

'No. He transported the Temple of Solace from Jebal Maar in the far east and placed it where it has stood ever since. Then he stamped his feet in vexation at losing – djinn don't like to lose – and vanished, leaving only the sand.'

'So men believe.' The envoy shut the lid on the box with a snap and continued walking. 'Have you seen the scrolls, Commander?' he asked almost casually.

The scrolls were what he had come for; they were what Maya

wanted, it seemed, above all else. An image of the scrolls he had seen at the artists' workshop flashed into his mind – exquisite, disturbing, decorated with lizards and snakes, the text in a language he could not read.

'They are very beautiful,' he said eventually, noticing Red lean towards him almost hungrily. 'So I am told . . . by the Hafiz.'

Red nodded and frowned – a hint of disappointment, Gregor wondered.

'Given that this is a game, effendi,' Gregor said, 'how valuable would those scrolls be to one who had them?'

Red stopped and appraised Gregor with his calculating eyes.

'Given that it is a game, which I beg you to believe it is not, you would be wise to consider them to be of incalculable value. And of incalculable danger.' He turned, looking back towards the palace. 'And now if you are done with me, Commander, may I go to my quarters? I wish to pray.'

58
Madu

Madu met Daniel at the main gate, explaining: 'The palace has been under a virtual state of siege since my mother's murder, I doubt you'd have been able to get in without my pass.'

'How have you been?'

Madu was at ease again; this was his domain and he was comfortable here and recognised by all. He was also, in the Sultan's mind, one of the few people who could not have been implicated in Shajah's death and so freed of the suspicion that had attached to everyone else in the place.

'We'll go this way.' He led Daniel through a low door into a narrow corridor that ended in spiral stone steps. 'These are the stairs behind the stairs in the palace behind the palace. They were made for the servants to move around without bothering the better folk. They're also quicker and far more convenient if you don't want to be noticed.'

'Nothing is what it seems in Tumanbay.'

'You might say that. Where are you staying?'

'At the general's house. He's been good to me.'

'Beware the kindness of generals.'

They had been climbing for some time when Madu took another side turn and led them out into a corridor wide enough to host a small tournament. Richly hung with tapestries that, on examination, celebrated the many varieties of love, there were locked doors at either end and no guards.'

'Where are we?'

Madu produced an elaborate key. 'The Sultan has allowed me the use of my mother's old chambers. This is his private route to the hareem.'

'He's not concerned at you having access?'

'Hardly. We are united in grief for a great woman.'

He inserted the key and turned it.

'Well, you always said you were important . . .'

The rooms were in shadow and Madu strode across to the shutters, throwing them open with a clatter all along one great wall. The light flooded in and revealed the splendour accorded a First Wife in Tumanbay.

'Quite something.'

'Still smells of death to me.'

He pulled a cord, a series of levers turned and clicked, and two large palm-leaf fans on the ceiling began to swing back and forward, moving the heavy air.

'Do they know anything, about who might have . . .?' Daniel asked.

Madu said: 'If Gregor knows, he's not letting anything out. They say your sister must have seen what happened, but where is she?'

'Maybe she did it. Who knows, you could be locked in here with the brother of your mother's murderer.'

Madu rooted in a cupboard.

'I don't think so. Is she really your sister?' He got to his knees and peered into the recess. 'I knew she kept it somewhere in here. This is where she kept her most precious things. It was always locked. It was where she kept those damned scrolls that got her killed. Ahhh!' He pulled out a heavy crystal flask and poured for them both and drank. 'Very fine.'

'Fiery but good.'

'We could be executed for drinking this. You know my father had my elder brother beheaded for drinking alcohol.' He laughed. 'That's when I started drinking.'

'Fortunately I'm not a believer. Here's to us.'

They toasted each other and Madu felt a shiver of . . . what? He'd always loved those moments before something happened, when you didn't quite know if it would or wouldn't, but this one, this man Daniel, was more important than anyone he'd ever met. For a start, he'd saved his life, twice.

'So . . . uh . . . did you meet the general's daughter?'

'Yes, yes I did.'

'She's very beautiful, so they say.'

'Yes, she is.'

'No one's seen her. Well, no one at court. None of my friends, no one really. He keeps her locked away behind those big walls in his compound. He must like you a lot if he's allowed you to gaze on her beauty.'

'Or he might regard me as beneath notice. A slave, no more.'

'As are we all. The general certainly was, and look what happened to me.'

'You met me.'

'Did you like her?'

Daniel moved closer, his blue eyes intense.

'Would it bother you if I did think of her in that way?'

'Why should I care? Why are you smiling?'

'Put down that ridiculous bowl.'

He reached out, cupped the back of Madu's head and pulled him close and they were kissing. For a moment Madu wondered: did I do this, or did he? And then it didn't matter any more.

When they finally broke apart Madu said: 'I have been waiting so long for you to do that.'

'Was it worth the wait?'

'Oh yes, yes . . .'

They kissed again, broke apart, he stared into those *so* blue eyes.

'It's been a long time, Madu, my dear man.'

'It's been forever.'

They staggered to the couch, disentangling themselves from their clothing as they tripped and fell onto the diaphanous coverings and Madu thought for one brief moment: Well, Mother, I'm back!

Later, many hours later, as they lay together on the couch, Daniel said: 'The scrolls you talked about, that your mother had . . . What do you know about them?'

'A lot. I took the trouble to find out, I thought it might be useful one day.'

'Tell me.'

'I can do better than that . . .'

A pigeon flapped across the atrium. The guards had gone, presumably because his mother was no longer there to pay them. Madu stood under the broken cupola and shouted: 'Hello?'

'Eerie,' Daniel said. 'Strange to think it was once the most important place in Tumanbay.'

Madu shouted again and a door opened somewhere in the depths of the place and presently the small man, Bello, appeared.

'I want to see the Hafiz. Now,' Madu said.

'Ahh, so charming, so sad, so lost, the poor young man without his gracious lady mother. So many commiserations, my Lord. And this . . . Who is this blue-eyed fellow? We have not seen him before.'

'My name is Daniel. You are—'

'Merely ... Bello. At your service, my fine young men.' He sniffed and reached out a tubby hand as if to feel the air about them. 'Ahh, quite so, quite so. Good friends, then. Well, we like friends who like friends.'

'I don't like repeating myself,' Madu said. 'We wish to see the Hafiz.'

'So you do. I fear an appointment may be necessary.'

'For Shajah's son, I think not.'

Madu pulled his cloak aside to reveal a dagger. Fat Bello chortled.

'Ahhh, he shows me his naked blade, this brave swordsman – pricksmen both. Well, since you are who you are ... and for ...'

Gold appeared and disappeared into Bello's grasp, and they were conducted into the presence of the Hafiz.

The room was dark and stank like the urinals of far too many inns Madu had spent far too much time in during what he now considered his misspent youth. The Hafiz sat slumped before a table upon which a bottle stood next to an empty bowl.

'Have you come already? It's too soon.' The voice was still powerful, even this deep in drink. 'Do it now, then, in the name of mercy. Make it quick, make it fast.' He lurched to his feet. 'I should never have believed the bitch. God help me now.'

Madu pushed him back into his chair.

'The scrolls, where are they?'

'She took ... Said she'd keep until ... untilll ...'

'What secrets do they hold?'

The Hafiz shook his head and mumbled something indistinct. Madu slapped him; his head jerked to one side, saliva slid from his slack lips. Daniel reached past and filled the bowl and put it to the old man's mouth.

'Here, drink this.' The Hafiz sucked the liquor down like a baby. 'Go on, Madu, ask him.'

'Why my mother was killed?'

'The scrolls, of course.'

'Why are they so important?'

The Hafiz began to sleep with his eyes open, deep snores echoing from his skeletal frame. Madu made to slap him again but Daniel held his wrist.

'Let me.'

He leaned close to the old man's ear and whispered: 'Teacher, what do the scrolls say? What was their message? Teach us. Help us.'

'In the beginning . . . the Word passed down from the Maker of all that is . . . And all things that are not . . . And the Word became matter and matter was . . . was . . . and is.'

And finally the lids closed over the eyes.

'You will get nothing more from him now. He will not wake until the morning.'

'What about you? What do you know, Bello?'

'I am a student, Excellency, I only learn.'

'From him?'

'Oh, he was something once. If you had seen him then, you would not have treated him in this way. Then he would have destroyed you, young man.'

Madu pulled out the sword. 'And why should I not destroy you?'

'Ask your friend.'

Daniel put a restraining hand on Madu's shoulder.

'Leave him be. He knows nothing useful but wishes to be useful. Make him your man, Madu.'

'Very well. Bello, here . . .' More gold passed. 'Remember, you and your master are nothing in Tumanbay without a protector.

My mother is dead. You need a protector.'

'My gracious young lord, I am your ever-obedient servant.'

A bow executed with all the style of a practised courtier as Madu and Daniel departed. And when they had gone, a shrug. Bello jotted down details of the prince's visit on a scrap of parchment and concealed it in the sleeve of his robe – information for Commander Gregor.

59
Heaven

As it is appointed, the world turned under the heavens and the starry constellations came round in their turn and the moving town fell into sleep, but in the cage the two captives waited and when the boy arrived carrying a bucket, Heaven called out:

'Wait, please. I want to talk to you.'

He emptied the bucket, then paused by the cage, uncertain.

'What's your name?'

'It's Boy. You know that.'

'Your real name. My name is Heaven. Don't you have a real name?'

'It's not for here.'

'Then you're like him,' she said. 'He calls himself Slave and says he won't have a real name until he's free.'

'She speaks the truth, Boy.'

'What's that to me? Nobody gets away from them.'

'They won't matter soon,' she said.

'I can't stand around. I have jobs to do.' He picked up the pail.

'Wait. Listen, we're all going to die. And soon.'

He put the pail down.

'The first time we met, you asked if I was an angel come to take you away and I couldn't – but now I can. The plague is here, it's on Pamira and Rajik. I saw it before, on the ship where we were – my mother had it. I think she must be dead now, maybe they are all dead. But it hasn't touched us and it hasn't touched you, but it will and you will die. We'll all die if we don't run now.'

Wide-eyed, Boy stared at her, then picked up the bucket and went towards the tent.

She called after him: 'Under the chin, a red rash and lumps . . . On my mother's life, I swear it.'

He passed through the entrance and disappeared.

Heaven and Slave looked at each other and had nothing to say.

There was the faintest promise of morning in the east when the boy returned and walked up to the bars.

'Under the chin. The lumps too.'

'They are sick. They will die.'

'What about me? Can I catch it too?'

Heaven was going to say: no, you'll be safe with us – but that wasn't true for any of them.

'I don't know. Maybe, maybe not. The same for all of us but we will be safer if we are not close to the infection.'

The key appeared in the boy's hand and he unlocked the cage. A low growl came from the dogs; he spoke to them and they fell silent, watching with their pitiless eyes. Heaven and Slave climbed down from the cart.

'We need camels, provisions, we need . . .'

'Wait.'

Boy held up a hand, then whistled, a loud piercing tone that bought Rajik and Pamira stumbling from the tent.

'We trusted you,' Heaven wailed.

Rajik chuckled. 'Back in the cage, both of you. Boy, the dogs . . . Boy?'

The boy went to the end of the line to which the short leashes were attached and slipped it free of the iron cleat that secured it. He turned and faced Pamira and Rajik and spoke again to the dogs. They dropped to their bellies and began to slide like shadows across the ground, towards their owners.

Rajik bellowed: 'Be still, I'll flog the hides off your backs!'

Pamira seemed to understand sooner than her husband. She stuttered: 'We took you in.'

The dogs began to growl in a manner unlike anything Heaven had ever heard; the sound made her shiver. Rajik and Pamira ran back into the tent. Boy spoke quietly and the dogs streaked after them. High-pitched shrieks, two, three ... then a cry that was somehow even worse than the dogs: Pamira uttering a voiceless wail that carried the absolute understanding of what was happening to her now and what was going to happen in a few moments; a cry of desolation greater than all the deserts of all the worlds.

60

Manel

Manel knew her father had warned the blue-eyed man, Daniel, against any improper contact with her, and she respected his will as any daughter would. And as any daughter would, she knew the limits to that will and how to walk the perimeter without crossing the barrier. She hoped.

As the evening call to prayer sounded out for those believers in the city who followed the path, she waited in the courtyard by the gate until she heard the guard there refusing to let Daniel in, as the general was not at home. She summoned the man and told him to admit the visitor; he was an honoured guest and any disrespect would be reported to her father.

'Forgive our servants,' she said. 'Please, come in.'

'Thank you. I was beginning to wonder where I might settle for the night.'

'Like a bird,' she said.

'Like a bird indeed.'

His smile was open, friendly, respectful, everything she could
. . .

'It's very peaceful here after the city.'

The apricot trees were swaying in the evening breeze and the lamps were beginning to cast their magic glow across the tiles. She sat on the edge of a raised flower bed. He sat also, not too close, not too distant. His manners were, she thought, impeccable.

'The scent of the flowers is beautiful at this time of the evening,' he said. 'No wonder the poets tell us Paradise is a garden. It is a place to find oneself again. Who made such a wonderful place?'

She felt herself blushing. 'I . . . tried to make . . . a poor attempt but . . .'

'No, please, forgive me, but this is an oasis in the city. I think that only someone who has . . . great depths within, who has known both hope and suffering, could have made such a place.'

'You are far too kind, sir. I do not deserve . . . No, not at all. You are wrong, I cannot, I . . .'

She felt as if her whole body and soul were blushing and burst into tears. He stood up instantly. She hurried away, inside – deeply shaken and yet, somehow, pleased . . .

Later that night, shortly after General Qulan had returned home, the house resounded to the howls and cries of a youth being firmly and implacably beaten. After some time, Qulan appeared in the central chamber where he found Daniel waiting.

'General, I am sorry to disturb you.'

'Not at all. I was only helping my son remember that next time he will be present when his father returns home. What do you want?'

'I have some information that may be of use to you, sir.'

'Go on.'

61

al-Ghuri

The cloud-capped towers of Tumanbay were a riot of colour and movement; flags and banners fluttered gaily on the breeze and a thousand windows were filled with cheering citizens. The city walls were also lined a dozen deep with cheering crowds, many of them waving banners and flags made for this occasion. As the great gate opened, the streets revealed yet more deliriously happy folk welcoming back their victorious army; welcoming, above all, their glorious Sultan riding alone, at the head of his forces, the sun streaming off his golden armour like banners of light. The noise was immense – every bell in the city was ringing, peal after peal in concord with the mighty horns and trumpets of the army and the ground-shaking bass of the kettledrums.

Above the Great Eastern Gate, the Grand Vizier Cadali declaimed through a trumpet which magnified his words to heroic proportions:

'All hail our glorious Sultan. He brings us victory and peace! All hail al-Ghuri, Lion of Lions, Sultan of Eagles, Destroyer of Enemies, Father of the Peoples, Protector of the Poor ...'

On and on went the list of virtues, from the merely manly to the grandly godlike.

Al-Ghuri reined in his white charger and sat for a moment, regarding his city, basking in his glory. It had all been worth it – the plotting, the disposal of his elder brother, even the loss of Shajah – because they loved him, their Sultan; they gave their hearts to him, the Lion of Lions.

General Qulan cantered forward until he was level with his Sultan.

'Majesty, do I have permission to order your army to enter the city?'

'I hardly know what to say, General.'

'It is your victory, Majesty, your triumph.'

Truly it was; his tactics had turned the battle at the most crucial moment. He had seen more clearly than his commanders and the proof of it was on the spike of a lance: the head of Maya the Grim, long black hair loose in defeat, the face, even so, still handsome and his ... all his. Her eyes were shut. He wished there were some way to preserve life after beheading, so she could look down and taste the bitter aloes of her own defeat.

Qulan followed his gaze. 'Shall we show her to your people? Shall we let them cheer their great leader?'

'Very well, General, let us do so!'

Standing in the stirrups, Qulan raised his right hand and bellowed: 'The army will advance!'

On the command, the whole mass began to move forward. Al-Ghuri beckoned his nephew.

'Madu, ride with me.'

'The triumph is yours, Majesty. It's you the people want to see.'

He was delighted. 'Yes, and when we are done, have the bitch's head sent to my rooms.'

He looked up at her once more, swaying at the top of the lance – and she opened her eyes and looked back at him.

The smile fled from his face.

He opened his eyes, his heart thumping; even the scent of

'Flowers of the Desert Night' which infused his silken pillow didn't help to calm it. There was a pearly light creeping through the window shutters and he could hear the call to prayer sounding out over the city. He sighed; only a dream – but such a dream. Could it be a portent? He stretched and his right hand felt something on the pillow beside him. This time a cry of sheer terror escaped his lips. He leaped from the bed and staggered away from the awful thing.

The door burst open, a servant rushed in.

'Majesty, what is it?'

'Who was it?' he shrieked.

'What?'

'You were there all night in case I needed anything. Someone has come into my room and put it there . . .'

'Majesty, there was no one, I swear it.'

'You lie.'

'No one passed me.'

'You slept.'

'Impossible, Majesty.'

'Who can I trust?'

'Majesty, I have served you all my life.'

And yet there it was. A dagger, curved, the blue-black blade gleaming evilly. A warning, a dreadful warning. *We can get to you any time we want.* A warning and a message. *We could have killed you and we didn't.* What did it mean?

He picked up the weapon and shoved it out of sight in the depths of a cabinet, then locked the door on it and grasped the key in his fist.

'Guards! Guards!'

They could have killed him but they didn't.

The servant waited, white-faced and trembling.

Two of his personal guards crashed into the room, swords

334

drawn. Nobody must know that he was this vulnerable. The knowledge must die with . . .

'That man, he attacked me, he's a spy, a traitor. Throw him from the window.'

The servant fell to his knees. The guards paused but only for a moment – their habit was to obey. The servant barely struggled as they lifted him, opened the shutters and sent him falling to his death far below.

'You may go.'

They saluted and left him. They would not talk. They could not talk; their tongues had been torn out when they were selected as his guard. Their loyalty was absolute.

Al-Ghuri opened his fist and looked at the key that had locked away the mystery. It was time to act to show them – all of them – who he was: Lion of Lions, Sultan of Eagles, Destroyer of Enemies, Father of the Peoples, Protector of the Poor, and above all else, Sword of the Faith!

62
Gregor

Perhaps the bird of uneasy dreams had flown over the city that night, for when Gregor awoke in his deep chambers he was still carrying the weight of a journey made in sleep, over a high pass through deep snow, under a lowering sky which promised more snow before dark, before any chance of shelter. He was climbing, following the distant figure of Qulan, then there came a groan, as if the mountain itself was in pain, and everything seemed to tilt and shift and he was falling – turning slowly over and over in a cataract of white snow – falling farther and further away from hope. He screamed but the sound was lost in the wind – nobody would ever hear him, nobody would ever find him.

He woke with a feeling of dread in his belly, clambered from his cot and tipped a jug of cold water over his head and told himself it was just a dream. In his line of business there were often loose ends that tied themselves around the mind until . . .

A knocking at the door. Respectful, repeated, then insistent. He dried his face and turned the keys that secured his room. A guard, one of his men, held out his hand.

'Excellency, a messenger came. He told me I was to give you this.' In his palm lay a gold coin. 'The one who brought it said you would know.'

Gregor took the coin and dismissed the man. He had meetings

336

today. The Sultan needed his reassurance and he needed to establish his loyalty at a difficult time . . . and Effendi Red – what was he up to? He flipped the coin. It described a glittering arc and he snatched it out of the air. Yes, he had important meetings, but this was more important than any of them.

Good coffee is worth the effort and Ibn Bai loved making and drinking the first cup of the day – but not on this day, when the familiar pounding sounded at the front door just as he was about to take his first taste. Even so, he sipped as Commander Gregor erupted into the shady room.

'Coffee, Commander? It is the finest from—'

'Enough of your coffee. You sent your man with my coin.'

'I did.'

For once Ibn Bai felt that the balance between Gregor and himself was a little less than unequal, though he didn't for a moment underestimate the danger of the man who glowered impatiently at him across the coffee.

'Well, where is she?'

Ibn Bai finished the coffee, placed the cup on the tray and stepped back.

'Not here.'

Gregor slammed a fist onto the tray: coffee, cups, pot and spirit lamp all went flying.

'She came for her baby and you gave it to her? I told you what would happen if you betrayed me!'

Ibn Bai could have cooked up a second coffee on the heat of the fury that was coming off the commander.

'Do you think I would have called you if that had been so? Would I not have run to save my own worthless life?'

'You are a strange man, Ibn Bai, but you walk a narrow path. Please, enlighten me. Quickly.'

'Then come.'

Ibn Bai walked around the commander and into the baby's room, where the nurse stood beside the crib with the infant in her arms. Gregor followed.

'Mala has a message for you, Commander.'

'Well, girl?'

The nurse didn't answer.

'What's wrong with her?'

'She doesn't speak your language. Shall I question her on your behalf?'

'On your own behalf – my patience is short this morning, I do not have time for these games.'

Ibn Bai spoke rapidly to the maid in her own language.

'She says a spirit appeared in the night and gave her a message.'

'It is so,' the nurse said, 'even as I told you before.'

'What message?'

'The djinn told Mala that a man would come and that he is to take the baby to the City of the Dead.'

'This is absurd,' Gregor said. 'What is this place?'

His scepticism, if not his meaning, was clear enough to the nurse, who burst out: 'It is true, everyone knows there is a city of the dead down there.' She added in plain speech: 'Down, down, all many lost peoples down.'

'These are old wives' tales, to scare children and maids,' Gregor said. 'There's nothing in the catacombs except a few starving escaped convicts scrabbling in the dark.'

'Nonetheless, Commander, that's where you are to take her child.'

'Why should I?'

The nurse spoke again in plain. 'Mama say: You give me, I give you.'

The words echoed in his memory from that first meeting with Sarah: *You give me something and I give you something.*

'And if she is telling the truth, where do these djinns come from? How do they rise up from the underworld?'

The maid whispered to Ibn Bai, who said: 'The old Temple of Solace. She says that is where you will find what you seek.'

Gregor's first master in the art of spying and catching spies, and his predecessor as Commander of the Palace Guard, had set his pupil an exercise: every morning he was to walk around the palace and establish the ever-shifting position of the officials and courtiers – who was up, who down – and he was not to do this through the reading of reports or conversation or threats but through his skin, as the old master put it.

'Absorb the feelings, Gregor, as if you were a sponge on a reef in the Sea of Corals. Sift the air as if they were currents of seawater. Taste them, don't place any demands or expectations, simply accept what you feel and, above all, learn to trust those feelings.'

It had taken years – even after he had betrayed his master and assumed his place – before he had come fully to trust those feelings, but now he accepted them as the most important aspect of his work. Research, reports, betrayals and confessions were an invaluable tool, but the ability to sniff out treachery – or, on this morning, the icy grip of failure and its consequences – stood above them all. After he had emerged from his interview with the jurists, everything had changed.

Tumanbay's courtiers and officials were professionals in the art of survival and to a man and woman they had avoided his look, stepping out of his path, turning aside his greetings and sending apologies to his summons. They were seeing a man who was on the way out. The First Wife was dead, and the official who should have protected her was likely to be so himself unless he came up with some answers.

Even Cadali had smiled in sympathy after the meeting. He evidently no longer considered Gregor to be a rival. He had put a meaty arm about his shoulders and murmured, as if he didn't want anyone else to hear him talk with the plague dog.

'The Sultan will wish to see you this afternoon at the tenth hour, my friend. He is ... upset, nervous, he does not know which way to turn or who his loyal subjects are any more.'

'Except for you, Cadali?'

'Except for me, indeed. And you, Gregor, you would do well to have answers and not excuses this time. My advice was to run, you chose to ignore it.'

'And you chose to recommend the death sentence.'

'It would have been quick and clean, my friend. Much as I would have enjoyed seeing you under the torture, I am a compassionate man. I was doing you a favour.'

'One I hope to return, Cadali, in good time.'

'Or bad. Gregor, find out what happened or find a fast horse.'

The Vizier went on his way, leaving Gregor considering the matter in an alcove.

He needed something to offer, the fat snake was right about that. He had nothing. No suspects, no scrolls – surely the motive for the killing – and no picture in his mind of what had happened. Could he even trust his own guards? He had betrayed and murdered his master, and was certain there was no shortage of diverse hands in the Palace Guard ready to betray him and take his position. It was how things were done here. He might as well offer his throat to the knife as ask for help. He was on his own. He needed results and he needed them fast. Whatever the risk of searching for Sarah in this so-called underworld and of trusting himself to its denizens, it was better than arriving empty-handed – or worse, with lies and excuses – before al-Ghuri at the tenth hour.

Thus it was that Commander Gregor walked slowly across the square in front of the crumbling facade of the Temple of Solace. The baby gurgled; it had been fed before they left the slave merchant's house and seemed content. Away from the bustling markets and commercial sectors, this was a crumbling, unloved part of the city, a surviving corner of the old world, rarely visited by most of Tumanbay's inhabitants, who had little interest in the ancient beliefs and cultures. As Gregor approached there was no one around apart from an old beggar squatting on the temple steps with his bowl. As he got closer Gregor saw the fellow had empty eye sockets, presumably the better to excite the generosity of temple goers, not that he seemed to be having much luck.

'Do you seek solitude at the Temple of Solace, my son? For it does not look as if you need alms or food.'

'How do you know what I look like, old man? You've no eyes.'

The ancient cackled as ancients have cackled since the dawn of time.

'There are more ways of seeing than with those lumps of jelly, young man. I sit and I listen and I smell . . .' He sniffed. 'I have served here for many years, there's not much I haven't met.'

'Looks more like begging to me.' Gregor was getting impatient with the old fake, but just in case he said: 'So what do you see?'

'A fine man in the pomp of his years. Clever, powerful, with a baby –' he sniffed – 'full of mother's milk – and yet a man who has lost something.'

Gregor's sword whispered from its scabbard, the point hovering at the old man's throat.

'It seems you know a sight too much for your own good.'

'All I know, sir, is what you tell me yourself. And what you have lost, what sews a thread of fear in the cloak of power and privilege you carry about you – that is something else, from long ago.' With a forefinger he moved the point away from his throat. 'Your sword will be like my stick, it will be your guide when you need it.' He sniffed and nodded.

Gregor sheathed the sword. 'Tell me something useful or be damned.'

'Alms for the temple.'

A coin flipped into the bowl.

'Gold, master?'

'I expect value for my money or next time the sword won't go home unblooded. I want to get into the undercity.'

'No,' the old man said, 'you do not.'

Gregor waited. Somewhere, high above on the temple spires, he could hear a banner cracking in the wind, but no hint of a breeze reached them down here. At length the beggar sighed.

'Very well, effendi. Enter the temple, go to the wooden stair. At the foot of the steps are tiles, very beautifully patterned – one of the patterns is a keyhole. Find it, use this key, leave it in place, shut the hidden door behind you.'

A key, as long as a man's forearm, had appeared in the beggar's hand. Gregor took it; it weighed no more than a feather.

'I'll need to keep the key to get out again.'

'You won't get out, not on your own.'

The beggar had told the truth. The keyhole took some finding in the pattern, but on turning the key, a spring had lifted the tiles, revealing spiral steps leading down into darkness. He crouched down, cradling the sleeping child against his thigh, while he struck the flint to light the lantern Ibn Bai had thrust into his hands as he was leaving the house. He was grateful for the slave trader's foresight.

342

Holding the lantern up, he moved slowly down, each step a step into the unknown. And then there were no more steps – the floor was level and he was in a narrow passageway. As he moved along it, he could hear a distant and constant rumble, like a huge millstone grinding, and it was warm, hot even; a trickle of sweat ran down his nose and he wiped it away. The baby stirred uneasily and began to wriggle in his arms.

'Be still,' he said.

It didn't seem to work. The child started to cry and Gregor rocked her back and forth, trying to soothe her as he crept forward. Ahead, the passageway opened up and then divided into two. Gregor stopped, unsure of how to proceed.

'Hello?' he called out, and heard his voice, and the child's cry, echo all around. He waited, listening for any response.

As he continued along the larger of the passageways, he became aware of a draught, pushing against him, as if urging him back. But he continued. He had the baby, and Sarah wanted that more than anything. Her need was his defence.

Just as the child sank back into sleep, the lamp blew out and they were in absolute darkness. It pressed close about him; he could feel it like spiders' webs wrapping him, trapping him . . . He thrust the thought aside and drew his sword, holding it before him, recalling the beggar's words with a wry smile. The fellow definitely knew more than he should.

'Hello? Hello?' he called out several times, moving by feel alone, his fingers on the roughcast wall, each step a step into the unknown.

'Hello?'

Nothing. Then something. He stopped and listened intently: footsteps, running, far off, echoing through the passageways. Then behind him – he spun around. What was it? Again, closer – a child's laugh.

'Who's there?' Gregor called. 'Hello?'

Silence again. Gregor sighed and continued in the darkness, no longer sure if he was moving forwards or backwards. If this was some kind of fool's errand, he decided, he would return with his Palace Guard and have the whole place filled in.

He heard footsteps close by, approaching fast. He stopped and leaned against the wall. Then he felt a sudden rush of air as a body passed close to him.

'You, stop! In the name of the Sultan, make yourself known.'

A laugh again. He moved forward, waving the end of his sword. It touched stone. He slid it left – more stone; right – nothing. He shuffled towards the turn, felt the stone, then felt nothing; grit under his feet . . . and at last a voice – an old woman.

'Who comes?'

He called: 'I mean you no harm.'

A laugh, shockingly close to his ear – he swung his sword: nothing.

'Harm? What harm?' A younger voice, and a third, from behind: 'Who could harm us?'

The old woman again: 'We are the people, this is our place.'

'Ours alone.'

He swung to face the invisible presence behind him.

'I am looking for someone. If you help me there will be no trouble.'

The old woman: 'Trouble – you say that to *us*?'

Laughter snickered around him, gleeful and more than half insane. He could do nothing but go on. He stepped forward.

'A slave girl. Sarah. I have her child here. Sarah, I'm looking for Sarah.'

This time the ancient voice questioned: 'Why do you look where you cannot see?'

'She is under my protection.'

344

A wave of laughter, mocking. The baby started to cry again. 'The child, give us the child.'

He waved his sword in a pattern, hoping to cut off any advance. Even so hands touched him, brushed across his face; fingers ran down his back, pulled his hair, held his wrist in a grip as cruel as the questioner's pincers and made him cry out and let go of the baby – and then they were gone.

'Wait, the child, give her back, she's mine, I need her . . .'

Was he begging? Truly he was lost down here. He lowered his sword, slipped it back into the scabbard – it would do him no good – and took a breath, trying to find himself again. This damned darkness was no help at all. He should have brought a lamp.

'Where are you? Show yourselves. I am the Commander of the Palace Guard.'

He walked forward, hit something. Bars, metal bars and a door clanged shut behind him.

'Not down here, you're not.'

What a fool!

He had walked into a trap like the rawest recruit.

'I'll have you arrested. I'll . . .'

He stopped. A caged man making threats in the darkness. It was absurd and chilling at the same time.

The old woman spoke again. 'We know who you are, Gregor. Welcome to the grave.'

'I warn you . . .' he said.

'Your warning days are over, dearie.' The old woman's voice came back at him.

A masculine voice, deep as the pit in which he was trapped, boomed out: 'Now you must answer the charges.'

Gregor scoffed. 'What are you talking about? Let me see you, show yourselves.'

Metal striking stone – sparks flying and dying in the darkness – and again; fire drawn from flint and steel, flame leaping
up yellow behind glass, at first one lamp then two, three, lights
appearing all around him, revealing rock looming away into
the darkness, lighting the wall of pale faces before him, rank
upon rank of them, the old, the young, the vigorous and sick, the
dark-mirror image of Tumanbay gazing at him with a voracious
hunger.

The crone, and truly she was well-named, stood nearby hanging on to a tall stick, her body shrouded in dark robes.

'Ankur will be your judge. I will play the Sultan and pass
sentence.'

Were they really going to do this?

'It's madness,' Gregor said. 'Who are you people? You have
no right. I know nothing of any crimes. Who are you to try me?'

Figures emerged out of the crowd and walked towards him.
Men, women, children standing in a semicircle . . .

'I have the right, for you took my husband and I never saw
him again . . . You took my brother and he was hanged for no
crime save hunger . . . My sister, dishonoured by your police . . .
by your order . . . at your hands . . . in your cellars . . . under your
torture . . .'

So many fathers, mothers, wives and husbands, sons and
sisters and daughters and brothers . . . and the dreary litany of
accusation, the record of his public career laid before him.

'And now –' the booming voice of Ankur 'the judge', enthroned
upon a vast rock that glittered in the lamplight with veins of
quartz – 'now you must answer for the lives you caused to be
snuffed out in your torture chambers or to waste away in your
cells. For the families that suffered and starved and lost all they
had, and yet were innocent of any crime.'

Well, they could only kill him once – he hoped – so he

might as well go down as the man he was.

'Everything I did was for the greater good of Tumanbay. This was policy, not accident.'

A shiver ran through the multitude.

'There are enemies everywhere. If we once show weakness, anarchy rules. There must be control or nothing is possible.'

The crowd parted and a boy emerged. He was a child of no more than eight, wearing clothes, now dusty and frayed, that spoke of the middle classes of Tumanbay. Possibly the child of an official, Gregor thought.

'And what about poor Basim?' the child asked.

'Basim?'

Gregor shook his head. He had no idea what the boy was talking about.

'Officer of the Palace Guard. Your officer. A good soldier. Loyal to his masters. Strangled in the palace dungeons.'

'He must have done something or he would not have been there in the first place.'

The 'judge' leaned forward. 'The prisoner should remember where he stands at this moment. He is not helping his case.'

'Damn my case and damn you too. Basim – who in the seven hells is Basim?'

The boy came right up to the bars. Gregor could have reached through and grabbed his robe. He even thought about it until a young man appeared holding a scimitar and, grinning, shook his head.

'Don't, or I'll have your hand, Gregor, as sure as you had my brother's head on a spike over the Great Gate.'

The boy went on: 'My father Basim made one mistake. He allowed a man to see the Sultan.'

'Yes, I remember him now. He failed to do his job. The man threw a severed head down in front of our beloved ruler. It was an insult not just to him, but to Tumanbay. This officer failed to protect the Sultan.'

The crone stepped forward. 'As you failed to protect the Sultan's First Wife. And yet you escaped punishment above.'

'I'll not take any more part in this farce!' Gregor shouted. 'Who are you? The dregs and drainings of the city. Do your worst. I wouldn't waste my spit on you.'

'Then you have condemned yourself to the worst we can do.'

The boy regarded Gregor with a calm stare which, like his words, seemed far too old for one of his age.

'Gregor,' he said, 'my father rarely talked about his work – he didn't want his family to know such things – but I do remember once he told us that the great Commander Gregor was afraid of nothing . . . except bats. So be it.'

He stepped back and, as he did so, the lamps began to go out one by one. There was a rustling as of leathery wings, a chittering as of tiny claws on quartz rock, a million tiny lights as the last flames of the lamps caught the bright feral eyes of a multitude of bats, and then there was darkness and they were all about him.

And Gregor screamed.

63

al-Ghuri

The Sultan was anxious. The Vizier Cadali, adept at reading his master's moods, had no idea why but was, as ever, alert to the possibilities of the situation. His first concern: to place a body between him and the Sultan, so he sent for Theros, the physician, who immediately read the direction of the wind and was extremely uneasy.

'Why, Majesty,' Theros asked, summoning up all of his scholarly gravity, 'do you not care to eat?'

As if explaining something obvious to a child, al-Ghuri said: 'These are the very same sort of dates that poisoned my nephew. How can I trust them?'

'You ate them yesterday, Majesty.'

'And this is today.'

'True, true. But consider, Majesty, your taster has eaten them and there he stands, quite well.' Actually the man had a distinctly wan look about him, but then he always did. Imperial Taster wasn't a position that promised longevity in Tumanbay. 'Perhaps you are out of sorts. An enema ...' Theros suggested tentatively.

'Enema! Always it's the enema with you. But you are wrong. Not enema but enemies – I have enemies all around me. The hand that offers dates hides the dagger in its sleeve.'

349

Theros nodded sagely, but he had no idea what the Sultan was talking about.

'You have been under a great strain,' he said.

'From your idiocies!'

'My Lord, perhaps these petals from the Rose of—'

'Gahhh!' Al-Ghuri knocked the dried petals from the physician's trembling grasp. 'Get out, get out, I'm done with you!'

Leaving petals and dignity behind, Theros scurried for the door, passing General Qulan with a muttered: 'Bad day, storms ahead.'

Qulan raised an eyebrow and said, 'May I enter, Majesty, or do you wish to be alone?'

Regarding him through narrow, suspicious eyes, al-Ghuri beckoned him in.

'I wish to be safe, General. These fools . . . I can't have them around me any more. I am accounted a man able to read other men and yet now . . .'

Languidly he reached out and took a date from a silver bowl on the groaning breakfast table and ate it. Qulan walked forward and stood waiting.

The Sultan's eyes were suddenly very round and he whispered: 'I just ate a date without even thinking.'

'They look very good, Majesty.'

'Well, you wouldn't poison dates that looked like rubbish, would you? One moment of inattention . . . if they are poisoned.'

He slumped back onto his couch.

Without being asked, Qulan reached out, picked up a date and popped it in his mouth.

'Well, then,' he said, spitting the stone out, 'we'll both be dead men.'

But the suspicion of Sultans is not to be easily set aside.

'Maybe you know which dates are poisoned and which are not.'

'If you can tell dates apart, then you are a shrewder judge than I am, Majesty. May we get to business and leave our digestions to God?'

'Very well, General. Go on.'

'My scouts have informed me that Maya's forces have crossed into Emerald Province.'

Al-Ghuri picked up a date and ate it.

'So you say.'

'We need to hit her as soon as we can, and hit her hard.'

Al-Ghuri seemed unconvinced. 'Perhaps we should concentrate on finding these scrolls. That's what Maya wants. If we have them, they will give us time.'

'Time for what? We don't need time, she does.'

Al-Ghuri leaned forward and emphasised his words, tapping the table as he spoke.

'She already has spies in the city. They know all we do. They killed my First Wife.'

'If Maya's spies killed her, then they already have the scrolls.'

'What do you mean?'

'They were in Shajah's possession.'

The Sultan reared back, as if Qulan's words bore real poison.

'Nonsense. How can you know such things?'

'I am your general. It is my business to know such things.'

Al-Ghuri regarded 'his' general. How much does he know, he wondered. Does he know about this morning, the dagger? Is this the beginning of his move to take the Empire?

The silence stretched until Qulan broke it.

'I know what I must to defend Tumanbay, and your throne, Majesty.'

'Does His Majesty's throne need defending?'

351

Cadali's question hung in the room unanswered. No doors had opened, no curtains moved – he had appeared from nowhere, unless he'd been there all the time.

'Yes, where is your brother, General? We need to double the guards. Treble them. Where is Commander Gregor?'

'Yes, where is Commander Gregor?' echoed Cadali. 'We were meant to meet this morning to discuss the Sultan's security but –' he tilted his head, eyeing Qulan if he were to blame for Gregor's absence – 'he was nowhere to be seen.'

'And the envoy?' the Sultan enquired. 'I thought Gregor was keeping an eye on him.'

'Effendi Red is waiting outside. Shall I call him?'

'I don't want to see him. We have nothing to offer until we find what he seeks.' Al-Ghuri took another date, regarded it, handed it to Cadali, who examined it and put it back in the bowl. 'He would hardly ask for it if, as you say, General, he has it already.'

Qulan could contain himself no more: this was a council of fools.

'Majesty, these scrolls are no more than an excuse, created to confuse us, put us on the wrong track. She seeks to divide and undermine our resolve. Whatever we offer, she will want more until finally her armies stand outside our walls. We must act and act now!'

'That is one course of action, of course,' Cadali said, 'but there are others. It seems to me this rush to arms betrays our fear of Maya. In fact, we are not afraid of her. This city has stood for a thousand years, it shows our power, it *is* our power. We'll root out her spies and find these . . . these scrolls, or whatever she says is so important to her, and then we'll see.'

'No, Majesty, let me meet her in battle. We'll cut off her damn head, put it on a lance and then,' Qulan said, pointedly looking at Cadali, '*then* . . . we'll see.'

Al-Ghuri contemplated his general and Vizier sombrely. No doubt Tumanbay would stand whatever course of action he took, but what about him, Sultan al-Ghuri? Would *he* still stand? What of the dagger – was it his Vizier who placed it on his pillow? His General? And where was his spymaster? Who could he trust?

'Majesty,' Qulan continued, breaking the uneasy silence, 'give me permission to go back to my army and—'

'Your army? No, no, no. No! I want to keep you close, General. Cadali, tell the envoy to come back tomorrow. I don't want to see him.'

Cadali bowed. 'As you wish, Majesty.'

Al-Ghuri slumped back onto his couch.

'And send me the physician,' he called out as Cadali disappeared from sight.

64

Wolf

Wolf was feeling uncomfortable under the stony, suspicious gaze of the guard outside the Council Chamber. If he didn't stop soon, he was going to have to teach the fellow a lesson. He got up from the bench where he was sitting and started forward as the chamber door burst open and Qulan came through at speed, not bothering to close it behind him. Wolf fell in beside him.

'What happened in there, General? Are we ready to ride?'

'No. We're not going back to the army.'

'That's crazy.'

Qulan held up a hand and shook his head. He said no more until they had left the palace and were in the stables where their mounts were waiting. It was still early and the sun hadn't yet reached the high walled yard. Piles of manure steamed and pools of water and urine puddled the cobbles. Wolf took a deep breath.

'No damned perfumes here, just honest horse shit and pools of piss.' He beamed.

Qulan spoke quietly. 'The Sultan is a frightened man, scared for his own life. A man who is afraid to die will never be any good in a fight. Our greatest weakness is our leader. There, I've said it – treason.'

'More like horse sense,' Wolf grunted. 'You know where my loyalty lies. There's been too much talking, it's time to act.'

354

'What are you saying, Wolf?'

'We return to the army. Prepare for battle. We engage and destroy Maya's army. If the Sultan can't give the command, you must.'

'It will be difficult for both of us to leave, they will be watching.'

'Then order the army to come to us. Send a messenger. Now. Do you have a man you can trust?'

'One of my servants. Not a soldier. No one will notice.'

'Then do it and be damned to the consequences.'

'Or be damned to us.'

65

Manel

'The last time we talked, Manel, you were upset. If it was anything I said . . .'

Daniel left the sentence unfinished but she felt again that oddness, that mix of emotions long suppressed, that had struck her so strongly that first night when she had burst into tears. Part of her despised herself for giving way to emotion so easily. Her father would not have approved, quite beyond his fury had he known of the conversation itself, and yet Daniel seemed so . . . attuned to her feelings, so unlike her father and the few other men she had met.

She smiled and said, 'It was nothing you said. Don't concern yourself.'

'I am concerned. You have been kind to me, Manel.'

'No, no, it was . . . It wasn't . . .'

They both laughed.

'I'm sure it was,' he said. 'I am happy that you are happy. When you laugh . . .' He blushed, shook his head. 'I'm getting this all wrong.'

'You can talk about laughs and smiles all you want.'

He reached out and touched her shoulder. It was the first time she had ever been touched by a man who wasn't her father or her little brother.

'And kisses, Manel – what if I were to talk about kisses?'

A door opening and closing, footsteps approaching.

They moved rapidly apart and she said: 'My father is not here, I am afraid. I do not know when he will be back. I will inform him of your visit.'

Daniel bowed slightly, his head to one side, smiling.

'Thank you.' He turned to go.

Manel felt that the subterfuge was an acceptance of the words between them, the touch, the idea of kisses . . .

Qulan entered the room.

'No, wait, Daniel, I am here. Manel.'

'Father.'

He barely nodded to her.

'Daniel, I need you, with me now.'

He strode into the inner, more private room, what he called his war room, where campaigns were planned.

Daniel looked at her, his blue eyes intense.

'You didn't answer my question.'

Manel leaned forward, held up her head and, for an eternal moment, their lips touched and then he was gone.

'Coming, General.'

'Sit down. Your friend Madu, how is he?'

The room was in twilight, long drapes excluding the morning sun.

'He seems well enough, General.'

'Does he have ambitions?'

'Hard to tell. He's inclined to sit and write poetry and enjoy himself but . . .'

'Stay close to him, Daniel. He could be useful to us.'

'To "us", General?'

A dagger lay on the low table. No decoration, all business. Qulan laid his right hand across the blade of blued steel.

'That's right. I'm going to save Tumanbay. Does Madu trust you?'

'It's hard to be certain.'

'I need to know. Find out.'

66

Gregor

Gregor was woken by his own coughing. He was alone. It was dark. His heart was still racing as if it might burst, but he breathed slowly and deeply, and gradually it settled. He was lying in the dust, on a rough stone floor. His hands felt heavy, weighted down by something. As he adjusted his position to sit up, he heard a scraping sound echo through the chamber. Someone was coming.

No. Silence.

He moved again and the sound returned. It was the chain attached to the manacles about his wrists. He pulled at it, taking in the slack, and then gave it a hard tug. It held firm.

He lifted his hands to his face, ran his fingertips over his flesh. It was rough and scabbed. The bats – a million claws tearing at his flesh. He shuddered and remembered the pain, but felt none now. The wounds had healed over – he must have been here for some time. But he recalled nothing beyond the bats. He could smell the sour stink of vomit, his own fear dredged from his belly. He was thirsty, so thirsty.

He stood up and waited, listening for any sounds, any movement.

Nothing.

His thoughts seemed to be moving like clouds across his

mind – he found it impossible to control them or to concentrate on anything for longer than a few moments. Had they given him some potion, a spray, smoke – there had been smoke from the lamps – something that would have disordered his senses? He tried to remember ... but the sheer overmastering fear blotted out everything. Often enough, he had extorted confession by discovering the hidden fear of his subject, working on it, building it until they would do anything, betray anyone, to avoid it. Now he knew what it felt like to be strapped on the torture table facing the worst thing in the world.

How long had he been standing? He didn't know. He'd forgotten. His legs were feeling weary. It must have been a long time. He sat down and leaned against the wall; the only sound was the chain and his breathing. His breathing, that was all there was – darkness and breath, nothingness and life, side by side, there was nothing else. He closed his eyes and felt sleep pulling him away towards other worlds, other lives.

It was a disturbed sleep. Every time he moved, the scraping of the chain woke him and he jerked up, waiting for someone to return, his heart frantically beating against the wall of his chest. Once he fancied he heard the baby crying some distance away, getting closer.

He tried to concentrate, listening hard, but drifted back into sleep – a baby crying in a hut, the wind howling outside, and he, Gregor, and three or four brothers and sisters, huddled together eating roots that his father had gathered.

'Wait a few more days,' his mother had said, but his father was determined.

'The snows are coming,' he said, 'He will have his best chance if we do it now.'

His older sister was looking at him as if she knew something he didn't, and as his father put on his boots, she shared her remaining food with him and ruffled his hair. He tried to brush her hand away, but she wouldn't let go. Now she was pulling at his hair. He cried out and reached up, and the chain knocked against his head. He felt a sharp pain, but it wasn't from the chain, it was from a bright light held close to his face. He could smell the lampblack, the oil ...

When his eyes adjusted he could see several people staring down at him. White faces hanging in the darkness like ... severed heads floating there. They moved in and out of his vision. One had ancient leathery skin, another an opaque, cloudy eye, a third, a gaping wound where an ear should have been, and ...

'Sarah,' Gregor muttered, his voice cracked.

Her blue eyes were unmistakable. And then she was gone, and there was a grinning, toothless, old woman. She was holding up a cup.

'Are you thirsty?' she asked.

Gregor muttered his thanks and reached out. As he did so, she tipped the water onto the floor. Gregor tried to thrust his head beneath it to capture a few drops, but the old woman's grip on his hair was firm.

'You won't be seeing us again,' she said at last, releasing him.

Gregor slumped to the floor. He could feel the dampness against his cheek and stuck out his swollen tongue to lick the moist dirt. He lay there for a while, his eyes closed, listening, expecting the worst. But what he heard was footsteps retreating. He opened his eyes and saw shadows slithering around the uneven ceiling of the cavern as the group dispersed.

'What do you mean?' he cried out. 'Where are you going? I need water. Please!'

He was alone once more. Was this his sentence? To be shackled to a wall in darkness, scrabbling for cockroaches to eat until

Part Five

67

Madu

Kids on kites were flying over the city walls. Madu could hear their shouts of pleasure and warning as the long lines to those on the ground risked getting tangled. He knew a number of skyrats died every year, but he had always rather wanted to join the company of those who flew free above the city and its concerns.

'Well, I'm glad you've found something more interesting than me to look at,' Daniel said.

He was lying on the couch, naked. Madu left the window and sat beside him, leaning forward to kiss him deeply, enjoying the roughness of his cheeks.

'I should shave.'

'I don't mind your stubble,' Madu laughed. 'I'm a soldier. I'm used to it.'

'Not used to this, I think.' Daniel grasped him and Madu gasped. 'The good soldier always has his lance to hand.'

After they rolled apart and Daniel had fetched a copper bowl of warm water and cloths, Madu said: 'It's how my father died.'

'In bed with his lover?'

'Under the hand of the barber.'

'He was al-Ghuri's brother, yes?'

'Elder brother. Good ruler too, so everyone says. Al-Ghuri was obsessed by my mother and they plotted together.'

'She wasn't the First Wife then?'

'No, she was young, down the list, but beautiful enough to attract jealousy.'

'And they killed him. How?'

Daniel carried the bowl to the window and emptied it out. An angry shout rose up from below and both young men laughed.

'They poisoned the blade of the barber's razor. One nick and the Sultan died in agony hours later. They were never anywhere near and the barber was long gone, probably a paid assassin. Then they killed off the First Wife and the rest of the hareem and the children. There were a lot of them. Is it any wonder I hate this place? It's a pit of snakes.'

'It's that all right,' Daniel said.

He was knotting his belt. Madu took hold of it and pulled him close and kissed him.

'I never wanted to be Sultan, I just want us to be together and for everyone to leave us alone.'

'My dear man, that's not going to happen, not in this world.'

'I'm serious, this isn't some kind of joke, Daniel. We can make it happen.'

'How?'

'Run away.'

Madu could see Daniel considering it and then he said: 'Madu, you are the cleverest man in Tumanbay!' He laughed delightedly and kissed Madu. Once, twice and, 'Three for luck if we are actually stupid enough to try this.'

'But you're still a slave,' Madu said. 'I'd be all right, but if they caught you, they'd execute you.'

'Then we'd better not get caught.'

Madu couldn't be sure . . . did he mean it? Did they really love each other? He certainly loved Daniel, he had no doubt about that.

'Seriously, Madu, I will go anywhere with you, just say the word.'

'The word is, "I love you".'

'That, my dear man, is three words,' Daniel said, moving away.

'Where are you going?' Madu asked.

'My work. Serving Tumanbay. We can plot and plan later,' he said, and disappeared out of the door.

68

Manel

Manel thought she would go anywhere with blue-eyed Daniel. She'd never felt like this before.

She said: 'And when will the battle commence?'

What she wanted to say was: Kiss me, hold me, take me away from here.

Daniel put the tiny coffee cup down with exaggerated care.

'When your father wishes it to begin, then it will begin. This is a very beautiful cup. At first it seems plain but when you look closely, it reveals many details and you understand that decoration and show mean very little when set against true beauty.'

'It was given to him by . . . by . . . I forget.'

'By someone who appreciated beauty.'

The sound of water falling in the bowl of the fountain in the gardens outside was very loud, and the sound of doves and the sound of a bell somewhere far across the city.

'When it happens, this battle . . .'

She wanted to say: you will take care – but how stupid to ask a soldier to take care.

'General Qulan knows his business, you need have no fear for him.'

'For you,' she said. 'For you, for you.'

And realised she had spoken aloud, so what was there left to lose. Her modesty was gone. She threw her arms around him. Feeling him, his body, his heartbeat and breath ...

She felt his arms holding her but he said, urgently: 'Not here, my dear woman, not in your parents' house.'

'I don't care, I would do anything.'

His hands took her upper arms – firmly but so respectfully – and pushed her gently away.

'Then be wise for me, dear Manel, and let us act with care and make a future for us in which we will be free to love and hold and ... flourish.'

He kissed her once, twice and 'three times for the luck' – and then they were apart, on different sides of the room (how had Daniel done that?) as Qulan entered.

As usual lately, he was gruff and snapped, 'Where is your brother?'

'I haven't seen him this morning, Father. Do you wish coffee?'

'Yes, now. Is he using his time wisely, to better himself? Good day, Daniel. Have you the maps I requested?'

'Yes, General. I will get them at once.'

'You ...'

Qulan fixed a servant with his terrible eye. The man's knees quaked.

'Master?'

'Get my son. If he's still in bed, beat him. Beat him anyway, he should be up and about. Why was I cursed with a lazy son who—?'

He was interrupted by hammering at the door to the compound, as if ten battering rams were at work out there. Manel made a move to go and see what was happening but he held her back with a gesture.

'Daniel, see to it.'

This time, Manel felt the sound of the fountain in the silence was ominous rather than promising. Absently she poured her father coffee and absently he drank it. Presently Daniel returned with two officers from the Palace Guard. Qulan stood.

'What do you want?'

The senior officer took a sheet from the satchel he carried.

'General Qulan, you are to come with us.'

His voice quavered; to Manel it looked as if he were scared half to death.

'Why?'

The officer cleared his throat but when he spoke his voice was husky with nerves.

'Are you going to come peacefully or shall I call my men?'

Daniel had slipped to the far corner of the room, where two spears and a shield, antique but still functional, served as a soldierly decoration. He reached out for one. Qulan shook his head. Daniel's arm fell to his side, his hand empty.

'Am I to understand that you are arresting me. By whose authority?'

The officer held out the sheet of parchment. His hand shook.

'The Sultan's.'

Qulan took the sheet and ran his eye down it.

'I see, it is like that.'

'Sir, General!' the officer burst out. 'I served under you at the Pharmeon Fields and the Bridge of Montuk. I don't want to be here but it is my duty to obey my orders.'

An appeal to duty. It was, Manel thought, the one thing that would ensure her father accompanied the guards without trouble.

Daniel stepped forward. 'General, what should I do?'

'Do nothing. Serve the Sultan loyally. And look after my family.'

'My life on it, General.'

Pushkarmi entered the room, her hair still undone and falling about her shoulders.

'Husband, what is . . .?'

Manel moved to her mother's side and took her hand.

'Guards,' she whispered, 'from the palace.'

Qulan joined them. 'It seems, my dear, I may have to leave you.'

Manel felt her mother tense, straighten her back, lift her chin and look at the guards with a cold, hard stare. She was a woman who would allow no one to intimidate her.

'What will be, will be,' she said. 'Let them know that General Qulan has never done an ignoble act nor a disloyal one.'

Qulan nodded, even his stone face visibly moved.

'Remember what I told you if this day ever came?'

'All will be done as you wish, husband.'

He moved close to his wife. Manel saw his lips moving but stepped back as her brother careered into the room and came to a standing stop just short of the guards. Pesha had been a skyrat for some months and his clothes and style reflected this, though fortunately his father remained ignorant of the fact. Manel had long feared the explosion that would come when he found out – but now everything was changed.

'Father, what's happening?'

'Ah, Pesha, you join us at last.'

'Who are these men?'

'Messengers, no more. Now, my boy, I had wanted more time to prepare you for this world. I may have seemed harsh, you will understand why one day.'

'General . . .' The officer waved the warrant ineffectually. 'We need to go.'

'Of course. Pesha, take care of your mother and sister. I place that duty upon you, my son.'

Tears in his eyes, Pesha nodded. Qulan strode to the door, looked around the room, fixing it in his mind's eye, and walked out, followed by the Palace Guards who scurried in his wake. Manel, Pushkarmi, Pesha and Daniel remained frozen until the compound gate slammed. Then daughter and son cleaved to their mother and the three of them held each other as if each might fall if the others let go for an instant.

Manel said: 'Daniel, find out what you can.'

'There must be some mistake. I'll go to the palace.'

'Be careful.'

'Don't worry, I know a way . . . a secret way.'

Their eyes met and said what their lips could not and then he was gone.

Pushkarmi took a deep breath. 'Very well, we have work to do. Your father's papers, the gold he has in store, all this must be moved, hidden . . . Hurry now, hurry.'

69

Madu

Through winding valleys where storm
Denies the lover's quest,
Cross wave girt ocean and endless seas,
Where sailors bold reclaim the west . . .

Was 'wave girt ocean' right? Surely that meant waves around the edge rather than everywhere. Madu sucked the end of the feather and plunged the nib into the ink pot. 'Wave raddled oceans'? No, hardly. 'Wave specked'?

Closer but not right. It needed to show how the lover overcame perils and obstacles to obtain—

A knock, *their* knock. He slipped the pen into the pot and let Daniel in. He could see at once that something was wrong.

'The Sultan has had the General arrested.'

'I'd heard something. I tried to get a message to you. It's all gone insane here – no one knows what's happening.'

'But, Qulan?' Daniel was pale, shocked, something Madu had never seen before. 'He's the most loyal of the loyal.'

'They say he's been plotting to march the army on Tumanbay.'

'Who says?'

'The Vizier Cadali.'

'I simply don't believe it's true, Madu. I've been in his house.

I would know if he'd planned anything like this. You know the man. He simply wouldn't do that.'

Madu went back to his desk. 'The Sultan is seeing traitors everywhere. They say he's started to wear armour in bed! What are you looking at?'

Daniel was leaning out of the window. 'There are soldiers down there. Palace Guards.'

'It's a purge. I heard there have already been executions. I don't know. It's all . . . hateful really.'

'Are you safe?' Madu heard real concern in Daniel's voice and his heart leaped a little.

'I think he trusts me, even though I was with the army. Besides, I would have been first. In these things you always kill the heir first.'

'At least that's good news. I have to go.' He ran his hand quickly through Madu's hair and then hurried to the door. 'I need to get a message to Wolf before this beast consumes us all.'

Madu tapped the nib against the edge of the ink pot and wrote:

Through winding valleys where storm
Denies the lover's quest,
Across all-consuming wave and endless sea,
Where sailors bold reclaim the west . . .

Yes, that was better, that's how poetry was done: sheer inspiration.

70
Wolf

Dawn was creeping across the windowsill and placing its rosy fingertips upon the buttocks of Wolf the Barbarian as he stirred and the covers fell away. He grunted and woke, sitting and climbing out of the rumpled bed in one easy movement. He stood for a moment, looking at Shamsi, and was about to climb back in when she too woke and turned over and smiled more brightly than the dawn itself.

He said, 'I don't like sharing you with other men.'

'No more than you like sharing your horse with other men?' She slipped past him, took a robe from the chair and put it on. 'Wine or water?'

'It's not the same at all. Water in the morning.'

'Prove it to me.'

She poured two cups of water from a crystal jug and passed him one.

'I will, but first—'

'You have to get back to your horse?'

'It's the first lesson a man must learn if he wants to lead others. After a raid, first you attend to the horses, then to your men, only last do you see to yourself. Besides, we have a job to do.' He drank off the cup in one draught and handed it back to her.

She filled it again. 'Maya is a dangerous enemy who needs to be taught a lesson.'

'So go and teach her, my Barbarian, and then come back to me.'

'It's not that simple.'

'Somehow it never is with men,' she said sadly.

'The Sultan is afraid. He wants to talk peace. He won't let us go back to the army so General Qulan has ordered the army to come to Tumanbay. They've been marching for a while now. She'll be coming. We need to prepare.'

'Then I suggest you put some trousers on!'

He did, and his shirt and jerkin and boots, rapidly, efficiently, talking as he dressed.

'Yes, we went against the Sultan's order, but he's not my Sultan and someone has to act or she'll just walk in through the gates.'

'And when you come face to face with this Queen Maya or whoever she is, what are you going to do?'

'When that moment comes, I will know.'

He squatted in front of the mirror and attended to his hair with far more ceremony than he'd devoted to his dressing.

'She's beautiful, they say.'

'You've met her?'

'Of course not. I've heard her beauty is—'

'I've heard she has spies everywhere.' He stood, looming over her. 'Maybe you are one of them.' There was no tenderness now in his eyes.

'I'm just a whore.'

'Who renders men weak so she can steal their secrets?'

Taking his sword belt from the back of a chair, he buckled it on.

'You're beginning to scare me,' she said, backing away.

He reached out . . . and touched her nose with his forefinger and laughed.

'I would not scare you for the world. Forgive my rough manners – I am no better than my horse.'

'A stallion . . .' she began, when a thunderous knock rattled the door in its frame.

'That doesn't sound like your madam's hand. Who's there?' he called.

In answer the door burst open and half a dozen uniformed men crowded into the room. Shamsi gave a cry. Wolf rested a hand on the hilt of his sword.

'What do you want?'

One man, evidently an officer, stepped forward. He held a scroll.

'You are to come with us by order of the Sultan. He wishes to see you.'

He brandished the scroll as if it might protect him. His men stepped forward and two of them placed their hands on Wolf – and moments later picked themselves up off the floor.

'No one arrests me.' His sword was in his hand. 'Shamsi, step back. Now!'

Two more men moved forward, their swords out and ready, if not enthusiastic.

Shamsi shouted: 'No, Wolf.'

He looked at her. Looked back at the officer and his men pressing carefully forward.

'You don't take me to see the Sultan. I go of my own free will. Shamsi, wait for me.'

Sliding sword back into scabbard, he walked past the guards and out of the door. They scuttled after him. Shamsi heard the rattle of gold coins thrown onto a wooden floor coming from below, and then the front door opening and slamming. She hurried to the window in time to see him striding along the street, guards in pursuit. He stopped at the corner and looked back at her. What was in his eyes, she could not say, but in her own heart there was a gleam of hope.

71

Qulan

Chains clanking, Qulan strode along the corridor surrounded by guards, the two officers walking ahead, eager to be done with this task. He looked right and left, through the arches, at the endless roofs and towers of the palace stretching away to the inner walls and, beyond that, the skyline of the city to which he had devoted his life. And for which he might soon lose it. Well, he had nothing to regret, he had done his duty as he saw it. He also saw a slovenly collar on one of his guards and snapped at the man: 'You, adjust your collar. You look a mess.'

Instinctively the fellow tightened the fastening.

'Yes, General.'

Qulan smiled to himself.

The party stopped before the great doors. The officer lifted the brass handle and let it fall with an echoing thud. The doors began to creak open. The whole procedure was designed to impress and awe the visitor. Qulan yawned.

A voice from within boomed: 'Bring him forward!'

The guard with the collar took hold of the manacles. Qulan glared at him and he let go.

'I will walk unaided.'

And he entered the Council Chamber. This time there was no breakfast table and no dates or apples – only the Sultan, his guards, trebled in number, and, as always, the Vizier, who commanded: 'Stand there.'

Qulan moved a little to one side.

'Here?'

'There!'

'Here?'

'I think you are making light of the situation in which you find yourself, General.'

'And what situation would that be? Is here better?'

'There, where His Majesty can see you. Now kneel. Make him kneel!'

Shrugging off the guards, Qulan lowered himself to his knees.

'I will kneel myself before the Sultan. My loyalty always has and always will be to him.'

'Aye,' Sultan al-Ghuri regarded his general balefully, 'I relied on your loyalty above all. And yet, here we are.'

'Here we are, Majesty, while time runs out.'

'I relied on you, yet you are the one who betrayed me. And I gave you the power to do so.'

'Actually your late brother promoted me to—'

'Enough. Do you deny that you sent orders to the army to march on Tumanbay?' He brandished a sheet of parchment. 'Here, I have your treacherous letter here, taken from the man you sent. Even so, the army marches . . .'

Qulan reflected on his wisdom in sending three riders in different directions and at different times.

'. . . yes, it marches on Tumanbay. As we speak. To depose me!'

Cadali leaned on his staff – that was a new addition, maybe he thought it lent him gravitas – enjoying Qulan's discomfort. It was probably his men who had intercepted one of the messengers.

'They are marching to defend the city, Majesty.'

Cadali laughed – a breach of protocol which he stifled with

his sleeve before orating: 'You are a traitor, Qulan. A disgrace to your uniform and your Sultan!'

Al-Ghuri leaned forward as if examining one of the glass retorts in which he distilled his fragrances.

'Does Maya even exist, General? Is it all an illusion? Is she no more than the scent of threat in which to hide your plotting?'

'Her armies are real, Majesty. They are winning city after city.'

Al-Ghuri looked unconvinced.

'Have you heard from the Governor of Emerald Province? No, because it has gone over to Maya virtually to the man and woman. She has barely had to fight a battle yet.'

Smooth Cadali glided forward. 'Majesty, if I might advise, it is better not to listen to the lies of—'

'You are being protected from the truth by these sycophants.'

Cadali laughed. 'The lies of a traitor who is trying to save his own skin.'

'Why are you doing this, Cadali? To gain power? Over what? The ruins of a city? Maya's forces move fast, ours move slowly. We must be in place to stop them and that means protecting the city, not allowing them to outflank us.'

The doors crashed open behind Qulan and Wolf appeared, holding two limp guards by the scruff of their necks, having used their heads to batter his way in. He dropped them and advanced on al-Ghuri, who slipped behind his throne with remarkable speed for a torpid man.

Qulan continued talking: 'The world is changing and fast. I have been trying to save us all.'

Wolf stood beside his general. 'He speaks the truth. My riders have seen it. Majesty, you are a fool and soon you will be a dead fool if you do not listen.'

He pulled his sword as if he were ready to do the job himself. Guards burst into the chamber and surrounded both men, spears at the ready. Wolf regarded the forest of spikes surrounding them and laughed.

Cadali bellowed over the clatter of armour and the shouts of the guards.

'Sheathe your sword! No one uncovers a blade in the presence of the Sultan!'

'And then what?' Wolf said 'Your jackals stick us like pigs? No thanks, I'll meet my gods, sword in hand.'

'Put your sword away, Wolf, we can do no more than live to fight again.'

The barbarian looked at the general, then shrugged, touched his thumb to the edge of his blade, drawing a jewel of blood, and slid the sword back into the sheath.

He growled: 'I was wrong. Tumanbay is not worth fighting for.'

'Take them away,' al-Ghuri said.

He slipped back round to the front of his throne and sat again.

'You heard His Majesty, take them away, lock them up.' Cadali waved his staff. 'Hurry, hurry . . . Get them out of here.'

The guards backed the two men through the door at spear point; they were taking no chances. The last Cadali heard was Wolf, roaring oaths and then, unaccountably, laughing. It sent a chill up his spine and made the thick flesh of his back ripple unpleasantly.

'Is it true, Cadali? Have you been hiding the truth?'

'From your all-seeing eye, Majesty? How could I? I was always against granting such great powers to Qulan. No one man should control an army. Unless it is you, Majesty,' he added hurriedly.

'Very well. Form a committee of the General Staff, let them . . . bring the army back, yes, that is good sense at least. Let's have them under our eye. But no one man in command, mark me well, Vizier. We shall divide and rule and then . . . then . . .'

He ran out of words and sank back, wheezing.

'Then,' Cadali took up his words, 'then we shall show why Tumanbay has stood a thousand years and will stand a thousand years more.'

'I know Tumanbay will survive. That's not my concern. I want this city locked tighter than the hareem – no one in or out without proper papers, a curfew after evening prayers until the dawn call. Double the street patrols. Call up the civil reserve. And find Gregor . . .'

He clapped. His personal guard formed a ring of steel about him as he stood.

'Do you suspect Gregor, Majesty?'

'I suspect you all, you fat fool. Now get on with it.'

72

Heaven

Night comes fast to the desert and with it comes the cold. The three sat around a miserable fire, hugging themselves to keep warm. They had travelled fast, with Slave and Boy often jogging beside the camel they had stolen, putting a good distance between themselves and the moving town. They had headed a little north of west, as Slave put it, hoping sooner or later to strike the city, but Heaven was beginning to lose hope, and though she said nothing, it was clear the others had read it in her eyes. Boy was resolutely cheerful and his dogs had hunted and found them desert rodents to cook over what scraps of wood they could gather.

Slave threw another on the fire. The last. Flames flicked feebly at the scrap of meat skewered on its stick.

'It won't last long,' she said.

Slave grunted. 'Would you rather be back in the cage? Wood is hard to find.'

'You said that last night and the night before.'

'And I'll probably say it tomorrow night and the night after that.'

Boy stood up. 'Over there!'

Slave was on his feet in a flash, Rajik's sword in his fist.

'Where? Who?'

'No, not there, there, far away . . . There!'

'On the horizon?' Heaven said.

'Like morning but in the wrong place.'

Heaven stood and peered. 'Yes, light. I can see light where there shouldn't be any light.'

'Is it the city?' Boy said.

Slave grunted again. Heaven had noticed he was doing a lot of grunting, mostly when it saved him having to answer questions.

'Are those the lights of Tumanbay?'

'How should I know? You ask too many questions. Maybe you need a good slapping.'

The dogs growled quietly from the darkness.

Heaven said: 'Stop it, we're a family. You have to stop behaving like you're a king or something.'

He put the sword back on the ground.

'I was a king once.'

'Well, you're not any more.'

Slave thought about it and then answered.

'Yes, it's Tumanbay,' he said. 'We'll be at the gates tomorrow.'

Boy stood and walked to the edge of the light cast by the fire. He held up his right hand and the dogs appeared as if he had summoned them by magic. He spoke some words and after a moment they ran off barking into the darkness.

Heaven said: 'Why did you do that, they were your dogs?'

'They were their own dogs. I gave my promise to them that if they helped us reach our journey's end, they would be their own masters and make their own way.'

'We could have sold them,' Slave said.

'They were not for sale.' He walked back to the fire and

crouched close to the guttering flames. 'Tomorrow, then, we'll see Tumanbay?'

'We will. So better sleep while there's still heat in the fire.'

He pulled his robe close about himself and lay down, curled around the sword, his hand resting on its hilt.

73

Gregor

Gregor had only once felt so alone. It was the last time his father had taken him out into the gloomy, barren mountains. He thought they were on a hunting trip, a last, desperate attempt before the winter set in to collect food for their family. The mist was closing in and his father, whom he remembered being a kind man, led the young Gregor across a river and down a valley he had not been to before. They stopped beside a small wooded area and his father pointed towards the snowy peaks in the distance.

'Villeppi is that way,' he said. 'There are opportunities there for strong, clever boys.'

Then he told Gregor to wait there for him while he checked his traps.

Gregor waited as the mist darkened. It was cold and it started to rain. But Gregor stayed put, as his father had instructed. After a while, he called out for him. But his father didn't return that night.

In the morning, Gregor tried to retrace their footsteps. Snow was falling and, seeing a wolf, he decided to return to the safety of the woods. Cold and hungry, he foraged for roots, but the ground was frozen and hard. There were days when he ate no more than leaves and grass.

On the third or fourth evening, he smelled something

familiar: meat cooking on a fire. He followed the aroma, his mouth watering, until he came to the edge of a clearing. There, he saw a small boy, about his age, perhaps a little younger, sitting beside a campfire, chewing on a rabbit leg. His back was turned, allowing Gregor to approach unseen. As he got closer he noticed something was wrong with the boy's leg; blood was seeping out from rags wrapped round it.

This was an opportunity. Gregor leaped forward and snatched the piece of meat from the surprised boy's hand, then ran back towards the woods. But before he got there, he felt himself being pulled to the ground. Surely the injured child had not been able to give chase, he thought, or to bring him to the ground with such force. Rolling over he saw the face of another, older boy, looking down at him furiously. He grabbed the rabbit leg from Gregor's hand and kicked him in the ribs.

'Get away!' he shouted.

Gregor scrambled to his feet and retreated to the woods. He waited there all night, watching the two boys.

In the morning, they packed up their meagre belongings and moved off through the wood. Gregor followed.

'Let me join you,' he pleaded from a distance. 'Three is better than two. I can help.'

His ribs hurt like never before. It must have been a heavy kick. He tried to keep up, but now he was alone again, on his back, staring up at the fading light, a stinging pain in his hands and wrists . . .

And then the light appeared to move and there was a baby crying.

'Drink,' a soothing voice said, and Gregor felt a cup lifted to his lips.

He gulped the water down. It was like a river flowing through him. But who had come to save him? Was it his sister? Had she found him in the open and brought him home? He felt her soft hands holding his as she washed his wounds. Tentatively, he moved his fingers, then his hands. They felt light and – hadn't they been manacled?

He sat up and looked around. He was in the caverns beneath the city but now there were rugs and cushions beneath him and Sarah was kneeling beside him, carefully bandaging his wounded hand. The baby was nearby, held by an older woman.

Gregor closed his eyes and slumped back, trying to recall what had happened. After a moment, he opened them again and looked at her.

'Why are you helping me?' he asked.

Without taking her blue eyes off her task, she said quietly, 'Because, in your way, you were kind to me.'

Gregor shook his head. 'I'm not kind to anyone. I used you, you were my tool.'

She poured some oil from a small bottle onto her hands and started to gently rub it onto his wrists. It stung and he involuntarily pulled back.

'Be brave,' she said. 'It will soothe the pain.'

Her kindness took him off balance. This slave, who he had cared nothing for, who knew who he was, what he was . . . He shook his head to clear his mind. He needed to understand what was happening.

'They think you killed her,' he said. 'Shajah, the First Wife.'

She didn't respond.

'Did you find her body?' Gregor asked. Still nothing. 'You found her there, strangled, and you ran away because you thought they would blame you?'

He watched her for any sign of an answer.

'Did you see anyone else there?'

Slowly, almost imperceptibly, she shook her head.

'It's all right. I believe you. Did they kill her for the scrolls?'

'No,' she said.

'You saved the scrolls? That's why you had to escape from the palace. Do you have them here?'

She got up and turned to the woman holding the baby. Gregor reached out, frustrated, and grabbed hold of her gown. Instead of trying to break free, she took Gregor's hand in hers and looked at him with those striking blue eyes.

'You can't do that any more,' she said.

After a few moments, he lowered his hand.

'Everything you desire to know, you shall know,' she said. 'You do something for me, I'll do something for you. Remember?'

'I brought your baby,' Gregor said.

She lifted a hand to her lantern and the cave dissolved once more into darkness.

'Sarah!' Gregor called. He could hear the baby gurgling, footsteps receding. 'I risked my life to bring you your baby!' he bellowed.

'And you are free,' she replied from some distance away.

Gregor got up. He was unbound – free to go where he wished. But he had no idea how to get out of this labyrinth of darkness. He had once interrogated the sole survivor of an army battalion that had been sent down to clear the city beneath the city of vagrants and criminals. They became lost and wandered through the darkness for years, going blind, eating insects. All but one were never seen again.

'Sarah!' Gregor called out again.

Frantically he put his hands to the wall and felt his way in the direction he sensed she had gone.

After some time – he couldn't say how much – he became aware of light ahead.

'Hello,' he called out, approaching. He heard whispers and stopped to listen.

'Is it him?' a woman's voice asked.

'Yes,' said another. It sounded familiar.

'Sarah?' Gregor called out. 'Is that you?'

'Yes,' she replied. 'Come. There's someone who wants to see you. Come into the light.'

The floor of the passage here curved downwards and as Gregor approached, the darkness receded and the light emerged from the horizon like the dawn. He found himself at an open door looking into a small furnished room. There was a table and two chairs, and a couch against a wall, and food and plates and things on shelves; it was a home of sorts.

Seated at the table were a woman and a young boy, both with their heads turned to look at Gregor with interest.

'Sarah, what's happening?' Gregor asked, though he couldn't see Sarah there.

'This is my son,' said the woman.

The boy looked familiar. Gregor tried to delve into his fractured memory to recall where he had seen him.

'You had a dream,' the boy said.

It wasn't a question. His voice had an odd tinge to it, as if the small body were inhabited by a far older being.

'What are you talking about? What dream?'

'About your brother, something that happened a long time ago. Snow and ice. An injured boy. A murder?'

Gregor felt a surge of anxiety. Had he been crying out in his sleep, he wondered.

'That dream brought you to me. My name is Frog.'

And then Gregor remembered.

'Before . . . You were at my "trial", yes?'

'It's of no matter,' the Frog replied. 'But yes, I am the son of the man whose name you couldn't remember.'

'Basim,' the woman said. 'Basim. Basim was my husband and a good father. And a loyal soldier.'

'What do you want with me?'

They continued to look at him silently.

'It's Tumanbay,' he said. 'That's how it works here.'

Neither of them moved.

'If you want to kill me, just do it.'

The boy pushed his chair back and rose to his feet. He went over to his mother and kissed her on the forehead. She whispered something into his ear that Gregor couldn't quite hear, then he picked up a lantern and walked past Gregor and back into the passageway.

'Where are you going?' Gregor asked.

The boy stopped and turned. 'We have a journey to go on, you and me.'

'More riddles? I'm done with this,' Gregor said, but he knew this sounded hollow.

'It doesn't matter,' the boy said. 'You have no choice. Everything will happen as I have seen, just as I saw my father's death . . . oh, and the moment of my own death and my mother's too. And yours, Gregor, Master of the Palace Guard. I've seen your death too. I wanted to kill you for what you did, but I couldn't because I have had a vision and I need to tell the Sultan about it. You will take me to him.'

What a curious child, Gregor thought. But he was right about one thing. He didn't have a choice if he wanted to get out of this pit and back into the world of the living.

'I will do my best to help you,' Gregor said. 'But even I am unable to guarantee the Sultan will see you.'

The Frog held out his fist, opened it to show a gold coin, possibly the one Gregor had given to the blind man when he had entered the city beneath the city through the Temple of Solace.

'See the coin,' he said. 'If I turn my hand, it will fall.'

He did so and the coin fell and landed dully on the stone beneath.

'So it is written and so it will be.'

And after a pause, a very childish smile appeared on his face.

'You like her,' he said.

'Who?'

'The lady with the blue eyes. You like her a lot.'

'I don't know what you mean,' Gregor said.

The Frog cocked his head and considered Gregor for a few moments.

'I liked my father a lot too.'

Gregor was unnerved by the boy. He was impossible to read. How did he know so much? And was this a threat? Was he saying that harm would come to Sarah and her child down here, if he did not do the boy's bidding?

'Come on,' the Frog said. 'We have to go.'

He turned and continued along the passageway.

And Gregor followed.

74

Qulan

A holy man had once told Qulan that dreams were messages from the gods. Qulan had responded that whenever he ate cheese late at night he had dreams; did that mean cheese was a god? The fellow had no answer. As far as Qulan was concerned, dreams were the leftovers from the meal of waking life, scraps that were best swept up and thrown away for the pigs to eat. And yet, in his cell, in the gloom, where there was little difference between night and day, his dreams had been strong and rich, a banquet of the dark hours, he decided.

Over the first two nights of his incarceration, he had dreamed of those years long ago when he was a boy in the mountains. Why had those scenes come back to him now? He had seen his father, a dour brutal man who worked as a woodsman and often drank his pay away at the local inn before coming home and using his fists on his wife and family. It was not considered anything unusual – it was surely a man's right to exercise his authority, and so what if he broke his wife's collarbone or split his daughter's nose? Over the years, Qulan had taken his share of pain, often stepping forward to save his mother from the fist blows. And, over the years, he had grown and gained muscle and sinew of his own, working in the great woods, and a slow resentment at the life they lived had burned in him until one night it flared.

A cold and cheerless night it was, on the edge of winter, the ground already hard with an iron frost. He had waited under the stars for his father to come weaving back from the inn, past the pile of root vegetables that had been dug from the family's strip of the common ground: long pale root beets, bulbous at the top, tapering away to a narrow tail. They were poor eating but had a weight to them, and as his father staggered singing and steaming over the field, young Qulan had wrapped his hand around the tail of a good heavy root and stepped forward.

His father had bunched his fists and laughed at the boy with an evil joy, but his pleasure in the violence to come didn't survive the first hit of the frozen beet. It broke his cheek and he went down on his knees, trying to mouth obscenities through smashed bone. The boy lifted his weapon and brought it down twice more. There was the sound of collarbones cracking like ice breaking – and then a dull thud as the skull was broken and the drunk man fell face down and the life drained out of him. Qulan had stood for a long time under the stars as his father's blood froze at his feet, then he turned and left the hut, the village, the life he would bear no longer.

Many village boys had left their families to find a future and a hope across the mountains in far Tumanbay. Qulan had long wanted to go but his father had not allowed it, jealous of his power over his family. Now there was nothing stopping the boy and, shouldering the pack and provisions he'd hidden away over the past moons, he had made his way south, climbing, always climbing up towards the high passes.

On the third day he had fallen in with Varsi, a boy three or four years younger than himself, lying by the side of the track, the snow around him stained with his blood. Perhaps it was a memory of his father's blood that had caused Qulan to stop, to help the younger boy open the bear trap that had closed on his ankle. Perhaps it was his guilt at leaving his mother and sisters and brothers to fend for themselves in this cold season. Perhaps it was just the need to do something good for another person, but he set about making a crutch from a fallen tree and, shouldering Varsi's pack along with his own, they had set off together.

Progress was slow and Qulan was beginning to wonder if he had made a stupid mistake as the big soft flakes of snow began to fall again and the wind got up and tore at their inadequate clothing. They were huddled over an inadequate fire, trying to cook a stringy rabbit, when a third boy had come out of the night, intent on stealing their food. Qulan had given him a kicking and sent him on his way but in the morning he was still there, squatting in the snow a stone's thrown from the camp, his hungry, grey eyes burning. Qulan had ignored him but when Varsi and he had packed and started off along the trail, the boy followed.

'Two's better than one and three's better than two,' he called after them. 'Let me come with you.'

All morning he had been there behind them. When they stopped at midday and Qulan gratefully lowered Varsi to a fallen branch, the boy caught up.

'What happened to him?' he asked.

'Bear trap,' Qulan said.

'Going over the mountains, are you?'

'To Villeppi,' Varsi said. 'I know the way, I have a plan, I saw a map once and I know how to get there.'

'That true?' the visitor asked.

'True, I've seen it,' Qulan said. 'This late in the year, with the snow, there's no way to read the land, follow the track. We need the map.'

'I can help carry,' the visitor said.

Qulan appraised the boy. There was something feral about

him – a thin, tall child with eyes as cold as the grey snow clouds lowering above them.

'You can't do it all by yourself,' the boy persisted, indicating Varsi's leg. 'You'll never make it.'

After a moment, Qulan simply nodded.

'You can call me Gregor,' the boy said, throwing his pack down and sitting on the log between them.

Despite his injury, Varsi had become their token, something greater than each of them, making them stronger together. They would get through this hellish journey – they would conquer the high passes and go down to the coast and find a new future in Tumanbay. And yet it was not to be. Varsi had fallen to his death in a blizzard. Qulan had been worried that the loss would destroy Gregor, who had been with the younger boy when the tragedy happened, but from that moment the weather had improved. They had crossed the highest point and, almost as if it were Varsi's last gift to them both, they were heading down towards the plains and the coast and the port of Villeppi.

On waking from the second dream, Qulan swore that for a moment he could smell the snow like cold steam around his head. He told himself to not be a fool. There was much to think about: the state of the city defences, his brother Gregor. Where was he? Why had he not got a message through? Had he been arrested too? Was Cadali in charge now? He prayed this was not so; the man was a capable politician but no general. Like most of his kind he could see no further ahead than his own immediate advantage. No, it was all down to Gregor. The two of them had worked together since that long ago morning; Gregor had always been the planner, the man who had a knife concealed beyond the knife he had concealed. It was up to him now. Qulan just hoped he was in a position to do something.

75

Heaven

'The wall that protects the city is a wonder of the world, my friends.'

The camel driver had joined them mid-morning as they approached the city. A cheery fellow with a caravan of two dozen beasts he intended to sell in the city, Jahan was also a fount of information and, as he said: 'A man who spends many nights alone in the desert spends nothing, so when he meets good companions, why, he is liberal indeed.' And they were happy enough to listen to his chatter as the walls grew taller and the towers of Tumanbay appeared through the heat haze, at first wavering like a mirage and then becoming solid, almost impossibly tall and elegant with their minarets and domes, many, Jahan told them, topped with gold that would never lose its glitter and shone in the sun like a thousand fires.

'Yes, yes, the city is a wonder but first consider these walls, for what is a house without a good wall, eh?'

'How tall are they?' Boy asked.

Of their little party he was the most obviously interested, and it was to him that Jahan answered.

'Thirty-five cubits, my young friend, but that is the least of it – these walls are castles in their own right. Within them are barracks, offices, watch-keepers' houses – yes, whole houses – and granaries, more than on the fingers of all our hands, stuffed with grain and every other provision the mind can think of. Water too – cisterns filled from perpetual springs that are as clear as melted snow from the high peaks. And even that is not the end of it, for there are warehouses containing machines of war, mangonels and catapults and bows so vast that only a giant could pull them.'

Boy, ever practical, asked: 'But if only a giant could use them, what is the point of having them, since there aren't any giants?'

'Tell me that when you have seen half of what these old eyes have witnessed. But I will take pity on your youth. These bows are mounted on carts and pulled by teams of men winding levers so that more men may lay arrows as big as pine trees.'

'How big are pine trees?' Boy asked. Jahan ruffled his hair.

'Truly are you a boy. They are big. But I must leave you now, I have camels to sell in the markets. Princess, if you will alight?'

Boy spoke to their camel and it kneeled, allowing Heaven to step down. They had sold it to Jahan for a reasonable price. They would not need it in the city, so best get rid of it now. Jahan bowed deeply to each of them, wished them a long life and led his string off into the crowds gathered around the foot of the walls.

It was a city in its own right – a tent city with stalls and livestock pens, even slaves for sale and crowds of folk buying, selling or merely watching. A stallholder called as they entered the melee: 'Sweets ... and coffee, falafal and cool water, the finest sherbets, sweet cheeses and soured onions, mint tea, tea from the spice roads of the far east.'

Boy said: 'I'm hungry.'

'You're always hungry,' Slave said.

'We can eat when we get to my father's house,' Heaven said, 'like kings and queens.'

'I'd settle for breakfast,' Boy said.

The stallholder beamed: 'Kofta, the finest.'

Heaven slipped a coin from her belt. 'Three of those, and a water skin.'

'Very wise, with pine nuts – and the coolest, finest water to be—'

'Passed through a camel, most like,' Slave said.

'Ah, my friend, for a man with such a sweet, young wife you've a sour nature. Here you are, sweetheart!'

They sat in the shade of a grove of lemon trees and ate and drank without worries for the first time in a long time.

'Mmmm . . . Does everything taste this good in Tumanbay?' Boy said. 'And how do we get in?'

'See there?'

Slave pointed to a vast wooden gate studded with iron bands. It was closed and guarded. At its foot a far smaller gate was set into the wall and here people were queueing and entering. The queue wasn't moving very fast, so they decided to finish their breakfast while standing in line. As they moved slowly closer, they could see an official and a couple of guards at the gate. People were presenting something.

'What are papers?' Boy asked.

'What?'

'That's what he's saying. I could see his lips moving. Papers.'

'A pass or permission to be or go somewhere,' Slave said.

'I'll talk to him,' Heaven said.

They entered the gate and found themselves facing a narrow passage where only one person at a time could pass.

The official at his desk said: 'Papers.'

'We're together. My father lives in the city. His name is—'

'Papers. Don't hold up the queue.'

'His name is Ibn Bai. He'll pay whatever is necessary, if we can only go through.'

'No papers, no entry. Orders. Time of peril, they're much stricter now.'

'I was kidnapped and—'

'Move back, please. No papers, no entry. Officer.'

'But you don't understand!' She was getting angry. The other two pulled her back as the guard advanced.

'No trouble,' Slave said. 'We'll go. Come on.'

'It's not fair!' she wailed, as they emerged and hurried past the shuffling line, all of whom did have papers. 'We're so close!'

'There must be other ways,' Boy said.

'We'll think of something.' Slave let go of her arm. 'How much have you got left? We might be able to bribe our way in.'

'Ahhhh, it can be soooo very hard, eh?'

A tall man, as tall as Slave, but thin, as if he had once been a short man and had been stretched three times his length. His bony wrists extended beyond his sleeves – his clothes were of light colours and many-layered – and his long hands bore rings of silver and gold. He smiled. A lot.

'To come all this way to the greatest city in the world only to find . . .' He snapped his fingers with a dry crack which caused Boy to jump. 'Boff! There is no way in. Used to be easy, you could walk through free as the Sultan himself.'

'Used to be?' Heaven asked.

'There have been, how would you say, problems! Out on the borders. Rumours of war. As a consequence, everything has been –' he wrung his hands as if winding a screw – 'tightened. Terrible for trade, of course, but there you are. As they say.'

'And here we are,' Slave said.

'As they say,' echoed Boy.

'Indeed they do, they do, my pretty lad. Terrible times for us merchants. Like your father, my dear young lady? I heard you say he was in business here?'

'Oh yes. Perhaps you know him? Ibn Bai of the House of Abi Talib. He's very well respected.'

'And he trades in?'

'Slaves.'

'I'm sure we've met, the name is, as it were . . . And these are your followers?'

'We are friends. We have no papers . . .'

She left the sentence unfinished, realising that this man knew very well what they wanted. The only question was the price to be paid.

'There is always a way and, if I may say so, I, Grassic, will be more than happy to aid the daughter of a fellow merchant.'

'Grassic?' Slave said. 'What kind of name is that?'

'The kind that denotes who I am, a man who may be trusted to help—'

'We have money,' Heaven said.

'No, no, no, not necessary.'

'Then what do you want?' Slave said.

'We are happy to help people who will, at some time in the future, be happy to help us, do you see? No catch, favours beget favours – a network of those who—'

'Help each other,' Boy said.

'Exactly. Talk it over between yourselves. Take it or, if you wish, leave it. My tent is over there, do you see, the blue . . . stands out, don't you think? I shall be there conducting business among my friends for my friends. Peace be upon you.'

He did something with his body, between tying it into a knot and bowing, as he retreated backwards and then was gone.

'I don't trust him,' Heaven said.

Slave said: 'Of course you don't. Neither do I, neither does Boy, but we still need to get into the city. I'll talk to him.'

Heaven said: 'You're sure?'

'I'm sure of nothing except that we can't wait forever outside the walls. If there is a war we'd be caught between the city and whoever the enemy might be.'

'Maybe Rajik was right,' Boy said, 'and Tumanbay is finished.'

Slave looked up at the walls, at the towering gate.

'Does it look finished? Wait here.'

Once he was lost in the crowd, Boy said: 'I don't trust him either.'

'I think I do,' Heaven said. 'We've been through a lot together.'

'He wants to kill a man.'

'You killed Pamira and Rajik.'

'Not me. The dogs, they killed them. I just—'

'Nothing is just "just", in this world,' she said.

Boy turned away and looked at the desert. 'We could go somewhere else, find a better place.'

'Don't you see, I have to know about my mother. If she's alive. I have to know.' There were tears in her eyes and she turned angrily away. 'I have to know and I want to see my father. That's all. Go if you want, I won't stop you.'

When she turned back he was still there.

Neither of them said anything more until Slave returned and announced: 'I've worked it out with him. Come.'

'How? What did he want?' Heaven said.

Boy followed on with: 'That's what I want to know.'

They had to hurry to keep up with Slave, who was threading his way through the crowds towards the blue tent.

'We are pledged to perform certain tasks once we are in the city. For three moons. When that time has passed, our obligation will be paid, whether he has called on us or not.'

'If we don't do what he asks?' Heaven said.

'We will, they will ensure it. We are not the only people they have working for them.'

Heaven knew there was something deeply wrong with this whole idea.

'I'm not going to do it.'

Slave didn't pause. 'Don't. I'll do it alone or with the boy. Either you have to trust me or ... find your own way home.'

She wanted to – she truly wanted to – but could she? Didn't she need Slave's strength, his desire for revenge? It wasn't fair, none of this was fair. She looked at Boy.

'What do you think?' she whispered.

'We're both kids. What chance would we have alone? They'd eat us up and I don't have the dogs.'

Slave waited by the flap of the tent. They stood frozen for a moment, then joined him.

'Just trust me,' he said, and they went inside.

In her head, Heaven heard the words echo: Nothing is ever just 'just'.

'Ahhhh, very good, my dears. You are sensible. Wait a moment and all will be done. Passes. You two are brother and sister, yes? Oh, such a lovely couple you make.'

Using a pair of clippers, he clamped a tiny lead seal onto a sheet.

'Is that it?' Slave asked.

'Oh, trust Grassic, eh? Works every time. Look through it. You can read? Good.'

'As they say.'

'You are a man who appreciates the nature of the jest, sir, so you are.'

'The money?' Slave said.

Grassic threw a pouch onto the table – it was heavy and clinked. Coins?

Heaven said, 'I don't understand?'

Grassic offered a smile that was far too long with far too many teeth in it.

'You don't have to, dear. You merely need to be able to lie on your back with your legs apart, and I'm sure you can manage that. You'll make a fine show with your little brother. I know customers who will pay well for that!'

Boy made for the door but he was too slow. Slave had him and slipped manacles on his wrists, then pinned him to the table. Heaven's arms were jerked suddenly, painfully back in a long-fingered grip, and she felt metal on her wrists, too tight, too painful. She screamed.

His face pressed against the table, Boy said: 'What's he done?'

'Sold you,' Grassic said.

Slave slipped the pouch under his robe.

'I'm done with you at last. All your whining, from the first moment we came ashore, whine, whine, whine. You and the boy, I don't need you and I don't want a family. Right? And now I'm rid of you both, at a good price too.'

Heaven spat at him – caught him full in the face. He wiped the saliva away.

'I hope you die!'

Grassic slipped a hand under her robe and ran it down her arm. It was like being caressed by a camel spider. She shuddered.

'Don't worry, everyone's a slave in Tumanbay. Who knows where you might end up?' She spat at him. He tightened his grip. 'Behave or I might have to discipline you. I might have to anyway. Is everything satisfactory, my friend?'

Slave nodded. 'Perfectly. Let us shake hands upon it, as we do in my country.'

The long hand slithered out from under Heaven's robe and was offered. Slave took it.

'We are in agreement, as they say.'

The men shook – Grassic went to release his hand but nothing happened.

They stood facing each other, then Grassic grunted. 'Uhh-hhnnnn . . .' and Slave crushed his hand.

Heaven could hear the long bones splintering. A thin cry came from the man's throat, like the cry of a child having a nightmare. Slave dropped the hand that hung at the end of that long forearm like a sack of bones, reached out for Grassic's neck and wrenched it once, as if it were a chicken's neck and he an efficient butcher. Grassic dropped to the floor. Slave bent, extracted keys and unlocked both sets of cuffs. Heaven and Boy stood stock-still in shock.

Slave said: 'You didn't think I'd actually sell you? Now, shall we test those papers before his friends come back.'

76
Gregor

Gregor was lost, dependent on a child, being led by the hand this way and that, and he didn't like it one bit.

The Frog pulled. 'This way.'

'How do you know? I can't see anything.'

'You get used to it, your eyes start seeing after a while and then it's all right, you can find your way, as long as you can remember your way. Stop here, reach out.'

Gregor felt the iron rungs of a ladder. Something solid at last.

'We climb now,' the boy said. 'It's not far. Look up – can you make it out?'

He did, he could: a very faint crescent . . . no, a circle of light.

'That's where we go. It'll let us out in the vegetable and fruit market. Can't you smell it?'

He could: greenery, fresh lemons? He began to climb towards the light, the world he knew, away from the dark, until he was hunched with his shoulder braced against the iron grating.

Frog called from below: 'Push, it should be easy.'

It was: the slightest shove and the iron hinged up as if it were on a counterweight. Daylight drenched him like rain in the desert as he hauled himself out and reached down for the boy and pulled him up. They both stood blinking behind a great pile of sacks: almonds from the Valley of Shan. A porter appeared with a barrow upon which he piled three sacks and, without any hint that he'd noticed the newcomers, wheeled them away whistling tunelessly.

The Frog grinned. 'See, it's like we don't exist. Now, when can I see the Sultan?'

Gregor realised that up until this moment he hadn't actually thought about how the boy might see al-Ghuri, or even if the boy should see al-Ghuri; maybe it would be better if Gregor took a message. Down there, with Sarah coming to his aid, it had all seemed possible, but now, in the world of things and men, he could not help having doubts. He had something to offer the Sultan: he knew where the scrolls were, even if he didn't have them under his hand. He could, possibly, obtain them. That was solid, but this boy ...

'Follow me,' he said, 'keep close.'

'It's all right,' the boy said. 'You'll see.'

The ways of the palace were many and mysterious and Gregor knew them all, so it was no trouble gaining admittance and taking the Frog back to his apartments. Or it would not have been if the place weren't crawling with guards, one of whom bellowed: 'You two, stop! How did you get—?' before he recognised his commander.

'Sorry, Excellency, didn't ...' He took in Gregor's injuries but said nothing. 'We've been ordered to detain and question—'

'Ordered? By who? Last I knew, I gave the orders.'

'But you've not been here for days, Commander. The Sultan has taken personal control of the Palace Guard so, uh ...' The fellow was at a loss.

Gregor said: 'You'd better carry on, then. I shall be in my rooms.'

He grabbed the Frog's hand and dragged him quickly past the

guard, down a flight of steps and through his own door, which he slammed thankfully shut, wondering exactly how long he'd been away.

'Half a moon,' the Frog said.

'What?'

'You've been away half a moon – that's what you're wondering, isn't it?'

The boy wandered around the room, picking things up and putting them down again in the wrong places.

'Don't touch anything.'

'Why?'

'Just don't.'

The Frog regarded him, head on one side, a finger picking his nose, and said, 'When can I see the Sultan?'

'No one can just "see the Sultan". Things have to be arranged. You'll have to wait. There are protocols. Do you know what that means?'

He turned away and caught sight of himself in the sliver of mirror on the wall; he looked a mess.

'I'm hungry.'

'I'll send for something,' Gregor said, moving to the door. 'And don't touch anything.'

The Frog picked up a thumbscrew. 'What's this?'

Gregor felt strangely embarrassed to have left such an implement out for a child to see.

'A cracker for walnuts,' he said. 'Put it down.'

The Frog said: 'I'm bored.'

Gregor had a thought. 'Here's a riddle. Boys like riddles, don't they? How can two women meet two men and say to them: "Greetings to our two sons and our two husbands and the sons of our husbands."? That should keep you busy for a while.'

Without a pause the Frog said: 'Each man married the

mother of the other one after she'd lost her first husband, so they were their two sons, their two husbands and the sons of their husbands.'

He went back to the thumbscrew. Gregor gave up and stalked into his private chambers to wash and change his clothes.

Feeling a good deal more prepared, he hurried to the Receiving Room where he hoped the Sultan would be at this time, dealing with matters of state, or at least trying out new scents on his courtiers.

The doors were closed and guarded more heavily than usual. Something out of the ordinary was certainly happening but . . .

'What a surprise . . .'

The oily tones of Cadali, followed by the man himself, oozing from the throne room through a barely cracked door. Al-Ghuri's voice could be heard shouting angrily before the door closed.

'Everyone has been looking for you, Gregor. Where have you been?' And then, noticing his bandaged hand, 'What happened to you? An argument with your secret lover perhaps?'

'I don't intend to explain myself to you, Cadali. I need to see the Sultan.'

'You look like you've been in a brawl in some low inn. I only have your best interests at heart, my friend – and trust me, you need to keep out of the Sultan's way, at least for now.'

'Trust you, Cadali? Why would I do that?'

'Because His Majesty has uncovered a plot.'

The greasy bastard was enjoying this; he could hardly wait to deliver the fatal blow.

'What? Who?'

'General Qulan has ordered the army to march on Tumanbay.'

'I don't believe it.'

'Family loyalty is all very well, my friend, but facts are facts. The army is returning to the city, your brother and this barbarian horseman of his have been arrested. If I were you, I'd stay in your rooms until we get to the bottom of it.'

'Arrested?'

'You are not usually so slow on the uptake, Gregor. Yes, they are both in the cells. If you wish to avoid—'

'I have a boy.'

'Really. How interesting. I have many . . .'

'This child is special. He has dreams.'

'Are you all right, Gregor? You seem dazed? Perhaps your injuries are worse than you thought. You really do need to rest.'

'No, the boy needs to see the Sultan.'

Gregor could see a smile of refusal appearing on Cadali's face, but the Vizier's words died on his lips as he thought of a better idea, one clearly calculated to end Gregor's influence in the palace for good.

'Very well, bring your special boy and his dreams. I'm sure we will all be most interested to hear of your contribution to the present emergency, Gregor.'

77
Madu

Madu had never been good at waiting and now it seemed harder than ever, stuck in a stinking stable not knowing if Ahmed, the young stable slave, would be able to carry out his mission. He trusted the lad but in these times, with the whole world turned upside down, nothing was certain. He kicked loose straw from under his feet and then kicked it back again. He recited his latest poem and decided it needed more work. He counted the patterned bricks that composed the feed trough, twice, and then, at blessed last, Ahmed pushed open the stable door and Daniel was there.

'What on earth are you doing here, my dear man? I can think of you in many strange places, but a stable?'

'I've been waiting for you.'

'Of course, but it's not safe. And who is the boy?'

'Ahmed works here in the stables. We are ...' He paused, suddenly feeling shy. 'We know each other.'

Ahmed grinned and mimed an act which could have got them all executed, but with such glee that both men laughed.

Madu went on: 'He can get us horses.'

'Why?'

Madu felt a surge of excitement. This was the moment when everything would change. Daniel would see that he too could plan and act for both of them, for a new future.

'What we talked about, getting away. My mother has – had – a small palace in the mountains. She knew she could escape there any time, only she never had the chance. We do.'

Madu was good at gauging people's responses; it had kept him uninjured on many occasions, but he was unable to read anything in Daniel's expression. Certainly not the excitement he expected.

'Don't you see? It makes perfect sense while there's such confusion in the palace. We can go tonight, escape all this plotting—'

Daniel held up a warning hand. 'Stop, Madu. We have to keep clear heads or we could end up—'

'No one will see us if we go under cover of the darkness.'

'No, no, no. You mustn't draw attention to yourself. The Sultan is . . . half mad with suspicion, he sees threat everywhere. You say you are safe because of your mother, I say that isn't true. They've trebled the guards on the gates, no one goes in or out without papers at any time of the day or night.'

Out in the great yard grooms were exercising horses, their hooves striking sparks from the cobbles. They were beautiful beasts, owned by the greatest houses and clans of Tumanbay, and half a dozen of them belonged to his mother – to him now. There they were, waiting, and once again his plans had been cast aside. It had been that way his whole life: everyone telling him to be responsible, to grow up, but as soon as he produced an idea, they turned away, as Daniel was turning away now. A great tide of anger and resentment was rising within him.

'You don't want to go, do you? You never wanted to go. You lied to keep me, that's all, because I was useful.'

Daniel reached out; he struck the hand away.

'You're nothing to me now.'

'You're not a fool, Madu, and I have never used you. I love you.

415

Plain and simple – only nothing is ever simple in this cursed city. Yes, if you go tonight I will come with you. We may, if we are lucky, be together in your palace in the hills. Only think – how long will they leave us be? You are the son of a Sultan, the nephew of a Sultan. Your mother was First Wife. Because of who you are, you will always be part of this great game of empires they have played for centuries in Tumanbay. The choice for you and for those that love you is simple – are you a player of the game or merely a piece on the board? I have watched you learning so much in the army and since. I have seen a boy become a man, a man with strength and vision and power. This could be your moment.'

Horses passing in a long line, high stepping, manes flowing in the wind, the grooms merely touching the reins as they wheeled their mounts and retraced their steps; horses passing back through the ranks in what seemed a confusion, as if there must be collisions, animals rearing up, riders falling – but none of that happened and out of disorder came order. The ranks parading in perfect lines. Madu felt his heart rising within him; that tide which had threatened to overwhelm him just a moment ago was now a glorious rising sea bearing his ambitions ever upwards.

'Could I do it? Alone?'

'You would not be alone, my dear man, never alone again.'

'You could be my Vizier.'

'And we shall change the law so the Sultan must definitely sleep with his First Minister. Come, let us go back. Ahmed, my boy . . .'

Gold glittered in Daniel's hand. Ahmed reached out for it with a grin, then staggered slightly, looked at his empty hand with a puzzled frown and fell to the straw. A needle-thin dagger slipped back under Daniel's robe.

'I'm sorry.'

'What did you . . . ?' A sea of glory, a sea of blood. 'You killed him, Daniel.'

'He was dead from the moment you came asking for horses. He's a boy for hire, he owed you no loyalty, I do, that's why I took his death on myself. You are clean of it, Madu, my Sultan. Now, we need to hide him under the straw. When they find him, they'll assume one of his customers got nasty.'

78

Qulan

The noon bell rang far away. It hung in a belfry atop the tallest tower in the palace and could still be heard in the lowest oubliette. Qulan smiled to himself; it was designed to let even the most despised prisoner know that he was still part of Tumanbay and would answer to it. That no matter for how long he'd rotted in his call, he was not forgotten and that sooner or later he would answer for his crimes, whatever they may be. After trial and sentencing he would either be transported to the camps far away in the provinces, where he would rot with other guilty souls, or be posted to the labour battalions where his career would be hard and short – for even in a slave economy there were those tasks that slaves, who represented cash, would not be set to. Cleaning the sewers of the city, for instance: Qulan had seen shambling chain gangs of poor wretches marched to the cisterns of the main sewer – men who knew that only a few of them would survive the day. It was no surprise that many chose to end their own lives rather than risk a dark stinking death underground.

A fate, Qulan wryly reflected, that could be his, left to rot in this place. He knew every inch of it by now; his daily regime ensured that he exercised body and mind, walking around his cell endlessly, recreating marches and landscapes from his military career in minute detail. He also plotted the cell itself: the curved shape of the oubliette; the brickwork; the iron staples in the wall; the door set high above steep steps; the number of steps; the number of bricks in each quadrant . . . the distance to the tiny grating on the curve of the ceiling, which opened two floors above and allowed just enough light through for him to perform his daily tasks. On and on, a refusal to let his mind dwell on dangerous thoughts. Thoughts of home, yes, but even more, concern about the situation in the Empire and the city itself. Maya was no myth. Whatever power she had, or seemed to have, was drawing more adherents to her cause every day. He knew that towns were already going over to her on the marches of the Empire. Soon it would be cities, whole provinces. He needed to be at the head of his men, preparing for the coming battle!

He smashed his fist against the wall in impotent fury, then breathed deeply and calmed himself. He could do nothing where he was; he only hoped Gregor was still free. There had been no word, no message even. He checked each of his two daily meals for some sign but there was nothing. He sat on the stone sleeping area cut out of the wall of the cell and rested his head on his closed fists. How long? How long . . .?

79
The Prophecy

Before the door to the Receiving Rooms, Gregor told the Frog to wait.

'No, I'll come with you.'

The boy slipped under the arm of a guard and walked into the presence.

Cadali, in his usual spot by the throne, beckoned.

'Gregor, come, come. Stand there where His Majesty can see you – where we can all see the man who has been so elusive of late.'

He walked to the centre of the room. No point in being modest, this was either going to work or . . . He never liked 'ors', too many damned possibilities.

'You are responsible for the Sultan's security, Commander, and yet you . . . vanished. I can put it in no other way. You were not here when a plot was discovered through . . .' He smirked, enjoying this. 'His Majesty's great acumen. You failed in your duty. Explain yourself.'

'Majesty . . .'

Al-Ghuri lifted one ponderous eyelid and turned his gaze upon Gregor; the eye was all-knowing and all-seeing. That at least was the story they lived by, and the Sultan had survived plots in the past, had indeed inspired plots in the past; there wasn't much he didn't know about the art of betrayal. Gregor had best choose his words carefully – he didn't have much of a hand to play here.

'... I have been working behind the scenes, not sitting in the palace drinking tea and filling my belly.'

Cadali stepped in smoothly. 'I have been beside my Sultan while you have been ...'

Gregor let the silence fill the room as Cadali's satisfaction swelled to monstrous size and ...

'I have located the scrolls stolen from your late First Wife Shajah, Majesty.'

... deflated like a pig's bladder stuck with a hundred needles. Cadali's eyes popped.

Al-Ghuri said: 'You have this thing, these scrolls that are talked of, Commander?'

'I know where they are, Majesty.'

Al-Ghuri snapped: 'I know where they are – they are lost. The question is—'

'The scrolls don't matter.' A boy's voice, cutting across the angry moment.

'Who is this child?'

'This is the boy who has been making prophecies.' No harm in writing the legend a little larger than fact might allow. 'He has attained considerable fame. His reputation has spread far and wide. His predictions are remarkably accurate.'

Cadali guffawed. 'A circus performer? That's what you offer the great al-Ghuri at this time of crisis? Oh, Gregor, Gregor, what has become of you?'

The Sultan leaned forward, a tiny speck of interest in his expression at this novelty. At least it would not prove threatening.

'What do they call you, boy?'

'Frog.'

'And what do you want, Frog?'

'To tell you about the dreams you've been having.'

Al-Ghuri sat back, his expression now one of menace.

'What do you know about my dreams?'

In a clear voice the boy said: 'You dream of victories and when you wake, you fear the hand of the assassin.'

Even Cadali gasped at the words. Two of the guards moved forward, ready to cut the child down at the first hint, but al-Ghuri did not give any command. Rather, he got up from his throne, stepped down from his plinth and crossed the floor, his sandals flapping like duck's feet, Gregor thought. He squatted in front of the Frog and looked directly into his eyes.

'Tell me more about my dreams.'

'You are riding next to your general, at the head of a great victory parade.'

'Where are we?'

'Tumanbay.'

'I have had such a dream . . . but any ruler might.'

'But in truth, your general will be riding in your dust and you will be beside her. She will be there.'

'Maya?'

'Yes, Maya.'

'And I will be at the head of the armies?'

'And all the people of Tumanbay will see you.'

'And this is your prophecy – this is what will happen?'

'There will be a sign just before.'

'What sign?'

'Birds will gather in the midday heat. Then you will know that what I say will come to pass.'

'Give me a sign now!' the Sultan asked, hungry for certainty.

The boy looked at the Sultan curiously. 'What would you like?'

'Something, anything, some magic so I know what you say is true.'

The Frog held up his hands, palms out and empty. Al-Ghuri got to his feet with a groan or two, his expression now petulant; of the two, it seemed to Gregor that the Frog was the older.

'A sign, give me a sign, do something.'

The Frog did a little dance, shuffling his feet, ending with a bow and a flourish.

'What sort of sign is that?' al-Ghuri demanded, losing patience.

Cadali stepped in. 'He is a trickster, Majesty, he knows nothing. These dreams, anyone could make up such stuff.'

'Take the boy away, give him a good beating.'

The Sultan shuffled back to his throne, his sandals more duck-like than ever. Gregor was feeling distinctly uncomfortable. Was he the fool here?

'Leave him to me,' he said, taking the Frog by the arm and firmly guiding him out of the room. 'I'll see to it myself.'

'There was something on your pillow when you woke!' the Frog shouted back.

'Stop,' the Sultan ordered.

Gregor let go of the Frog. The Sultan approached.

'What was on my pillow?' There was apprehension in his voice. 'Think well, your life will depend on your answer.'

The Frog looked at Gregor, who nodded slightly, encouragingly; then about the room at all the officials and slaves, their eyes fixed on him; then to the Sultan, Lion of Lions, Sultan of Eagles, Destroyer of Enemies, Father of the Peoples, Protector of the Poor, Sword of the Faith, now no more than a hand's width away – the most powerful ruler on earth revealed as an anxious old man.

'A dagger,' the Frog said eventually. 'Unsheathed, with emeralds and a horse's head on the hilt.'

423

He might have been talking of a child's toy, so everyday was his tone, but the effect on al-Ghuri was instant and extraordinary. He paled, lifted his right hand to his heart and croaked: 'Go on.' The Frog noticed perspiration about his temples.

'You had your servant killed,' he continued, 'so no one would know about it. You fear everyone around you, you don't know who to trust, you can't sleep.'

'Who put it there?' the Sultan asked urgently.

The Frog closed his eyes, scrunching up his face as if trying to remember or to conjure up an image.

'I see the colour red,' he said.

'And the general who rode beside me. In your . . . your prophecy, your dream . . . will he betray me?'

The Frog tilted his head and frowned as if surprised by the question.

'What do *you* think?' he asked.

'He is in the cells now, how could he betray me?'

'Then you have answered your own question.'

'But . . . but is he loyal?'

'He is loyal to Tumanbay.'

'But is he loyal to *me*?' His voice was getting increasingly urgent.

'Oh yes, he would die for you because the Sultan and Tumanbay are one.'

Al-Ghuri stared in wide-eyed astonishment at the boy. It was as if time itself had stopped. No one present moved. They were waiting for the Sultan to respond. Then al-Ghuri turned to Cadali.

'Release General Qulan now,' he said quietly.

'But, but . . . Majesty,' Cadali stuttered, 'I must advise—'

'Release the general!' Now he was screaming 'Release him now! And I'm ready to see Maya's envoy. Bring him.' He had rediscovered his courage. 'Give that boy a pomegranate, give him an orchard, give him a horse, one of my whites.'

'I want to go home,' the Frog said.

'And keep him here in the palace. I will need him later.'

The Frog looked up at Gregor. 'You promised.'

'The Sultan has spoken,' Gregor said. 'Come, you can rest in my rooms.'

He didn't spare Cadali a glance as they left.

The doors were opened by two guards, one of whom muttered: 'Good to have you back, Commander.' Gregor nodded.

As the doors closed he could hear the Sultan exulting.

'I will lead my army myself. I will defeat Maya in battle and rip her living heart from her chest and squeeze it until blood soaks the sand red.'

80

Qulan

Time, he decided, is like distance. There's no point if a march has no destination; no point if the waiting has no end. He was measuring his days in the growth of his beard. If he didn't get out soon, he'd look like the Hafiz. His thoughts turned to his garden. He resolutely cut them short. There was no garden, no family, no army, no officer corps, no campaign to plan, no battle, no victory. There was only the here and now, another day – if day it was – another routine to follow. Walk three paces, turn, walk three paces . . . Turn, walk three paces, turn . . . Check the spider's web up near the grating. Clever creature, that was good strategy. Everything goes towards the light, however dim. And yes, there was a fly ensnared; the spider was busily wrapping it in silk to preserve it for later. Well, that was one thing you could always be sure about in this damned hole: there would be a later.

He walked on, three paces by three paces . . . He was recreating the walk off the mountain after they had lost Varsi. He and Gregor, both half-starved but drawn on by the first trees – firs sturdy enough to survive the high passes – lichen, then scrubland, gorse, grasses, green leaves and brown boughs and, one miraculous day, the green of high meadows and shortly after that, goats among the mountain oaks. They were just approaching a wily old she-goat with rocks in their hand, ready to kill themselves their first good meal for weeks when he heard footsteps approaching and the jingle of keys. The door opened halfway up the wall of the bottle-shaped cell. A guard appeared in the square of the door.

'You are free to go, General Qulan. The Sultan commands you to resume your duties.'

He climbed the steps, blinking as he emerged into the corridor. The guard handed him his sword.

'This way, General.'

A door opened along the passage and Wolf climbed out. He had spent his time re-plaiting his hair in a different style. When his sword was handed back, he made to stab the guard who scuttled clear. Wolf laughed.

'So, this is how Tumanbay treats her allies, eh? What's happening?'

'Seems like we may be free to do our jobs again. If you want to. I wouldn't blame you if you took your people back to the high country and I wouldn't stop you either.'

Wolf shrugged. 'Well, there's a fine woman here who I would be sorry to lose, so I think I'll stay for now.'

'Then we have work to do.'

81

Ibn Bai

Ibn Bai walked through the great central slave market but his mind really wasn't on the job. He'd had trouble recently, concentrating on business; his concerns were more for the child and her mother, down there in the undercity, and for Commander Gregor, that devious and dangerous man. Even so, old habits die hard and he stopped here and there to look over what was on offer.

'Ibn Bai, is it you, my friend?'

'It is indubitably me,' he said, 'but who ...? Mitra? From the market at the harbour? You've moved up in the world.'

'A man cannot stay still, Ibn Bai, or ... he goes nowhere. I am expanding. My nephew is handling the port end of the business now, channelling the product to the farm markets, the fighting pits or, only the best, to the House of Mitra, here at the centre of all things. Are you buying? I have a new consignment from the south ... or from the mountains. Fine house servants ...'

Ibn Bai shook his head. 'Not at the moment, Mitra.'

Mitra blew a long fart through his ample lips. 'I tell you, Ibn Bai, strictly between us, business is terrible, has been ever since all this invasion talk – armies and call-up and everything in the air, falling who knows where. Business loves stability, eh?'

'They say the Sultan will destroy this Maya.'

'They say the moon lives at the bottom of a well – but I don't believe it.'

He looked around, checking to be sure no nosy ears were listening in. There were those in the city who made a good living out of informing on disloyal citizens.

'Hard for everyone, I suppose,' Ibn Bai said, though he wasn't really interested in the conversation.

'And I've got to keep on feeding them,' Mitra said. 'No one else is going to. Some traders, they've begun cutting their losses, you must have heard the whispers?'

'I've not really been much involved with the business lately.'

Mitra mimed an exaggerated throat-cutting. 'What else can they do. But not me, not yet. Too much invested. Oh, how did the blue-eyes turn out? Did you manage to tame the man?'

'Got a good price for him. Probably in the fighting pits by now.'

'And the girl with the babe in arms? Surprised you took them both. I suppose it ended up with the dogs, though she was pretty enough.'

'No, stop, I don't want . . .' Ibn Bai shook his head. 'Sorry, Mitra. It's a bit of a story.'

'Well, I'm not exactly run off my feet at the moment. Boy . . .' He called to a lad lounging by one of the cages. 'Tea, now! Ibn Bai, sit at my table here, drink tea with me, tell me your sadness, for I can see it is so.'

He gestured widely and they both sat down.

'Speak,' Mitra said.

'I lost my wife and child. They were coming to join me here in Tumanbay and the ship . . . my ship became their final resting place.'

'Ibn Bai, no! Such a misfortune. What happened?'

'Plague. It was a ship of the dead when it finally came to shore. So many dreams . . .'

Mitra clicked his tongue in sympathy.

'She was to be married, my Heaven . . . I had found her a good match and all was . . . ashes. Burned as the ship was burned in the harbour.'

'Aye, aye, I remember the day, the black smoke rising above the port. And to think, it was your ship. Ha, the ways of God are hard for men to bear and yet bear them we must.'

'All that is the past now,' Ibn Bai said. 'It was not to be.'

The tea arrived; they drank it in silence and, out of the silence, Ibn Bai said: 'I looked after the child.'

Mitra asked: 'Child? Which . . .? Ah, the slave girl's child, you mean?'

'But then she too was taken from me. Life raises a man only to throw him down again.'

'It does, it does. Honey cake?'

Ibn Bai waved the cake away. 'Perhaps it is my fate to be alone, as we all are in the end.'

'Surely there is a purpose to everything that happens in this world, Ibn Bai, if only we could understand it.'

'Then it would take a wiser head than mine. Thank you for the tea, my friend, and for the talk, it has eased my heart a little. I hope business picks up for you.'

'It is in God's hands. Are you sure you don't want to see the new stock?'

'Next time, perhaps.'

As he wandered away, Ibn Bai wondered if there ever would be a next time. Perhaps for him it was time to retire from the world and read his books and contemplate . . .

'Excuse me, Excellency.'

He had almost bumped into a young woman, robed and hooded.

'What is it, girl, what do you want of me?' A beggar? 'I have no alms to give today.'

'Have you nothing to give to your daughter, Father?'

He began to shake and tremble before he even began to think – she pulled her hood back.

He began to cry before he even found the words to say: 'But you are dead, I saw you burn, I saw the ship . . .'

He began to fall before he could even reach out to touch her beautiful, so dearly beloved, so deeply mourned face. Strong hands caught him before he touched the ground – and then he touched her face, and clasped her to him. Her tears and his joined, father and child together.

'We were looking for you. I did not know where you lived but we thought you would come to the market sooner or later, and here you are and here we are.'

'Is he really her father? We found him?'

A boy, scratching his dirty hair with his head on one side and a lopsided grin on his face.

The big man, who gently set Ibn Bai down, said: 'Yes, Boy, we did.'

Ibn Bai, the tears still streaming down his face, said: 'Indeed, my boy, my splendid boy. My dear man,' to the big fellow, 'you have found me.'

'These are my friends, Father.'

'Then they are my friends too.'

The big man smiled, an odd sort of smile that Ibn Bai couldn't read.

'And my house is your house and all that is mine is yours, for you have found my daughter who was lost. Your name, sir.'

'My name is No-Man. This –' a hand laid on the boy's shoulder – 'is Boy.'

'Come now to my house and grant me one favour. Let me walk with my daughter for I have – even in this time of joy – sad news to give her.'

Heaven took his arm – there was a strength in her that both Slave and Boy noticed; it had been growing over the past days but now its flowering would soon come. They heard her say: 'She is dead, isn't she? The plague.'

Slave held Boy back a moment. 'Let them have their time.'

Boy said: 'Your name is No-Man, then?'

'It is for now.'

'Aaaand you were a slave. That's what she said. Aaaand you kidnapped her from her father's ship, which means—'

Slave held a finger to his lips. 'Shhhhhhh . . . Enough for now, we have come to a place where we may rest.'

82

Red

Effendi Red regarded Gregor with curiosity.

'Where have you been, Commander? They have been looking for you.' He took in Gregor's bandaged hand but said nothing.

'Now they have found me, and asked me to summon you to the Council Chamber. If it is not inconvenient?'

'My convenience is of little matter.'

He was sitting in a chair by the window of his chamber, a board open before him on which pieces were laid out. He picked one up and placed it on a horizontal marker next to a smaller piece, which he then removed from the board.

'I don't recognise the game, effendi.'

'No, I dare say you do not.' He stood. 'I am ready. Shall we go?'

As they left Gregor said: 'You don't lock your door? Were you not given a key?'

'Probably the same one you have.'

There was no answer to that.

'And may I ask who your opponent is.'

'Opponent?'

'In the game you were playing.'

'It is not a game.'

He would say no more and after a few failed attempts on Gregor's part, they walked in silence. Only as they approached the Council Chamber did Red say: 'I presume they have been found, then?'

'The scrolls?'

'What else?'

'I'm certain His Majesty would wish to be the first to share the news with you.'

The doors opened as they approached. Al-Ghuri was on his throne, his guards surrounding him. Cadali stood to one side, his arms folded.

Red strode to the centre of the room and, ignoring protocol as usual, said: 'I hope you had a restful night, Majesty?'

'I did, despite your intentions.'

Everything about the Sultan spoke of a new confidence; he was like the younger man Gregor remembered in the first days after the coup, who still had everything before him.

'My "intentions", Majesty?'

'The knife on the pillow that morning. I imagine it was your work?'

Red offered empty hands to the throne. 'None of my doing. I would say that if my queen had wished to kill you . . .' He left the threat unsaid. 'Set your mind at rest, Majesty, she wishes you no harm. She wishes to be your friend. You showed great wisdom in restraining your army and arresting General Qulan. All she wants are the scrolls. So, if you will hand them to me, I shall convey—'

'Nothing at all.'

'Majesty, I do not understand . . .?'

'You know what. Gregor, place Effendi Red under guard, convey him to the cells and lock him up. He should find that easy enough to "understand".'

'I am Maya's envoy. You can't do that. Protocol—'

'You are the envoy of a dead governor's wife who will shortly meet the end she deserves. I know the future, I have nothing to fear. I am ready for battle and I will march at the head of my troops and destroy your whore-bitch queen. Take him away.'

Red went without a struggle. His demeanour was calm; he might have been walking in a lemon grove on a warm afternoon for all the notice he took of the guards, the descent into the cells, the manacles placed on his wrists and ankles. He sat calmly and nodded to Gregor as the door was shut and locked. Walking back to report that the man was securely housed, Gregor thought back to the board and the pieces that were moved and removed, and wondered: if it wasn't a game, then what was it?

83

Gregor

'Put your sword away,' the Frog said, 'and keep walking. No one will hurt you while you are with me.'

He sounded pleased with himself. He should; he'd long been plaguing Gregor with demands to go home, which had invariably been answered with the simple mantra: 'The Sultan wants you here, here you will stay.'

Which he had, eating vast amounts, fiddling and moving everything and complaining until the last day or so, when he had announced smugly: 'I have seen it – we will go soon.'

And here they were, the boy holding Gregor's sleeve, leading him into the sibilant darkness. He could smell bat droppings, which meant bats, and despite himself, he shuddered. It was all very well to face your fears but thousands of the little horrors was something else. Still, it had amply confirmed his own use of the technique. Simply find the worst thing in the world for your subject – it could be as mundane as cloves of garlic or as exotic as the ragiffa worm – and then . . .

'We are here,' the Frog said.

'Where?'

A door resolved itself as it opened onto a lighted chamber beyond. They stepped over the chittering of cockroaches and a woman came forward, arms open, to enfold the boy.

'I knew you would come back, my little Frog.'

The Frog mumbled into her bosom until she let him go and he finished: '. . . told you I would.'

'You see, I have brought him back, as I promised,' Gregor said.

'Perhaps, perhaps not. What do you want?'

'The woman Sarah and her baby. I have news of her brother, she will want to hear.'

The woman looked to her son: 'Should I, Frog?'

'Yes, Mother, take him, keep a good hold so his foot does not stray. Goodbye, Gregor.'

The woman took his wrist in a grip as firm and friendly as manacles.

He said: 'Have you seen my future, Frog? Will I live, will I prosper? Have you seen it?'

Frog merely smiled and said: 'It doesn't matter, since it is written. So it will be.'

Gregor shouted back: 'Why can't you damned prophets ever be clear about anything?'

This time the Frog laughed in the enfolding darkness.

They walked for what seemed an endless time, Gregor's senses utterly dislocated, until it was only the woman's strong grip that kept him upright and moving forward. At last, she stopped and let him go. He flailed wildly, trying to touch her, grab her, get some kind of grip on himself and her and then, out of the darkness, flame – great sheets of writhing fire and a blast of heat that sent him staggering backwards. He shielded his eyes against the shattering brightness, but nothing could protect his ears from the roar like a thousand dragons. A line came into his mind: It is a dreadful thing to be in the hand of the living Gods. And then it was gone and he was left with the after-image of dancing flames and a buzzing in his ears.

'It is the Chasm.' Sarah's voice. 'No one knows how deep it

is – there are fires down there that burn perpetually. Sometimes they make themselves known to us, so we do not forget. Come, this way.'

Her touch was like ... a butterfly's, he thought, barely there and yet reassuring. She led him into a chamber where gradually lamps resolved out of the fires that burned in his eyes. When she let go of his hand he felt a certain regret.

'You deserted me last time,' he said, 'before I could give you news of your brother.'

'What news?'

'Do you have the scrolls?'

'Oh, Gregor, still trying to trade? Have you learned nothing?'

'I am the Sultan's representative and he demands their return. They belong to the state of Tumanbay.'

'You should hear yourself. You sound like a little boy beating his chest and threatening to kill dragons.' She smiled at him and her face was suddenly beautiful. Why had he never noticed before? 'When all the time you should have been a little boy attentive at his lessons. There is none so ignorant as he who believes he knows everything.'

'I know there are no dragons,' he said.

'Really? Then there is no Sultan's representative down here either. If you want the scrolls it is for yourself, yes?'

'I can help you, Sarah, you and your baby. I have houses in the city where you will be safe. You can see the sun, breathe the fresh air, be free.'

'I'll no longer be your slave?' she asked.

'Whatever you want will be yours. Give me the scrolls, tell me what you know about Shajah's death.'

'You don't understand, Gregor. I am not free to leave here. I cannot simply walk away.'

'Why not?'

She glanced around nervously and signalled for Gregor to speak quietly.

'I can arrange it, Sarah. I have men who can hide in the shadows, we will rescue you.'

'People who can see in the dark,' she whispered, 'have no fear of men who hide in the shadows. And there are others – not just those of the undercity but something far stronger, far more demanding. Sit beside me. Listen, I will tell you a story.'

She sat and after a moment's hesitation, he sat beside her; he could feel her presence, her warmth, the smell of her . . .

'There was a teacher,' she said, 'who, rather than sit in the temple, went to the marketplace one day and told the people, "There is only one God. He doesn't want gold or jewels and vast temples and statues. He wants the hearts of men and women. Men and women who are not afraid to die for their beliefs because they know they will die blessed." And he wrote all these things down on two scrolls, and over the years these scrolls became the most sacred relic to believers who do not believe in sacred relics. And that is why the Sultan will lose and Maya will win.'

'I don't understand, Sarah. What does it mean?'

'It's a story, that's all,' she said. 'That people tell themselves so they aren't frightened in the dark.'

Was she frightened? Looking at her face in the fragile lamplight, surrounded by the darkness, he felt a great concern – something he had not felt in his life for a long, long time, something he thought had been lost on that mountain pass. He wanted to save her. He could save her. And yet he knew she was more than she seemed. Could he trust her? Could he trust his heart? He never had, and all his experience told him that he should be wary of everything she said, all that she was. And yet, and yet . . . his lost heart called to him still.

'Who are you, Sarah?'

'Aren't you a man who discovers such things?'

'Can I trust you?'

She said, simply, 'Yes.'

'Then show me. Give me the scrolls now.'

'First, you must do something more for me. A message to Ibn Bai. So that he knows the baby and I are safe. Bring his answer and then I will give you what you want.'

'I am not your messenger!' But I am, he thought, that's exactly what I am. 'And you will tell me what you know?'

She stood and handed him a folded sheet of vellum.

'I promise you will find as much of the truth as there is to be found, Gregor.'

A young man entered. A scimitar hung at his waist.

'You will be guided by this one,' Sarah said.

'And your brother, don't you want to know about him?'

She nodded.

'His fortunes are improving every day. He has done well, assistant to General Qulan.'

She smiled but she seemed distant, as though preoccupied, or just scared, Gregor thought.

He felt a hand on his shoulder and turned.

'This way,' said the young man, indicating the door.

Gregor nodded, then looked back to Sarah. But she disappeared into the darkness. As he followed the young man, he reflected that those who no longer fear the dark may not fear anything else either . . .

84

al-Ghuri

A boom like the crack of doom sounded over the Field of War, where they were testing the cannon. There were two great bronze and iron beasts with mouths as wide as a man's arm span, that could throw a projectile a league or more. The first, the *Hand of the Sultan*, had just spewed flame and smoke and, with a great rushing of wind, sent an iron ball far across the field to crash into a barracks building which Cadali hoped someone had remembered to evacuate. The walls were smashed into a thousand pieces and the whole structure vanished in a cloud of dust. Sultan al-Ghuri, peering through a brass telescope, cooed his satisfaction.

The *Hand of the Sultan* lurched back on its carriage from the recoil, but even before it had come to a rest the gunner's mates, half-naked and blackened with gunpowder residue, were straining at the ropes to pull it back into firing position. The loading platform, necessary to allow the crew to reach the height of the muzzle, was pushed into place by more straining backs, and the barrel hissed and belched steam as a wet sponge on a long oaken handle was shoved down to cool and clean it out. Powder sacks and wadding followed and were tamped into place. Finally, rather than a cannonball, a round metal canister as tall as Cadali, filling the width of the barrel, was lowered and carefully rammed home. As the gun was traversed, its companion, the *Hand of God*, roared out and bucked backwards in its turn, sending a cloud of powder smoke across the field. There was a scent of sulphur and eggs and Cadali wrinkled his nose in distaste. Far away another building collapsed.

The cannon had been imported at great expense from a land beyond the Middle Sea where they possessed the secrets of such workings. The Sultan was convinced they would deliver him a quick victory over this insolent woman. He said as much, when Cadali enquired as to who would run the city during the coming hostilities.

'I'll hardly be away for long. My *Hands* will strangle the life from her scrawny neck.'

Ever the courtier, Cadali replied: 'And you will return victorious but the city must have a proper authority. What if these so-called spies of Maya engineer a revolt?'

The crew of the *Hand of God* were busy cleaning and reloading their charge now. Al-Ghuri kept his gaze upon the two monsters.

'And you suggest?'

Was he smiling? Could Cadali make out the edge of a grin? Surely not.

He said: 'Possibly Gregor. After all, he is Master of the Palace Guard, but . . . Where has he been? What has he been up to? Has he, indeed, been totally honest with you? And then there's Madu. The young man has come on wonderfully since his time in the army, but he is young and there is his personal life . . .'

A second canister was lowered into the barrel of the *Hand of God*. The crews began to traverse both barrels, aligning them with a great wooden pavilion far away across the field. It had been used by al-Ghuri's brother when he reviewed the troops. The present Sultan had never liked it and never used it.

'Go on, Vizier.'

'I have served you long and well.'

'Really?'

Cadali was adept at reading the sound of a word, its pronunciation, for signs of pleasure or displeasure; but then al-Ghuri was equally adept at disguising the sound of a word.

'Do you doubt it, Majesty?'

'And yet . . .' A squeaking in the air; it was a gunner screwing down the long sight on the nearest cannon. 'And yet General Qulan went to prison. Was it not on your advice?'

'My Lord, any man might – in his wish to serve – perhaps exceed . . . And there was the matter of the messages sent to the army . . .'

'Yes, there was suspicion but you, I believe, added weight to the scale. Your counsel was wrong.'

'But my concern was always for you, Majesty. If there was excess, it was excess of loyalty. Perhaps I got it wrong but . . .'

Al-Ghuri turned. No smile; now there was a frown of anger, the brows drawn close and dark, the eyes glittering with menace.

'Did you get it wrong, or did it go exactly as you wished until the boy prophet made all things clear to me?'

For a moment, the loudest sound to be heard was Cadali swallowing.

'I wonder what it would be like for a man to be standing in front of the *Hand of the Sultan* or the *Hand of God* when they fired their canisters full of needles?'

He nodded and then the loudest sound to be heard was the loudest sound Cadali had ever heard: both cannon firing together, delivering a rain of needles that sliced the distant pagoda into ribbons. It hung there like a tissue paper ghost for a moment, and then the wind blew it away into nothing.

'I never liked that building,' the Sultan said, but neither man heard anything; they had both been temporarily deafened by the roar. The lesson, however, and its deadly weight, sounded loud

443

and clear in the Vizier's head and he remembered . . .

A child of six years watching his house burn, hearing the screams of his mother and father as they burned too, and the wails and pleas of his brothers and sisters as they were gathered up in nets laid across the saddles of the slavers' horses and ridden down to Villeppi to be sent for sale in Tumanbay. He had felt . . . He had felt nothing. Numbed by the horror of it all, as he was numbed now by the sheer vast concussion of these great engines of war. And yet the child had, after moons, begun to emerge as himself again and make his way in a strange city. Today time was a luxury he did not have. He needed to mend things with his ruler now.

'Majesty,' he bellowed as they descended the platform, 'as always you show us the way!'

'I do, I do,' al-Ghuri said.

'And if you wish it, I will stand before the guns willingly and die for you because you are Tumanbay and everything to me. You raised me up, I stand only in your estimation.'

'Get to it, man.' The Sultan's carriage was approaching.

'I am, it would be true to say, hated by all in the palace.'

'For your ambition, Cadali.'

'And all of my ambition and my hopes and my power reside in you. You are the only sun of my world, I owe nothing to any other. Can that be said of General Qulan, of Commander Gregor?'

In a cloud of dust the carriage came to a halt. A groom leaped down and opened the door and lowered the steps.

'I have reinstated General Qulan, Commander Gregor delivered the miraculous boy to me. Do you dare to say I am wrong, Vizier?'

'Not for a moment, Majesty. Your wisdom is well known. You are a great king. We are all your tools. Your decisions are always right. But consider – Qulan and Gregor owe you and Tumanbay their service but in the end, their loyalties lie with each other. From childhood they have relied upon and supported each other. You know they have both acted without your express command. They may be your tigers, but tigers have been known to turn. As for me, I have no one, no friend, no ally except you, Majesty. You hold me like a tiny spider on a shovel over a roaring fire. You may destroy me at any moment ... but them ... I only say – be wise, beware the brothers.'

One foot on the step, al-Ghuri paused. Finally, he nodded and climbed in, the door shut and the carriage departed. Cadali allowed himself a smile.

85

Gregor

The cells beneath the palace of Tumanbay had been built to impress their unwilling guests with the sheer power of the state that loomed above them and pressed down with the weight of a million blocks of stone. Even Gregor felt a certain disquiet as he descended the flights of steps down into the abyss, the flaming sconces on the walls sending his long shadow creeping before him. A disquiet increased by the knowledge of the world beneath this world where the woman Sarah waited.

She had said: 'I promise you will find as much of the truth as there is to be found.'

That could mean anything at all. Undoubtedly she knew ... what? She must have been there when Shajah died, or she was the cause of that death, or she found her mistress dead and ran with the scrolls that he had commanded her to deliver. Was he allowing his feelings for her – and he was beginning to have to admit to himself that the jurist's question was not without its truth – to influence his actions? If he were to be honest – he almost laughed aloud at the irony of it all – he could remember looking forward to their meetings not alone for her information, which was of minor value, but for her company. He had not travelled in the land of the heart since

... since his last glimpse of his sister and underground he had, for a moment, confused his sister and Sarah ... He shook the thought away. This was all undiscovered country and there was no profit to be had here. There was a job to do, so best do it.

Guards snapped to attention as he passed. They could doubtless hear his footsteps approaching. He shivered; it was cold down here in what was, his brother had once said, his natural realm. Sometimes, even on the hottest days, there was a mist that snaked about the stone corridors, carrying the sour stink of defeat. He stopped before a cell door, nodded to the guard, unlocked it and entered.

Effendi Red looked up just as calmly as he had when he had been relaxing in his chambers. He had a candle, a stone bottle of water, some uneaten bread on a tin plate. He sat on a stone bench, one foot tucked up under his robe. He might have been reading or dictating letters home.

'Have you come to free me?' He laughed. 'Of course you haven't. You've come to ask me a question.'

'You think you know my business better than I do,' he asked?

'Probably, yes.'

And probably the bastard is right, Gregor thought.

What he said was: 'Then I imagine you can give me the answer without hearing what I have to say?'

'Yes.'

'Then be so kind as to do so, effendi.'

Red smiled. 'You know the answer without hearing what I have to say. But if you insist—'

'I could have it torn out of you, with pincers and hot lead.'

'Very simply put, your best chance of surviving what is going to happen, will be to deliver the scrolls.'

447

'Unlike your chances, which are getting shorter by the moment.'

Not a flicker betrayed any response from the envoy; he might have been carved out of ivory, blood ivory. Whereas Gregor knew he had betrayed himself uttering a pointless threat. He was losing his touch.

'My brother will defeat Maya and then you will die, I guarantee it, effendi.'

'I look forward to the moment with interest. Don't be the fool you are not, Commander. Cadali is out of favour, but who is in? Your brother? Perhaps. Young Madu? Maybe. Gregor? You are a man who sits down at the gaming table with nothing in your purse, my friend.' He swooped to his feet like a great black and red bird, his robes billowing around him, and called to the guard: 'My visitor is leaving.'

Gregor turned on his heel and went without a word. Making his way back up the steps he thought: Maybe it is time to get out from under, to look to the future. He was right in one thing: without the scrolls I have nothing; with them I can sit down at the table with Maya herself.

Did that mean he had already betrayed Tumanbay in his heart? But he had no heart; that had been killed on a snowy pass when two lost children had faced their end before even seeing their beginning. Or was something yet more devious driving him back to the dark labyrinth of the undercity? For as every good spy knows, at the heart of every labyrinth there lies ... either treasure or a monster – salvation or defeat.

Sarah or the scrolls; Sarah and the scrolls. But would she deliver them up to him? Was she able to make her own decisions down there? Every instinct told him she had not been lying when she hinted at her lack of freedom; the dwellers below hadn't survived by being kind, as he knew to his cost. On the other hand, she had lied about her upbringing. But all slaves did, and who, at this time, would want to admit to having been brought up in Amber Province. The fate of Sarah had become chained to the fate of the scrolls, and to save one he must save the other.

86

Qulan

Qulan had refined his plans. In fact the plans had been long refined in his mind, and the time had been spent persuading the Sultan to accept them. The prophecy of the boy Frog, produced from who knows where by his brother Gregor, had, as Wolf put it, 'rammed a spear shaft up the Sultan's arse and made him stand like a man for once.'

The army had halted the march back to the city and now waited thirty leagues from the great walls, where it would be joined by the Sultan and his staff in due course. It was all taking far too long for Qulan's liking but at last new armour had been fashioned for al-Ghuri, fragrances had been created, auguries had been read by the Hafiz, who was to accompany His Majesty (unless he could weasel out of it), and a ceremonial departure had been hastily arranged for the twelfth day of the red moon, an auspicious time for victory. There was to be a reception the next day at the palace, when the whole enterprise would be launched.

The night before, Qulan dined with Wolf and Daniel in his war room. The big barbarian was eager to get back to his riders – their regular dispatches made it clear Maya's forces were on the move; she had gathered her people into one great company that spread, like a dark stain, across the desert sands, leaving only small garrisons to hold the cities she had taken.

Rolling up the map, Qulan said: 'Your riders will play the decisive role in the battle to come, Wolf. Their task, to turn her forces at the moment of greatest peril and expose her flanks, will not be achieved without losses. Likely major losses, so I say to you again – Tumanbay has not treated you well, you owe the city nothing.'

Wolf downed a flagon of wine and grinned at Daniel, as if he were playing the barbarian.

'I give you my loyalty, General. And I am not in the habit of breaking my word. As for dying, what would battle be without the risk of it? A game played for counters, not gold.'

'Very well, then. I shall expect everything of you and your riders.'

Wolf stood. 'You'll get it. Permission to rejoin my comrades?'

Qulan stood too. 'Granted. We'll follow you with the sun the day after tomorrow. As long as the Sultan can get up in time.'

They sat in silence until they heard the sound of hooves in the compound and the gate opening. Qulan poured more wine for them both.

'I haven't had a chance to thank you yet.'

'I was only doing my duty, General.'

'My family were not your duty. Pushkarmi tells me you were a support for them all.'

'Fortunately it was only a short time.'

'You didn't know that. I thank you, Daniel,' he said formally.

Equally formally, Daniel relied: 'It was my privilege.'

'Good. Now, I asked you to get close to the Sultan's nephew.'

'Madu and I are firm friends, sir.'

'What's he like, the young man? I've seen him at court, in the army – my feeling is that he's entitled and weak, though not without charm when he needs to deploy it.'

'He was thinking of running away. His mother had a palace in the mountains. He thought it would offer peace and safety. I persuaded him it was his duty to stay.' Daniel sipped his wine and took a lump of bread and dipped it in the salt and olive oil. 'I assumed that you would not have asked me to be his friend to no purpose?'

'Do you object to that?' Qulan asked.

'In this world we are all to be used . . .' He put the bread in his mouth, chewed and swallowed. 'And, if we are fortunate, to use.'

'Yes, I agree. Now I am going to ask you to give up this battle.'

Daniel half rose, his fist clenched. 'That's impossible! Battle is where a man can prove himself, show his worth.'

Qulan felt the young man was still cool under his anger. Was it real? Hard to tell. He was a thinker, this Daniel, a planner, possibly an intriguer. In any case a man to have on your side, rather than against you.

'I ask this because I believe I can trust you, my boy. War is unpredictable. The whole art of it lies in being able to adapt. Even so, men die. In defeat, in victory, even by accident. I have seen two hundred men lost because a bridge collapsed. Whatever happens, Tumanbay must have stable leadership and that means a succession, not a scramble for power.'

'The Vizier? Your brother?'

'I think times are changing. I would feel more comfortable if I knew that someone I trusted – someone who might well become part of my family – were standing at young Madu's side.'

There: circumstances change cases. He had told Daniel he would kill him if he even thought of Manel, and now he was cementing his loyalty with the promise of his daughter's hand. So it goes.

'You think he'll be needed?'

'I don't know. Nobody knows the future but the wise man will be as prepared as possible to meet it when it comes knocking at the door.'

'Then you can count on me, General.'

87

Madu

The palace was in the state of orderly confusion that indicated great events were taking place. Servants were ferrying dishes from the kitchens to the throne room, trailing clouds of steam; perfume braziers were placed by windows and doors, wafting the Sultan's new scent, 'The Taste of Victory at Dawn's First Light'. There was music, the lilt of the oud, multi-stringed and plangent, and the rhythm of kidskin drums. The Palace Guard, Gregor's guard, were in their ceremonial uniforms directing those summoned to the presence – old families and new, merchants and traders, a few foreign guests – and Cadali, hovering uneasily near the doors, trying both to be seen and not-seen, a trick that appeared to be beyond even his talents. It had been rumoured that the Sultan had turned on his Vizier with considerable fury after the Frog's prophecy and the release of Qulan.

This is the last place I want to be, Gregor thought, *and the first place I must be.* The noise was considerable and he had to raise his voice to greet the Vizier.

'Not at the centre of things, Cadali?'

'And you were not anywhere to be seen, Gregor? But that's what we've come to expect from you these days—'

'My absence was due to my work.'

'Oh yes, Maya's spies. Perhaps you are getting a little too close to them, Gregor.'

A group of Abyssians entered, their long plumes brushing the crystal chandeliers that glittered with candles.

'Let's hope they don't ignite,' Gregor muttered as they went by, then: 'I hear, Cadali, that your work has been less well received by the Sultan of late? Stories of crawling on the floor, weeping tears of remorse, begging. Was there begging? I do hope so.'

Cadali smiled with benign hate. 'I think you were misinformed, Commander.' He paused to bow to a member of a princely clan as he entered, and Gregor reflected that nowhere he knew of had the smile become so devalued as in Tumanbay. 'Mistakes were made, apologies were offered and graciously accepted by His Majesty.'

'Grovelling, then – tell me at least there was grovelling?'

'Enjoy your evening. Ah, Highness . . .'

He attached himself to a large Circassian and drifted away in her wake. *What is that slimy, conniving bastard up to now?* Gregor wondered. The Vizier was all too calm after his disgrace.

Across the room Daniel and Madu stood by the big window and observed the tension between Gregor and the Vizier.

Madu said: 'There's no love lost between those two, but then there never was. They both supported al-Ghuri, but Cadali had worked happily for my father.'

'He adapted,' Daniel muttered. 'A considerable skill in this society. What about Gregor?'

'Second-in-command of the guard – his commander was mysteriously killed during the coup. Ah, looks like things are happening. Here comes my uncle now.'

The music stopped and started again with the Sultan's Anthem. Everyone came to a momentary halt as he swept in surrounded by his guard. A gong sounded and the guard peeled away to circle the throne, revealing the Hafiz in His Majesty's wake, swaying somewhat, even with the support of his acolyte Bello.

'Probably drunk,' Madu whispered.

'Certainly smells like it.' Daniel sniffed. 'We could do with some of your uncle's poison right now.'

As if in answer to the words, perfume billowed into the room, obscuring the Hafiz for a moment. He coughed and spat. The monk, Bello, hastily put his shoe on the gobbet and ground it into the carpet. Cadali appeared from the crowd and turned to address the room.

'His Holiness will bless the mighty enterprise of our beloved, far-seeing, wise and warlike Sultan Abu'l Abass al-Ghuri, Lion of Lions, Sultan of Eagles!'

Madu muttered, 'Greasy bastard. He thinks he's home clear.'

'We'll see,' Daniel said. 'Here he goes.'

The great voice of the Hafiz commanded the room in a way the man himself never could.

'God has said that an idolater will come out of the east who will preach in His name, though she is the furthest of all souls from His mercy.'

'Probably written by the fat monk,' Madu said.

'Her flag will be the darkness and as the darkness is vanquished always by the light of dawn . . .'

'If the smirk of satisfaction on his face is anything to go by, I should think so,' Daniel said.

'. . . so her heresy will, after its false victories, end in defeat and misery. Her followers shall be cast down and cast out. Runaways, outcasts, gamblers, murderers and fornicators, they will be scattered to the four winds.'

'Do you think he means us?' Madu asked.

'And the righteous shall be lifted up to glory in His sight.'

'Only God knows. I note he left out drunks.'

'Wise man.'

The Hafiz took a deep breath, ready to launch forth again, but no one was listening any more. After a short while he drifted away to a couch and sat and put out his hand, into which Bello placed a tea bowl.

'Arak, I'd bet.' Madu said.

'Another sin,' Daniel said, 'and another fat man.'

'Madu, dear boy.' Cadali was smiling as he placed himself between them. 'I hear you are not going with the army? All got a bit much for you, has it?'

'Like you, I serve at the Sultan's command.'

'And will –' the Vizier rippled his shoulders towards Daniel – 'your companion be remaining behind too?'

'I too serve in that capacity, Vizier.'

'Which capacity would that be, my blue-eyed friend. One that requires you to have free access to Prince Madu at all times of the day . . . or night?'

'I would say –' Madu leaned close between his friend and the Vizier – 'that in time of war gossip should be beneath us – though I have to admit, Cadali, that you do set a low precedent.'

'Are you really thinking of running away, Madu? You and your friend here? Gossip I know, but . . . there was a body in the stable, a lad known to have been an . . .' He waved a searching finger in front of Madu. 'What would the word be . . .? Ah yes – an intimate of yours?'

Daniel said coldly, 'Tumanbay is a dangerous city, Vizier Cadali. Even the greatest must be careful here, don't you agree?'

'I agree that what seems to be solid is often like the Sultan's perfume, merely a mist. Now if you will excuse me, His Majesty is about to speak.'

457

He slipped into the crowd and moments later appeared by the throne. The music ceased, the guards crashed the butts of their lances against the floor and conversation echoed to silence. Cadali stepped forward.

'Across the whole world the name of Tumanbay will resound to the fame of—'

Al-Ghuri stood. Cadali ceased speaking at once. The Sultan spoke forcefully and briefly.

'I will crush this rebellion. While I am leading our victorious forces, the Grand Vizier Cadali will be my voice . . .'

Cadali positively expanded.

'. . . and will advise my nephew Madu, who will sit upon the throne as my regent. Together they will preserve the balance that has been so important a part of Tumanbay.'

Cadali's usual pasty complexion paled even further.

'Majesty, surely . . . If I may be permitted to say, Madu is so young, so . . .'

A master of the moment, the Vizier picked up the signs at once – the lowering of the Sultan's forehead, the narrowing of his eyes, a vein pulsing on the jaw – and switched direction with the alacrity of a skittering insect escaping a hungry lizard.

'But of course, Majesty, if it is your will then it will be my deep pleasure to offer my obedience and . . .'

Daniel caught the eye of General Qulan across the crowded room. He raised an eyebrow as if to say: *Did you know about this?*

With the slightest of shrugs, the general sent back: *The wise man takes every possibility into account!*

Madu looked as if he was about to be sick, and was going to turn on his heel and run for it before disgracing himself.

Daniel said: 'You see? You'll show them all now what a leader you can be.' He squeezed his arm reassuringly. 'And I will be with you always, my dear. And you can make that bastard Cadali bow before you!'

Al-Ghuri wriggled a ring from one forefinger and held it up.

'I will place this ring upon his finger. Come, Madu, and accept your destiny.'

A light seemed to go on behind Madu's eyes. He walked confidently forward, taking control of the whole room, kneeled before the Sultan.

'Majesty, I accept this ring and swear on all I hold sacred, on the ashes of my dear mother –' uncle and nephew shared a moment of memory and tear of loss – 'that I will serve you and serve Tumanbay faithfully.'

A respectful murmuration of applause flowed through the crowd as al-Ghuri raised Madu up and the two men stood together. A silence fell. Madu stepped half a pace forward.

'I call upon the Grand Vizier Cadali to kneel and kiss the ring to show we are united in service.'

A gleeful smirk of pleasure flowed across the assembled guests; there was hardly a man or woman present who hadn't, at some time, suffered or lost money or face at the hands of Cadali.

As the Vizier kneeled, Madu whispered: 'You know, Cadali, nothing I could think of saying could ever improve on the pleasure of this moment.'

After the kiss, Cadali stood. 'A cloth to wipe away the past, a rose to sweeten the present, a kiss to greet the future.'

Standing behind his brother, Gregor muttered: 'He swallowed that with some style.'

'That's because he's thinking about the next battle – the one he can win rather than the one he's just lost. The man's not a fool. Ah, our Sultan is about to speak.'

Madu and Cadali on either side, al-Ghuri said: 'We shall march on the dawn of the blood moon. Beside me, at the head of our armies, to show this woman that God fights with us, will be His Holiness the Hafiz!'

The silence following his words was broken as the bowl of arak dropped from the hands of the Hafiz and smashed on the floor.

88

Slave

Ibn Bai, Heaven, Slave and Boy, and the thousands of other citizens who crowded the streets and the walls of Tumanbay, could
see the spectacle plainly.

Four ranks of spearmen marched in the vanguard, the wicked
steel points of their weapons catching the sun and sparkling like
stars in the daylight. Around them bannermen in their hundreds carried the flags of the Sultan and the city, a riot of strange
devices and bright colours, the silk and canvas swirling and
snapping in the cool dawn winds coming off the desert. Behind
them, horns of brass and silver, fashioned like serpents twisted in
a hundred bizarre shapes, blasting out what, to Ibn Bai, sounded
like the sound of dyspeptic elephants, but then he'd never had an
ear for music. Drums followed – huge kettles, hefted by camels,
hammered by mighty muscled riders in red fezzes.

Heaven had to shout to make herself heard above the thunder:
'Who's in charge? Where's the Sultan?'

'There, there, in the chariot!'

It was of gold, drawn by a dozen white horses, the Sultan's
own, runners with drawn scimitars keeping pace and the Sultan
himself standing behind the driver, not acknowledging the
crowds but peering out at the desert where victory awaited.

'Isn't he rather small?' Boy said.

'Size isn't important in sultans,' Ibn Bai said. 'He has the loyalty of all Tumanbay. And there's General Qulan on the horse – the greatest general in the world!'

The general was riding with a small group of officers, taking care to keep well behind the Sultan's chariot and its dust so as not to dim his glory. Behind them came mounted pikemen, swaying on their camels, then horse cavalry and finally a cart – draped in cloth of gold and scarlet, pulled by monks hauling on silken cords, bearing a throne on which a figure sat slumped, his wispy white beard and hair blowing in the wind. Beside him stood a small, fat fellow who was waving at the crowd with one of the old man's floppy hands.

'That's the Hafiz,' Ibn Bai explained. 'He's a very holy man.'

Slave said: 'He looks like a very drunk man, to me.'

'Is that why he's tied to the chair?' Boy asked.

'Perhaps he doesn't want to go to war,' Ibn Bai said.

'I think he's being sick,' Boy said.

Later, after the parade had passed and the great gates of the city had shut behind them, Boy said he was hungry – as usual – and Slave took him to the market in search of something to eat.

Heaven and her father walked home together and she said: 'Why did we have to come?'

'I thought it would be interesting for the boy. And to see the Sultan—'

'No, here, to Tumanbay. If we'd stayed at home they could have had their war and Mother would still be alive and . . . we would be happy and . . .'

She shook her head, tears on her cheeks. He took her hands and looked into her eyes, so like her mother's. He felt his own tears rising and hugged her to him.

'It's not for us to know God's plans. All I know is that my

daughter was a girl when I left and is now a woman. Do you remember the orchard in our old house, in the autumn when the leaves were blown on the winds? So are we all. The best we can wish for in this world is that we come to a happy end.'

Cracks – there were definitely cracks in the plaster of the new wall, and Ibn Bai had sent for the builder. After all, he had paid well and added a larger than usual bribe, never mind the extra for the baby. He considered he was owed and strode to the door, ready to give the fellow a piece of his mind. Though, of course, with the usual discretion . . .

'Arem, my friend, it seems there is a crack in my— You?'

'I believe so.' Gregor bowed.

'Excellency, I never—'

'Expected I would survive the underworld? May I come in?'

The man had a way of asking that sounded very much like a command to Ibn Bai's ears.

'Yes, of course, come through. I will tell them to prepare—'

'I need nothing beyond . . . Ah, who is this?'

Heaven entered the room, a coffee cup in her hand. She regarded Gregor levelly.

'A pearl that is lost and found,' Ibn Bai said. 'My daughter Heaven.'

'The gods have indeed been kind to you. But the plague ship – it was burned in the harbour . . .'

Before Ibn Bai could answer, Heaven stepped in. 'I was not on it.'

The room had got suddenly cooler, or maybe it was Ibn Bai himself and the apprehension he felt now that Gregor had fixed his attention on Heaven.

'And yet here you are,' Gregor said.

Ibn Bai wished there were some way he could warn his

463

daughter about this man and the danger he represented. Nothing good had ever come from his arrival in this house.

'There was a storm. I was washed overboard. A fellow passenger saved me.' Once again her gaze was level. 'I would have drowned. Even so, we couldn't get back to the ship. We were washed ashore. We had . . . so many adventures. It was like the old tales.'

Was she daring him to question her story? If so, she was taking a dangerous chance.

Ibn Bai said: 'It was a complete surprise when—'

Gregor held up a hand and he fell silent.

'In a storm, you were on deck?'

She nodded.

'And a fellow passenger dived in to save you?'

'Yes.'

'On deck. Out in the open. I am surprised your mother allowed it. Or the captain – surely he would have been more careful of his employer's . . . family.' Like a scorpion catching the eye of its intended victim, he went on, circling closer. 'You do not strike me as a disobedient daughter?'

She smiled at him. 'Oh, I was younger then, effendi.'

'And you survived in the seas until . . . you drifted ashore?'

Why was he so interested? Surely Heaven's story had nothing to do with him – or did he sense, as Ibn Bai had himself, that what he had been told was not all the truth?

'I . . . I don't know. It's hard to remember.'

Gregor crossed the room until he was standing very close to Heaven.

'I'm sure that if you put your mind to it, something will come.'

'A . . . life raft.'

Ibn Bai wrung his hands – Gregor wanted something and was using Heaven as a piece in his play. Perhaps he didn't even need her but he couldn't resist: where pressure could be applied, he would always apply it, no matter who suffered.

'A life raft. Really? And yet they did not pick you up but left you to . . . sink or swim as fate decreed?'

'That is what she said.'

It was Slave. A presence equal to Gregor's, he occupied the room with absolute authority. Had he been listening outside? He stood beside Heaven. Gregor now faced the two of them.

'This is the gentleman who saved me.'

'How fortunate. I am told many sailors do not know how to swim. You are . . .?'

'My name –' he paused as if thinking, and then nodded slightly – 'is Akiba.'

Heaven went pale.

'Gregor, Master of the Palace Guard.'

'Gregor. I will be sure to remember it.' He stepped forward.

Gregor either had to step aside or come into contact with the larger man. He turned and said to Ibn Bai: 'Perhaps I will have that coffee.'

Ibn Bai clapped and sent the servant to prepare it.

'Were you travelling far, Akiba?'

'From Alkube-Lan. Are you a traveller, sir?'

Had words been blades, Ibn Bai felt, there would have been blood on the floor this morning.

'Not really. It's merely that there is something familiar . . . Have we met before?'

'I think not.'

'I was in the kingdom of Bornu some time ago. You have the look of . . . the place.' He shrugged. 'Do you know it?'

'By reputation. I was never there. Isn't it a province of Tuman-bay now?'

'We have a long reach and a great appetite.'

465

'For other people's lands? So I have heard.'

The conversation had surely come to a point where something must happen to shatter the moment for good or ill. Heaven stepped around Akiba, standing between the two men.

'But you have come to see my father, effendi. we will leave you. Akiba, there was something I wanted to show you.' She placed a hand on his arm. He bowed.

'You will excuse me, effendi.'

'Of course. I hope we meet again.'

'I'm sure we will.'

As they left the room, Gregor called after them: 'Congratulations.'

Akiba turned back. 'Sir?'

'On surviving. It is a great art, to survive.'

'Perhaps that has yet to be ascertained.'

And they were gone.

'Strange friends your daughter has, Ibn Bai.'

'Who am I to question the works of providence?' he said. 'The baby was taken from me and in return, I am given my daughter. Now how may I help you, Commander? Ah, here is your coffee.'

The maid presented the little cup on a tray. Gregor waved it away.

'I need you to write a reply to this.' He handed Ibn Bai a sheet of paper.

'From Sarah. She is safe?'

'She is safe.'

'And so you are a messenger now?' Ibn Bai knew he had gone too far the moment the words had left his lips. 'Forgive me, I spoke out of order.'

'Once I would have cut your throat for that, but times change. Write your reply.'

466

They went to the library, where Ibn Bai placed the letter on a writing stand.

'She tells me that all is well and that I am to write to her that I have not been harmed and that if I do, she will give you what you desire. May I ask what you desire, Commander? Is it to do with the scrolls you talked of, or is there something else?'

Gregor took up the quill, wetted the nib in the ink pot and handed it to Ibn Bai.

'Write on the reverse of the words she sent. That I have kept my word.'

As the nib scratched against the vellum, Ibn Bai thought there was something different about this man Gregor today. Surely before, he would not have allowed No-Man, or Akiba as he had announced himself, to face him down, for that is what had happened. Nor would he have been a messenger. In the past, Ibn Bai had seen men surprised and caught by emotions they did not know they possessed – by love, by care, by affection – no wonder soldiers distrusted them. Was Ibn Bai seeing a man under the harrow of such feelings?

He finished the letter, scattered sand across it and handed it to Gregor.

'You will go back down there, Commander?'

'I will go where it is necessary, Ibn Bai. You have been true to your word, I believe. Perhaps we shall meet again, though I think you would rather be done with me for good. These are strange times, who knows how things will come out in the end. Goodbye.'

He bowed and said not another word as Ibn Bai escorted him out of the house, and waited at the compound gate until he had melted into the ceaseless crowd that flowed everywhere through Tumanbay's streets.

Akiba stood watching from an upstairs window. He took

Rajik's sword and secured it to his belt, covering himself and it with a burnous.

'What are you doing?' Boy said.

'I'm going out.'

'He's the one, then?'

'He's the one.'

Boy followed him downstairs. Heaven was in the main room talking with her father. They both looked up, knowing something was wrong.

'He's going to kill that man,' Boy said.

Heaven said: 'You can't.'

'That also is yet to be ascertained.'

'It will come back on us,' Heaven said. 'On my father, on all of us. Is that what you want?'

'It is what I must do.'

Part Six

89

Bello

Great epics without number have been written about battles, mostly by people who weren't present. If they had, and if they'd survived, their accounts would, at best, have been a series of glimpses accompanied by terror, triumph and the urge to run because, as most brave men or women will tell you, in battle, to advance fearlessly, to stand against a deadly foe while the arrows rain around you and thud like hailstones into your shield, to ram the butt of your pike in the ground and hold the shaft steady as a mounted rider plunges down upon you, is a form of insanity. And yet still men fight, battles happen, victories are made and lost.

Thus considered the monk, Bello, at what came to be known as the Battle of the Caterpillar. He'd long thought of himself as a scribe, a recorder of his times; he'd been writing the Hafiz's speeches for years and had recently embarked upon an epic retelling of the history of Tumanbay. Now, through no effort of his own – indeed his personal attitude to the battle was even less enthusiastic than the Hafiz's, if only because the Holy Man was drunk and dead to the world – he found himself present at a moment of history. And as a historian, a recorder of great events, he knew this day presented him with a chance that could make his name shine forever in the annals of the city. The great battle, they would say in years to come – go and look it up in Bello!

For that everlasting fame, he was prepared to brave anything, so he dug a hole behind a dune, emptied his bowels, tightened the belt of his robe, mounted a donkey and made his way to the field of battle, picking his way behind the waiting troops, to the rise where the great General Qulan, the hero of his tale, was gathered with his staff. He had resolved there would be no terror and lunacy, no confusion and fear in his account: only mighty-thewed heroes, clean heroism, far-sighted tactics and the complete triumph of Tumanbay.

He had no idea how wrong he was going to be.

The armies had been in position since dawn. Water carriers were running up and down the ranks of Tumanbay's soldiers with skins, ensuring each man had a drink as the sun rose higher and the heat became more intense. Qulan was notable among commanders for ensuring his armies had the best attention, demanding in return the highest performance from them. It was a case of mutual respect – and certain death for any man who deserted his post.

On this morning, even Bello could see that Qulan's forces held the better position, ranged in a great crescent across the firmer ground where sand gave way to shale and the rocky outcrops of a plateau. They were facing west, the sun rising over their heads, shining directly into the eyes of Maya's advance.

A bare league separated the front lines. The dust had subsided; both armies could see each other plainly. From Tumanbay's ranks, orchestrated by the sergeants waving their staffs of office, came great bellows accompanied by the roar of the drums: *Oooooyah-hh! Ooooooyahh!* You could feel the excitement, the blood rising, the desire to be at the enemy's throat. Bello scribbled a hasty note to that effect.

General Qulan growled an order: 'Hold them, above all hold them. Let her make the first move.'

The order passed from officer to officer, sergeant to sergeant, sounding along the ranks: 'Hold steadyyy, hooooold steadyyy! Let her come, let her come!'

A joker shouted: 'Yes, let her come and we'll kick her fat arse all the way back to Amber!'

Derisive laughter sounded and Bello heard Qulan again: 'Good, they're salty and ready to go.'

Maya's ranks were silent. No answering jeers or cheers came from them. Only black-robed figures darting here and there among soldiers who stood with an eerie stillness, lances barely wavering in the rising heat, black banners unmoving. To Bello they gave an impression of deadly seriousness. He dismounted and climbed a rock to get a better view. Who were they, where did they come from, these thousands who flocked to her banner? He felt a moment of uncertainty. However, one look at General Qulan, steady and confident on his white stallion, restored his belief.

In the far distance, to one side, Bello was aware of light reflecting brilliantly off armour. A platform had been erected on a hilltop there, from which Sultan al-Ghuri could observe the great battle. Bello had left the Hafiz there earlier, slumped on a velvet couch at the rear of the platform, and had given orders to the servants to keep an eye on him; he would be needed at the moment of victory to bless the army and the commander. Bello had already written the speech and had it in his satchel.

A ripple of movement disturbed the stillness of Maya's forces. The front ranks kneeled, revealing massed bowmen, arrows nocked and aimed at the sky.

Someone said, 'Here it comes.'

'Shields up!' General Qulan shouted.

Once again the order was repeated down the lines, and thousands of hide-covered, bronze-studded shields locked together to make an impenetrable shell over the army of Tumanbay.

Everyone was silent now, waiting for the battle to begin.

You could hear the faint hum of the wind on the taut bowstrings of Maya's archers. Qulan spoke quietly to a barbarian who waited with his horse.

'Go now. Tell Wolf that once she advances, hit her flank and hit it hard. He'll know the moment.'

The rider nodded, leaned forward, whispered to his horse and was away with barely a sound.

'Come on, come on,' an officer said.

Still nothing happened. It was as if the whole world was frozen for a tiny moment in which, somehow, a whole battle could take place, had taken place, and yet no one had seen it happen because . . . what was happening was unthinkable, impossible.

'Something's wrong with our men,' Qulan said.

Gaps had begun to appear in the shield wall above the Tumanbay forces – at first a few, then more and more, as men fell, stabbed under the arm by those standing next to them, by their comrades. The great army was collapsing in on itself, as if it had been eaten out from the inside and there was nothing to support the frame. Banners dipped, lances swayed and lowered. There were cries – shouts more of surprise than anything else – and still they went down, man after man, open to the blades of their fellows with their shields held above them, offering no protection. Soldiers depend on each other, knowing that the man next to them has their back as they have his; it is a system based and braced upon trust and, strangely in such a warlike profession, love, and when that goes, there is nothing.

Later, when he had time to consider it, Bello felt it was like watching raindrops on a window – two drops close to each other and one would bulge slightly at the edge, reaching out until it touched the other and simply absorbed it. And then there would be one drop.

General Qulan pulled his sword and rushed forward, shouting: 'To me, Tumanbay, to your general! Stand by your banners, stand by your brothers!'

But there were no banners and no brothers, only thousands of men writhing on the ground in their death throes. Above them, their once-brothers sheathed swords, dropped bows unfired, lowered lances, deserted cannon unshot.

Bello saw the desolation of hope, an army defeated from within. It had all happened so quickly – a great reversal of fortune that would, it struck him, make an astounding chapter in his history, as long as he survived to write it. He clambered off the rock and back on his donkey, hoping that the beast wouldn't have turned traitor.

Riders were approaching: the barbarian horsemen – General Qulan's horsemen. They wheeled their horses in a circle around the general. Their commander dismounted and walked up to him.

It was no good; no matter how much heart and bowels told him to flee, Bello had discovered something more powerful than fear: the sheer intense curiosity to know what happened next. He urged the donkey forward so he could hear the two men.

'Wolf, what in God's name are you doing?' General Qulan asked. 'I need your cavalry to attack their flank. What are they doing here? Get them into battle now. *Now!* Or all is lost.'

But the barbarian commander didn't move.

'What's wrong with you, man?' Qulan screamed, his face red with anger.

'It's over, General,' the barbarian said calmly.

'What are you . . .?' Qulan stared at him, disbelieving.

'The battle is lost, General. Tumanbay is lost. It always was. As it was written.'

Bello was thrilled and appalled: two strong men held in a bond of honour and betrayal, neither giving the width of a little finger. Qulan's face like ancient rock, seamed and cracked by time; the barbarian commander, his stern, beautiful features framed with black plaits wound about with coloured cloth that fluttered in the rising breeze.

'I trusted you, Wolf. You betrayed me. You're a traitor.'

'No, General, I was never a traitor, I was hers from the beginning. Just as thousands of your men have seen her truth and set it against the rottenness . . .'

Bello didn't catch the rest because an officer on a horse grabbed the reins of his donkey.

'Monk, your master needs you, move . . .'

He was dragged away from the group surrounding Qulan as they urged their horses forward, closing the circle.

'My master – what? Who?'

The officer was galloping now, pulling Bello's donkey, who was evidently unused to moving at such speed and was straining at its lead, across the desert towards the Sultan's viewing platform.

'The Hafiz, you fat fool. Come, come . . .'

Bello presumed he was still in the hands of his own side; even so, he began planning what to say to his new employers, who surely would need the Hafiz and thus need his invaluable helper.

In the few moments he was able to look around before disappearing behind a hill, he could see the two armies flowing into each other, merging, the smaller becoming part of the larger. There was no cheering or celebration, only a workmanlike attitude as bodies were piled up, weapons stacked and animals led to one side, all under the direction of the men in black robes.

90

Akiba

A feeling of expectation, seasoned with a touch of anxiety, hung about the city and its people; they gathered in groups around market stalls, cafes, street corners and shaded doorways and muttered earnestly to each other, yet even these uncertain times had not brought any worshippers to seek the lonely solace of the Temple of Solace. The square before its ancient face was empty except for the old beggar, who sat as usual, his empty eye sockets seeming to be searching out potential donors, his bowl held up in insolent supplication, a slight smile visible under the raggedy beard that reached to his waist.

'Is there something that amuses you?' Gregor asked him.

'Everything amuses me, effendi.'

'Be specific.'

'What men and women want, if you like. What they desire and what they get.'

'Do you remember me?'

'I remember everything, effendi. Memory is all any of us have. You are from the palace.'

'Indeed. I need to go back down the winding stair.'

The toothless smile became a grin. 'Not possible.'

'Don't worry. I have my offering for your gods,' Gregor said, dropping a coin in the bowl.

'Still not possible. Do not reach for your sword, please.'

Gregor let his hand fall to his side.

'The key is gone, they have taken it. The people below wish to protect themselves from the war.'

Squatting, looking into the old face, Gregor said: 'There's going to be a great victory. As above, so below.'

The old man shook his head sadly. 'When they come, they will destroy this place. These old temples, our ancient beliefs … Tumanbay may be rotten at its core, but at least we have been allowed to remain. So many people from so many places have found a life in this city. The newcomers will change all that.'

He reached out and pulled Gregor towards him. The darkness of his eye sockets seemed to engulf all time, all space.

'Something terrible is coming …' he whispered. 'Something unthinkable.'

A shadow fell across the ancient's face.

'Commander Gregor, isn't it?' came a voice from behind.

Gregor spun around. The fellow was big – very big – and though he was smiling broadly, the smile was cold. Gregor knew all about cold smiles; they were his stock in trade.

'How pleasant to happen upon you. My name is Akiba, if you recall,' he said, holding out his hand. 'We met at the house of the slave trader.'

Had this man been following him?

'The shipwreck,' Akiba added.

After a moment, Gregor took his hand and smiled back.

'Ah yes, the champion swimmer.'

'And you were telling us about your time in the kingdom of Bornu.'

'Was I?'

'You were governor there, I believe?'

'Yes. Forgive me, I have important business to attend—'

'And now you are Master of the Palace Guard.'

The big man stood squarely, facing Gregor, like a street fighter. He looked absurd, in clothes typical of a slave trader, but too tight, no doubt borrowed from his host. He wore a sword and was carrying the three-pronged slaver's staff – the type used to shepherd the merchandise into pens – and Gregor could see his eyes flickering to the sides as if surveying the square. For accomplices, perhaps? Or witnesses?

'If you will excuse me,' Gregor said, bowing politely.

He nodded to the blind man – absurdly – and started walking towards the street at the far end of the square, where he could see a few traders with their donkeys and carts, unloading their merchandise for the day.

'I'll walk with you,' Akiba said, falling into step with Gregor. 'If you don't mind.'

Gregor kept his hand near the hilt of his sword. He had felt uneasy about this man from the moment he set eyes on him at Ibn Bai's house some days before. There was something familiar there, but he couldn't place him. Even so, as they walked he was careful to keep a blade's width between them.

'I have a confession to make.' That smile again. 'I said I'd never been there – to Bornu. That isn't so. I know the country well.'

'I see,' Gregor said, walking faster.

Akiba reached out and touched Gregor's shoulder. Gregor glared at him.

'Don't you recognise me?' Akiba asked.

'There are many people in Bornu. I didn't meet all of them.'

'No, of course. You must get that all the time.'

'What?'

'When you have been somewhere and people say, "do you know so and so?" Of course, you wouldn't remember, would you?

You're a governor, an important man. You're not going to meet everyone. Of course you're not.'

They were approaching the corner of the square, where it met the streets that fed into the great trunk road of the city. Gregor could see the crowds, the dust thrown up by wagon wheels. He quickened his pace.

'But kings . . .' Akiba continued. 'Even the kings of these places are but insignificant, dirty wretches to be kicked and abused like stray dogs by the grandees of Tumanbay.'

'I wish you a good day, ' Gregor said, changing direction abruptly.

But Akiba moved faster and stood before him, barring his way.

'Did you meet any kings?' he asked.

They remained still for some moments, eyes locked, smiles frozen, an uneasy game of do or dare, each waiting for the other to make a move.

'Who are you?' Gregor asked.

Then the big man raised his arm and pulled up his sleeve.

'Recognise this?'

The crest of the gates of the Empire, burned into his flesh with a branding iron.

'Property of Tumanbay – that's me,' said Akiba.

Of course. Gregor remembered the day he had travelled to the mountains of Bornu. They were called something like 'the Mountains of the Moon' – some nonsense like that. Tumanbay wanted to mine silver there and the local tribe had objected. Their gods would be offended, they had said.

He had met the king – no more than a tribal leader really, Gregor recalled – but he considered himself regal and appeared with a retinue of followers, surrounded by the usual shabby pageantry. Whatever Gregor had offered on behalf of the Sultan had been refused. And he had offered a lot. This so-called king had the same look on his face then as he did now – obdurate, stubborn, deadly. Fortunately, on that day, Gregor had an army at his back and the matter had been settled swiftly, efficiently. The survivors had been put to work in the new mines. Today it was just him, and he wasn't confident he could overcome the fellow on his own. If Gregor made a move and failed – if he didn't kill him on the first strike – this man could pick him up and break his spine across his knee.

'No hard feelings, eh?' Akiba said. 'After all, just think of all that Tumanbay has given us in return. Civilisation, protection, culture. I was just a "bush-dweller" then – I think those were your words, Commander – so really I should be grateful.'

'We are all slaves,' Gregor said.

'Yes, you call yourselves slaves, but where are your chains?'

Gregor could see the man's fingers caressing the hilt of his sword. Was he planning murder or assault? He needed to defuse the situation somehow, quickly.

'There's a coffee house over there,' he said, gesturing past Akiba's shoulder.

He could see guards of the street patrol moving along the stalls, checking the papers of the various merchants. He knew he could deal with this menace if he could just get him a little closer to the main street and attract the attention of the guards.

'I've often thought about Bornu,' he said, signalling to Akiba to come with him. 'What happened there. Mistakes were made, I'm sure, but now there might be something I can do to help. We could talk about it over mint tea, honey cakes, are you partial to . . .?'

Akiba dropped to his knees.

'What are you doing? ' Gregor asked, shocked by the sudden move.

'Touching the feet of the man who brought civilisation to our lands, who converted us savages to the true path and showed us the way of the future.'

'Get off me. Take your hands off me,' Gregor hissed, pulling out his sword as he fought to free himself from the man's grip.

He fell to the ground and they struggled in the dust. Gregor thrust blindly with his weapon and managed to break free. He staggered back onto his feet.

'What do you want from me?' he asked, incredulous.

Akiba rose slowly to his feet, regarding him coolly, and then held up his right hand. Streaks of blood rolled from his fingers down his arm.

'You cut me. I'm bleeding,' he said, still smiling.

'What do you want?' Gregor asked again, aware of the ground vibrating beneath his feet. He turned to see a camel train approaching fast.

'Make wayyyyy! Make wayyyy!'

Gregor stepped back just as the first beast galloped past. He could see Akiba on the other side, waiting, his sword now in his hand. He breathed deeply, calming himself. He didn't need this distraction but it looked like he was going to have to settle it one way or the other.

More camels, snorting and honking, saddlecloths flying, shite falling, dust rising; Gregor backed against a wall. When the camels finally passed and the dust settled, the two of them faced each other, side on, blades constantly moving, each searching out a weakness in the other's defence, an opening.

But this was Tumanbay, and even in these days of war and anxiety, two men in the street with naked blades promised entertainment. Magically a crowd appeared around them – fifty, a hundred eager watchers. Gregor could hear bets being laid as they circled each other.

'Two on the big man ... Three on the commander, I know him ... Four on the first hit ...'

But there were other noises too, and the crowd was being rudely shoved aside by the guards of the street patrol.

The officer in charge stepped forward, trying to break up the altercation.

'No naked blades in the street!' he screamed, beckoning his men to help. 'Down! Lay them down *now!*'

Akiba took in the tall hats of the guards and, in a moment, slipped into the crowd.

'Commander Gregor. Sorry, effendi, we didn't know it was you,' said the officer. 'Do you need our assistance?'

Gregor scanned the faces around him. Just as magically as it had appeared, the crowd was vanishing and Akiba along with it.

'No,' Gregor said. 'A common criminal, nothing more. I'm fine. Carry on with your work.'

91

al-Ghuri

Sultan al-Ghuri, Lion of Lions, Sultan of Eagles, Destroyer of Enemies, Father of the Peoples, Protector of the Poor, Sword of the Faith, was leaning against the side of the platform, squinting out towards the field of battle.

'Why isn't General Qulan ordering the advance?' he asked, to no one in particular.

He was surrounded by servants and staff. It was hot and his decorative gold and silver armour was chafing his skin. This was the time of day when he would normally take his rest, and he was tired and irritable.

'And where's the cavalry? They were meant to attack from the right flank,' he said, gesticulating and pacing across the platform.

A slave mirrored the Sultan's every move, holding a sunshade above his head to protect his ageing skin from the harsh light.

'Ah ... Some answers, perhaps ...'

Several of his officers were approaching on horseback, the dust rising around them; one of their number followed in their wake, leading a donkey on which a fat monk was balancing precariously.

The officers dismounted and three climbed up onto the viewing platform and came to attention.

'What news?'

A pause. They looked at him. He looked at them.

'I'm sorry, your Majesty,' said the most senior, a Miralay colonel, gathering his breath. 'He was betrayed.'

'Who was?'

'General Qulan.' Another long pause. 'He has been captured. His army has gone over to Maya. All is lost.'

The Sultan froze, wide-eyed, absorbing what he had just heard. The officers shuffled uncomfortably and looked away – at the horizon, at the sky, at anything other than their Sultan.

'So?'

'So, Majesty?'

'So what do we do? What is the strategy?

'Majesty . . .'

The Miralay colonel fell silent; one of his companions, a Yuzbasi in a tattered uniform, poked him and mumbled: 'Go on, we don't have much time. We need to do this.'

'What? Do what?' the Sultan demanded.

The Yuzbasi officer stepped forward. 'They will abuse you, Majesty. Even in death.'

'Even in death? What do you . . .?' He didn't like the shifty glances the officers were giving each other.

'You will be used as a symbol of Maya's triumph,' the officer continued. 'They will hang you from the gates.'

'So what are you saying? We need to withdraw?' he asked, a tinge of hope in his voice. 'Is that what you are saying?' But somehow he knew it wasn't.

'There's no way out,' a third officer said. 'We are surrounded. An ant couldn't get through, Majesty, never mind a man on a horse. You must submit to . . . to . . .'

The Sultan stared at him, his face suddenly drained of colour.

'Where's the Hafiz?' the colonel shouted. 'It's his job, that's what he's here for. You! Monk!' He pointed to Bello, who was struggling off his donkey. 'Get your master now!'

Bello scurried towards the tents behind the platform. He had already spotted the Hafiz, sitting in a large drum, a bemused expression on his face. He appeared to have sobered up. Bello reflected, it only needed the fall of an empire to do it.

'Holiness, there's work for you. They need you.'

'From all I saw they need a miracle.'

He belched sourly as Bello helped him to his feet and handed him his staff, reasoning that three legs would be better than two.

'The officers say there's something you have to do, that it's your job.'

He could see knowledge returning to the old man's eyes, and a complete lack of fear; this moment had restored some of the power Bello had admired as a young novice in a faraway land. The rising wind of change had fanned the flames and there was fire there – for how long, he couldn't say.

'Majesty.' The Hafiz stood, somehow magnificent, before al-Ghuri, who was now slumped despondently in a chair surrounded by his staff. 'According to the immemorial customs of Tumanbay, the Sultan must not – nay, may not – fall into the hands of the enemy to suffer upon his head their insults and derision. That head must be cut from his body and concealed – to be buried in the sands of the great desert, where no man may find it.'

The Sultan didn't respond. He simply closed his eyes as if shutting out the world.

'There is no choice, Majesty,' said the colonel. 'But rest assured it will be a clean cut and we will bury your head well. And when this is all over, we will come and retrieve it and give it . . . er, *you* . . . proper burial in the mausoleum of the martyrs.'

The colonel looked around for support. The other officers were nodding encouragingly. Al-Ghuri remained motionless, silent.

'It must be done now,' the colonel urged, 'before they get here . . . They will not be long.'

After a moment, al-Ghuri opened his eyes and stood up. He was the Sultan of Tumanbay, Lion of Lions, King of Slaves . . . It was not fitting to reveal to his subjects the terror he was feeling within. He smiled reassuringly at those gathered around and nodded.

'I'm sorry, Your Majesty, we need to act quickly.'

The colonel motioned to his staff waiting at the foot of the platform, where a stool, cushions and a prayer mat had been arranged on the sand.

'This way, Majesty.' The colonel gestured towards them. 'You, priest, come with us, we'll need a blessing and some absolution after this!'

Bello followed. First the defeat of Qulan, now the death of al-Ghuri. Such events would surely ensure the immortality of Bello's Chronicle!

'Are you sure about this?'

The Sultan was on his knees. One of the officers was holding a leather sack with a drawstring at the neck, just about large enough for a human head.

The chief of the Sultan's staff, a gloomy fellow, said: 'Rest assured, Majesty, it will be a clean cut. And your fame as al-Ghuri the Undefeated will echo down the ages.'

Bello was pushed forward. He kneeled by the Sultan and said: 'Shall we pray together, Majesty, in this moment of . . .'

He paused, unsure of what this moment actually was. Al-Ghuri pushed him away.

'A man can only die once and tonight I will be in Paradise. Lay on, and be quick about it.'

Bello scrambled clear – he didn't want to get the martyr's

blood over his robes. He had to admit, though, the Sultan was facing it all with courage.

Al-Ghuri lowered his head, suffered the clothing to be pulled from his neck, gulped a series of deep breaths . . . Lion of Lions, Sultan of Eagles, Sword of the Faith . . . Adulterer, Thief, Slayer of his own Brother . . .

'Try to relax, Majesty,' came a voice interrupting his contemplations.

It irritated him. How was he supposed to relax at a time like this? But he didn't want to die angry, so he said nothing and tried to think of the life to come. He wondered how he would be received there.

'Bow your head a little lower, please, Majesty. It will make for a cleaner . . . uhmmm . . .'

'Get on with it!' al-Ghuri hissed, no longer able to hold back his fear and fury.

The shadow of the sword lay across the sand. It rose up like the hand of a clock, ready to strike the end. And from the rocks behind them arose a great twittering, rushing, flapping flock of birds, speckled brown and white, their shadow mottling the sand, concealing the sharp contours of the scimitar's shadow, their call filling the silence, their very flight a tangible thing moving the air itself around them.

'What's that?' al-Ghuri shrieked, jerking his head up.

'Majesty, you need to keep still if—'

'In the heat of the day!'

He clambered to his feet. The executioner stepped back, confused, looking around for orders.

'The prophet boy told me –' the Sultan held his hands up, as if he would embrace the whole great flock that circled above him – 'when the birds fly in the heat of the day, then will you lead your army.'

The officers looked at him, unsure.

'We can still win!' he shouted, delighted. 'Now I understand.'

'Understand what, Majesty?'

'I will marry her. I have no First Wife. I will offer her marriage. It will legitimise her. Maya and I will rule Tumanbay together.'

The flock changed direction as one, swooping across the sky like a banner cracking in the wind, and then it was gone, as if it had performed its sacred task. Al-Ghuri strode past his astounded staff, flicked a hand at Bello.

'With me, priest, and bring the Hafiz too, he can officiate here and now.'

And he went forth, laughing, to face his destiny.

92
Madu

'Wake up. Wake up.'

Madu grunted and burrowed down under the covers. His head hurt, and so it should after last night. The amount of alcohol that had flowed would have condemned thousands in the old days – now, thank goodness, things were looser in time of war. He was the only victim. Daniel seemed able to drink any amount without effect, except on the variety and invention of his lovemaking.

The voice went on: 'Wake up, my love.'

And a hand shook his shoulder. He recognised the touch. Unfortunately, this morning it was neither arousing or loving, only urgent. The covers were pulled back.

'You have to get up.'

'Why?'

He blinked in the sunlight flooding through the windows of his old chambers; he had moved out of the First Wife's quarters in the hareem, not liking the many eyes that might be observing him. No point in courting trouble, Daniel had said.

Now he was pulling him upright and saying: 'Because you're the Sultan. You need to show them you're in charge or you won't be for long.'

Resisting the tug on his arm, pulling the cover over his shoulders, Madu said: 'I'm only the temporary Sultan. Let Cadali deal with things.'

'No, you have to deal with Cadali.' He leaned in and planted a kiss on Madu's lips. 'He needs to be dealt with. Before he deals with you.'

Madu escaped the grip and lay back, his hands behind his head, smiling seductively.

'You think he'd like to deal with me?'

'I'm sure of it, Madu. While the Sultan is away. And I'm serious, so listen to me.'

The room echoed to a series of loud knocks on the door.

'Don't answer. It's only the slave.'

But Daniel was already halfway across the room.

'Come back to bed,' Madu giggled. 'I order you. I am the Sultan.'

Ignoring him, Daniel opened the door.

'Yes?'

It was Cadali, a guard visible behind him in the corridor.

'Oh . . .' Cadali said, startled by Daniel's naked body. 'I was looking for our young Sultan.'

Daniel allowed the door to swing open, revealing Madu, now sitting up on the bed, the cover falling away from his torso. He'd been following a series of exercises laid down by Daniel and was proud of his new physique.

'I hope I'm not interrupting anything, Majesty,' Cadali said, craning his neck.

'You are actually.'

Cadali forced a smile.

'But since you're here, you may as well come in.' Daniel stood aside and Cadali took a few steps into the room. 'Throw me my robe, if you would, and my breeches.'

Cadali looked at the articles which lay in an untidy mess at the foot of the bed.

'I suggest you order your man to do that.' He flicked his head in Daniel's direction.

'So what do you want, Cadali?'

'I am here as a courtesy, Majesty. I thought you would wish to be the first to welcome him back.'

'Welcome who back?'

'Your uncle, the Sultan.'

Madu accepted the clothes from Daniel, sniffed the trousers, threw them aside and went to the hanging space where he chose another pair in royal blue silk. Let Cadali look at his arse – the bastard was enjoying this, showing that he knew what Madu did not.

'What are you talking about?'

'The army has returned. The wall guards have been reporting dust clouds on the horizon since dawn.'

Unspoken was the phrase: as you would have known if you hadn't been rutting on your bed with blue eyes here.

'Maya is defeated?'

'Sorry your reign has been so brief, though I doubt if anyone will have noticed. I shall be at the Imperial Gate to welcome him. You may join me when you have finished with your amusements.'

And he was gone, the guard slamming the door behind him.

Daniel said: 'Well, he does know how to make an exit, that man. Even so, we should hurry. Your uncle needs to see you, Madu, and you need to be seen.'

93
Caterpillars

A small group was waiting for Madu and Daniel when they reached the battlements over the Imperial Gates. The city had been stripped of men for the army and the walls were now manned by members of the Palace Guard in their gaudy ceremonial uniforms. They were releasing the levers that set in motion the massive counterweights controlling the doors. They were only opened on ceremonial occasions nowadays, and were slowly and painfully parting with a shriek of unoiled hinges.

Cadali welcomed Madu with an extravagant bow and gestured out towards the desert.

'Behold – the glorious army comes!'

The Vizier, Madu recalled, had a habit of lapsing into flowery language on great occasions.

Madu squinted at the rising sun.

'I can't see very much, it's too bright. Are those our banners? They don't look like ours.'

'Captured banners, probably. Displayed by the victors,' Daniel answered.

Madu could make out the Sultan's banner at the head of the army. Then, as a slight breeze cleared the dust away . . .

'I see him!' he shouted. 'My uncle. He's riding before them all, leading his army home.'

'Our great Sultan!' Cadali cried, flinging a flower he'd been holding over the edge of the wall. They watched it fall the long distance to the sand below.

'I don't see the general, though,' Daniel said.

'Well, he will be at the back organising the prisoners, I suppose,' Cadali said.

It was a magnificent sight. The army stretched back as far as the eye could see, as if marching out of the rising sun itself.

'But why has there been no word?' Daniel asked.

'Well, perhaps my uncle wants to be the first to announce his triumph,' Madu said.

'No, there should have been scouts sent ahead. There's something wrong.'

They stared out as the great mass of the army came on, closer and closer, the only sound that of marching: soft footfalls in the sand; the rasp of armour moving against armour; animals grunting; banners flapping in the wind.

'He's not moving,' Daniel said eventually.

'What do you mean?' Madu asked.

'He's not moving with the horse. Look!'

It was true. The Sultan appeared to be tilting to one side.

'The banner of Tumanbay,' Cadali said. 'It's upside down!'

And closer they got and closer still, and the gates creaked open wider and wider . . . and on they came, and on . . .

And if there was one thing growing up in the palace of Tumanbay had given Madu, it was an instinct for survival. Even at the worst of times, in the army when he might have died in the sand, he had found Daniel, and Daniel had given him the strength to go on, to survive. He was an instrument fine-tuned to threat, and at that moment every string was screaming.

He ran to the gate mechanism, where a team of guards were at work with nippers, controlling the rate at which the ropes ran over the wheels and through the blocks as the counterweights descended.

'Shut the gates!' he shouted. 'Shut them now! There's something wrong!'

No one moved. The ropes continued to slide through their blocks, the gates continued to open, the army got closer.

'I am the Sultan, listen to me!'

He grabbed hold of a rope in a futile attempt to hold it back. The guards were stolid, taking no notice of his frantic efforts.

'What's wrong with you, man?' he screamed, pushing one of them hard against the parapet. 'I am the Sultan!'

The soldier didn't resist, didn't answer. He just stared with expressionless eyes.

Madu felt a hand on his shoulder.

'Leave it,' Cadali said. 'They're not going to obey you.'

'What do you mean?'

In a voice like ashes, he said: 'Don't you understand? They are already here. They aren't going to shut the gates. They've been waiting for her. We have to get back to the palace.'

'Why?'

'Because . . .' Cadali was white as bleached linen, his lips bloody where he had gnawed them; he wrung his hands and looked as if he were about to vomit. 'Because we have to make her welcome,' he said eventually, and made for the steps leading down.

Madu looked desperately out at the figure of his uncle, sitting stiffly in the saddle, staring fixedly ahead, black-robed riders to either side. Behind him advanced the unstoppable, unimaginable mass of the wrong army. Daniel put his arm around him.

'I think,' he said gently, 'Cadali is right. We should go to the palace.'

'Shouldn't we run – to the mountains, my mother's . . .?'

Daniel shook his head. 'It's too late.'

*

Like water from the snows of the high peaks melting in spring, flowing down cliffs in intricate falls, through valleys, growing in size from stream to a mighty torrent, finally crashing into the dry river beds that stretch out into the scrubland and the desert edges, bringing new life and a new hope to riverbank and riverine plain, to wadis and wells, so did the armies of Maya enter into their kingdom. Or so it must have seemed to the thousands who lined the streets to welcome them – not, admittedly, with cheers, but with respectful salaams and bows and smiles, and palm fronds to shelter them from the heat of the sun, and dates and water as pure and clear as crystal. Some – many – waved to fathers, brothers and sisters who had gone out under one banner and now returned, alive, under another. Of those who were waiting for no one, whose fathers, brothers and sisters were not coming back, who had neither dates nor water, there was no sign. With the instinct of the city dweller, they knew very well which way the wind blows and they stayed indoors.

The vanguard of the army split away from the main body and, still silent, marched through the palace gates, which opened before them, into the Grand Courtyard, where they arrayed themselves in ranks behind a dais on which a throne had been placed. Sultan al-Ghuri was sat upon it, still unmoving, staring ahead as if frozen.

'Madu, you go down, go out and greet them. Greet her.'

'I'm not going out there, Cadali.'

They were at a window of one of the reception rooms, peering down at the Grand Courtyard. Gathered behind them was a collection of terrified palace officials.

'You have to,' Cadali urged.

'Why?'

'You're the Sultan. You have to persuade her we never wanted this war. We'll need gifts. Where are the servants?' he said, turning to a hapless official. 'Tell them to . . . to prepare a banquet. Everyone loves a banquet. And gold, we need . . .'

Below, a figure moved forward. Wearing black robes, he was fearfully tall and thin, the hand that held his staff of office long, sparely fleshed, unadorned by rings or bracelets. He stepped up onto the dais and stood beside the Sultan.

'People of Tumanbay . . .' His voice echoed around the walls of the courtyard. 'Here is your Sultan. The revered ruler of the most powerful empire in the world. Cast your eyes on him now. You have much to fear.'

'What can we do?' Madu sounded desperate.

'You need to go out there,' Cadali replied. 'You,' he repeated, in case the point was lost on Madu.

'No . . . I can't. I just can't.'

'Right. You decline my advice. In that case, I must order the Palace Guard to throw open the doors—'

'You will do no such thing!'

Cadali was pacing around, trying to remove some of the rings from his fat fingers.

'We need to surrender ourselves up to Maya. Yes. We need to convince her that . . . that . . .' He yelped in fear as the doors behind them crashed open. 'Gregor! Where have you been? You're supposed to be in charge of the Palace Guard? Where are they? Why aren't they protecting us?'

Gregor ignored him and approached Daniel.

'Blue Eyes,' he said. 'You're the brother, aren't you?'

Daniel nodded.

'She is safe . . . Your sister and her baby. They are both . . .' Gregor fell silent. Blue Eyes seemed uninterested.

Gregor looked out at the mass of black-robed soldiers lining the courtyard, and noticed the figure seated upon the throne.

'What is that?'

'The Sultan,' Cadali said.

'I know *who* it is, you fat fool – *what* is it? Is he alive? What have they done to him?'

'It's called the Way of the Caterpillars,' Daniel said. 'They've skinned him and stuffed him with straw.'

'How the walls of Tumanbay have crumbled,' the voice outside boomed, 'before the simple belief of the faithful. How have all your riches, your merchants, your whores saved you? Where are they now . . .? Where are your armies, where are your leaders? Where is your general?'

He fell silent – a silence broken by the grinding of the iron-rimmed wheels of a large cart bearing a cage, pushed forward by black-robed figures over the flagstones. Within the cage, General Qulan, manacled wrist and ankle, holding one of the bars to steady himself. He stared ahead, as expressionless as the Sultan.

Cadali hissed: 'So, Gregor, it seems that your brother has failed the Empire as much as you have.' He groaned as he dragged a gold and amethyst ring over a swollen knuckle and slipped it into a pocket.

The tall man held his staff out towards the cage.

'General, where are your tactics, your plans? Where is your brilliant strategy?' Figures emerged from the ranks behind him, wearing the uniform of Tumanbay. 'Where are your loyal men? The men who would die for you?'

The soldiers surrounded the cage. Each man had an amphora and they emptied them through the bars, onto the thick straw under Qulan's feet.

'They are gone, General, all consumed by the wrath of God, as you will be consumed by the fire of Maya's vengeance.'

Cries and wails arose from the crowd of palace servants.

Gregor turned and headed for the door.

'Where are you going?'

'We still have something.'

'We have nothing! And nothing will save your brother now. We must submit, all of us, utterly . . .' A gold chain of office fell from under his robe, followed by a pearl bracelet. 'Gregor . . . Come back, you fool, you'll try and you'll die.'

But Gregor was gone. Cadali slumped into a chair. There was nothing to do but await his fate.

Daniel took Madu's hands in his. 'I want you to go to your room, Madu, lock the door. You will be safe. I will come for you in time. Everything will be all right if you trust me.'

Looking into his lover's face, Madu realised that he didn't know him at all. He also knew, with an absolute certainty, that his only chance of coming through this alive lay in trusting the tall, blue-eyed stranger who held his hands and his heart.

'Go now, Madu. I will be with you soon.'

Gregor ran down the stone stairs into the prison depths of the palace. Many of the sconces that usually burned and lighted the gloomy passages had gone out; most of the guards were absent, and those that remained were slouching against the walls, a lost expression on their faces. Outside the envoy's cell there was no one at all – the door stood ajar; it was empty. Gregor cursed and hammered a useless fist against the wood of the door. Too late.

'Commander?' A young guard at the far end of the passage, his sword in his hand. 'What's happening? They say she's here . . . in the city. Is it true?'

'It's true enough. You're the one who was guarding the envoy. Where is he?'

'I moved him, down the passage. He was talking to me. All the time. Telling me that I should . . . that she was . . . I didn't want to hear. I put him at the end so I didn't have to listen.'

Gregor was impressed. The only guard still at his post, a virtual boy.

'What's your name, son?'

'Hero, Excellency.'

'Good job, Hero. I'll remember you. You remember me. Give me the keys then go home, lose your uniform.'

Effendi Red sat as he had the last time Gregor had seen him, on the stone bed, one leg tucked under his robes. His wrists and ankles were manacled. His expression, in the dancing light of the sconce in the passage, was calm. He nodded.

'Is she here?'

'She's here. Get up.'

'As you wish.' He stood. 'What do you want, Commander? Your hand keeps reaching for your sword, then you pull it back. Do you want to kill me? No. Then what? Do you even know? Is there, somewhere, a desire that you dare not acknowledge yet?'

Gregor could see exactly why the guard had moved this man out of his hearing. There was something insidious about his voice, beguiling, reeling you in . . .

Gregor pulled his sword and punched Red in the face with the pommel guard. The envoy fell backwards onto the stone bed, blood falling from a torn cheek, one eye already black and swelling.

'Did you guess?' Gregor said. 'Now come with me if you want to live.'

'As you say.' Red heaved himself up. 'Where are we going?'

'To see your damned mistress.'

As Gregor emerged from the palace, pushing the envoy ahead of him, the Grand Square was silent and still. Maya's troops stood barely moving. Black-robed figures flittered here and there along the ranks, and the four traitors in the uniform of

Tumanbay stood holding torches at each corner of the cage in the middle of the courtyard, where General Qulan waited, his feet in the oily straw. Behind him, Sultan al-Ghuri sat on his throne, his skin stretched tightly over its stuffing, a few wisps of straw protruding from under his closed eyelids and from his nostrils. This close, Gregor could see that his lips had been sewn shut, the thread pulled up at each corner, giving him a smile he'd never exhibited in life.

The envoy's chains dragged across the stone flags as Gregor pushed him forward. It was the loudest sound there, and echoed horribly back from the walls.

'Maya!' he bellowed. 'Here is your trusted servant! He will die here before you if you burn General Qulan!'

Nobody answered, nobody moved. He looked for her, for this queen. Was she one of the expressionless faces that lined the courtyard? Was she even here?

'Why would she care if I live or die?' Red said, his voice raspy and dry. 'She has so many envoys. As for me, I am not afraid of death. I can think of no greater honour than to die in her service and be ensured a swift passage to Paradise.' He might have been talking about replanting a flower bed.

Gregor hit him again with the pommel guard. He went down in a clatter of chains and a flutter of black and red robes, then struggled to his knees. No one interfered. Gregor went forward to the cage.

Qulan sat inside, his face bloodied and bruised, his uniform torn.

'Well, brother,' Gregor said, 'I tried to save you but I think ... I think this is the end.'

Qulan shrugged. 'I'm a soldier, death is no stranger to me.' He grinned as he had when they were crossing the mountains all those years ago. 'We've come a long way, you and I, Gregor, and

I suppose we got most of what we wanted as boys.'

For a moment, it was as if they were standing on the high peaks again, looking down at the endless snows and an unknown future. They had indeed come far, achieved much, the two of them, and yet it had started with a lie. Gregor thrust the memory aside but it would not go: it had started with a lie, could it end that way? Did he not owe his brother the truth at this last moment?

A moment broken when Qulan said: 'I am glad to see you here even if it was a stupid thing to do.'

Gregor reached up, took his brother's hand – and slid a long, thin dagger under the straw. It would be quicker and less painful than burning to death.

Qulan nodded his appreciation. 'Always the practical man,' he said.

'Don't use it before you have to,' Gregor whispered. 'There may be a chance, just a small . . .'

His voice broke at the sight of his brother's calm, reassuring look. He let go and went back to his prisoner, who had clambered to his feet. The bruise now covered the whole side of his face.

'The scrolls we talked about,' Gregor said urgently. 'If I had them—'

'Then things might be different? Is that what you wish?'

'They're important to your queen, yes?'

'Yes.'

'Is she here? Somewhere in the city, in this square?'

'She is here. Believe that.'

'I can get them for you . . . or I can cast them into a chasm where they will burn and they will be forever lost. Believe that.'

'Very well. Unchain me. You have a master key, you can do it.'

It was true. This man knew altogether too much; Gregor had the feeling that all of this was a play of some sort, a ceremony in which everything was happening as had been ordained for centuries. He unlocked the shackles. Red massaged his wrists as they fell away. It was a small – human – gesture and somehow made Gregor feel better, as if a man might actually have a chance of changing things here.

'Very well, Effendi Red, you are free. Now, what do you have for me?'

'The true believer is free even in the deepest captivity.'

Gregor hit him again.

'I don't want your shitting philosophy, Red, I want an answer.'

'Very well. You have until sunset to bring me the scrolls. Or it won't just be the general – the whole city will be consumed in flames.'

Gregor ran back to the cage.

'We will meet again, brother,' he said. 'In this world, I promise.'

Qulan nodded. 'You always knew what to do, Gregor.'

'Yes. And I have to tell you something because if I don't tell you now ...'

'Time is short, Commander. Don't waste it,' came Effendi Red's voice from behind.

'Brother, go!'

'I killed Varsi.'

Qulan frowned and shook his head, confused.

'In the mountains. I said he had tripped and fallen to his death. But the truth is I pushed him. He was slowing us down. I didn't think we would make it unless ...'

He could see the anger and disappointment in Qulan's face.

'I did what I had to, brother. Varsi was too great a burden – we would all have died out there in the snow. It was necessary.'

'I would not have done it, Gregor, no matter how necessary.'

'And we would have died before we even started. We wouldn't have had any of this, brother. We would never have even seen

Tumanbay, let alone served it. And that's why I had to, brother – that's what I've always done. What was necessary for us to survive.'

He turned and walked back towards the palace, past Effendi Red, whom he afforded barely a glance.

'I won't let you down this time, brother,' he said.

Once inside, he started to run, through corridor after corridor, past the Hall of Mirrors, the Gold Room, the menagerie, the collection of sculptures from the ancient world, and down into the sunken garden towards the Archway of the Martyrs.

He left the palace by the Traitors' Gate. It was somehow suitable on this day of all days. A guard leaned against the wall outside, cleaning his nails. He looked at Gregor, his commander, recognised him, shrugged and returned to his occupation.

'Are you supposed to be guarding this gate, Pamender?'

'No more commands. We're all dead now.'

Gregor left him to it, making his way through a series of alleyways behind the palace and emerging onto one of the main thoroughfares that cut through the city. It was always busy here but something was different; everyone was heading in the same direction, towards the city gates. People were carrying whatever possessions they could manage. A cart trundled past piled with furniture. A young girl was perched on the back, holding two chickens.

As he pushed his way against the flow of humanity, Gregor felt an arm on his shoulder.

'Not this way, friend,' said a terrified-looking man trying to pull him back. 'Don't you know there is trouble?'

Gregor ripped his arm free.

'Everything's trouble,' he spat, and thrust him away so he tripped and went down with a cry, under the feet of the mob.

Gregor pushed on: he had told Qulan the truth at last, something he never thought he would do in this life. Now he had to find Sarah; she had the scrolls and they could save his brother's life if he could get them in time – if he could find her, if she was safe, if she would listen to him . . . No, too many questions. He didn't need them. He put his head down, butted an elderly couple aside, smashed his fist into the face of a fat merchant and ran. Now was the time for action. For what was necessary. That was what he did – what he'd always done – and nothing had changed. Had it?

94

Manel

Manel heard the knocking as she waited by the fountain under the quince tree. She had been waiting for something ever since the servants had gone. One minute they were there, then they were gone; only her nurse and a few old retainers were left. No one else cared to be associated with the defeated commander of Tumanbay's armies. The knocking continued. Maya's men, come to arrest the family of an enemy? Looters? Refugees? Clutching an antique dagger, she unlocked the wicket gate and stepped back.

'Manel, that knife has a blade like a razor, please . . .'

The knife dropped from her fingers and she took his hands in hers.

'Daniel. Daniel. Daniel.'

He smiled reassuringly. 'We could stand here all day but I'd rather get off the streets.'

'Of course, I'm sorry, I wasn't thinking, come in . . .' He stepped through and she locked the door behind him. 'Is there any news of my father?'

One glimpse of his expression told her it was not good.

'Is your mother here, your brother?'

'Of course. Inside. Come.'

That he had come to them was a joy for her; the news he must be carrying was a horror. Caught between her heart and the world of war, Manel felt as if she were being pulled apart. How could they go on in the face of what had happened? Daniel's hand rested for a moment on her back as he ushered her through into the house; the touch thrilled her. She had asked herself: how could they go on? And yet now, more than anything, she wanted him, she desired him – she wanted to go on with him.

'Mother, it's Daniel. He has news.'

Pushkarmi rose; Daniel bowed to her.

'My respects to you, and to your house.'

'And to you, Daniel. You are welcome. If your news, I fear, is not.'

Pesha burst into the room, carrying a scimitar far too big for him. A look from his mother subdued his warlike spirits. He went to stand beside her, looking very young.

Daniel said: 'He lives – that is first and foremost.'

Manel felt as if an invisible bird had flown from her breast, carrying a cargo of worry and fear. *He lives!*

Pushkarmi said: 'Does he live in honour or infamy?'

Manel wanted to say, I don't care, he lives! but she knew how deeply honour mattered to both her parents.

'You need have no fear of dishonour, madam. From what we know, and much is still unclear, he was betrayed – the army had been infiltrated by Maya's followers. They never offered even a sword in resistance but turned on their brothers – the army killed itself. Qulan was betrayed, taken prisoner and is now held in the palace, so I have heard and so I believe.'

Pushkarmi stood unmoving, and Manel knew what an effort it cost her.

Pesha waved his sword and said: 'I swear I will avenge my father. Whatever the cost, I will have her head.'

His voice, newly broken, turned to a squeak for the last few words. Even so, Manel could have hugged him for his courage.

Daniel smiled. 'Well spoken, young man. Your father would be proud of you. And I must tell you, there is hope. The general has many friends – aye, and enemies too – who respect him.'

'They will kill him,' Pesha spluttered. 'They will cut off his head.'

'Hush, my son.' Pushkarmi placed a hand on the boy's shoulder. 'Listen to our friend. Go on, Daniel.'

'It may be that Maya or her advisors will be content if your husband accepts an honourable retirement.'

'It doesn't sound like Father,' Manel said.

Daniel grinned. 'Forgive me. Yes, I agree, but there would be no shame. His reputation would not suffer. It may be that a word from his wife and daughter would be a help in the matter, but let's not talk of what we cannot know. For now he lives. I have to go. I will return when I know more.'

Manel saw him to the gate. They did not speak until they were standing in its shadow and the wicket was unlocked.

She said: 'Is it true? Is there a chance for him?'

'I believe there is.'

'What will happen, Daniel, to all of us?'

'That is in other hands than ours. What will be, will be. But know, Manel, you are in my thoughts, I care very much for you.'

'My heart is a traitor.'

'How so?'

'Even with my father in their hands, I cannot stop thinking of you, Daniel. Hold me, please.'

He took her in his arms, resting his chin on the top of her head so she could feel as well as hear his voice.

'I hold you in my arms, my dear woman, and I hold you in my heart.' He stepped back. 'Now, pick up the dagger you dropped and if anyone tries to get in other than me, use it.'

Their eyes met, their lips met for a moment, Manel felt their souls touch and then he was gone. She locked the gate and picked up the dagger.

He was right, she thought, its edge was as sharp and fine as a razor, you wouldn't even feel it as it cut your throat.

95
Madu

If time had been frozen like water formed into glass, Madu wrote,
*then time began again to the sound of a thousand mirrors smashed,
a million shards falling like rain upon marble, bringing forth a new
and terrible future.*

He could hear it as the pen moved over the thick double-laid
paper. Other sounds too, marking a work of relentless destruction. He'd crept out of his room, despite Daniel's advice, and
watched from secret windows in hidden passages he'd known
since childhood, as Maya's black robes set about the treasures
of the Sultan's palace. The Hall of Mirrors, the great galleries of
sculpture from all the world's history, the gardens and – most
horrible of all – the screams of the animals in the zoo as they
went down under the relentless hammers and knives. He had
retreated to his rooms and tried to find escape in poetry, and felt
like a traitor doing so. He pushed the paper away, drank deeply
of a white spirit in a ruby bottle, feeling it burn its way down his
throat – and almost vomited it back up when the handle of the
room door began to turn. Had he locked it? Who . . .?

'Madu, it's me. Let me in.' A moment and Daniel was in the
room and in his arms. 'What's been happening here?'

'They're destroying everything. The great garden, the art . . .
all of it. We have to get out, Daniel. My mother's villa in the

mountains. I know of ways we can leave, get through the walls too. We'll find—'

Daniel stopped the rush of words with a gentle touch.

'Madu, stop, think. You have to keep your head now or you'll lose it for sure. There's nothing against you.'

Madu broke free and went back to the bottle. He swigged and offered it.

'I'm the Sultan. It's just a matter of time.'

Daniel waved the spirits away. 'We need clear heads, my dear man. You aren't the Sultan, al-Ghuri was. He was a tyrant. He murdered your father and stole your mother. Maya has avenged you.'

'I was complicit.' Madu slumped onto a sofa. 'I hated my father. I knew about the plan. I could have told him but I didn't.'

'Ahhh, Madu, you're choked by guilt and regret. Think what it would be like to lose that, to see it . . . disappear as mist burns away before the sun.'

'It never will.' He reached for the bottle but Daniel stayed his hand, holding his wrist in a grip as firm as steel. 'Remember the army, when you stood up and spoke to Qulan and you were fearless?'

Had he? It seemed to Madu that it had been Daniel who spoke out, but . . . maybe he was right, maybe Madu had said . . .

Daniel let go of his wrist, held his hands each side of his head – such warm capable hands – and looked into his eyes.

'Is this the end?' Madu asked.

'Live each moment. It's all we truly ever possess and when it is past, not all our efforts, not all the power of Tumanbay, nor Maya herself, can take it away.'

96
Gregor

The market, when Gregor finally reached it, was empty; he could still hear the crowds howling and bellowing in their quest for escape, but they had done their worst here and left. Stalls were smashed to splinters, canvas torn in shreds that fluttered in the wind, fruit was trodden underfoot, fine cloth mashed into puddles of wine and water. Barrels lay on their sides, spilling their cargoes of olives and fish in brine and vinegar and oil; lamb and other meats smouldered on abandoned grills, filling the air with the stink of burned flesh. Only the chickens and geese, rabbits and oak squirrels thrived here now, freed from smashed cages, wandering among the ruins, pecking and eating their fill.

He tried to recall their route when the boy, Frog, had led him out of the underworld. His powers of recall were great, but everything had changed since he had seen the place and the waymarks he could have used – merchants' banners, the corner pavilions of the market guards – had all been destroyed. In the end it was accident that found him his way: spilled wine and vinegar flowing along a gutter and emptying down into the sewers – through the grille he had opened when ascending. It should have had a counterweight but when he pulled at the bars it wouldn't shift.

He stood astride, grasped with both hands and pulled again,

shouting out with the effort. Still nothing. He tried again, then stood, gasping for breath. *Think, Gregor, think.* 'Time is short, don't waste it,' the envoy had said. He forced himself to stop and calm his breathing.

Of course, it made sense – there would be a lock or a catch. He kneeled and let his fingertips run along the iron rim of the drain cover. Once, twice around and there – an irregularity. He pressed it, pulled at the cover and it rose easily, revealing the ladder down into the darkness and the sound of water flowing sluggishly. He took a few precious moments to make himself a torch from rag and oil and cooking implements and then descended. There was no point in asking whether or not he was being a fool: he simply had no choice.

Once down, he lit his rags in their makeshift sconce and started out in what he hoped was the right direction. He shouted as he went, trusting that someone would hear and come for him. Of course, in this world trust was in short supply; he might find himself wandering forever.

'You should not be here, you are not wanted or welcome. We do not want your war or your woe. The way is closed, how did you enter?'

The same sibilant whisper as before, the same presences all around him. Hands twitched the torch out of his grasp and propelled him forward. He had no idea if they were following the same route. It seemed to go on for a long time, but at least there were no bats. At length they came to a lilting circle of light cast by an oil lamp. Sitting beside it, the boy Frog. Just visible in the darkness behind him, the young man with the naked scimitar. It was almost a comfort to think there was still someone who considered him a threat.

'Hello, Gregor. You have come back to us.'

'So you see. No oranges or dates, I'm afraid.'

'Yes, you are afraid.'

'A man would be a fool not to be in these times, Frog. It's all change up there.'

'Tell me.'

'I've no time. I need to find the woman, Sarah. Where is she? Don't make me wait, Frog, and don't think your swordsman back there will stop me.' His sword was in his hand. He stepped forward into the circle of light. 'Tell me or I will hurt you.'

The Frog laughed and waved his protection back into the shadows.

'No you won't, and you won't find what you want down here either.'

'If you have hurt her, I swear I will have your life and the life of everyone in this pit.'

'You see, Gregor,' the boy laughed, 'I was right, you do like her. What will you feel if you never see her again? If they cut her head off like they did to my father?'

'If I don't find her they are going to burn my brother alive. I need to see her, she has something. If she . . .'

The Frog held up a restraining hand. 'She has gone to where she came from.'

'She's alive?'

'She is alive in your heart, Gregor.'

He held his sword out at arm's length, its point within a fingernail's width of the boy's throat.

'I've had enough of your mystical horse shit.'

The Frog didn't try to move away from the point – he seemed for a moment almost to sleep; his eyes clouded over and then refocused on Gregor with a new intensity.

'You will find her with her child in the city above.'

'They let her go?' Gregor said. 'She's not been harmed?'

'I don't know, effendi. That isn't how it works. You surely

understand that much. The woman is where she is safe now.'

He turned his head, blew out the candle and vanished in the dark.

Subtle hands took hold of Gregor and guided him.

Where she was safe. Where she was safe . . .?

Of course!

515

97
Red

His robes dusty and torn among the black figures surrounding him, Effendi Red pushed open the great doors of the Council Chamber and led his retinue inside. Cadali stood by the throne. This, he knew, was his chance to make an impression. To explain how useful he could be: a man who knew all the secrets, the short cuts, who knew how things worked – and, more importantly, how they could be taken apart, since destruction was obviously more in Maya's line than construction.

'Your Eminence . . .' No harm in a bit of flattery. 'Honoured Effendi Red, I have them all here as you requested.' He opened the great brass-bound ledger that lay on the table before him. 'The record of all the palace officials, from the highest to the lowest. We have always prided ourselves here in Tumanbay on our efficiency. Chamberlains, the law courts, the civil adminis-tration, trade, public officials . . .'

Red waved him to silence.

'You appear to be a useful fellow, Cadali.'

'I have been waiting my whole life for the opportunity to serve my queen.'

'Really?'

Yes, that was rather laying it on a bit thick; after all, Maya had only appeared on the scene recently.

'Well, my Lord, I was feeling an unsatisfied desire, a long-felt wont, something missing from my life that, only now, at the dawn of a glorious new age, do I feel will be satisfied at last.'

The black robes, who had spread out around the chamber examining drawers, cupboards, chests – locks seemed to be no bar – stopped and turned their pale faces, hooded in darkness, towards him like a convocation of skulls. Why were they all so thin, so still? He swallowed nervously. Would he have to lose weight to fit in? Well, he could do it, he could do anything to survive. He checked his hands – no more rings, thank goodness. He pointed to a bag on the table beside the ledger.

'My rings, my jewellery, my chains of office – I offer them up to Maya. I understand that these so-called riches mean nothing. I have and I wish no worldly goods of my own. I was a victim of circumstances.'

One of the black robes took the bag, tipped it out. The gold and garnets, the diamonds and silver shone as the skeletal fingers made an account, noting everything in a small book, then scooped them back into the bag, which vanished under his robes. What now? Cadali looked around, he needed ... he needed ... Madu, entering the room with the blue-eyed bugger. Well, they'd certainly get rid of him; these religious types always hated any kind of pleasure.

'Effendi Red, this is Madu, he was acting Sultan. In him resides the corrupt degeneration of the old regime. Vice is written on his visage!'

'Maya wishes that he stay on the throne.'

'Where I am sure he will be able to learn, under my supervision, the true path of virtue and together—'

Red snapped his fingers and a young soldier stepped forward. He came to attention before the envoy and bowed.

'This soldier is one of my finest. If encouraged in the right way, he will make a fine leader one day. His father serves in Maya's court. His mother has worked for many years in Maya's service. They are good people.'

'Yes, yes, I have no doubt they are. A fine young man, to be sure.'

Where was this going? What did Red have in mind?

'Kill yourself,' Red said.

The soldier took a dagger from the scabbard strapped across his chest and plunged it, two-handed, into his stomach. His face was without expression as he fell.

Cadali's stomach turned over and came within a heave of delivering up his breakfast. The temperature in the room dropped like a desert night and an icy sweat crept over his body. This was the most serious thing he had ever seen.

'If Maya chooses you to serve, then you will serve, in whatever way she wishes. You understand?'

'Yes.'

'Life and death are no more than a doorway to the eternal. Do you, Madu of Tumanbay, understand this?'

'I do.'

Blue Eyes glanced at the Sultan and a smile passed between them. Cadali could see their hands touch.

The soldiers at the door parted and the Hafiz swayed in, supported as usual by his fat monk. What was the fellow's name? Bello? Surely Red would dispense with the old drunk?

'Your Holiness, how are you?'

'His Holiness is a little unwell.'

'Please, sit. Maya wishes to see you clearly.'

Bello guided the Hafiz skilfully around the corpse and the spreading pool of blood, to a chair, where he subsided with a sigh.

Cadali peered around the room. *See him clearly?* he thought.

Was she here, in this room? In person? Did she have extraordinary powers? He shivered again.

'How was your journey?' Red addressed the Hafiz but the monk answered.

'We were treated well, effendi. His Holiness said prayers while al-Ghuri was stripped of his . . . skin. A coach was provided for our transport back to the city, and we were assured that Maya valued our contribution and His Holiness's . . . how should I put it? . . . position as the leader of the faith.'

The Hafiz belched and dribbled into his beard.

Bello hastily added, 'I mean that the faith is ensconced in his sacred person –' another belch – 'and it is not for us to judge the choice of the Almighty.'

'Enough. Maya has a question for Your Holiness.' He leaned close to the old man, wrinkled his nose.

Cadali listened. Was there a whisper in the room, a woman's voice, silvery like moths' wings in the moonlight?

'Is Maya the Sword of the Faith under your guidance? Is she justified by the faith?'

The Hafiz's lips moved. A husky whisper that was impossible to make out. Red leaned closer.

'What did you say?'

'He says yes!' Bello was exultant. 'Yes, yes, yes, yes!'

98
Gregor

Ibn Bai had always thought of himself as a reasonable man. However, it was becoming harder by the day to exercise that faculty due to the simple fact there was no peace in the house; and without peace in the house, even the greatest of philosophers would have found it difficult to be reasonable – and Ibn Bai was far from that and far from calm.

The problems had begun shortly before the news of the Battle of the Caterpillars, when Akiba, as he must now call him, had left the house in pursuit of Gregor – in Ibn Bai's eyes the most dangerous man in Tumanbay. He intended to kill him in revenge for some terrible wrong done to him and his people. Neither Heaven nor Boy had agreed with the idea, believing it would only bring more trouble. It made no difference to Akiba and he was gone for most of the day and night. When he returned, he had blood on his hands. He had insisted that he had not harmed Gregor.

'He is alive, I give you my word.'

Ibn Bai had tried to get out of the big man exactly what Gregor had done to wrong him.

'He took something from me – he took everything from me.' Beyond that, Akiba would say nothing.

Heaven had left the room and had barely spoken to any of

them since. Even Boy was shut out and an atmosphere hung about the house like the scent of uneasy drains.

Now, days later, they were virtual prisoners behind the walls of the compound. Outside the crowds raged and tore at each other, the city, Paradise itself, in their frantic efforts to escape. Akiba and Ibn Bai had patrolled the walls to guard against thieves and worse. Fortunately, Ibn Bai had not been called upon to wield the sword he felt so uncomfortable carrying, and Akiba's very presence, looming above the parapet, discouraged any incursions.

It was the hour after noon and Ibn Bai was making coffee, watching over the little pot as it heated and the thick black liquid bubbled up towards the rim for the third time.

Akiba wandered in from his patrol and said: 'How weak this great empire has proved to be. How fat and lazy it has become. No wonder Maya simply walked in. I have no doubt the man Gregor will have run, like all of them, or will be keeping his head down in some corner of the palace.'

Ibn Bai muttered: 'If I know Gregor, he'll have a plan.' He whipped the little pot off the flame, gave it a final tap with a wooden spoon and tipped the coffee into his cup. 'Now that, my friend Akiba, is how you make a good cup of—'

A hammering at the gate. A very recognisable hammering at the gate.

'Surely,' Ibn Bai said as he hurried across the compound to open it – the servants had vanished to a man and woman, 'the ancients spoke the truth, we live in a world of eternal recurrence. Good day, Commander Gregor, you were just in my thoughts.'

'Where is she?'

'Not here, I can assure you.'

Which was the moment Boy chose to wander out of the house to see what the noise was, carrying a baby.

'Well, she was here but—'

521

Gregor pushed him aside, strode across the courtyard to Boy. 'Where is the mother of that child?'

Holding the baby close, Boy shook his head and said something in a language Ibn Bai didn't recognise. Gregor grasped his hair and lifted him off his feet. He howled, the baby screamed.

'She came, she left the child, she said she had to go to the palace!' Ibn Bai shouted.

Gregor swung Boy round. Ibn Bai managed to catch the baby as she slipped from his grip.

'You're lying, all of you! I want the truth!'

An arm snaked around Gregor's neck, in it, a knife. Akiba's voice: 'The truth is that you are going to die.'

Gregor dropped Boy. He twisted in the big man's grip but couldn't move. The knife blade lay against his throat. Heaven burst from the house.

'No, Akiba, not here, you promised.'

'I am sorry, Heaven. It has to be, the man must die.'

Ibn Bai could see the muscles in his arm tensing. Gregor spoke quietly and clearly.

'If I die, you die too. The blade against your thigh is a pinprick – but a poisoned one. We will see Paradise together.'

'What do I care, as long as you are dead. My wife, my children, my people will be able to rest, knowing I have done what I promised in their name. I have nothing except my desire for that to be done.'

'You have everything!' It was Heaven, shouting at him. 'I am carrying our child!'

Ibn Bai staggered backwards, hit the edge of the pool and sat down in the water.

'A child?'

'It's true – here, growing.' She held her hands over her belly. 'Our child, Akiba.'

Neither man said a word or made a move. They were a statue in the courtyard, barely breathing. And Ibn Bai, that reasonable man, still holding the baby, pulled himself up out of the water and stood dripping and said: 'I have a suggestion. We do not have to be enemies, not today. Next year, who knows? But today I will count to three and you will both drop your knives at the same time.'

No answer from either of them, then the baby – Sarah's baby – cooed and chortled, as if it were all a game. Akiba's knife fell to the stones.

'Gregor, he has dropped his weapon, please—'

'Why should I? One nick and what future then?'

'Let him go!'

It was a cry torn from the heart of every mother in every war in every age of the world. A cry, but not a plea. Heaven had known suffering and pain, loss and now, with a new hope in sight, the words she spoke had a new authority. It was a command and the tiny spike fell from Gregor's grip and rang on the ground.

'Thank you, Your Excellency.'

Gregor strode out into the street without a word. Ibn Bai, Heaven and Akiba all stared at each other wordlessly.

Boy laughed and said: 'Another baby, that'll be fun!'

99
Wolf

The Street of Jars, otherwise known as 'lechers alley' at the centre of the brothel district, was silent and empty. The doors of the many houses of pleasure were locked shut, the window shutters closed. The fall of an empire was often taken to sanction the rise of anarchy – drunkenness and pleasure given their head as folk celebrated the breakdown of law – but not in Tumanbay, not under the cold hand of Maya, it seemed. Even the irrepressible spirit of the city's bad boys and girls was subdued: above there were no kite flyers, no shouts of joy; and below, no rough encounters, no heads in gutters and legs akimbo, no cries of pleasure or pleasurable pain – only silence.

Broken at last by the sound of hooves thudding over packed sand. A flurry of movement as the rider pulled up his mount, slid out of the saddle and strode to one of the many blank-faced doors. He raised his fist and hammered at the thick wood. No answer. He hammered again and again, the blows echoing along the street. At last a voice, ancient and tremulous, answered.

'We're closed.'

He hammered once more. A flap in the door at head height was unlatched and opened. Ancient eyes looked out.

'I told you, we're closed.'

'I was here a while ago with a girl called Shamsi. I paid in gold. I paid well. Send her out now or I'll return with Maya's police. You don't want that.'

The flap shut. He waited, leaning against the roughcast wall. He was in no hurry and certainly not scared of being stopped by anyone's police. When a group of black-robed figures passed along the street, taking note of the houses and their various signs, he merely nodded to them and they went on their way.

There was a rattle of locks and keys and finally the door opened. The girl, Shamsi, was thrust rudely out of the darkness within, tripping as she crossed the step. The man caught her, helped her up. She looked at him.

'I said I would come back.'

She was scared – but spoke anyway.

'They say it was a barbarian called Wolf who betrayed the general, who sold Tumanbay to Maya.'

He shrugged. 'It was no betrayal. We were always on Maya's side, even before we'd heard of her. Palaces and riches mean nothing to us. We carry everything we possess on our horses. Gold weighs us down. We have been waiting for her for centuries.'

'How can that be?'

'We live between the earth and the sky. When one of us leaves this world, we are offered to the sky. We don't cling to the earth like the people of Tumanbay.'

'But don't you feel anything for the general? He must have trusted you.'

The barbarian stood for a while, arms crossed, head lowered, considering. Eventually he spoke.

'General Qulan is a man among men. In another life I think he would have believed too. In this one, he was honest and I am proud to name him my enemy. Of all the people I have known in this city I would save only two – and one I cannot help.'

'And the other is a whore,' Shamsi said. 'I am the corruption of

Tumanbay, I am everything your mistress Maya despises.'

'She is not my mistress. Yes, I believe in her, but so do I believe in the mountains and the plains. Maya is what must be at this time – you, Shamsi, can be anything you wish. You are so light you can ride on my horse and it will be as if there is only one rider. Will you come with me?'

'Can I trust you, Wolf?'

'Until death.'

He swung himself into the saddle and held out his hand. Without hesitation she took it. He pulled her up and they rode away, leaving the Street of Jars, otherwise known as 'lechers alley', to its silence and emptiness.

100

Gregor

Why did I let him live? Of all the many I have killed, why him?

Gregor had passed through the Bulpass Quarter and was running along Maduk Highway towards the palace, hardly noticing that the chaos and panic had now subsided and the street was all but empty. A stray dog stopped to watch him for a moment before sauntering across the deserted road.

And why . . . her . . . ?

His thoughts kept turning to Sarah.

She is the key to everything. She has the scrolls, she can save Qulan, she can save . . . me.

He entered the palace as he had left it, through the Traitors' Gate. The passageway reeked of strong liquor and the guard was now unconscious and slumped against a wall. Gregor stepped over him and into the passages of the palace.

She would have approached from the front entrance, and it would have taken her some time to explain her mission to whoever was at the gates. She would have asked to see whoever was in charge, said it was of the utmost importance and kept the box close to her. The likelihood was that Maya's officers would simply detain her. It might be hours or days before anyone thought to notify Effendi Red of her request. He no doubt had other things on his mind as he oversaw the plundering of the palace.

But finding Sarah, taking possession of the scrolls and delivering them to Red was the only thing that would save Qulan. And Gregor had the advantage of being able to move about the palace almost unnoticed.

As he passed through the corridors, it became clear to him that the usual order had disintegrated into a state of panic during his short absence. He turned a corner to see a courtier running frantically towards him, his clothes dishevelled.

'Go back,' the man pleaded, pulling Gregor along with him. 'They are killing people. Go back!'

Seeing that Gregor was intent on continuing, he let him go and ran on, shouting at anyone he encountered.

There was the sound of hammering and crashes coming from ahead. Gregor approached and saw a group of black robes, heavy mallets in their hands, knocking down and smashing statues from the Sultan's priceless collection gathered from the ancient world.

He moved on unseen towards the throne room. As he passed the entrance to the hareem he heard whimpering and stopped. Several dozen pairs of terrified eyes looked out at him from a small dark room. He noticed children too, their mothers' arms around them, and one woman was nursing a baby. The wives and children of the palace, their lives about to expire.

'Help us,' one of them pleaded, seeing from his dress that Gregor was a palace official. 'We have nowhere to go.'

'Our babies . . . Help us . . .' said another.

'You need to wait,' Gregor said firmly.

He could do nothing for them now.

'But our children. She will take her revenge on . . .'

He didn't have time for this but he stopped – not really knowing why – and shifted a wooden cabinet away from the wall. Behind it there was a small door, invisible to anyone who did not know it was there. Gregor did. Now he pressed the release catch and opened it – a cold, musty wind blew through it.

'In here, all of you. Go left and down the winding stairs, then go left again and down again. It will lead you to a shallow stream that flows through a culvert. Follow it, you'll be in the city, lose yourselves. Don't come back.'

Like deer frozen in the bowman's eye they stared at him.

'*Go! Go!*' he bellowed, and then ran on.

He hurried swiftly past the Hall of Mirrors, now carpeted with shards of glass reflecting a terrible brightness, and darted through a panel in the wall and along one of the narrow servants' passageways that took him to the reception room outside the throne room, where Effendi Red had set up his headquarters.

When he emerged, he saw her waiting there, an ornate box in her hands. It was the one he had seen in the workshop of the brothers Angellotti. She seemed composed and unafraid, despite the chaos, despite Maya's guards looming around her.

'Sarah . . .?' Gregor called out, rushing to her. 'What are you doing . . .?' Taking her by the arm, he guided her back towards the protection of the passageway. 'This is too dangerous. These people – you don't know what they are capable of.'

'I have the scrolls.'

She handed the box to him. He took it.

'Now come, quickly.'

He was aware of activity – of soldiers passing by, of orders being given, of Maya's senior commanders going in and out of the throne room – but no one seemed to pay much attention to him or Sarah. Perhaps they didn't matter any more. Maya's forces were so supremely confident, they would get around to dealing with everyone eventually.

'Go down here,' he said, 'and wait for me at the end of the passageway. You'll be safe for a while. I have to deliver this to

Maya's envoy and then I'll come. I'll look after you. I swear. I was wrong, wrong about everything . . .'

'Do you know what they are?' she asked.

'What?'

'The scrolls?

'Myths, histories, something past. It doesn't matter. I don't care what they are, just what they can do for me now. It's the past. It's dead and gone.'

'You give me something. I give you something.'

'I don't understand.'

'But you will.'

'What are you talking about?'

Something in her manner was making Gregor feel uneasy.

'Not the past, not histories, not myths . . . The opposite, in fact – the future.'

Gregor stared at her, confused.

'How can a scroll possibly depict—?'

'Perhaps you'll have a part to play in that future, Gregor, Master of the Palace Guard.'

The doors of the throne room swung open and Effendi Red appeared.

'Ah, you are here . . .' he called out.

Sarah leaned in to Gregor and embraced him.

'We shall see each other again,' she said quietly into his ear.

'Yes, yes, I'll be back as soon as I can,' he replied, trying to reassure her, though he knew something was wrong.

After a moment, Sarah released him and he stepped forward into the light, holding up the box.

'I have the scrolls, Effendi Red.'

'Good. Put them there,' the envoy said, gesturing to an oval table in the middle of the room, seemingly unconcerned. Gregor put the box down.

'So, this is it. This is what has caused so much anguish. This is what you asked for. Now keep your side of the agreement and release my brother.'

But the envoy ignored Gregor, instead keeping his eyes on Sarah.

'It's been a long time . . .' he said, then added, 'my wife.'

'Yes,' Sarah replied, approaching him.

He touched her head and closed his eyes as if in a blessing. After a moment, he took her hand.

'And our child?' he asked.

'Our child is safe, husband.'

Gregor watched, a million questions rushing through his mind – questions he could not quite formulate and which eventually made their way to his mouth as simply, 'Sarah . . .?'

But the young woman was no longer interested in him; her blue eyes were fixed on her husband, Effendi Red.

'The city is ours?' she asked.

'The city is ours.'

'As it is written so it shall be . . .'

There were only a few moments in Gregor's life when he felt as though he was looking down on himself from above. It had happened after his first kill, long ago in the mountains, when he had convinced himself that the death of the crippled boy, Varsi, was not betrayal but survival. It was happening again now. He was looking down on this place and time, when everything he had come to expect was confounded. He hadn't seen it coming – and now it was too late.

He was looking down at a fool.

Acknowledgements

Tumanbay came into existence after Jeremy Howe and Gwyneth Williams at the BBC saw the potential in a few paragraphs we submitted. By commissioning the first audio drama series – then the second and third and fourth – we were given the chance to build the universe of Tumanbay. A lot of people were involved. Over a period of several years, the actors who appeared in series one came back for more, and then more again. Rufus Wright *is* Gregor for us; Matthew Marsh, Cadali; Olivia Popica, Heaven; Chris Fulford, Qulan; Raad Rawi, Sultan al-Ghuri; Nabil Elouahabi, Ibn Bai; Aiysha Hart, Manel.

Other actors came and went but were none-the-less part of this extraordinary journey into another world and I'd like to thank them for being part of it: Anton Lesser, Tara Fitzgerald, Alexander Siddig, Hiran Abeysekera, Nina Yndis, Sarah Beck Mather, Danny Ashok, Gareth Kennerley, Peter Polycarpou, Akin Gazi, Antony Bunsee, Albert Welling, Deeivya Meir, Nathalie Armin, Laure Stockley, Sirine Saba, Akbar Kurtha, Christian Hillborg, Alec Utgoff, Stefano Braschi, John Sessions, Annabelle Dowler, Sky Yang, Tanya Ravljen, Vincent Ebrahim, Byron Mondahl, Lara Sawalha, Flaminia Cinque, Zaqi Ismail, Anjli Mohindra, Jonas Khan, Jacob Krichefski, Tia-Lana Chinapyel, Amir El-Masry, Finn Elliot, Humera Syed, Yusuf Hofri, Muzz Khan,

Farshid Rokey, Alexander Arnold, George Georgiou, Marlene Madenge, Vivek Madan, Carl Prekopp and Dolya Gavanski.

It was producers Emma Hearn and Nadir Khan who worked out how to record what we had written, sound designers Steve Bond and Eloise Whitmore who built the world in audio, alongside Jon Ouin, Ania Przygoda, James Morgan, Andrea Gomez and the brilliant composer Sacha Puttnam. There were also other writers who stepped in to guest-write episodes; Andrew Mulligan, Ayeesha Menon and Mac Rogers. Lorraine Aston read an early draft and made many valuable suggestions. We want to thank them all.

When we started to write *Tumanbay* as a novel, we were encouraged by Euan Thorneycroft of AM Heath and Emad Akhtar, Publisher at Orion Books, who helped us shape the novel and challenged us to dig deeper into the characters and their world.

We would also like to thank our agents Georgina Ruffhead, Georgia Glover of David Higham Associates and Tanya Tillett of The Agency.

And finally, the Old Man of the Mountains who whispered many secrets into our ears.

JSD & MW

Credits

Orion Fiction would like to thank everyone at Orion who worked on the publication of *City of a Thousand Faces* in the UK.

Editorial
Emad Akhtar
Lucy Frederick

Copy Editor
Steve O'Gorman

Proof Reader
Kate Shearman

Audio
Paul Stark
Amber Bates

Design
Debbie Holmes
Joanna Ridley
Nick May

Editorial Management
Charlie Panayiotou
Jane Hughes
Alice Davis

Production
Ruth Sharvell

Marketing
Jennifer McMenemy

Publicity
Stevie Finegan

Finance
Jasdip Nandra
Afeera Ahmed
Elizabeth Beaumont
Sue Baker

Rights
Susan Howe
Krystyna Kujawinska
Jessica Purdue
Richard King
Louise Henderson

Contracts
Anne Goddard
Paul Bulos
Jake Alderson

Sales
Jen Wilson
Esther Waters
Victoria Laws
Rachael Hum

Ellie Kyrke-Smith
Frances Doyle
Georgina Cutler

Operations
Jo Jacobs
Sharon Willis
Lisa Pryde
Lucy Brem

Keep reading to discover more from
Walker Dryden in the next in the
Tumanbay series . . .

The Poisoned Throne

An ordinary man, perhaps a little less than average height, wearing an undistinguished brown robe, sandals that were anything but new, walking with a pronounced limp, a slight smile on his face as if he were recalling a pleasant memory. In his wake, soldiers, armoured and armed. For a moment it was hard to tell if they were escorting the small man or arresting him; only when he stopped for a moment at a crossroads, and the soldiers came to attention, did it become clear that he was in charge. He looked one way and then the other, pulled a sheet of vellum from his sleeve, consulted it and set off towards the affluent residences of the Bulpass Quarter. His escort followed. There were six of them, but their presence hardly seemed necessary. As the small party progressed, the streets before them emptied of pedestrians, stallholders, of anyone at all, until the way was clear. The small man looked benignly at the closing doors and shutters, the heels of children running for shelter, the shrouded women pulling back into the shadows, the canvas covers of stalls hastily lowered, and walked on. After the party had passed, the streets slowly came back to life, though it was notable that no one appeared to comment on what had just happened; quite the contrary – they treated it as if nothing had happened at all.

So intent were the small party upon their destination that they did not notice the figure following them, possibly a beggar or some shopkeeper condemned for selling short measures by Maya's police. He took care to stay a street or so behind them and to keep his face hidden in the shade of his hood.

In due course, the small man came to a halt before the door of a prosperous house and lifted the ornate knocker that proclaimed the owner to be a member of the guild of olive importers.

The door opened, a servant peered out and the small man said pleasantly: 'Peace be upon you.'

'And upon you, effendi.'

'I am sorry to disturb you so late in the afternoon. Is the master at home?'

'He is resting. I can . . .'

The small man held his hand up.

'Let him be. It is the child of the house I wish to speak to.'

The servant said nothing but her eyes widened.

'Please, don't be alarmed. It is a small matter.'

He stepped forward. Without thinking, the servant opened the door and he entered the house, followed by two of his escort. The others remained in the street.

The master of the house, far from resting, was standing behind the door where he had heard the conversation.

'You wish to speak to my son? He is saying his prayers.'

The small man clasped his hands across his narrow chest.

'Good. I'll wait, if it's convenient? Oh, please, excuse my escort. I have walked from the palace and in these times . . . well, I'm afraid it is necessary.'

He smiled apologetically, then turned to a woman who entered the room, scolding her husband.

'What are you thinking? Making a holy man stand, not offering him refreshment.' She kneeled to touch the small man's feet.

'It is an honour to receive you, Holiness, into our home. Food, drink? You must be—'

'We have need of nothing,' he said, reaching down and touching her head. 'Sister, please don't . . . Ahhhh.' A smile appeared on his face as he spotted a boy peering around the edge of a door at the far end of the chamber. 'This must be your son. Come, child, there is nothing to be frightened about.'

The boy slid round the door reluctantly. His father hurried over and took his shoulder and led him into the room. Now the small man sat down on a settle and patted the cushion beside him.

'Come, sit with me here. We need to talk.'

The mother said: 'Malik, sit with the holy father.'

The boy looked at the soldiers standing against the wall of the room.

The small man said: 'Oh, don't mind them, Malik. They won't let me leave the palace without them trailing behind. Can you imagine it, eh?'

He chuckled and a tiny smile appeared for a moment on the boy's face as he sat.

'Good. Now, how do you like school?'

'It's all right . . .' the boy mumbled shyly.

'Ah, you are one of the lucky ones. I didn't have such a good education as you. Tell me about your teacher.'

A silence in which the only sound was the ticking of a clock. Such novelties, imported from over the Middle Sea, were popular with the merchant class. The father was looking as if he wished he'd never seen the thing, or could throw it out now.

'What do you call him?'

'Master Odot.'

'Master Odot. Good, good . . . And Master Odot teaches you

about the scriptures? Tells you how a young man should live his life according to God's law?'

'Yes.'

The small man's head tilted, his eyes narrowed as he appraised the child. Eventually he said, 'I have heard he tells other things too.'

The boy's cheeks began to redden. He looked to his father, who nodded encouragingly.

'Tell the holy father everything, Malik,' he said. 'You have nothing to hide.'

His mother approached with a servant carrying a tray of refreshments.

'Now, Holiness, please don't insult us by declining our hospitality. It is hot and—'

'No,' the small man snapped.

'But you must be—'

'I said no!'

Without taking his eyes off the boy, he waved her away.

'Stand beside your husband,' he commanded. 'Tell the servant to go.'

She gave her husband a concerned look and then nodded to the servant, who left the room.

'You look worried, Malik,' the small man said, warmth returning to his voice. 'Don't be. Do you know what makes us strong? When I say strong, I mean without fear of what might happen to us?'

The boy shook his head.

'No? It is the truth that makes us strong. God's gift to us. That is why I, Barakat, have a reputation for never uttering a lie. Never. That is my strength. That can be your strength too. Do you understand me?'

He paused, waiting for a response. Eventually the boy nodded.

'We have brought our son up to always tell the truth, Holiness,' the father said. 'Haven't we, Malik? Tell him . . . tell him.'

'You see, it has come to my attention,' Barakat continued, now addressing the parents, 'that there is a heretic in your son's school.' He was almost apologetic.

The mother burst out: 'I swear we know nothing of this.'

'Of course, of course. How could you? You are not trained. You expect that when you send your children to school, their teachers will show them the true path. We are living in dangerous times. Not everyone is who they seem to be.'

'Are you saying that our son's teacher . . .?'

'He has visited,' Barakat said, nodding sadly.

'What?'

'This house.'

'Uhm, Malik was falling behind . . . in his recitations. We paid for extra lessons . . .'

'Of course, I understand.' Baraket took the child's hand in his. 'If only all parents were so diligent, my work in Tumanbay would be unnecessary.'

'If our child has done anything wrong,' the mother cried, 'tell us and we shall beat him!'

Baraket turned back to the boy, still holding his hand.

'Soldiers came to your school today, looking for your teacher. Where was he?'

The child now had his chin pressed against his chest and his eyes squeezed shut, as if trying to shut out all around him.

'Did someone tell him soldiers were coming?' Gently, he squeezed the boy's hand – not causing pain, rather reassuring him. 'You can tell me, Malik. I know already. I know everything. I just need you to tell me so I know you are a good boy. You know where Master Odot went, don't you?'

'No, that's not . . . How could he?' his mother cried.

Barakat hissed at her impatiently, then leaned close to the child and whispered: 'You have a chance to save yourself, Malik. We know everything already.'

'He's just a child,' his mother wept.

'Every child, every teacher in every school, every soul is important to us, especially one so young as yours.'

Malik was sobbing now, sucking in heaving breaths, his shoulders convulsing.

'You are feeling distressed. It is natural to feel distress. You are trying to hide from God, but nobody can hide from God. I am His eyes. God sees all and all will answer to Him. You know how to save yourself. So I will ask again – where is the master?'

The boy seemed to calm. Without a word, he lifted his head, opened his eyes and looked into Barakat's. Then he raised his arm and pointed at the door by which he had entered. Baraket nodded; the soldiers hurried through into the rooms beyond.

'No,' his mother said. 'He's confused. You are confusing him.'

She clasped her husband's arm, as if she might collapse. Baraket let go of the boy's hand and rose to his feet. From the adjacent room came the noise of searching – the crash of furniture overturned, cupboards ripped open . . . After a moment, the soldiers returned.

'Nothing, Holiness.'

The parents breathed again. Baraket waved at the house door and one of his men opened it. Those he had left outside entered now, with a figure in the robes of a teacher struggling in their grip. He was howling for mercy, an inarticulate wail of sheer terror.

'Climbing out of a back window, Holiness, as you said.'

The mother rushed to clasp her son. Baraket observed for a moment with vague interest, as she hugged him and ran her hands through his hair.

'Take the parents too,' he said eventually.

It took three soldiers to prise the mother's grip from her child. The father stood stunned, looking at the clock, as if it alone was the author of all their misfortunes.

'And the child?' asked one of the soldiers.

'Leave him, he has saved himself.' He sat for a moment beside Malik, like a kindly uncle. 'You see, God takes care – God takes care of all. The truth sets you free.'

He limped out, leading his men and their prisoners into the afternoon sun.

From his position across the street behind the gnarled trunk of an ancient fig tree, the shrouded figure of Gregor watched the sad procession and knew that sooner or later he would have to face this man Barakat, and that upon that confrontation the fate of Tumanbay would depend.

'The truth will make you free,' he muttered, 'or the truth will destroy you . . .'